PENGUIN CLASSICS

A MODERN INSTANCE

Edwin H. Cady began to work on William Dean Howells for an M.A. thesis project in 1939. He is the author of *The Road to Realism: The Early Years of William Dean Howells, 1837–1885; The Realist at War: The Mature Years of William Dean Howells, 1885–1920; The Light of Common Day; Howells as Critic;* and books on John Woolman and Stephen Crane, among others. Mr. Cady is also the founder and first general editor of *A Selected Edition of William Dean Howells.* He has taught at Syracuse and Indiana universities and is now Andrew W. Mellon Professor Emeritus in the Humanities at Duke Univerisity.

A Modern Instance

BY

William Dean Howells

With an Introduction by
EDWIN H. CADY

PENGUIN BOOKS

PENGUIN BOOKS
Published by the Penguin Group
Viking Penguin Inc., 40 West 23rd Street, New York, New York 10010, U.S.A.
Penguin Books Ltd, 27 Wrights Lane, London W8 5TZ, England
Penguin Books Australia Ltd, Ringwood, Victoria, Australia
Penguin Books Canada Ltd, 2801 John Street,
Markham, Ontario, Canada L3R 1B4
Penguin Books (N.Z.) Ltd, 182–190 Wairau Road,
Auckland 10, New Zealand

Penguin Books Ltd, Registered Offices:
Harmondsworth, Middlesex, England

A Modern Instance first published in
the United States of America by James R. Osgood and Company 1882
This text of *A Modern Instance* first published in
the United States of America by Indiana University Press 1977
This edition first published in The Penguin American Library 1984
Reprinted in Penguin Classics 1988

LIBRARY OF CONGRESS CATALOGING IN PUBLICATION DATA
Howells, William Dean, 1837–1920.
A modern instance.
(The Penguin American library)
"This text . . . was established by David J. Nordloh
and David Kleinman"—T.p. verso.
Bibliography: p.
I. Title.   II. Series.
PS2025.M6   1984   813'.4   83-13461
ISBN 0 14 039.027 8

Printed in the United States of America by
R. R. Donnelley & Sons Company, Harrisonburg, Virginia
Set in Baskerville

This text of *A Modern Instance* was established by David J. Nordloh
and David Kleinman.

Quotations from all letters by William Dean Howells are used by
kind permission of the Heirs of William Dean Howells,
Professor William White Howells, literary executor.

Contents

Introduction

A Modern Instance came at one of the crucial moments in William Dean Howells's career. Insofar as people are able to control their destinies, he planned matters that way. He had just completed a happy decade, packed with hard but successful work, with celebrity and social life, with famous friends whom he was able to help in a number of professional ways. He had edited a great magazine, the *Atlantic Monthly*. He had built an extraordinary home. He had exerted influence in the political as well as the intellectual life of his country. He had established himself nationally, even internationally, as a novelist and critic.

He knew that, creatively, he had crossed a threshold into a new, more mature period. It was high time to resign his editorship of the *Atlantic,* with its demands that he give himself away piecemeal to other authors, review books by the dozens, and carry executive burdens. The time had come to realize the stirrings and perceptions, urgent and vivid and important, that were newly surging up from the depths of his creative being.

During the 1870s, Howells had written *Their Wedding Journey, A Chance Acquaintance, A Foregone Conclusion, The Lady of the Aroostook,* and *The Undiscovered Country,* among others. It was a body of distinctive, interesting work for which he would still be remembered had he died in 1880. But in the eighties he was to produce *A Modern Instance, Indian Summer, The Rise of Silas Lapham, The*

Minister's Charge, Annie Kilburn, April Hopes, and *A Hazard of New Fortunes,* among others. The novels of the two periods speak of worlds that are different, artistically as well as substantively. Howells criticism demonstrates how difficult it is to reconcile those worlds into one coherent account. And the first, though not the least, of the novels of the new manner, the new artist, the new period, was *A Modern Instance.* In spite of much wavering and hesitancy to choose in after years, Howells always kept a spot in his heart in which to feel it perhaps his "best."

What we know of the sources of *A Modern Instance* tells us how charged with creative energy was the imagination freed by the break away from the *Atlantic,* effective 1 March 1881, Howells's forty-fourth birthday. He had already given James R. Osgood, his agent, a prospectus for the novel. (Howells had learned to handle the business side of authorship by keeping ideas for novels in his head, perhaps for many years, and not writing until a publisher had contracted for the serial and book publication rights.) The prospectus was supplied for the Scribners on 18 February 1881, and they bought the novel to serialize in their smart new *Century Magazine.* Yet Howells had been working on the theme and characters for half a decade. Years later, in rather casual conversation with an interviewer in 1908 regarding the centrality of the "practical and modern" in fiction, Howells described the epiphany that gave rise to the novel: "*A Modern Instance,* Mr. Howells said, came to him after witnessing a performance of Janauschek in Euripides' play *Medea.* 'I said to myself, "This is an Indiana divorce case," ' said Mr. Howells, and the novel was born."

Though Howells talked for years about his "New Medea," considerations of which *Medea* he saw (or knew) or of what relations might exist between "classical" figures and Howells's moderns, are largely irrelevant. Long having known, at least in German translation, the Euripidean text, Howells, inveterate theatergoer, saw Grillparzer's *Medea* in Boston in 1875 and the epiphany occurred. What lighted up his imagination, however, was "practical and modern." Far from perceiving a narrative in any way "classical," he saw "an Indiana divorce case." To get it right, he would visit a courthouse in session in Crawfordsville, Indiana, and see the proceedings for himself, practically, immediately. *Medea* somehow pulled a trigger, but the cannon that roared was *A Modern Instance*. The effective source lay in the author's deepening perceptions about contemporary life. The tragic condition he glimpsed was a pattern of crisis in human values in the United States at that instant.

A Modern Instance was Howells's first chance to experiment with a novel on the large scale. Previously he had, except for "travel" elements, kept his fiction tight, concentrated on a few characters under intense focus. But *A Modern Instance* stretches geographically from the Maine woods to dusty Arizona. In between, its cameras scan life in a Yankee small town, at several levels in the urban world of Boston, and all about the square before a Hoosier county courthouse.

Far more important than mere geography, however, is the broad spectrum of Howells's characterizations and major themes. *A Modern Instance* turned out to be, both intellectually and intuitively with regard to conditions within American culture, a far-reaching book. No other novel matched it. As has been said before, the realist conducted his imaginative transactions principally through character: *A Modern Instance* provides a prime example of how character may become theme and theme character.

In proposing his book to the publisher, Howells had emphasized that "just as the question of spiritualism was the moving principle of *The Undiscovered Country*, so the question of divorce will be that of The New Medea," a question to be treated "tragically" (Lohmann, 2, p. 277). As Howells warmed to his work, however, he found that he had struck another fresh, fictive "principle." Journalism was a theme almost untreated in American fiction, and it was one Howells knew from his country roots, his practice as a news-paperman in a provincial center during a great election, and at the intellectual pinnacle of New York opinion-making. Important leaders in the field like E. L. Godkin, Whitelaw Reid, and John Hay were his friends. He had kept close to the younger journalists in Boston; partly because of the *Atlantic,* a number of the best Boston professionals were among his friends. "I am making the hero of my divorce story a newspaper man," he confided to C. D. Warner. "Why has no one struck journalism before?" (Lohmann, 2, p. 295).

As subjects or indeed thematics, divorce and the new jour-nalism provided almost radical "principles" for the American novel. They lent strength, appealed to immediacies almost sensational, certainly shocking to the staid. Nonetheless, in *A Modern Instance* neither divorce nor journalism became much more than an organizing principle, a vehicle for the novel's real advances upon contemporary American character, upon conditions in the culture, and upon acute dislocations in ethical sensibility. What *A Modern Instance* is "about" is those conditions and dislocations—concerning which readers are left to draw the most useful conclusions they can reach after the novel has presented its whole narration to them.

In its exact, vivid registrations of American life (local color) lies one of the great strengths of Howells's novel. Another resides in the rich, widely varied cast of *dramatis personae.* From Kinney, the camp cook, to Clara Kingsbury, the socialite, they are sharply focused, revealingly angled pictures of hu-man beings. Though they are "simple, separate persons" exactly registered, each also represents classes and conditions, historical circumstances, lost chances, or struggling potential-ities in American life.

In making the novel go—in controlling the marionettes on the artist's stage—some of Howells's most interesting characters serve as what Henry James called *ficelles:* strings that make the marionettes move. When a novelist can fascinate his reader with *ficelles* and yet get their indispensable business done, as Howells can with Kinney or Clara Kingsbury or Olive Halleck, that is first-class artistry. The central and thematic characters, those in support of whom the novel weaves all its textures, are really only three: Marcia Hubbard, Bartley Hubbard, and Eustace Atherton. Through them the narrative "principles" of *A Modern Instance* are acted out, presented.

The most general and fatal error in criticism of Howells is sleepily to miss his irony. Pluralism and many-mindedness linked with a vivid imagination and strong emotions characterized Howells. Therefore he was habitually, helplessly, ironic. He loved ironists and was loved by them, and his work deals in virtually every variety of irony. The single-minded or the lazy-eyed cannot read far into Howells. They are apt, having tried, to report their failure to discover depth.

To contrast *A Modern Instance* with its opposite number among Howells's novels of the 1870s is to uncover a web of ironies. The paired work is *A Chance Acquaintance* (1874), first among his true fictions of the seventies. Its portrait of Kitty Ellison, fascinating to Henry James, launched discussion of "the American Girl" (which after 1879 became "Daisy Millerism") as a topic of international debate. But much more to the point is the fact that Howells intended *A Chance Acquaintance* (and perhaps most of his fiction) as a study of democracy.

Howells explained his insight, perhaps his central creative impulse, to Henry James as he understood it in 1873: "I conceived the notion of confronting two extreme American types: the conventional and the unconventional." By "conventional" Howells meant agreeing with the rules, habits, standards of what would become society-page society, "the Four Hundred," or "Proper Boston," of club-men, debutantes, and their families. Though such considerations may seem remote from our times, they are not; translated into our conditions, they persist. Even Howells's terms remain live

issues, one way or another, in American life until after the
Second World War. "Now conventionality is, in our condition of things, in itself a caricature," Howells explained to
James; and so the conventional Bostonian "hero" had to be a
"stick" with a "necessary, cool assumption of superiority"
over small-town, unconventional Kitty Ellison. Against Miles
Arbuton's snobbishness Kitty feels "provoked" to "reprisal."
She "cannot very well help 'sassing' him . . ." (Mildred
Howells, 1, pp. 174–75); and her final, justified resentment of
the psychic injuries inflicted on her by Arbuton's "code"
leads to an "unhappy ending," rather daring in a comedy of
manners.

Variations upon that theme would continue to appear in
Howells's fiction at least as late as *The Landlord at Lion's
Head,* of the middle 1890s. In the course of working out the
early variations that dominated the fiction of the seventies,
Howells learned a great deal about his themes.

Commenting to his father on 20 April 1873 about the good
reception given *A Chance Acquaintance,* Howells put an
important gloss on his remarks to James. The novel "sets me,"
he wrote, "forever outside the ranks of mere *culturists,*
followers of an elegant literature, and proves that I have
sympathy with the true spirit of Democracy" (Lohmann, 2,
p. 24). The remark was calculated to please his father, with
whom relations had become a little strained over matters
theological. But the context was introspective, his habits of
communication home were candid to the point of being
confessional, and there is no reason to doubt his sincerity.

The remarks to James and to William Cooper Howells
together cast light deep into *A Chance Acquaintance,* and
that light reflects back into *A Modern Instance.* The creative
impulse that carried *A Chance Acquaintance* up to the surface of its creator's conscious mind sprang from depths of
American idealism familiar to the life of the early Republic,
from perceptions often called "Jeffersonian." Some of them

were fixed in the amber of Royall Tyler's *The Contrast*. They found voice in Timothy Dwight's *Greenfield Hill*. Americans, they said, echoing Crèvecoeur's famous "What is an American?," may be defined by their difference from Europeans. Americans have broken the historical chains of European cruelty, oppression, bloodshed, and crime. Americans are properly free and virtuous, poor and simple. Like citizens in the most admirable days of Rome, Americans have republican virtue. They risk corruption and degradation when they expose themselves to Europe. The unhappiest of folk are Europeanized Americans. They have lost virtue and simplicity without really attaining sophistication or cultivation. The thematics stay about the same from *The Contrast* to *The Portrait of a Lady*.

Like the primitivisms concerning the happy farmer and the small town, belief in the superiority of rustic virtue was a prime article of American faith. Many a cultural revolt to the contrary notwithstanding, those primitivisms persist in secular American dogma today. Given the radicalism of William Cooper Howell's periods of devotion to "Loco foco" Jacksonianism, to communitarian Utopianism, and to abolitionist libertarianism, there is no occasion to wonder at the reverence with which his son spoke to him of "Democracy." It is easy to see how the author's vision glorified Eriecreek, Pennsylvania, with the traditions of antislavery and wartime sacrifice. It is easy to see why his vision exalted the "unconventional" American girl and the men of her family but ironically undercut the hyper-Anglophilic, "Europeanized" and so "conventional" Miles Arbuton, together with all his world. Howells never committed treason against Boston. He had never pledged it his loyalty.

Just as when the British fifers played their surrender tune at Yorktown, by the time the wheel of Howells's creativity had revolved round to the 1880s and *A Modern Instance*, this revolution was at least halfway "The World Turned Upside

Down." What the shaping eye behind *A Modern Instance* had seen was that the terms in which human experience had seemed definable in *A Chance Acquaintance* (and all its noble republican tradition) were now inapplicable, if not dead.

MARCIA

Her doom had been sealed when the religious faith that animated the founders of the New England town and its culture died. Equity's condition had become precisely what Emily Dickinson, the hidden poet of Amherst, Massachusetts, predicted: "the abdication of belief makes the behavior small." Marcia's "village atheist" father, the most vital mind in town, devoted his days to flogging a dead horse; and her mother retreated into anomie. Equity, despite the brave Jeffersonian ring to its name, had become "a dry mock," one more irony. In it hope and virtue were obsolete. The young life strained against frozen patterns of dead promise until, as Sherwood Anderson was many years later to see in *Winesburg, Ohio,* they twisted folk into "grotesques." Squire Gaylord was such, his wife another; and so Marcia at last became, not saved by her complex adventures with the city or the great world outside. From first, in her perfect "indiscipline" of emotions and egotism, to last, in her bitter withdrawal, which united her mother's anomie with her father's hardness, Marcia demonstrates how thoroughly "Equity" is played out. Thus the novel, because Howells knew exquisitely well how central an American dream "Equity" had once been, dramatizes loss and failure.

The dry rot of Equity, creating a cultural vacuum, left Marcia confused about sexual issues. Father's spoiled child, she was accustomed to getting what she wanted; and that worked neatly so long as what Marcia wanted was what Father approved. But when what Marcia wanted became Bartley and Father forbade him, a classically Electral situation arose.

Marcia flared into self-destructive rebellion. Howells no more knew Freud in 1882 than Sophocles knew Freud in 402 B.C., but all three understood certain tendencies in human behavior.

A like point holds for Marcia's passionately sexual behavior. It is patent in the text, and one cannot doubt that Howells knew it was. What he needed to do was to encode it well enough to hide it from sexually innocent eyes yet allow sexually sophisticated readers to find it. (An important new treatment of this subject in Howells may be found in Elizabeth Prioleau, *The Circle of Eros,* 1983.) But the idea that Howells was "afraid" or "too prudish" or "too squeamish" to deal with sexuality, in particular female sexuality, is a vulgar error. Marcia's problem with her powerful sexuality arose from her heritage in Equity of naiveté. Without the discipline of understanding or commanding her sexuality, she became its victim. The bankruptcy of "unconventional" culture undid her; and, again, she had not the resources of even elementary religious culture to help her.

Moving to Boston, then, brought Marcia the experience of deep culture shock. Howells's narrative of that shock registers one of the most typical and distressing human experiences of our era, one now almost universal. When the old, decayed culture, or what remains of it, must be left behind or has been stripped away around you, what can you do? Where can you go? Who shall you be? "I feel like an old graveyard ghost," laments the Okie farmer bulldozed off his land in Steinbeck's *Grapes of Wrath.* Marcia in effect went sleepwalking in Boston.

Marcia alternated in response from meek submission to a habit of personality that would eventually destroy her. When Bartley misbehaved, especially when he baited her with cold malice, she exploded into demonic tantrums of wounded egotism and sexually jealous frenzy. The habit grew on her until at last, never enabled by faith, reflection, or valid self-correction, she lost all answerable connection to ordinary life. The demon she had made possessed her. That is a psychic progression Hawthorne might have liked; but there was a difference between Howells and Hawthorne, and indeed between Howells and his Swedenborgian father. Howells was a believing and professing agnostic at the moment of writing *A Modern Instance*, and the demon he imagined possessed no superhuman, supernatural, or "spiritual" dimension. Indeed, much the same thing happened in the imaginations of Howells and Henry James at about the same time. Each, having forsaken his father's Swedenborgian theology, continued to borrow metaphors from it. But the metaphors worked in what William James would call "this-worldly" dimensions.

BARTLEY

Except for that Hoosier courtroom scene, which appears to have stood in the original *donnée* of the novel, "The New Medea" could have been staged in Equity, making the novel an ancestor of the Tilbury Town, Spoon River, or Winesburg, Ohio, stories. It was in transferring the central action to Boston that Howells made it *A Modern Instance*, an exemplum of the way things are now. Bartley Hubbard, however, would have been Bartley and just about the same anywhere. Bartley was not a villain. There wasn't enough to him to furnish forth villainy. He was just a run-of-the-mill scoundrel with nothing much in him but a large, tender ego and a great deal of shallow cleverness. He had not an unselfish bone in his body, nor one that wasn't lazy. Is he not a modern man? Is he not *the* modern man, the "new man," a foregone failure? After George Washington Cable had read the January 1882 installment of the novel in the *Century* (through Chapter VII), he wrote from New Orleans to praise its "fine, clear exposition of our national 'smart Aleck' and his results. . . . Ah! if you knew what I have suffered from the unchallenged predominance of America's Bartley Hubbards you could understand the grateful delight with which I behold them with a ring in their nose at last."* Bartley could have been the whole procession, a modern instance all by himself.

Bartley is the first fully drawn worshipper of William James's "bitch-goddess Success" in American fiction. He is the new "success" type (who would so confuse later writers like Norris and Dreiser and London). Cozy, he is quick to spot a hole and dive through it to advantage. Easy-going, cynical, he lives by an unrationalized code of social Darwinism. When he can, he will "take" anybody for anything and in any way; he will exploit and devour; never a lover or giver, he lives psychically and professionally by grasping and extorting. He is the perfect candidate for Whited Sepulchre, Arizona.

When *A Modern Instance* opens, Bartley is, though mildly, already demonic. Swedenborgian doctrine, shared by W. C. Howells and Eustance Atherton, held that the daily cumulation of moral actions, either loving and giving or selfish and exploitative, massed up through the years to create an individual moral being dominantly either angelic or demonic. From childhood Bartley had let his egotism indulge itself, blotting up kindness, neglecting gratitude, loyalty, reciprocity, love, and duty. As early as college he had achieved, as his generous, self-sacrificing friend Halleck perceived, "no more moral nature than a baseball."

In that phrase from Quaker "plain speech" for which we seem to have no equivalent, there is something about Bartley Hubbard that "speaks to the condition" of the male American and his guilts. As may be easily proved, Howells's habit in imagining characters was to fold together characteristics from half a dozen or more people he knew, homogenize them well, and add the ingredients necessary to make the character "work" in his novel. Like Faulkner, for instance, Howells used recurrent characters and altered their ages, circum-

* George Washington Cable to Howells, 21 January 1882. Houghton Library, Harvard University, Cambridge, Mass.

stances, histories, and even their temperaments to serve different fictions. Why not?, as Faulkner demanded. The characters belong, after all, to their creator: only the artist "knows" them.

But scarcely half of *A Modern Instance* had been serialized before Mark Twain, lost in admiration at the portrayal of the drunken scoundrel Bartley, claimed emphatically that Howells had taken Bartley from Sam Clemens. Promptly denying it, Howells said he had used himself for Bartley. Various critics have adduced other models that have seemed to them probable. It has not been an exercise notably productive of useful insights. Perhaps much more to the point is the frequency with which students have felt the compulsion to say, in conference with a professor or even in an examination essay, "I am Bartley Hubbard. I never realized it before I read the novel, but I act like Bartley all the time."

About the new journalism as Bartley and Witherby and Ricker and the working press knew it, one who runs might read. Between 1876 and 1983 nothing has changed but the financial scale and the media. For every Ricker there are a dozen Bartleys and Witherbys in the field, and there is no hope in them. Howells's study of journalism, historically fascinating, became a vehicle for the main insight, which was moral. Kinney, the common man's Thoreau, plays his part as *ficelle*, moving events most powerfully to Bartley's catastrophe. Likewise, newspaper life comes to have mainly a technical function in *A Modern Instance*. It carries Bartley to the pure deviltry of his climactic fall. When he has robbed trusting Kinney, defied Ricker, broken with Witherby, and wrecked his career, he is ready for the tornado of malice with which he will destroy his marriage and deliver himself irretrievably "to the ruin he had chosen."

ATHERTON

The opportunity then arises not so much to judge and condemn Bartley Hubbard as to understand what Bartley and his instance can tell us about ourselves and certain realities in modern life. To provide that opportunity, Howells brought Boston into the novel, and the key Bostonian, *raisonneur* not for Howells but for "the conventional," is Eustace Atherton. What has Atherton, a lawyer and giver of laws, to say to Bartley Hubbard and Bartley's instance—which happens to involve a number of Atherton's friends and clients? What if he should at last have nothing, really, to offer? What if he too were somehow demonic, or at least partly so? Then the condition of the modern world would have become ominous indeed.

It cannot be accident that Eustace Atherton's name, Anglophilic and genteel, faintly too conventional, should echo the name of Miles Arbuton. Where *A Chance Acquaintance* warmly believed in Kitty Ellison and Eriecreek and in the democratic traditions of the "unconventional," *A Modern Instance,* with its bleak picture of dead and frozen Equity, no longer believes. Does there, then, remain hope in the city? Does the water of life flow in Boston—Boston vulgate, Boston bohemian and commercial in its journalism, Boston "Proper," with all its exclusivities and conventions in place? Can Marcia find happiness or Bartley salvation in Boston? If not, what good is conventional urban civilization? If Eustace cannot answer such questions, perhaps nobody can. He is a Daniel come too eagerly to judgment, perhaps a Pharisee. But he will end in the humiliation of sighing, like an agnostic, " 'Ah, I don't know! I don't know!' "

Because too many good critics have not seen it, the point has to be made that Atherton never spoke for Howells in the novel. The published correspondence shows unmistakably that W. D. Howells settled into a determined agnosticism during the 1870s and stayed agnostic through the composition of *A Modern Instance.* He felt forced to confess disbelief in Swedenborg to his disappointed father. Since Eustace Atherton's unnamed faith, well understood by his friends, is unmistakably Swedenborgian, there is no reason to suppose that

Howells accepted Atherton's rigid moralism. Indeed, the
novel implicitly condemns moralism as a sin of presumption.

In the early seventies, Howells's determination, after com-
pleting a course of theological reading, was that he would try
"to be humble and true and charitable" (Lohmann, 1, p. 390)
but had to abandon theology. The confusion regnant at the
heart of matters in conventional Boston reveals itself when
Halleck asks Atherton to judge for him, in fact to judge him.
Considering what Atherton should have known, it astonishes
one that he consented to play God, to act like God the judge,
the law-giver, the inflicter of penitential pain upon gentle
Ben Halleck. Such smugness, such comfort in self-regard, such
spiritual arrogance, figure in the Gospels as the sins of
Pharisees. Far enough extended, they would become the sin
of Lucifer himself. Surely one might behave demonically in
that line of misconduct as in any other. Atherton was in profound danger of becoming a deep-frozen demon, as Marcia
Gaylord and her father were fire-demons of egotism and
vengeance.

It roused the derision of Henry Adams to look back upon
the generations of his grandfather and father and see how the
old, conventional folk had rested in "the Boston solution."
Boston, notwithstanding the gifted rebels who flouted it, was
satisfied that it had found the solution to the ills of humanity.
The resulting attitude of cool superiority to perturbed, un-
tidy, seeking, suffering human nature irked Kitty Ellison,
who felt compelled to "sass" the Boston solution. By the time
of *A Modern Instance,* when in fact Boston had no solution
at all for realities like perishing Bartley and soul-starved
Marcia, Boston assurance began to seem almost criminal. In
fact, Boston conventionality seemed to have nothing to offer
its own (like Halleck) except wealth. And money as a cause
had not been supposed to play any part in the Boston
solution.

The absurdity of the situation Clara Kingsbury acts out

deliciously, her days "divided between the extremes of squalor and of fashion," her outreach to Boston squalor the howling irrelevance of her "Indigent Children's Surf-Bathing Society." One of the targets of her fund-raising has a speech that explains everything about why one of Howells's most perceptive contemporaries insisted that a good title for the series of his Boston novels was "Boston Under The Scalpel." Her victim says:

> "Clara Kingsbury can say and do, from the best heart in the world, more offensive things in ten minutes than malice could invent in a week. Somebody ought to go out and drag her away from that reporter by main force. But I presume it's too late already; she's had time to destroy us all. You'll see that there won't be a shred left of us in *his* paper, at any rate. Really, I wonder that, in a city full of nervous and exasperated people like Boston, Clara Kingsbury has been suffered to live. She throws her whole soul into everything she undertakes, and she has gone so *en masse* into this Indigent Bathing, and splashed about in it so, that *I* can't understand how we got anybody to come to-day. Why, I haven't the least doubt that she's offered that poor man a ticket to go down to Nantasket and bathe with the other Indigents; she's treated *me* as if I ought to be personally surf-bathed for the last fortnight; and if there's any chance for us left by her tactlessness, you may be sure she's gone at it with her conscience, and simply swept it off the face of the earth" [pp. 187–88].

It is of course part of Clara's problem that wealth blinds her to the realities of squalor. That same wealth, when he attains to it by marrying Clara, turns a sharp irony against Eustace Atherton. The harshest of his condemnations of Ben Halleck fall from Atherton's lips in scenes of almost painful luxury as he exults in the delights of his breakfasts—exquisite surroundings, perfect food, all warmed by Clara's devotion. Bleak judgments fall from him in the midst of all the best that love, luck, and wealth can buy. The dramatic irony becomes intolerable.

One is forced back upon the New Testament to catch exactly the quality of this strain of irony in *A Modern Instance*. What does it mean that nemesis caught Bartley in "Whited Sepulchre, Arizona"? That is a pun on "Tombstone," a place grubbily real enough but already notorious for its gunmen and bad men, romanticized in *The Police Gazette* and the dime novels. Where else ought a Bartley to get his packet? "Whited Sepulchre," however, also plays upon a familiar New Testament verse. In Matthew XXIII, Jesus denounces "the scribes and the Pharisees" for ecclesiastical arrogance, oppression of the poor, and, worst of all, hypocrisy. The sermon made "Pharisee" a byword. One of the most telling images speaks from verse 27: "Woe unto you, scribes and Pharisees, hypocrites! for ye are like unto whited sepulchres, which indeed appear beautiful outward, but are within full of dead men's bones, and of all uncleanness."

Although a kind of scribe and an expert hypocrite, Bartley was not conspicuous for ecclesiastical pomposity. Eustace Atherton, however, finds himself driven to ever "higher ground" in judgment, even denunciation, of poor Halleck. He grows subtly, reconditely Swedenborgian, grandly appropriating the highest ground of the Boston solution also—and all amid the luxuries of his breakfast room. Thus, in the final scene, again at breakfast, even scatterbrained Clara can quote him against himself, until she tells him, " 'Oh, how hard you are!' " Then Eustace Atherton is at last routed into self-question and the admission, " 'Ah, I don't know!' " Had he "known" and said too much, from too portentous a ground, too careless of the pain he inflicted? Was he in danger of a sort of Pharisaical demonism of his own? The narrative gives us warrant to suppose that perhaps he was, and therefore he cannot speak for Howells himself.

In fact, Atherton's final analysis of Halleck's case reveals flaws in his vision. He has not a true use of his eyes. Like a "conventional" myopic of Howells's seventies novels, Atherton argues for a genetic moral aristocracy, which Halleck belongs to and must heroically maintain against common humanity. Like a "neoromantic" delusionist of Howells's novels of the eighties, Atherton holds that, though "another sort of man" might marry the widowed Marcia, Halleck could not: it would be a "lapse from the ideal" (p. 453). By the middle years of the decade, Howells the ironic realist would proclaim "the superiority of the vulgar."

Certainly Atherton at his highest-flown moments matched up not at all with the author who had pledged to be humble and charitable and true. Certainly Atherton ran dead against principles of conduct proposed in later Howells novels: that human beings have a duty to observe a rule of "the economy of pain"; that, since we never know enough to condemn, we have a duty not to judgment and vengeance but to a "law of mercy." Certainly Howells promised the Scribners not "to write a *tendency-romance*"; and certainly his faith in the laws of art in fiction forbade his ever doing the moralizing: it was the function of art to compel the reader to do the moralizing.

Even divorce in *A Modern Instance,* then, serves as a large objective correlative for the main burden of the novel. The theme of divorce, like the theme of journalism, helps to carry the burden of Howells's moral insight to the climax of the novel. Carefully "unmoralized," the burden of the narrative is that (as of a hundred years ago) modern American life had rushed beyond moral, religious, or cultural control. Every modern instance, it suggests, will reveal the same truth.

Howells's creative insight, running, by the way, far ahead of his ordinary discursive perceptions, had showed him for the first time what danger menaced American democracy. The early republican faith in rural-agrarian America had failed. The "Boston solution" had failed. The domestic lares and penates no longer prevailed. The old gods were dead. Commercial sharpness and the cheap emptiness of *l'homme moyen sensuel* were answerably confronted by nothing in the modern instance. The imagination of W. D. Howells had anticipated by twenty years some of what were to be the informing insights of *The Education of Henry Adams*. In the depths of his imagination, he was one of us.

—Edwin H. Cady

Suggestions for Further Reading

1. Scudder, Horace E. "A Modern Instance." *Atlantic Monthly,* 50 (Nov. 1882): 709–13.
2. de Wagstaffe, W. "The Personality of Mr. Howells." *Book News Monthly* 26 (June 1908): 739–41.
3. Howells, Mildred, ed. *Life in Letters of William Dean Howells.* 2 vols. New York: Doubleday, Doran, 1928.
4. Cady, Edwin H. "The Neuroticism of William Dean Howells." *PMLA* 61 (March 1946): 229–38.
5. Gibson, William M., and Arms, George. *A Bibliography of William Dean Howells.* New York: New York Public Library, 1948.
6. Carter, Everett. *Howells and the Age of Realism.* Philadelphia: Lippincott, 1954.
7. Cady, Edwin H. *The Road to Realism: The Early Years, 1837–1885, of William Dean Howells.* Syracuse, N.Y.: Syracuse University Press, 1956.
8. Gibson, William M. "Introduction," *A Modern Instance.* Boston: Houghton Mifflin, Riverside Edition, 1957.
9. Fryckstedt, Olov. *In Quest of America: A Study of Howells' Early Development as a Novelist.* Cambridge: Harvard University Press, 1958.
10. Bennett, George N. *William Dean Howells, the Development of a Novelist.* Norman, Okla.: University of Oklahoma Press, 1959.
11. Foster, Richard. "The Contemporaneity of Howells." *New England Quarterly* 32 (March 1959): 54–78.
12. Vanderbilt, Kermit. *The Achievement of William Dean Howells: A Reinterpretation.* Princeton, N.J.: Princeton University Press, 1968.

13. Sweeney, Gerard M. "The *Medea* Howells Saw." *American Literature* XLII (March 1970): 83–89.

14. Lynn, Kenneth. *William Dean Howells: An American Life*. New York: Harcourt Brace Jovanovich, 1971.

15. Cady, Edwin H. *The Light of Common Day: Realism in American Fiction*. Bloomington: Indiana University Press, 1971.

16. Girgus, Sam B. "Bartley Hubbard, The Rebel In Howells' *A Modern Instance*." *Research Studies* 39 (December 1971): 315–21.

17. Halfmann, Ulrich. *Interviews With William Dean Howells*. Arlington: University of Texas at Arlington, 1973.

18. Lewis P. Simpson. "The Treason of William Dean Howells." In *The Man of Letters in New England and the South*, 85–128. Baton Rouge: Louisiana State University Press, 1973.

19. Howells, W. D. *A Modern Instance*. Vol. 10 of *A Selected Edition of W. D. Howells*. Bloomington: Indiana University Press, 1977. See especially "Introduction" by George N. Bennett, and "Textual Apparatus" by David J. Nordloh.

20. W. D. Howells. *Selected Letters*. Edited by Lohmann, Christof, et al. Boston: Twayne Publishers. See especially Vol. 2, 1873–1881, with introduction by George Arms (1979); Vol. 3, 1882–1891, with introductions by Robert C. Leitz, III, and Richard H. Ballinger (1980).

21. Wright, Ellen. "Given Bartley, Given Marcia: A Reconsideration of Howells' *A Modern Instance*." *Texas Studies in Literature and Language* 23 (Summer 1981): 214–31.

22. Habegger, Alfred. *Gender, Fantasy, and Realism in American Literature*. New York: Columbia University Press, 1982.

23. Prioleau, Elizabeth. *The Circle of Eros: Sexuality in the Work of W. D. Howells*. Durham, N.C.: Duke University Press, 1983.

A Note on the Text

This edition is a photo-offset reproduction of the text established by David J. Nordloh and David Kleinman, published by Indiana University Press in 1977 as Volume 10 of *A Selected Edition of W. D. Howells*. The following typographical errors have been corrected with the permission of the original editors: page 101, line 33, "Bartly" to "Bartley"; page 105, line 35, "home" to "home'"; page 199, line 1, "my wife" to "'my wife"; page 215, line 15, "superflous" to "superfluous"; page 291, line 27, "squire" to "Squire"; page 416, line 6, "society" to "society'"; page 428, line 31, "capitivity" to "captivity"; page 439, line 25, "squire" to "Squire"; page 448, line 30, "attained" to "attainted."

A Modern Instance

I

___

THE VILLAGE stood on a wide plain, and round it rose the mountains. They were green to their tops in summer, and in the winter white through their serried pines and drifting mists, but at every season serious and beautiful, furrowed with hollow shadows, and taking the light on masses and stretches of iron-gray crag. The river swam through the plain in long curves, and slipped away at last through an unseen pass to the southward, tracing a score of miles in its course over a space that measured but three or four. The plain was very fertile, and its features, if few and of purely utilitarian beauty, had a rich luxuriance, and there was a tropical riot of vegetation when the sun of July beat on those northern fields. They waved with corn and oats to the feet of the mountains, and the potatoes covered a vast acreage with the lines of their intense, coarse green; the meadows were deep with English grass to the banks of the river, that doubling and returning upon itself still marked its way with a dense fringe of alders and white birches.

But winter was full half the year. The snow began at Thanksgiving, and fell snow upon snow till Fast Day, thawing between the storms, and packing harder and harder against the break-up in the spring, when it covered the ground in solid levels three feet high, and lay heaped in drifts that defied the sun far into May. When it did not snow the weather was keenly clear and commonly very still. Then the landscape at noon had a stereoscopic glister under the high sun that burned in a heaven without a cloud, and at setting stained the sky and the white waste with freezing pink and violet. On such days the farmers and lumbermen came in to the village stores, and made a stiff and feeble stir about their doorways, and the school children gave the street a little life and color, as they went to and from the academy in their red and blue woollens. Four times a day the mill, the shrill wheeze of whose saws had become part of the habitual silence, blew its whistle for the hands to begin and leave off work, in blasts that seemed to shatter themselves against the thin air. But otherwise an Arctic quiet prevailed.

Behind the black boles of the elms that swept the vista of the street with the fine gray tracery of their boughs, stood the houses deep-sunken in the accumulating drifts, through which each householder kept a path cut from his doorway to the road, white and clean as if hewn out of marble. Some cross-streets straggled away east and west with the poorer dwellings; but this that followed the northward and southward reach of the plain, was the main thoroughfare, and had its own impressiveness, with those square, white houses which they build so large in northern New England. They were all kept in scrupulous repair, though here and there the frost and thaw of many winters had heaved a fence out of plumb, and threatened the poise of the monumental urns of painted pine on the gate-posts. They had dark-green blinds of a color harmonious with that of the funereal evergreens in their dooryards; and they themselves had taken the tone of the snowy landscape as if by the operation of some such law as blanches the fur-bearing animals of the north. They seemed proper to its desolation, while some of more modern taste, painted to a warmer tone, looked, with their mansard roofs and jig-sawed piazzas and balconies, intrusive and alien.

At one end of the street stood the Academy with its classic façade and its belfry; midway was the hotel with the stores, the printing-office and the churches, and at the other extreme, one of the square white mansions stood advanced from the rank of the rest, at the top of a deep-plunging valley, defining itself against the mountain beyond, so sharply that it seemed as if cut out of its dark wooded side. It was from the gate before this house, distinct in the pink light which the sunset had left, that on a Saturday evening in February a cutter, gay with red-lined robes, dashed away and came musically clashing down the street under the naked elms. For the women who sat with their work, at the windows on either side of the way, hesitating whether to light their lamps, and drawing nearer and nearer to the dead-line of the outer cold, for the latest glimmer of the day, the passage of this ill-timed vehicle was a vexation little short of grievous. Every movement on the street was precious to them and with all the keenness of their starved curiosity these captives of the winter could not make out the people in the cutter. Afterwards it was a mortification to them that they should not have thought at once of Bartley Hubbard and Mar-cia Gaylord. They had seen him go up towards Squire Gay-lord's house half an hour before, and they now blamed them-selves for not reflecting that of course he was going to take Marcia over to the church-sociable at Lower Equity. Their identity being established, other little proofs of it reproached the inquirers; but these perturbed spirits were at peace, and the lamps were out in the houses, (where the smell of rats in the wainscot and of potatoes in the cellar strengthened with the growing night) when Bartley and Marcia drove back through the moon-lit silence to her father's door. Here, too, the win-dows were all dark, except for the light that sparely glimmered through the parlor blinds; and the young man slackened the pace of his horse, as if to still the bells, some distance away from the gate.

The girl took the hand he offered her when he dismounted at the gate, and as she jumped from the cutter, "Wont you come in?" she asked.

"I guess I can blanket my horse and stand him under the wood-shed," answered the young man, going round to the ani-mal's head, and leading him away.

When he returned to the door the girl opened it, as if she had been listening for his step; and she now stood holding it ajar for him to enter, and throwing the light upon the threshold from the lamp which she lifted high in the other hand. The action brought her figure in relief, and revealed the outline of her bust and shoulders, while the lamp flooded with light the face she turned to him, and again averted for a moment, as if startled at some noise behind her. She thus showed a smooth low forehead, lips and cheeks deeply red, a softly rounded chin touched with a faint dimple, and in turn a nose short and aquiline; her eyes were dark, and her dusky hair flowed crinkling above her fine black brows, and vanished down the curve of a lovely neck. There was a peculiar charm in the form of her upper lip: it was exquisitely arched, and at the corners it projected a little over the lower lip, so that when she smiled it gave a piquant sweetness to her mouth, with a certain demure innocence that qualified the Roman pride of her profile. For the rest, her beauty was of the kind that coming years would only ripen and enrich: at thirty she would be even handsomer than at twenty, and be all the more southern in her type for the paling of that northern color in her cheeks. The young man who looked up at her from the doorstep had a yellow moustache, shadowing either side of his lip with a broad sweep like a bird's wing; his chin, deep cut below his mouth, failed to come strenuously forward; his cheeks were filled to an oval contour; and his face had otherwise the regularity common to Americans; his eyes, a clouded gray, heavy-lidded and long-lashed, were his most striking feature, and he gave her beauty a deliberate look from them as he lightly stamped the snow from his feet, and pulled the seal-skin gloves from his long hands.

"Come in!" she whispered, coloring with pleasure under his gaze; and she made haste to shut the door after him with a luxurious impatience of the cold. She led the way into the room from which she had come, and set down the lamp on the corner of the piano, while he slipped off his overcoat, and swung it over the end of the sofa. They drew up chairs to the stove, in which the smouldering fire, revived by the opened draft, roared and snapped. It was midnight, as the sharp strokes of a wooden clock declared from the kitchen; and they were alone together and all the other inmates of the house were asleep. The situation, scarcely conceivable to another civilization, is so common in ours, where youth commands its fate, and trusts solely to itself, that it may be said to be characteristic of the New England civilization wherever it keeps its simplicity. It was not stolen or clandestine; it would have interested everyone but would have shocked no one in the village if the whole village had known it; all that a girl's parents ordinarily exacted was that they should not be waked up.

"Ugh!" said the girl, "it seems as if I never should get warm." She leaned forward, and stretched her hands toward the stove, and he presently rose from the rocking-chair in which he sat somewhat lower than she, and lifted her sack to throw it over her shoulders. But he put it down, and took up his overcoat.

"Allow my coat the pleasure," he said, with the ease of a man who is not too far lost to be really flattering.

"Much obliged to the coat," she replied, shrugging herself into it, and pulling the collar close about her throat. "I wonder you didn't put it on the sorrel. You could have tied the sleeves round her neck."

"Shall I tie them round yours?" He leaned forward from the low rocking-chair into which he had sunk again, and made a feint at what he had proposed.

But she drew back with a gay, "No!" and added, "Some day, father says, that sorrel will be the death of us. He says it's a bad color for a horse. They're always ugly, and when they get heated, they're crazy."

"You never seem to be very much frightened when you're riding after the sorrel," said Bartley.

"Oh, I've great faith in your driving."

"Thanks. But I don't believe in this notion about a horse being vicious because he's of a certain color. If your father didn't believe in it, I should call it a superstition. But the Squire has no superstitions."

"I don't know about that," said the girl. "I don't think he likes to see the new moon over his left shoulder."

"I beg his pardon, then," returned Bartley. "I ought to have said religions. The Squire has no religions."

The young fellow had a rich caressing voice, and a securely winning manner which comes from the habit of easily pleasing; in this charming tone and with this delightful insinuation, he often said things that hurt; but with such a humorous glance from his softly shaded eyes that people felt in some sort flattered at being taken into the joke, even while they winced under it.

The girl seemed to wince, as if, in spite of her familiarity with the fact, it wounded her to have her father's skepticism recognized just then. She said nothing, and he added, "I remember we used to think that a red-headed boy was worse-tempered on account of his hair. But I don't believe the sorrel-tops, as we called them were any fiercer than the rest of us."

Marcia did not answer at once, and then she said with the vagueness of one not greatly interested by the subject, "You've got a sorrel-top in your office that's fiery enough if she's anything like what she used to be when she went to school."

"Hannah Morrison?"

"Yes."

"Oh, she isn't so bad. She's pretty lively; but she's very eager to learn the business, and I guess we shall get along. I think she wants to please me."

"*Does* she! But she must be going on seventeen, now."

"I dare say," answered the young man carelessly, but with perfect intelligence. "She's good-looking in her way, too."

"Oh! Then you admire red-hair."

He perceived the anxiety that the girl's pride could not keep out of her tone, but he answered indifferently: "I'm a little too near that color, myself. I hear that red hair's coming into fashion, but I guess it's natural I should prefer black."

She leaned back in her chair, and crushed the velvet collar of his coat under her neck in lifting her head to stare at the high-hung mezzotints and family photographs on the walls, while a flattered smile parted her lips, and there was a little thrill of joy in her voice. "I presume we must be a good deal behind the age in everything, at Equity."

"Well, you know my opinion of Equity," returned the young man. "If I didn't have you here to free my mind to, once in a while, I don't know what I should do."

She was so proud to be in the secret of his discontent with the narrow world of Equity, that she tempted him to disparage it farther by pretending to identify herself with it. "I don't see why you abuse Equity to me. I've never been anywhere else, except those two winters at school. You'd better look out: I might expose you," she threatened fondly.

"I'm not afraid. Those two winters make a great difference. You saw girls from other places—from Augusta and Bangor and Bath."

"Well, I couldn't see how they were so very different from Equity girls."

"I dare say they couldn't, either, if they judged from you."

She leaned forward again and begged for more flattery from him with her happy eyes. "Why, what *does* make me so different from all the rest? I should really like to know."

"Oh, you don't expect me to tell you to your face!"

"Yes, to my face! I don't believe it's anything complimentary."

"No, it's nothing that you deserve any credit for."

"Pshaw!" cried the girl. "I know you're only talking to make fun of me. How do I know but you make fun of me to other girls, just as you do of them to me. Everybody says you're sarcastic."

"Have I ever been sarcastic with you?"

"You know I wouldn't stand it."

He made no reply, but she admired the ease with which he now turned from her, and took one book after another from the table at his elbow, saying some words of ridicule about each. It gave her a still deeper sense of his intellectual command when he finally discriminated, and began to read out a poem with studied elocutionary effects. He read in a low tone, but at last some responsive noises came from the room overhead; he closed the book, and threw himself into an attitude of deprecation with his eyes cast up to the ceiling.

"Chicago," he said, laying the book on the table, and taking his knee between his hands, while he dazzled her by speaking from the abstraction of one who has carried on a train of thought quite different from that on which he seemed to be intent, "Chicago is the place for me. I don't think I can stand Equity much longer. You know that chum of mine I told you about: he's written to me to come out there and go into the law with him at once."

"Why don't you go?" the girl forced herself to ask.

"Oh, I'm not ready, yet. Should you write to me if I went to Chicago?"

"I don't think you'd find my letters very interesting. You wouldn't want any news from Equity."

"Your letters wouldn't be interesting if you gave me the Equity news; but they would if you left it out. Then you'd have to write about yourself."

"Oh, I don't think that would interest anybody."

"Well, I feel almost like going out to Chicago to see."

"But I haven't promised to write yet," said the girl, laughing for joy in his humor.

"I shall have to stay in Equity till you do, then. Better promise at once."

"Wouldn't that be too much like marrying a man to get rid of him?"

"I don't think that's always such a bad plan—for the man." He waited for her to speak; but she had gone the length of her tether, in this direction. "Byron says:

        " 'Man's love is of man's life a thing apart—
          'Tis woman's whole existence.'

Do you believe that?" He dwelt upon her with his free look, in the happy embarrassment with which she let her head droop.

"I don't know," she murmured. "I don't know anything about a man's life."

"It was the woman's I was asking about."

"I don't think I'm competent to answer."

"Well, I'll tell you, then. I think Byron was mistaken. My experience is that when a man is in love, there's nothing else of him. That's the reason I've kept out of it altogether, of late years. My advice is, Don't fall in love: it takes too much time." They both laughed at this. "But about corresponding, now: you haven't said whether you would write to me, or not. Will you?"

"Can't you wait and see?" she asked, stealing a look at him, which she could not keep from being fond.

"No, no! Unless you wrote to me, I couldn't go to Chicago."

"Perhaps I ought to promise, then, at once."

"You mean that you wish me to go."

"You said that you were going. You oughtn't to let anything stand in the way of your doing the best you can for yourself."

"But you would miss me a little, wouldn't you? You would try to miss me, now and then?"

"Oh, you are here, pretty often. I don't think I should have much difficulty in missing you."

"Thanks, thanks! I can go with a light heart, now. Good-by!" He made a pretence of rising.

"What! Are you going at once?"

"Yes, this very night—or to-morrow. Or no, I can't go to-morrow. There's something I was going to do to-morrow."

"Perhaps go to church."

"Oh, that, of course. But it was in the afternoon. Stop! I have it! I want you to go sleighriding with me in the afternoon."

"I don't know about that," Marcia began.

"But I do," said the young man. "Hold on: I'll put my

request in writing." He opened her portefolio, which lay on the table. "What elegant stationery! May I use some of this elegant stationery? The letter is to a lady—to open a correspondence. May I?" She laughed her assent. "How ought I to begin? Dearest Miss Marcia, or just Dear Marcia: which is best?"

"You had better not put either"—

"But I must. You're one or the other, you know. You're dear,—to your family—and you're Marcia: you can't deny it. The only question is whether you're the dearest of all the Miss Marcias. I may be mistaken, you know. We'll err on the safe side: Dear Marcia:" He wrote it down. "That looks well, and it reads well. It looks very natural, and it reads like poetry— blank verse; there's no rhyme for it that I can remember. Dear Marcia: Will you go sleigh-riding with me to-morrow afternoon at two o'clock sharp? Yours—Yours sincerely, or cordially, or affectionately, or what-ly? The Dear Marcia seems to call for something out of the common. I think it had better be affectionately." He suggested it with ironical gravity.

"And *I* think it had better be Truly," protested the girl.

"Truly, it shall be, then. Your word is law—statute in such case made and provided." He wrote "With unalterable devotion, Yours truly, Bartley J. Hubbard," and read it aloud.

She leaned forward, and lightly caught it away from him, and made a feint of tearing it. He seized her hands. "Mr. Hubbard," she cried in undertone, "let me go, please."

"On two conditions—Promise not to tear up my letter, and promise to answer it in writing."

She hesitated long, letting him hold her wrists. At last she said, "Well," and he released her wrists on whose whiteness his clasp left red circles. She wrote a single word on the paper, and pushed it across the table to him. He rose with it, and went round to her side. "This is very nice. But you haven't spelled it correctly. Anybody would say this was *No*, to look at it; and you meant to write *Yes*. Take the pencil in your hand, Miss Gaylord, and I will steady your trembling nerves, so that you can form the characters. Stop! At the slightest resistance on your part, I will call out and alarm the house; or I will"— He put the pencil into her fingers, and took her soft fist into his, and changed the word, while she submitted, helpless with her smothered laughter. "Now the address. Dear"—

"No, no!" she protested.

"Yes, yes! Dear Mr. Hubbard. There, that will do! Now the signature: Yours"—

"I *wont* write that. I wont, indeed!"

"Oh, yes you will. You only think you wont. Yours gratefully, Marcia Gaylord. That's right. The Gaylord is not very legible, on account of a slight tremor in the writer's arm, resulting from a constrained posture, perhaps. Thanks, Miss Gaylord, I will be here promptly at the hour indicated"—

The noises renewed themselves overhead; some one seemed to be moving about. Hubbard laid his hand on that of the girl still resting on the table, and grasped it in burlesque alarm; she could scarcely stifle her mirth. He released her hand, and reaching his chair with a theatrical stride, sat there cowering till the noises ceased. Then he began to speak soberly, in a low voice. He spoke of himself; but in application of a lecture which they had lately heard, so that he seemed to be speaking of the lecture. It was on the formation of character, and he told of the processes by which he had formed his own character. They appeared very wonderful to her, and she marvelled at the ease with which he dismissed the frivolity of his recent mood, and was now all seriousness. When he came to speak of the influence of others upon him, she almost trembled with the intensity of her interest. "But of all the women I have known, Marcia," he said, "I believe you have had the strongest influence upon me. I believe you could make me do anything; but you have always influenced me for good; your influence upon me has been ennobling and elevating."

She wished to refuse his praise; but her heart throbbed for bliss and pride in it; her voice dissolved on her lips. They sat in silence; and he took in his the hand that she let hang over the side of her chair.

The lamp began to burn low; and she found words to say, "I had better get another," but she did not move.

"No; don't," he said; "I must be going, too. Look at the wick, there, Marcia: it scarcely reaches the oil. In a little while it will not reach it, and the flame will die out. That is the way the ambition to be good and great will die out of me when my life no longer draws its inspiration from your influence." This figure took her imagination; it seemed to her very beautiful; and his praise humbled her more and more. "Good-night," he said, in a low, sad voice. He gave her hand a last pressure, and rose to put on his coat. Her admiration of his words, her happiness in his flattery filled her brain like wine. She moved dizzily as she took up the lamp to light him to the door. "I have tired you," he said, tenderly, and he passed his hand around her to sustain the elbow of the arm with which she held the lamp; she wished to resist, but she could not try.

At the door he bent down his head and kissed her. "Good-night, dear—friend."

"Good night," she panted, and after the door had closed upon him, she stooped and kissed the knob on which his hand had rested.

As she turned, she started to see her father coming down the stairs with a candle in his hand. He had his black cravat tied round his throat, but no collar; otherwise he had on the rusty black clothes in which he ordinarily went about his affairs: the cassimere pantaloons, the satin vest, and the dresscoat which old fashioned country lawyers still wore, ten years ago, in preference to a frock or sack. He stopped on one of the lower steps, and looked sharply down into her uplifted face, and as they stood confronted, their consanguinity came out in vivid resemblances and contrasts; his high, hawklike profile was translated into the fine aquiline outline of hers; the harsh rings of black hair, now grizzled with age, which clustered tightly over his head, except where they had retreated from his deeply seamed and wrinkled forehead, were the crinkled flow above her smooth, white brow; and the line of the bristly tufts that overhung his eyes was the same as that of the low arches above hers. Her complexion was from her mother: his skin was dusky yellow; but they had the same mouth and hers showed how sweet his mouth must have been in his youth. His eyes, deep sunk in their cavernous sockets, had rekindled their dark fires in hers; his whole visage, softened to her sex and girlish years, looked up at him in his daughter's face.

"Why, father! Did we wake you?"

"No. I hadn't been asleep at all. I was coming down to read. But it's time you were in bed, Marcia."

"Yes, I'm going, now. There's a good fire in the parlor stove."

The old man descended the remaining steps but turned at the parlor door, and looked again at his daughter with a glance that arrested her with her foot on the lowest stair. "Marcia," he asked grimly, "are you engaged to Bartley Hubbard?"

The blood flashed up from her heart into her face like fire, and then as suddenly fell back again and left her white. She let her head droop and turn till her eyes were wholly averted from him, and she did not speak. He closed the door behind him and she went up stairs to her own room; in her shame she seemed to herself to crawl thither, with her father's glance burning upon her.

II

BARTLEY HUBBARD drove his sorrel colt back to the hotel stable through the moonlight, and woke up the ostler, asleep behind the counter on a bunk covered with buffalo robes. The half-grown boy did not wake easily: he conceived of the affair as a joke, and bade Bartley quit his fooling, till the young man took him by his collar, and stood him on his feet. Then he fumbled about the button of the lamp, turned low and smelling rankly, and lit his lantern, which contributed a rival stench to the choking air. He kicked together the embers that smouldered on the hearth of the Franklin stove, sitting down before it for his greater convenience, and having put a fresh pine root on the fire, fell into a doze, with his lantern in his hand. "Look here, young man!" said Bartley shaking him by the shoulder, "you had better go out and put that colt up, and leave this sleeping before the fire to me."

"Guess the colt can wait awhile," grumbled the boy; but he went out all the same, and Bartley, looking through the window saw his lantern wavering, a yellow blot in the white moonshine, towards the stable. He sat down in the ostler's chair, and in his turn kicked the pine-root with the heel of his shoe, and looked about the room. He had had, as he would have said, a grand good time; but it had left him hungry, and the table in the middle of the room, with the chairs huddled round it, was suggestive though he knew that it had been barrenly put there for the convenience of the landlord's friends, who came every night to play whist with him, and that nothing to eat or drink had ever been set out on it to interrupt the austere interest of the game. It was long since there had been anything on the shelves behind the counter cheerfuller than corn-balls and fancy-crackers for the children of the summer boarders; these dainties being out of the season the jars now stood there empty. The young man waited in a hungry reverie, in which it appeared to him that he was undergoing unmerited suffering, till the stable-boy came back, now wide awake and disposed to let the house share his vigils, as he stamped over the floor in his heavy boots.

"Andy," said Bartley in a pathetic tone of injury, "can't you scare me up something to eat?"

"There aint anything in the butt'ry but meat-pie," said the boy. He meant mince-pie, as Hubbard knew, and not a pasty of meat; and the hungry man hesitated.

"Well, fetch it," he said, finally. "I guess we can warm it up a little by the coals here." He had not been so long out of college but the idea of this irregular supper, when he had once formed it, began to have its fascination. He took up the broad fire shovel, and by the time the boy had clubbed to and from the pantry beyond the dining-room, Bartley had cleaned the shovel with a piece of newspaper, and was already heating it by the embers which he had raked out from under the pine-root. The boy silently transferred the half pie he had brought from its plate to the shovel; he pulled up a chair, and sat down to watch it; the pie began to steam and send out a savory odor; he himself in thawing emitted a stronger and stronger smell of stable. He was not without his disdain for the palate which must have its mince-pie warm at midnight; nor without his respect for it either: this fastidious taste must be part of the splendor which showed itself in Mr. Hubbard's city-cut clothes, and in his neck-scarfs, and the perfection of his finger nails and moustache. The boy had felt the original impression of these facts deepened rather than effaced by custom: they were for every day, and not, as he had at first conjectured, for some great occasion only.

"You don't suppose, Andy, there's such a thing as cold tea or coffee anywhere that we could warm up?" asked Bartley, gazing thoughtfully at the pie.

The boy shook his head. "Get you some milk," he said; and after he had let the dispiriting suggestion sink into the other's mind, he added, "Or some water."

"Oh, bring on the milk," groaned Bartley, but with the relief that a choice of evils affords.

The boy clubbed away for it, and when he came back the young man had got his pie on the plate again, and had drawn his chair up to the table. "Thanks," he said with his mouth full, as the boy set down the goblet of milk. Andy pulled his chair round so as to get an unrestricted view of a man who ate his pie with his fork as easily as another would with a knife. "That sister of yours is a smart girl," the young man added, making deliberate progress with the pie.

The boy made an inarticulate sound of satisfaction, and resolved in his heart to tell her what Mr. Hubbard had said. "She's as smart as time," continued Bartley. This was something concrete; the boy knew he should remember that comparison.

"Bring you anything else?" he asked, admiring the young man's skill in getting the last flakes of the crust on his fork: the pie had now vanished.

"Why, there isn't anything else, is there?" Bartley demanded with the plaintive dismay of a man who fears he has flung away his hunger upon one dish when he might have had something better.

"Cheese," replied the boy.

"Oh," said Bartley. He reflected a while. "I suppose I could toast a piece on this fork. But there isn't any more milk."

The boy took away the plate and goblet, and brought them again replenished.

Bartley contrived to get the cheese on his fork, and to rest it against one of the andirons so that it would not fall into the ashes. When it was done, he ate it as he had eaten the pie, without offering to share his feast with the boy. "There!" he said. "Yes, Andy, if she keeps on as she's been doing, she wont have any trouble. She's a bright girl." He stretched his legs before the fire again, and presently yawned.

"Want your lamp, Mr. Hubbard?" asked the boy.

"Well, yes, Andy," the young man consented, "I suppose I may as well go to bed."

But when the boy brought his lamp, he still remained with outstretched legs in front of the fire. Speaking of Hannah Morrison made him think of Marcia again and of the way in which she had spoken of the girl. He lolled his head on one side in such comfort as a young man finds in the conviction that a pretty girl is not only fond of him but is instantly jealous of any other girl whose name is mentioned. He smiled at the flame in his revery, and the boy examined, with clandestine minuteness, the set and pattern of his pantaloons, with glances of reference and comparison to his own.

There were many things about his relations with Marcia Gaylord which were calculated to give Bartley satisfaction. She was without question the prettiest girl in the place, and she had more style than any other girl began to have. He liked to go into a room with Marcia Gaylord; it was some pleasure. Marcia was a lady; she had a good education; she had been away two years to school; and when she came back at the end of the second winter he knew that she had fallen in love with him at sight; he believed that he could time it to a second. He remembered how he had looked up at her as he passed, and she had reddened and tried to turn away from the window as if she had not seen him. Bartley was still free as air; but if he could once make up his mind to settle down in a hole like Equity he could have her by turning his hand. Of course she had her drawbacks, like everybody. She was proud, and she would be jealous; but with all her pride and her distance she had let him see that she liked him; and not a word on his part that any one could hold him to.

"Hullo!" he cried, with a suddenness that startled the boy,

who had finished his meditation upon Bartley's pantaloons, and was now deeply dwelling on his boots. "Do you like 'em? See what sort of shine you can give 'em for Sunday-go-to-meeting to-morrow morning." He put out his hand and laid hold of the boy's head, passing his fingers through the thick red hair. "Sorrel-top!" he said, with a grin of agreeable reminiscence. "They emptied all the freckles they had left, into your face, didn't they, Andy?"

This free, joking way of Bartley's was one of the things that made him popular; he passed the time of day, and was give and take right along, as his admirers expressed it, from the first, in a community where his smartness had that honor which gives us more smart men to the square mile than any other country in the world. The fact of his smartness had been affirmed and established in the strongest manner by the authorities of the college at which he was graduated, in answer to the reference he made to them when negotiating with the committee in charge for the place he now held as editor of the Equity Free Press. The faculty spoke of the solidity and variety of his acquirements; and the distinction with which he had acquitted himself in every branch of study he had undertaken; they added that he deserved the greater credit because his early disadvantages as an orphan, dependent on his own exertions for a livelihood, had been so great that he had entered college with difficulty and with heavy conditions. This turned the scale with a committee who had all been poor boys themselves and justly feared the encroachments of hereditary aristocracy. They perhaps had their misgivings when the young man in his well blacked boots, his gray pantaloons neatly fitting over them, and his diagonal coat buttoned high with one button stood before them with his thumbs in his waistcoat pockets and looked down over his moustache at the floor with sentiments concerning their wisdom which they could not explore; they must have resented the fashionable keeping of everything about him, for Bartley wore his one suit as if it were but one of many; but when they understood that he had come by everything through his own unaided smartness, they could no longer hesitate. One indeed still felt it a duty to call attention to the fact that the college authorities said nothing of the young man's moral characteristics, in a letter dwelling so largely upon his intellectual qualifications. The others referred this point by a silent look, to Squire Gaylord.

"I don't know," said the Squire, "as I ever heard that a great deal of morality was required by a newspaper editor." The rest laughed at the joke, and the Squire continued: "But I guess if he worked his own way through college, as they say, that he hain't had time to be up to a great deal of mischief. You know it's for idle hands that the devil provides, doctor."

"That's true, as far as it goes," said the doctor. "But it isn't the whole truth. The devil provides for some busy hands, too."

"There's a good deal of sense in that," the Squire admitted. "The worst scamps I ever knew were active fellows. Still, industry is in a man's favor. If the faculty knew anything against this young man they would have given us a hint of it. I guess we had better take him; we sha'n't do better. Is it a vote?"

The good opinion of Bartley's smartness which Squire Gaylord had formed was confirmed some months later by the development of the fact that the young man did not regard his management of the Equity Free Press as a final vocation. The story went that he lounged into the lawyer's office one Saturday afternoon in October, and asked him to let him take his Blackstone into the woods with him. He came back with it a few hours later. "Well, sir," said the attorney, sardonically, "how much Blackstone have you read?"

"About forty pages," answered the young man, dropping into one of the empty chairs, and hanging his leg over the arm. The lawyer smiled, and opening the book, asked half a dozen questions at random. Bartley answered without changing his indifferent countenance, or the careless posture he had fallen into. A sharper and longer examination followed: the very language seemed to have been unbrokenly transferred to his mind, and he often gave the author's words as well as his ideas.

"Ever looked at this before?" asked the lawyer, with a keen glance at him over his spectacles.

"No," said Bartley, gaping as if bored, and further relieving his weariness by stretching. He was without deference for any presence; and the old lawyer did not dislike him for this: he had no deference himself.

"You think of studying law?" he asked, after a pause.

"That's what I came to ask you about," said Bartley, swinging his leg.

The elder recurred to his book, and put some more questions. Then he said, "Do you want to study with me?"

"That's about the size of it."

He shut the book, and pushed it on the table towards the young man. "Go ahead. You'll get along—if you don't get along too easily."

It was in the spring after this that Marcia returned home from her last term at boarding-school, and first saw him.

III

BARTLEY woke on Sunday morning with the regrets that a supper of mince-pie and toasted cheese is apt to bring. He woke from a bad dream, and found that he had a dull headache. A cup of coffee relieved his pain, but it left him listless, and with a longing for sympathy, which he experienced in any mental or physical discomfort. The frankness with which he then appealed for compassion was one of the things that made people like him; he flung himself upon the pity of the first he met. It might be some one to whom he had said a cutting or mortifying thing at their last encounter, but Bartley did not mind that: what he desired was commiseration and he confidingly ignored the past in a trust that had rarely been abused. If his sarcasm proved that he was quick and smart, his recourse to those who had suffered from it proved that he did not mean anything by what he said; it showed that he was a man of warm feelings and that his heart was in the right place.

Bartley deplored his disagreeable sensations to the other boarders at breakfast, and affectionately excused himself to them for not going to church, when they turned into the office, and gathered there before the Franklin stove, sensible of the day in freshly shaven chins and newly blacked boots. The habit of church going was so strong and universal in Equity that even strangers stopping at the hotel found themselves the object of a sort of hospitable competition with the members of the different denominations, who took it for granted that they would wish to go somewhere, and only suffered them a choice between sects. There was no intolerance in their offer of pews, but merely a profound expectation, and one might continue to choose his place of worship Sabbath after Sabbath without offence. This was Bartley's custom, and it had worked to his favor rather than his disadvantage; for in the rather chaotic liberality into which religious sentiment had fallen in Equity, it was tacitly conceded that the editor of a paper devoted to the interests of the whole town, ought not to be of fixed theological opinions.

Religion there had largely ceased to be a fact of spiritual experience and the visible church flourished on condition of providing for the social needs of the community. It was practically held that the salvation of one's soul must not be made too depressing, or the young people would have nothing to do with it. Professors of the sternest creeds temporized with sinners, and did what might be done to win them to heaven by helping them to have a good time here. The church embraced and included the world. It no longer frowned even upon social dancing, a transgression once so heinous in its eyes; it opened its doors to popular lectures; and encouraged secular music in its basements, where during the winter oyster-suppers were given in aid of good objects. The Sunday School was made particularly attractive, both to the children and the young men and girls who taught them. Not only at Thanksgiving but at Christmas, and latterly even at Easter, there were special observances, which the enterprising spirits having the welfare of the church at heart, tried to make significant and agreeable to all, and promotive of good feeling. Christenings and marriages in the church were encouraged and elaborately celebrated; death alone, though treated with cut flowers in emblematic devices, refused to lend itself to the cheerful intentions of those who were struggling to render the idea of another and a better world less repulsive. In contrast with the relaxation and uncertainty of their doctrinal aim, the rude and bold infidelity of old Squire Gaylord had the greater affinity with the mood of the Puritanism they had outgrown. But Bartley Hubbard liked

the religious situation well enough. He took a leading part in
the entertainments, and did something to impart to them a
literary cast, as in the series of readings from the poets which he
gave, the first winter, for the benefit of each church in turn.
At these lectures he commended himself to the sober elders,
who were troubled by the levity of his behavior with young
people on other occasions, by asking one of the ministers to
open the exercises with prayer, and another, at the close, to invoke the divine blessing: there was no especial relevancy in
this, but it pleased. He kept himself, from the beginning,
pretty constantly in the popular eye. He was a speaker at all
public meetings, where his declamation was admired, and at
private parties, where the congealed particles of village society
were united in a frozen mass, he was the first to break the ice,
and set the angular fragments grating and grinding upon one
another.

He now went to his room, and opened his desk with some
vague purposes of bringing up the arrears of his correspondence. Formerly, before his interest in the newspaper had
lapsed at all, he used to give his Sunday leisure to making selections and writing paragraphs for it; but he now let the pile of
exchanges lie unopened on his desk, and began to rummage
through the letters scattered about in it. They were mostly
from young ladies, with whom he had corresponded, and some
of them enclosed the photographs of the writers, doing their
best to look as they hoped he might think they looked. They
were not love-letters, but were of that sort which the laxness
of our social life invites young people, who have met pleasantly, to exchange as long as they like without explicit intentions on either side: they commit the writers to nothing; they
are commonly without result except in wasting time which is
hardly worth saving. Every one who has lived the American
life must have produced them in great numbers. While youth
lasts, they afford an excitement whose charm is hard to realize
afterwards.

Bartley's correspondents were young ladies of his college

town, where he had first begun to see something of social life in days which he now recognized as those of his green youth. They were not so very far removed in point of time; but the experience of a larger world in the vacation he had spent with a Boston student had relegated them to a moral remoteness that could not readily be measured. His friend was the son of a family who had diverted him from the natural destiny of a Boston man at Harvard, and sent him elsewhere for sectarian reasons. They were rich people, devout in their way, and benevolent, after a fashion of their own; and their son always brought home with him for the holidays and other short vacations some fellow student accounted worthy of their hospitality through his religious intentions or his intellectual promise. These guests were indicated to the young man by one of the faculty, and he accepted their companionship for the time with what perfunctory civility he could muster. He and Bartley had amused themselves very well during that vacation. The Hallecks were not fashionable people, but they lived wealthily: they had a coachman and an inside man (whom Bartley at first treated with a consideration that it afterwards mortified him to think of); their house was richly furnished with cushioned seats, dense carpets and heavy curtains; and they were visited by other people of their denomination and of a like abundance. Some of these were infected with the prevailing culture of the city, and the young ladies especially dressed in a style and let fall ideas that filled the soul of the country student with wonder and worship. He heard a great deal of talk that he did not understand, but he eagerly treasured every impression, and pieced it out by question or furtive observation into an image often shrewdly true and often grotesquely untrue to the conditions into which he had been dropped. He civilized himself as rapidly as his light permitted. There was a great deal of church going; but he and young Halleck went also to lectures and concerts; they even went to the opera, and Bartley, with the privity of his friend, went to the theatre. Halleck said that he did not think there was much harm in a play; but that his people stayed away for the sake of the example: a reason that certainly need not hold with Bartley.

At the end of the vacation he returned to college, leaving his measure with Halleck's tailor, and his heart with all the splendors and elegancies of the town. He found the ceilings very low, and the fashions much belated in the village; but he reconciled himself as well as he could. The real stress came when he left college and the question of doing something for himself pressed upon him. He intended to study law, but he must meantime earn his living. It had been his fortune to be left when very young not only an orphan but an extremely pretty child, with an exceptional aptness for study; and he had been better cared for than if his father and mother had lived. He had been not only well housed and fed, and very well dressed, but pitied as an orphan, and petted for his beauty and talent, while he was always taught to think of himself as a poor boy, who was winning his own way through the world. But when his benefactor proposed to educate him for the ministry, with a view to his final use in missionary work, he revolted. He apprenticed himself to the printer of his village, and rapidly picked up a knowledge of the business, so that at nineteen he had laid by some money, and was able to think of going to college. There was a fund in aid of indigent students in the institution to which he turned, and the faculty favored him. He finished his course with great credit to himself and the college, and he was naturally inclined to look upon what had been done for him earlier, as an advantage taken of his youthful inexperience. He rebelled against the memory of that tutelage, in spite of which he had accomplished such great things. If he had not squandered his time or fallen into vicious courses in circumstances of so much discouragement, if he had come out of it all self-reliant and independent, he knew whom he had to thank for it. The worst of the matter was that there was some truth in all this.

The ardor of his satisfaction cooled in the two years following his graduation, when in intervals of teaching country schools he was actually reduced to work at his trade, on a village newspaper. But it was as a practical printer, through the free-masonry of the craft that Bartley heard of the wish of the Equity committee to place the Free Press in new hands, and he had to be grateful to his trade for a primary consideration from them which his collegiate honors would not have won him. There had not yet begun to be that talk of journalism as a profession which has since prevailed with our collegians, and if Bartley had thought, as other collegians think, of devoting himself to newspaper life, he would have turned his face towards the city where its prizes are won: the ten and fifteen dollar reporterships for which a four years' course of the classics is not too costly a preparation. But to tell the truth he had never regarded his newspaper as anything but a makeshift, by which he was to be carried over a difficult and anxious period of his life, and enabled to attempt something worthier his powers. He had no illusions concerning it: if he had ever thought of journalism as a grand and ennobling profession, these ideas had perished in his experience in a village printing-office. He came to his work in Equity with practical and immediate purposes which pleased the committee better. The paper had been established some time before, in one of those flurries of ambition which from time to time seized Equity, when its citizens reflected that it was the central town in the county and yet not the shire-town. The question of the removal of the county-seat had periodically arisen before; but it had never been so hotly agitated as now. The paper had been a happy thought of a local politician whose conception of its management was that it might be easily edited by a committee if a printer could be found to publish it; but a few months' experience had made the Free Press a terrible burden to its founders; it could not be sustained, and it could not be let die without final disaster to the interests of the town; and the committee began to cast about for a publisher who could also be editor. Bartley, to whom it fell, could not be said to have thrown his heart and soul into the work, but he threw all his

energy, and he made it more than its friends could have hoped.
He espoused the cause of Equity in the pending question with
the zeal of a *condottiere*, and did service no less faithful because
of the cynical quality latent in it. When the legislative decision
against Equity put an end to its ambitious hopes for the time
being, he continued in control of the paper, with a fair prospect of getting the property into his own hands at last, and
with some growing question in his mind whether, after all, it
might not be as easy for him to go into politics from the newspaper as from the law. He managed the office very economically, and by having the work done by girl-apprentices, with
the help of one boy, he made it self-supporting. He modeled
the newspaper upon the modern conception, through which
the country press must cease to have any influence in public
affairs, and each paper become little more than an open letter
of neighborhood gossip. But while he filled his sheet with
minute chronicles of the goings and comings of unimportant
persons, and with all attainable particulars of the ordinary
life of the different localities, he continued to make spicy hits
at the enemies of Equity in the late struggle, and kept the public spirit of the town alive. He had lately undertaken to make
known its advantages as a summer resort, and had published a
series of encomiums upon the beauty of its scenery and the
healthfulness of its air and water which it was believed would
put it in a position of rivalry with some of the famous White
Mountain places. He invited the enterprise of outside capital,
and advocated a narrow gauge road up the valley of the river
through the Notch, so as to develop the picturesque advantages of that region. In all this, the color of mockery let the
wise perceive that Bartley saw the joke and enjoyed it, and it
deepened the popular impression of his smartness. This vein
of cynicism was not characteristic, as it would have been in an
older man: it might have been part of that spiritual and intellectual unruliness of youth, which people laugh at and forgive and which one generally regards in after-life as something
almost alien to one's self. He wrote long bragging articles about

Equity in a tone bordering on burlesque, and he had a department in his paper where he printed humorous squibs of his
own and of other people; these were sometimes copied, and in
the daily papers of the State he had been mentioned as "the
funny man of the Equity Free Press." He also sent letters to
one of the Boston journals, which he reproduced in his own
sheet, and which gave him an importance that the best endeavor as a country editor would never have won him with
the villagers. He would naturally, as the local printer, have
ranked a little above the foreman of the saw mill in the social
scale, and decidedly below the master of the Academy; but his
personal qualities elevated him over the head even of the
latter. But above all, the fact that he was studying law was a
guaranty of his superiority that nothing else could have given:
that science is the fountain of the highest distinction in a
country town. Bartley's whole course implied that he was
above editing the Free Press, but that he did it because it
served his turn. That was admirable.

He sat a long time with these girls' letters before him, and
lost himself in a pensive reverie over their photographs, and
over the good times he used to have with them. He mused in
that formless way in which a young man thinks about young
girls; his soul is suffused with a sense of their sweetness and
brightness, and unless he is distinctly in love there is no intention in his thoughts of them; even then there is often no
intention. Bartley might very well have a good conscience
about them; he had broken no hearts among them, and had
only met them half way in flirtation. What he really regretted,
as he held their letters in his hand was that he had never got
up a correspondence with two or three of the girls whom he
had met in Boston. Though he had been cowed by their magnificence in the beginning, he had never had any reverence
for them: he believed that they would have liked very well to
continue his acquaintance; but he had not known how to open
a correspondence, and the point was one on which he was
ashamed to consult Halleck. These college-belles, compared

with them, were amusingly inferior; by a natural turn of
thought, he realized that they were inferior to Marcia Gaylord,
too, in looks and style, no less than in an impassioned preference for himself. A distaste for their somewhat veteran ways
in flirtation grew upon him as he thought of her; he philosophized against them to her advantage; he could not blame
her if she did not know how to hide her feelings for him. Yet
he knew that Marcia would rather have died than let him
suppose that she cared for him, if she had known that she was
doing it. The fun of it was that she should not know; this
charmed him, it touched him even; he did not think of it
exultantly, as the night before, but sweetly, fondly, and with
a final curiosity to see her again, and enjoy the fact in her
presence. The acrid little jets of smoke which escaped from
the joints of his stove from time to time, annoyed him; he shut
his portfolio at last and went out to walk.

IV

THE FORENOON sunshine, beating strong upon the thin snow along the edges of the porch floor, tattered them with a little thaw here and there; but it had no effect upon the hard-packed levels of the street up the middle of which Bartley walked in a silence intensified by the muffled voices of exhortation that came to him out of the churches. It was in the very heart of sermon time, and he had the whole street to himself, on his way up to Squire Gaylord's house. As he drew near, he saw smoke ascending from the chimney of the lawyer's office, a little white building that stood apart from the dwelling on the left of the gate, and he knew that the old man was within, reading there, with his hat on, and his long legs flung out toward the stove, unshaven and unkempt, in a grim protest against the prevalent Christian superstition. He might be reading Hume, or Gibbon; or he might be reading the Bible: a book in which he was deeply versed, and from which he was furnished with texts for the demolition of its friends, his adversaries. He professed himself a great admirer of its literature, and in the heat of controversy he often found himself a defender of its doctrine when he had occasion to expose the fallacy of latitudinarian interpretations. For liberal Christianity he had nothing but contempt, and refuted it with a scorn which spared none of the worldly tendencies of the church in Equity. The idea that souls were to be saved by church sociables, filled him with inappeasable rancor; and he maintained the superiority of the old Puritanic discipline against them with a fervor which nothing but its re-establishment could have abated. It was said that Squire Gaylord's influence had largely helped to keep in place the last of the rigidly orthodox ministers, under whom his liberalizing congregation chafed for years of discontent; but this was probably an exaggeration of the native humor. Mrs. Gaylord had belonged to this church and had never formally withdrawn from it; and the lawyer always contributed to pay the minister's salary; he also managed a little property for him so well as to make him independent when he was at last asked to resign by his deacons.

In another mood, Bartley might have stepped aside to look in on the Squire, before asking at the house-door for Marcia. They relished each other's company, as people of contrary opinions and of no opinions are apt to do. Bartley loved to hear the Squire get going, as he said, and the old man felt a fascination in the youngster. Bartley was smart; he took a point quick as lightning; and the Squire did not mind his making friends with the Mammon of Righteousness, as he called the visible church in Equity: it amused him to see Bartley lending the church the zealous support of the press, with an impartial patronage of the different creeds. There had been times in his own career, when the silence of his opinions would have greatly advanced him, but he had not chosen to pay this price for success; he liked his freedom, or he liked the bitter tang of his own tongue too well, and he had remained a leading lawyer in Equity when he might have ended a judge, or even a Congressman. Of late years, however, since people whom he could have joined in their agnosticism so heartily, up to a certain point, had begun to make such fools of themselves about Darwinism and the brotherhood of all men in the monkey, he had grown much more tolerant. He still clung to his old-fashioned deistical opinions; but he thought no worse of a man for not holding them; he did not deny that a man might be a Christian and still be a very good man.

The audacious humor of his position sufficed with a people who like a joke rather better than any thing else; in his old age, his infidelity was something that would hardly have been changed, if possible, by a popular vote.

Even his wife, to whom it had once been a heavy cross, borne with secret prayer and tears, had long ceased to gainsay it in any wise. Her family had opposed her yoking with an unbeliever when she married him, but she had some such hopes of converting him, as women cherish who give themselves to men confirmed in drunkenness. She learned, as other women do that she could hardly change her husband in the least of his habits, and that in this great matter of his unbelief her love was powerless. It became easier at last for her to add self-sacrifice to self-sacrifice, than to vex him with her anxieties about his soul, and to act upon the feeling that if he must be lost, then she did not care to be saved. He had never interfered with her church-going; he had rather promoted it, for he liked to have women go; but the time came when she no longer cared to go without him; she lapsed from her membership, and it was now many years since she had worshipped with the people of her faith, if indeed she were still of any faith. Her life was silenced in every way, and as often happens with aging wives in country towns she seldom went out of her own door, and never appeared at the social or public solemnities of the village. Her husband and her daughter composed and bounded her world; she always talked of them, or of other things as related to them. She had grown an elderly woman, without losing the color of her yellow hair; and the bloom of girlhood had been stayed in her cheeks as if by the young habit of blushing which she had kept. She was still what her neighbors called very pretty-appearing, and she must have been a beautiful girl. The silence of her inward life subdued her manner, till now she seemed always to have come from some place on which a deep hush had newly fallen.

She answered the door when Bartley turned the crank that snapped the gong-bell in its centre; and the young man who was looking at the street while waiting for some one to come, confronted her with a start. "Oh!" he said. "I thought it was

Marcia! Good-morning, Mrs. Gaylord. Isn't Marcia at home?"

"She went to church, this morning," replied her mother. "Wont you walk in?"

"Why, yes, I guess I will, thank you," faltered Bartley in the irresolution of his disappointment. "I hope I sha'n't disturb you."

"Come right into the sitting-room. She wont be gone a great while, now," said Mrs. Gaylord, leading the way to the large square room into which a door at the end of the narrow hall opened. A slumbrous heat from a sheet-iron wood-stove pervaded the place, and a clock ticked monotonously on a shelf in the corner. Mrs. Gaylord said, "Wont you take a chair," and herself sank into the rocker, with a deep feather cushion, in the seat, and a thinner feather cushion tied half way up the back. After the more active duties of her housekeeping were done, she sat every day in this chair with her knitting or sewing, and let the clock tick the long hours of her life away, with no more apparent impatience of them, or sense of their dulness than the cat on the braided rug at her feet, or the geraniums in their pots at the sunny window. "Are you pretty well to-day?" she asked.

"Well no, Mrs. Gaylord, I'm not," answered Bartley. "I'm all out of sorts. I haven't felt so dyspeptic for I don't know how long."

Mrs. Gaylord smoothed the silk dress across her lap: the thin old black silk, which she still instinctively put on for Sabbath observance, though it was so long since she had worn it to church. "Mr. Gaylord used to have it when we were first married, though he ain't been troubled with it of late years. He seemed to think then, it was worse, Sundays."

"I don't believe Sunday has much to do with it in my case. I ate some mince pie and some toasted cheese, last night, and I guess they didn't agree with me very well," said Bartley, who did not spare himself the confession of his sins when seeking sympathy: it was this candor that went so far to convince people of his good heartedness.

"I don't know as I ever heard that meat-pie was bad," said Mrs. Gaylord thoughtfully. "Mr. Gaylord used to eat it right along all through his dyspepsia, and he never complained of it. And the cheese ought to have made it digest."

"Well, I don't know what it was," replied Bartley, plaintively submitting to be exonerated, "but I feel perfectly used up. Oh, I suppose I shall get over it, or forget all about it by to-morrow," he added with strenuous cheerfulness. "It isn't anything worth minding."

Mrs. Gaylord seemed to differ with him on this point. "Head ache any?" she asked.

"It did, this morning when I first woke up," Bartley assented.

"I don't believe but what a cup of tea would be the best thing for you," she said critically.

Bartley had instinctively practiced a social art which ingratiated him with people at Equity as much as his demands for sympathy endeared him: he gave trouble in little unusual ways.

He now said, "Oh, I wish you would give me a cup, Mrs. Gaylord."

"Why, yes indeed! That's just what I was going to," she replied. She went to the kitchen which lay beyond another room, and re-appeared with the tea directly, proud of her promptness but having it on her conscience to explain it. "I 'most always keep the pot on the stove hearth, Sunday morning, so's to have it ready if Mr. Gaylord ever wants a cup. He's a master hand for tea, and always was. There: *I* guess you better take it without milk. I put some sugar in the saucer, if you want any." She dropped noiselessly upon her feather cushion again, and Bartley who had risen to receive the tea from her remained standing while he drank it.

"That does seem to go to the spot," he said, as he sipped it thoughtfully observant of its effect upon his disagreeable feelings. "I wish I had you to take care of me, Mrs. Gaylord, and keep me from making a fool of myself," he added, when he had drained the cup. "No, no!" he cried, at her offering to take it from him, "I'll set it down. I know it will fret you to have it in here, and I'll carry it out into the kitchen." He did so before she could prevent him, and came back, touching his moustache with his handkerchief. "I declare, Mrs. Gaylord, I should love to live in a kitchen like that."

"I guess you wouldn't, if you had to," said Mrs. Gaylord, flattered into a smile. "Marcia she likes to sit out there, she says, better than anywheres in the house. But I always tell her it's because she was there so much when she was little. I don't see as she seems over-anxious to do anything there *but* sit, I tell her. Not but what she knows how, well enough. Mr. Gaylord, too, he's great for being round in the kitchen. If he gets up in the night, when he has his waking spells, he rather take his lamp out there, if there's a fire left, and read, any time, than what he would in the parlor. Well, we used to sit there together a good deal when we were young, and he got the habit of it. There's everything in habit," she added, thoughtfully. "Marcia she's got quite in the way lately, of going to the Methodist church."

"Yes, I've seen her there. You know I board round at the different churches, as the schoolmaster used to at the houses in the old times."

Mrs. Gaylord looked up at the clock, and gave a little nervous laugh. "I don't know what Marcia *will* say to my letting her company stay in the sitting-room. She's pretty late, to-day. But I guess you wont have much longer to wait, now." She spoke with that awe of her daughter and her judgments which is one of the pathetic idiosyncrasies of a certain class of American mothers. They feel themselves to be not so well-educated as their daughters whose fancied knowledge of the world they let outweigh their own experience of life; they are used to deferring to them, and they shrink willingly into household drudges before them, and leave them to order the social affairs of the family. Mrs. Gaylord was not much afraid of Bartley for himself, but as Marcia's company he made her more and more uneasy toward the end of the quarter of an hour in

which she tried to entertain him with her simple talk, varying
from Mr. Gaylord to Marcia and from Marcia to Mr. Gaylord
again. When she recognized the girl's quick touch in the closing of the front door, and her elastic step approached through
the hall, the mother made a little deprecatory noise in her
throat, and fidgeted in her chair. As soon as Marcia opened
the sitting-room door, Mrs. Gaylord modestly rose, and went
out into the kitchen: the mother who remained in the room
when her daughter had company was an oddity almost unknown in Equity.

Marcia's face flashed all into a light of joy at sight of Bartley,
who scarcely waited for her mother to be gone before he drew
her towards him by the hand she had given. She mechanically
yielded, and then as if the recollection of some new resolution
forced itself through her pleasure at sight of him, she freed
her hand, and retreating a step or two, confronted him.

"Why, Marcia!" he cried, "what's the matter?"

"Nothing," she answered. It might have amused Bartley if
he had felt quite well, to see the girl so defiant of him, when she
was really so much in love with him, but it certainly did not
amuse him now: it disappointed him in his expectation of
finding her femininely soft and comforting and he did not
know just what to do. He stood staring at her in discomfiture,
while she gained in outward composure, though her cheeks
were of the jacqueminot red of the ribbon at her throat.

"What have I done, Marcia?" he faltered.

"Oh, you haven't done anything."

"Some one has been talking to you against me!"

"No one has said a word to me about you."

"Then why are you so cold—so strange—so—so—different."

"Different?"

"Yes,—from what you were last night," he answered with
an aggrieved air.

"Oh, we see some things differently by daylight," she lightly
explained. "Wont you sit down?"

"No, thank you," Bartley replied, sadly but unresentfully.

"I think I had better be going. I see there is something wrong"—

"I don't see why you say there is anything wrong," she retorted. "What have *I* done?"

"Oh, you have not *done* anything. I take it back. It is all right. But when I came here this morning, encouraged—hoping—that you had the same feeling as myself, and you seem to forget everything but a ceremonious acquaintanceship—why it is all right, of course. I have no reason to complain; but I must say that I can't help being surprised." He saw her lips quiver and her bosom heave. "Marcia, do you blame me for feeling hurt at your coldness, when I came here to tell you—to tell you I—I love you." With his nerves all unstrung, and his hunger for sympathy, he really believed that he had come to tell her this. "Yes," he added bitterly, "I *will* tell you, though it seems to be the last word I shall speak to you. I'll go, now."

"Bartley! You shall *never* go!" she cried, throwing herself in his way. "Do you think I don't care for you, too? You may kiss me—you may *kill* me, now!" The passionate tears sprang to her eyes, without the sound of sobs, or the contortion of weeping, and she did not wait for his embrace: she flung her arms round his neck, and held him fast, crying, "I wouldn't let you for your own sake, darling; and if I had died for it—I thought I *should* die last night—I was never going to let you kiss me again till you said—till—till now! Don't you see?"

She caught him tighter, and hid her face in his neck, and cried and laughed for joy and shame, while he suffered her caresses with a certain bewilderment. "I want to tell you now, I want to explain," she said, lifting her face, and letting him from her as far as her arms, caught round his neck, would reach, and fervidly searching his eyes lest some ray of what he would think should escape her. "Don't speak a word first! Father saw us, at the door last night,—he happened to be coming down stairs, because he couldn't sleep—just when you— Oh, Bartley, don't!" she implored, at the little smile that made his moustache quiver. "And he asked me whether we were engaged; and when I couldn't tell him we were, I know what he thought. I know how he despised me, and I determined that if you didn't tell me that you cared for me— And that's the reason, Bartley; and not—not because I didn't care more for you than I do for the whole world. And—and—you don't mind it, now, do you? It was for your sake, dearest!"

Whether Bartley perfectly divined or not all the feeling at which her words hinted, it was delicious to be clung about by such a pretty girl as Marcia Gaylord, to have her now darting her face into his neck-scarf with intolerable consciousness and now boldly confronting him with all-defying fondness, while she lightly pushed him and pulled him here and there in the vehemence of her appeal. Perhaps such a man, in those fastnesses of his nature which psychology has not yet explored, never loses, even in the tenderest transports, the sense of prey as to the girl whose love he has won; but if this is certain, it is also certain that he has transports which are tender, and Bartley now felt his soul melted with affection that was very novel and sweet. "Why, Marcia!" he said, "what a strange girl you are!" He sank into his chair again, and putting his arms round her waist, drew her upon his knee, like a child.

She held herself apart from him at her arm's length, and said, "Wait! Let me say it before it seems as if we had always been engaged, and everything was as right then as it is now. Did you despise me for letting you kiss me before we were engaged?"

"No," he laughed again. "I liked you for it."

"But if you thought I would let any one else, you wouldn't have liked it?"

This diverted him still more. "I shouldn't have liked that more than half as well."

"No," she said thoughtfully. She dropped her face awhile on his shoulder, and seemed to be struggling with herself. Then she lifted it, and, "Did you ever—did you"—she gasped.

"If you want me to say that all the other girls in the world are not worth a hair of your head, I'll say that, Marcia. Now let's talk business!"

This made her laugh, and—

"I shall want a little lock of yours," she said, as if they had hitherto been talking of nothing but each other's hair.

"And I shall want all of yours," he answered.

"No. Don't be silly." She critically explored his face. "How funny, to have a mole in your eyebrow!" She put her finger on it. "I never saw it before!"

"You never looked so closely. There's a scar at the corner of your upper lip, that I hadn't noticed."

"Can you see that?" she demanded, radiantly. "Well, you *have* got good eyes! The cat did it when I was a little girl."

The door opened, and Mrs. Gaylord surprised them in the celebration of these discoveries—or rather, she surprised herself, for she stood holding the door and helpless to move, though in her heart she had an apologetic impulse to retire, and she even believed that she made some murmurs of excuse for her intrusion. Bartley was equally abashed, but Marcia rose with the coolness of her sex in the intimate emergencies which confound a man.

"Oh, mother, it's you! I forgot about you. Come in! Or I'll set the table, if that's what you want." As Mrs. Gaylord continued to look from her to Bartley in her daze, Marcia added simply, "We're engaged, mother. You may as well know it first as last, and I guess you better know it first."

Her mother appeared not to think it safe to relax her hold upon the door, and Bartley went filially to her rescue: if it was rescue to salute her blushing defencelessness as he did. A confused sense of the extraordinary nature and possible impropriety of the proceeding may have suggested her husband to her mind; or it may have been a feeling that some remark was expected of her, even in the mental destitution to which she was reduced. "Have you told Mr. Gaylord about it?" she asked, of either, or neither, or both, as they chose to take it.

Bartley left the word to Marcia, who answered, "Well, no,

mother. We haven't yet. We've only just found it out ourselves. I guess father can wait till he comes in to dinner. I
intend to keep Bartley here to prove it."

"He said," remarked Mrs. Gaylord, whom Bartley had led
to her chair and placed on her cushion, " 't he had a headache
when he first come in," and she appealed to him for corroboration, while she vainly endeavored to gather force to grapple
again with the larger fact that he and Marcia were just engaged to be married.

Marcia stooped down and pulled her mother up out of her
chair with a hug. "Oh, come, now, mother! You mustn't let
it take your breath away," she said with patronizing fondness.
"I'm not afraid of what father will say. You know what he
thinks of Bartley—or Mr. Hubbard, as I presume you'll want
me to call him! Now mother, you just run up stairs, and put
on your best cap, and leave me to set the table and get up the
dinner. I guess I can get Bartley to help me. Mother, mother,
mother!" she cried, in happiness that was otherwise unutter-
able, and clasping her mother closer in her strong young arms
she kissed her with a fervor that made her blush again before
the young man.

"Marcia, Marcia! You hadn't ought to! It's ridiculous!" she
protested. But she suffered herself to be thrust out of the
room, grateful for exile in which she could collect her scattered
wits, and set herself to realize the fact that had dispersed them.
It was decorous also for her to leave Marcia alone with Mr.
Hubbard, far more so now than when he was merely company;
she felt that, and she fumbled over the dressing she was sent
about, and once she looked out of her chamber window at the
office where Mr. Gaylord sat, and wondered what Mr. Gaylord
(she thought of him, and even dreamt of him as Mr. Gaylord,
and had never, in the most familiar moments, addressed him
otherwise) *would* say! But she left the solution of the problem
to him and Marcia: she was used to leaving them to the settlement of their own difficulties.

"Now, Bartley," said Marcia, in the business-like way that
women assume in such matters as soon as the great fact is no

longer in doubt, "you must help me to set the table. Put up that leaf and I'll put up this. I'm going to do more for mother, more than I used to," she said, repentant in her bliss. "It's a shame how much I've left to her." The domestic instinct was already astir in her heart.

Bartley pulled the table-cloth straight for her, and vied with her in the rapidity and exactness with which he arranged the knives and forks at right angles beside the plates. When it came to some heavier dishes, they agreed to carry them turn about; but when it was her turn he put out his hand to support her elbow: "As I did last night, and saved you from dropping a lamp."

This made her laugh, and she dropped the first dish with a crash. "Poor mother!" she exclaimed. "I know she heard that, and she'll be in agony to know which one it is."

Mrs. Gaylord did indeed hear it far off in her chamber, and quaked with an anxiety which became intolerable at last. "Marcia! Marcia!" she quavered down the stairs, "what *have* you broken!"

Marcia opened the door long enough to call back, "Oh, only the old blue-edged platter, mother!" and then she flew at Bartley, crying, "For shame! For shame!" and pressing her hand over his mouth to stifle his laughter. "She'll hear you, Bartley, and think you're laughing at her." But she laughed herself at his struggles, and ended by taking him by the hand and pulling him out into the kitchen where neither of them could be heard. She abandoned herself in the extasy of her soul, and he thought she had never been so charming as in this wild gayety.

"Why, Marsh! I never saw you carry on so, before!"

"You never saw me engaged before! That's the way all girls act—if they get the chance. Don't you like me to be so?" she asked with quick anxiety.

"Rather!" he replied.

"Oh, Bartley," she exclaimed, "I feel like a child. I surprise myself as much as I do you; for I thought I had got very old, and I didn't suppose I should ever let myself go in this way.

But there is something about this that lets me be as silly as I like. It's somehow as if I were a great deal more alone when I'm with you than when I'm by myself! How does it make you feel?"

"Good!" he answered, and that satisfied her better than if he had entered into those subtleties which she had tried to express: it was more like a man. He had his arm about her again, and she put down her hand on his to press it closer against her heart.

"Of course," she explained, recurring to his surprise at her frolic mood, "I don't expect you to be silly because I am."

"No," he assented, "but how can I help it?"

"Oh, I don't mean for the time being; I mean generally speaking. I mean that I care for you because I know you know a great deal more than I do, and because I respect you. I know that everybody expects you to be something great, and I do too."

Bartley did not deny the justness of her opinions concerning himself, or the reasonableness of the general expectation; though he probably could not see the relation of these cold abstractions to the pleasure of sitting there with a pretty girl in that way. But he said nothing.

"Do you know," she went on, turning her face prettily round toward him, but holding it a little way off, to secure attention as impersonal as might be under the circumstances, "what pleased me more than anything else you ever said to me?"

"No," answered Bartley. "Something you got out of me when you were trying to make me tell you the difference between you and the other Equity girls?"

She laughed in glad defiance of her own consciousness. "Well, I *was* trying to make you compliment me; I'm not going to deny it. But I must say I got my come-uppance: you didn't say a thing I cared for. But you did afterwards. Don't you remember?"

"No. When?"

She hesitated a moment. "When you told me that my influence had—had—made you better, you know"—

"Oh!" said Bartley. "That! Well," he added carelessly, "it's every word true. Didn't you believe it?"

"I was just as glad as if I did; and it made me resolve never to do or say a thing that could lower your opinion of me; and then you know, there at the door—it all seemed part of our trying to make each other better. But when father looked at me in that way, and asked me if we were engaged, I went down into the dust with shame. And it seemed to me that you had just been laughing at me, and amusing yourself with me, and I was so furious I didn't know what to do. Do you know what I wanted to do? I wanted to run down stairs to father and tell him what you had said, and ask him if he believed you had ever liked any other girl." She paused a little, but he did not answer, and she continued. "But now I'm glad I didn't. And I shall never ask you that, and I shall not care for anything that you—that's happened before to-day. It's all right. And you *do* think I shall always *try* to make you good and happy, don't you?"

"I don't think you can make me much happier than I am at present, and I don't believe anybody could make me feel better," answered Bartley.

She gave a little laugh at his refusal to be serious, and let her head for fondness fall upon his shoulder, while he turned round and round a ring he found on her finger.

"Ah, ha!" he said after while. "Who gave you this ring, Miss Gaylord?"

"Father—Christmas before last," she promptly answered without moving. "I'm glad you asked," she murmured in a lower voice, full of pride in the maiden love she could give him. "There's never been any one but you or the thought of any one." She suddenly started away. "Now, let's play we're getting dinner." It was quite time: in the next moment the coffee boiled up, and if she had not caught the lid off and stirred it down with her spoon it would have been spoiled. The steam ascended to the ceiling and filled the kitchen with the fragrant soul of the berry.

"I'm glad we're going to have coffee," she said. "You'll have to put up with a cold dinner, except potatoes. But the coffee will make up, and I shall need a cup to keep me awake. I don't believe I slept last night till nearly morning. Do you like coffee?"

"I'd have given all I ever expect to be worth for a cup of it, last night," he said. "I was awfully hungry when I got back to the hotel, and I couldn't find anything but a piece of mince pie and some old cheese, and I had to be content with cold milk. I felt as if I had lost all my friends this morning, when I woke up."

A sense of remembered grievance trembled in his voice, and made her drop her head on his arm in pity and derision of him.

"Poor Bartley!" she cried. "And you came up here for a little petting from me, didn't you? I've noticed that in you! Well, you didn't get it, did you?"

"Well,—not at first," he said.

"Yes, you can't complain of any want of petting at last," she returned, delighted at his indirect recognition of the difference. The daring, the archness and caprice, that make coquetry in some women, and lurk a divine possibility in all, came out in her; the sweetness, kept back by the whole strength of her pride, overflowed that broken barrier now, and she seemed to lavish this revelation of herself upon him with a sort of tender joy in his bewilderment. She was not hurt when he crudely expressed the elusive sense which has been in other men's minds at such times: they cannot believe that this fascination is inspired, and not practiced. "Well," he said, "I'm glad you told me that I was the first. I should have thought you'd had a good deal of experience in flirtation."

"You wouldn't have thought so if you hadn't been a great flirt yourself," she answered, audaciously. "Perhaps I *have* been engaged before!"

Their talk was for the most part frivolous and their thoughts ephemeral, but again they were, with her at least, suddenly and deeply serious. Till then all things seemed to have been held in arrest, and impressions, ideas, feelings, fears, desires, released themselves simultaneously, and sought expression with a rush that defied coherence. "Oh, why do we try to talk?" she asked at last. "The more we say the more we leave unsaid. Let us keep still awhile!" But she could not. "Bartley! When did you first think you cared about me?"

"I don't know," said Bartley, "I guess it must have been the first time I saw you."

"Yes. That is when I first knew that I cared for you. But it seems to me that I must have always cared for you, and that I only found it out when I saw you going by the house that day." She mused a little time before she asked again, "Bartley!"

"Well."

"Did you ever use to be afraid— Or, no! Wait! I'll *tell* you first, and then I'll *ask* you. I'm not ashamed of it now, though once I thought I couldn't bear to have any one find it out. I used to be awfully afraid you didn't care for me! I would try to make out from things you did and said whether you did or not; but I never could be certain. I believe I used to find the most comfort in discouraging myself. I used to say to myself, 'Why of course he doesn't! How can he? He's been every where, and he's seen so many girls. He corresponds with lots of them. Altogether likely he's engaged to some of the young ladies he's met in Boston; and he just goes with me here for a blind.' And then when you would praise me, sometimes, I would just say, 'Oh, he's complimented plenty of girls. I know he's thinking this instant of the young lady he's engaged to in Boston.' And it would almost kill me; and when you did some little thing to show that you liked me, I would think, 'He doesn't like me! He hates, he despises me. He does, he does, he does!' And I would go on that way, with my teeth shut and my breath held, I don't know *how* long."

Bartley broke out into a broad laugh at this image of desperation, but she added tenderly, "I hope I never made you suffer in that way?"

"What way?" he asked.

"That's what I wanted you to tell me. Did you ever—did you use to be afraid sometimes that I—that you— Did you put off telling me that you cared for me, so long because you thought—you dreaded— Oh, I don't see what I can ever do to make it up to you if you did!— Were you afraid I didn't care for you?"

"No!" shouted Bartley. She had risen and stood before him in the fervor of her entreaty, and he seized her arms, pinioning them to her side, and holding her helpless, while he laughed and laughed again. "I knew you were dead in love with me from the first moment."

"Bartley! Bartley Hubbard!" she exclaimed. "Let me go! Let me go, this instant! I never heard of such a shameless thing!" But she really made no effort to escape.

V

THE HOUSE seemed too little for Marcia's happiness, and after dinner she did not let Bartley forget his last night's engagement. She sent him off to get his horse at the hotel, and ran up to her room to put on her wraps for the drive. Her mother cleared away the dinner things; she pushed the table to the side of the room, and then sat down in her feather-cushioned chair and waited her husband's pleasure to speak. He ordinarily rose from the Sunday dinner and went back to his office; to-day he had taken a chair before the stove. But he had mechanically put his hat on, and he wore it, pushed off his forehead as he tilted his chair back on its hind legs, and braced himself against the hearth of the stove with his feet.

A man is master in his own house generally through the exercise of a certain degree of brutality, but Squire Gaylord maintained his predominance by an enlightened absenteeism. No man living always at home was ever so little under his own roof. While he was in more active business life he had kept an office in the heart of the village, where he spent all his days, and a great part of every night; but after he had become rich enough to risk whatever loss of business the change might involve, he bought this large old square house on the border of the village, and thenceforth made his home in the little detached office. If Mrs. Gaylord had dimly imagined that she should see something more of him, having him so near at hand, she really saw less: there was no weather, by day or night in which he could not go to his office, now. He went no more than his wife into the village society; she might have been glad now and then of a little glimpse of the world, but she never said so, and her social life had ceased like her religious life. Their house was richly furnished according to the local taste of the time; the parlor had a Brussels carpet, and heavy chairs of mahogany and haircloth; Marcia had a piano there, and since she had come home from school they had made company, as Mrs. Gaylord called it, two or three times for her; but they had held aloof from the festivity, the Squire in his office, and Mrs. Gaylord in the family-room where they now sat in unwonted companionship.

"Well, Mr. Gaylord," said his wife, "I don't know as you can say but what *Marcia's* suited well enough." This was the first allusion they had made to the subject, but she let it take the argumentative form of her cogitations.

"Myes," sighed the Squire in long, nasal assent, "most too well, if anything." He rasped first one unshaven cheek and then the other, with his thin, quivering hand.

"He's smart enough," said Mrs. Gaylord, as before.

"Myes, most too smart," replied her husband, a little more quickly than before. "He's smart enough, even if she wasn't, to see from the start that she was crazy to have him, and that isn't the best way to begin life for a married couple, if I'm a judge."

"It would killed her, if she hadn't got him. I could see 'twas wearin' on her everyday, more and more. She used to fairly jump every knock she'd hear at the door; and I know sometimes, when she was afraid he wa'n't coming, she used to go out in hopes 't she sh'd meet him: I don't suppose she allowed to herself that she done it for that. Marcia's proud."

"Myes," said the Squire, "she's proud. And when a proud girl makes a fool of herself about a fellow, it's a matter of life and death with her. She can't help herself. She lets go everything."

"I declare," Mrs. Gaylord went on, "it worked me up considerable to have her come in some those times, and see by her face 't she'd seen him with some the other girls. She used to *look* so! And then I'd hear her up in her room, cryin' and cryin'. I shouldn't cared so much, if Marcia'd been like any other girl, kind of flirty like, about it. But she wa'n't. She was just bowed down before her idol."

A final assent came from the Squire as if wrung out of his heart, and he rose from his chair, and then sat down again. Marcia was his child, and he loved her with his whole soul. "Mwell!" he deeply sighed, "all that part's over, any way," but he tingled in an anguish of sympathy with what she had suffered. "You see, Miranda, how she looked at me when she first came in with him—so proud and independent, poor girl! and yet as if she was afraid I *mightn't* like it?"

"Yes, I see it."

He pulled his hat far down over his cavernous eyes, and worked his thin, rusty old jaws.

"I hope't she'll be able to school herself, so's't' not show out her feelings so much," said Mrs. Gaylord.

"I wish she could school herself so as to not have 'em so much; but I guess she'll have 'em, and I guess she'll show 'em out." They were both silent; after while he added, throwing at the stove a minute fragment of the cane he had pulled off the seat of his chair: "Miranda, I've expected something of this sort a good while, and I've thought over what Bartley had better do."

Mrs. Gaylord stooped forward and picked up the bit of wood which her husband had thrown down; her vigilance was rewarded by finding a thread on the oil-cloth near where it lay; she whipped this round her finger, and her husband continued: "He'd better give up his paper and go into the law. He's done well in the paper, and he's a smart writer; but editing a newspaper aint any work for a *man*. It's all well enough as long as he's single, but when he's got a wife to look after, he'd better get down to *work*. My business is in just such a shape now that I could hand it over to him in a lump; but come to wait a year or two longer, and this young man and that one 'll eat into it, and it wont be the same thing at all. I shall want Bartley to push right along, and get admitted at once. He can do it, fast enough. He's bright enough," added the old man with a certain grimness. "Mwell!" he broke out, with a quick sigh, after a moment of musing. "It hasn't happened at any very bad time. I was just thinking this morning, that I should like to have my whole time, pretty soon, to look after my property. I sha'n't want Bartley to do *that*, for me. I'll give him a good start in money and in business; but I'll look after my property myself. I'll speak to him, the first chance I get."

A light step sounded on the stairs, and Marcia burst into the room ready for her drive. "I wanted to get a good warm before I started," she explained, stooping before the stove, and supporting herself with one hand on her father's knee. There had been no formal congratulations upon her engagement from either of her parents; but this was not requisite, and would have been a little affected: they were perhaps now ashamed to mention it outright before her alone. The Squire, however, went so far as to put his hand over the hand she had laid upon his knee, and to smooth it twice or thrice.

"You going to ride after that sorrel colt of Bartley's?" he asked.

"Of course!" she answered with playful pertness. "I guess Bartley can manage the sorrel colt! He's never had any trouble yet."

"He's always been able to give his whole mind to him before," said the Squire. He gave Marcia's hand a significant squeeze, and let it go.

She would not confess her consciousness of his meaning at once. She looked up at the clock, and then turned and pulled her father's watch out of his waistcoat pocket, and compared the time. "Why, you're both fast!"

"Perhaps Bartley's slow," said the Squire, and having gone as far as he intended in this direction, he permitted himself a low chuckle.

The sleigh-bells jingled without, and she sprang lightly to her feet. "*I* guess you don't think Bartley's slow," she exclaimed, and hung over her father long enough to rub her lips against his bristly cheek. "By, mother," she said over her shoulder, and went out of the room. She let her muff hang as far down in front of her as her arms would reach, in a stylish way, and moved with a little rhythmical tilt, as if to some inner music. Even in her furs she was elegantly slender in shape.

The old people remained silent and motionless till the clash of the bells died away. Then the Squire rose, and went to the wood shed beyond the kitchen, whence he re-appeared with an armful of wood. His wife started at the sight. "Mr. Gaylord, what *be* you doin'?"

"Oh, I'm going to make 'em up a little fire in the parlor stove. I guess they wont want us round a great deal, when they come back."

"Well, I never did!" said Mrs. Gaylord. When her husband returned from the parlor, she added, "I suppose some folks'd say it was rather of a strange way of spendin' the Sabbath."

"It's a very good way of spending the Sabbath. You don't suppose that any of the people in church are half as happy, do you? Why old Jonathan Edwards himself used to allow 'all proper opportunity' for the young fellows that come to see his girls, 'and a room and fire, if needed.' His Life says so."

"I guess he didn't allow it on the Sabbath," retorted Mrs. Gaylord.

"Well, the Life don't say," chuckled the Squire. "Why Miranda, I do it for Marcia! There's never but one first day to an engagement. You know that as well as I do." In saying this, Squire Gaylord gave way to his repressed emotion in an extravagance. He suddenly stooped over and kissed his wife; but he spared her confusion by going out to his office at once, where he staid the whole afternoon.

Bartley and Marcia took the Long Drive as it was called, at Equity. The road plunged into the darkly wooded gulch beyond the house, and then struck away eastward, crossing loop after loop of the river on the covered bridges, where the neighbors, who had broken it out with their ox-teams in the open, had thickly bedded it in snow. In the valleys and sheltered spots it remained free and so wide that encountering teams could easily pass each other, but where it climbed a hill, or crossed a treeless level it was narrowed to a single track, with turnouts at established points where the drivers of the sleighs waited to be sure that the stretch beyond was clear before going forward. In the country the winter which held the village in such close siege was an occupation under which nature seemed to cower helpless, and men made a desperate and ineffectual struggle. The houses, banked-up with snow almost to the sills of the windows that looked out, blind with frost upon the lifeless world, were dwarfed in the drifts and seemed to founder in a white sea blotched with strange bluish shadows under the slanting sun. Where they fronted close upon the road, it was evident that the fight with the snow was kept up unrelentingly; spaces were shoveled out, and paths were kept open to the middle of the highway, and to the barn; but where they were somewhat removed, there was no visible trace of the conflict, and no sign of life except the faint, wreathed lines of smoke wavering upward from the chimneys.

In the hollows through which the road passed the lower boughs of the pines and hemlocks were weighed down with the snowfall till they lay half submerged in the drifts, but wherever the wind could strike them, they swung free of this load and met in low, flat arches above the track. The river betrayed itself only when the swift current of a ripple broke through the white surface in long, irregular grayish blurs. It was all wild and lonesome, but to the girl alone in it with her lover, the solitude was sweet, and she did not wish to speak even to him. His hands were both busy with the reins, but it was agreed between them that she might lock hers through his arm. Cowering close to him under the robes, she laid her head on his shoulder and looked out over the flying landscape in measureless content, and smiled, with filling eyes, when he bent over, and warmed his cold red cheek on the top of her fur cap.

The moments of bliss that silence a woman rouse a man to make sure of his rapture. "How do you like it, Marsh?" he asked, trying at one of these times to peer round into her face. "Are you afraid?"

"No—only of getting back too soon."

He made the shivering echoes answer with his delight in this, and chirruped to the colt, who pulsed forward at a wilder speed, flinging his hoofs out before him with the straight thrust of the born trotter, and seeming to overtake them as they flew. "I should like this ride to last forever!"

"Forever!" she repeated. "That would do for a beginning."

"Marsh! What a girl you are! I never supposed you would be so free to let a fellow know how much you cared for him."

"Neither did I," she answered dreamily. "But now—now the only trouble is that I don't know *how* to let him know." She gave his arm to which she clung a little convulsive clutch, and pressed her head harder upon his shoulder.

"Well, that's pretty much my complaint, too," said Bartley, "though I couldn't have expressed it so well."

"Oh, *you* express!" she murmured with the pride in him which implied that there were no thoughts worth expressing, to which he could not give a monumental utterance. Her adoration flattered his self-love to the same passionate intensity, and to something like the generous complexion of her worship. "Marcia," he answered, "I am going to try to be all you expect of me. And I hope I shall never do anything unworthy of your ideal."

She could only press his arm again in speechless joy, but she said to herself that she should always remember these words.

The wind had been rising ever since they started, but they had not noticed it till now when the woods began to thin away on either side, and he stopped before striking out over one of the naked stretches of the plain—a white waste swept by blasts that sucked down through a gorge of the mountain, and flattened the snow-drifts as the tornado flattens the waves. Across this expanse ran the road, its stiff lines obliterated here and there, in the slight depressions, and showing dark along the rest of the track. It was a good half mile to the next body of woods, and mid way, there was one of those sidings where a sleigh approaching from the other quarter must turn out and yield the right of way. Bartley stopped his colt, and scanned the road.

"Anybody coming?" asked Marcia.

"No, I don't see anyone. But if there's any one in the woods yonder, they'd better wait till I get across. No horse in Equity can beat this colt to the turnout."

"Oh, well look carefully, Bartley. If we met any one beyond the turnout, I don't know what I should do," pleaded the girl.

"I don't know what *they* would do," said Bartley. "But it's their lookout, now, if they come. Wrap your face up well, or put your head under the robe: I've got to hold my breath the next half mile." He loosed the reins and sped the colt out of the shelter where he had halted. The wind struck them like an edge of steel, and catching the powdery snow that their horse's hoofs beat up, sent it spinning and swirling far along the glistering levels on their lee. They felt the thrill of the go as if they were in some light boat leaping over a swift current. Marcia disdained to cover her face, if he must confront the wind, but after a few gasps she was glad to bend forward, and bury it in the long hair of the bearskin robe. When she lifted it, they were already past the siding, and she saw a cutter dashing toward them from the cover of the woods. "Bartley!" she screamed, "The sleigh!"

"Yes," he shouted. "Some fool! There's going to be trouble, here," he added, checking his horse as he could. "They don't seem to know how to manage— It's a couple of women! Hold on, hold on!" he called. "Don't try to turn out: I'll turn out!"

The women pulled their horse's head this way and that, in apparent confusion, and then began to turn out into the trackless snow at the roadside, in spite of Bartley's frantic efforts to arrest them. They sank deeper and deeper into the drift; their horse plunged and struggled, and then their cutter went over, amidst their shrieks and cries for help.

Bartley drove up abreast of the wreck, and saying, "Still,

Jerry! Don't be afraid, Marcia," he put the reins into her hands, and sprang out to the rescue.

One of the women had been flung out free of the sleigh, and had already gathered herself up, and stood crying and wringing her hands: "Oh, Mr. Hubbard, Mr. Hubbard! Help Hannah! She's under there!"

"All right! Keep quiet, Mrs. Morrison! Take hold of your horse's head!" Bartley had first of all seized him by the bit, and pulled him to his feet; he was old and experienced in obedience, and he now stood waiting orders, patiently enough. Bartley seized the cutter, and by an effort of all his strength righted it. The colt started and trembled, but Marcia called to him in Bartley's tone, "Still, Jerry!" and he obeyed her.

The girl who had been caught under the overturned cutter, escaped like a wild thing out of a trap, when it was lifted, and plunging some paces away, faced round upon her rescuer with the hood pulled straight and set comely to her face again, almost before he could ask: "Any bones broken, Hannah?"

"*No!*" she shouted. "Mother! Mother! Stop crying! Don't you see I'm not dead?" She leaped about, catching up this wrap and that, shaking the dry snow out of them, and flinging them back into the cutter, while she laughed in the wild tumult of her spirits. Bartley helped her pick up the fragments of the wreck, and joined her in her making fun of the adventure. The wind hustled them, but they were warm in defiance of it with their jollity and their bustle.

"Why didn't you let me turn out?" demanded Bartley, as he and the girl stood on opposite sides of the cutter, re-arranging the robes in it.

"Oh, I thought I could turn out, well enough. You had a right to the road."

"Well, the next time you see any one past the turn-out, you better not start from the woods."

"Why, there's no more room in the woods to get past than there is here," cried the girl.

"There's more shelter."

"Oh, I'm not cold!" She flashed a look at him from her

brilliant face, warm with all the glow of her young health, and laughed, and before she dropped her eyes, she included Marcia in her glance. They had already looked at each other without any sign of recognition. "Come, mother! All right, now!"

Her mother left the horse's head, and heavily ploughing back to the cutter, tumbled herself in. The girl from her side, began to climb in, but her weight made the sleigh careen, and she dropped down with a gay shriek. Bartley came round and lifted her in; the girl called to her horse, and drove up into the road and away.

Bartley looked after her a moment, and continued to glance in that direction when he stood stamping the snow off his feet, and brushing it from his legs and arms before he remounted to Marcia's side. He was excited, and talked rapidly and loudly, as he took the reins from Marcia's passive hold, and let the colt out. "That girl is the pluckiest fool, yet! Wouldn't let me turn out because I had the right of way! And she wasn't going to let anybody else have a hand in getting that old ark of theirs afloat again. Good their horse wasn't anything like Jerry! How well Jerry behaved! Were you frightened, Marsh?" He bent over to see her face, but she had not her head on his shoulder, and she did not sit close to him, now. "Did you freeze?"

"Oh, no! I got along, very well," she answered dryly, and edged away as far as the width of the seat would permit. "It would have been better for you to lead their horse up onto the road, and then she could have got in without your help. Her mother got in alone."

He took the reins into his left hand, and passing his strong right around her, pulled her up to his side. She resisted, with diminishing force; at last she ceased to resist, and her head fell passively to its former place on his shoulder. He did not try to speak any word of comfort; he only held her close to him; when she looked up as they entered the village, she confronted him with a brilliant smile that ignored her tears.

But that night, when she followed him to the door, she looked him searchingly in the eyes. "I wonder if you really do despise me, Bartley?" she asked.

"Certainly," he answered, with a jesting smile. "What for?"

"For showing out my feelings so. For not even trying to pretend not to care everything for you."

"It wouldn't be any use, your trying: I should know that you did, any way."

"Oh, don't laugh, Bartley, don't laugh! I don't believe that I ought to. I've heard that it makes people tired of you. But I can't help it—I can't help it. And if—if you think I'm always going to be so; and that I'm going to keep on getting worse and worse, and making you so unhappy, why you'd better break your engagement now—while you have a chance."

"What have you been making me unhappy about, I should like to know? I thought I'd been having a very good time."

She hid her face against his breast. "It almost *killed* me to see you there with her! I was so cold,—my hands were half-frozen, holding the reins,—and I was so afraid of the colt I didn't know what to do; and I had been keeping up my courage on your account; and you seemed so long about it all; and she could have got in perfectly well—as well as her mother did —without your help"— Her voice broke in a miserable sob, and she clutched herself tighter to him.

He smoothed down her hair with his hand. "Why, Marsh! Did you think that made me unhappy? *I* didn't mind it a bit. I knew what the trouble was, at the time; but I wasn't going to say anything. I knew you would be all right as soon as you could think it over. You don't suppose I care anything for that girl?"

"No," answered a rueful sob. "But I *wish* you didn't have anything to do with her. I know she'll make trouble for you, somehow."

"Well," said Bartley, "I can't very well turn her off as long as she does her work. But you needn't be worried about making me unhappy. If anything, I rather liked it. It showed how much you *did* care for me." He bent toward her with a look of bright raillery, for the parting kiss. "Now then: once, twice, three times—and good-night it is!"

VI

THE SPECTACLE of a love-affair in which the woman gives more of her heart than the man gives of his is so pitiable that we are apt to attribute a kind of merit to her, as if it were a voluntary self-sacrifice for her to love more than her share. Not only other men, but other women look on with this canonizing compassion; for women have a lively power of imagining themselves in the place of any sister who suffers in matters of sentiment, and are eager to espouse the common cause in commiserating her. Each of them pictures herself similarly wronged or slighted by the man she likes best, and feels how cruel it would be if he were to care less for her than she for him; and for the time being, in order to realize the situation, she loads him with all the sins of omission proper to the culprit in the alien case. But possibly there is a compensation in merely loving, even where the love given is out of all proportion to the love received.

If Bartley Hubbard's sensations and impressions of the day had been at all reasoned, that night as he lay thinking it over, he could unquestionably have seen many advantages for Marcia in the affair—perhaps more than for himself. But to do him justice he did not formulate these now, or in anywise explicitly recognize the favors he was bestowing. At twenty-six one does not naturally compute them in musing upon the girl to whom one is just betrothed; and Bartley's mind was a confusion of pleasure. He liked so well to think how fond of him Marcia was, that it did not occur to him then to question whether he were as fond of her. It is possible that as he drowsed, at last, there floated airily through the consciousness which was melting and dispersing itself before the approach of sleep, an intimation from somewhere to some one that perhaps the affair need not be considered too seriously. But in that mysterious limbo, one cannot be sure of what is thought and what is dreamed; and Bartley always acquitted himself, and probably with justice, of any want of seriousness.

What he did make sure of when he woke was that he was still out of sorts, and that he had again that dull headache; and his instant longing for sympathy did more than anything else to convince him that he really loved Marcia, and had never, in his obscurest or remotest feeling, swerved in his fealty to her. In the atmosphere of her devotion yesterday, he had so wholly forgotten his sufferings that he had imagined himself well; but now he found that he was not well, and he began to believe that he was going to have what the country people call a fit of sickness. He felt that he ought to be taken care of, that he was unfit to work; and in his vexation at not being able to go to Marcia for comfort—it really amounted to nothing less—he entered upon the day's affairs with fretful impatience.

The Free Press was published on Tuesdays, and Monday was always a busy time of preparation. The hands were apt also to feel the demoralization that follows a holiday even when it has been a holy day. The girls who set the type of the Free Press had by no means foregone the rights and privileges of their sex in espousing their art, and they had their beaux on Sunday night like other young ladies. It resulted that on Monday morning they were nervous and impatient, alternating between fits of giggling delight in the interchange of fond reminiscences and the crossness which is pretty sure to disfigure human behavior from want of sleep. But ordinarily Bartley got on very well with them. In spite of the assumption of equality between all classes in Equity, they stood in secret awe of his personal splendor, and the tradition of his achievements at college and in the great world, and a flattering joke or a sharp sarcasm from him went a great way with them. Besides he had an efficient lieutenant in Henry Bird, the young printer who had picked up his trade in the office, and who acted as Bartley's foreman, so far as the establishment had an organization. Bird had industry and discipline which were contagious, and that love of his work which is said to be growing rare among artizans in the modern subdivision of trades. This boy —for he was only nineteen—worked at his craft early and late out of pleasure in it. He seemed one of those simple, subordinate natures which are happy in looking up to whatever assumes to be above them. He exulted to serve in a world where most people prefer to be served, and it is uncertain whether he liked his work better for its own sake, or Bartley's, for whom he did it. He was slight and rather delicate in health, and it came natural for Bartley to patronize him. He took him on the long walks of which he was fond and made him in some sort his humble confidant, talking to him of himself and his plans with large and braggart vagueness. He depended upon Bird in a great many things, and Bird never failed him; for he had a basis of constancy that was immovable. "No," said a philosopher from a neighboring logging-camp, who used to hang about the printing-office a long time after he had got his paper, "there aint a great deal of natural push about Henry; but he stays put." In the confidences which Bartley used to make Bird, he promised that when he left the newspaper for the law, he would see that no one else succeeded him. The young fellow did not need this promise to make him Bartley's fast friend, but it colored his affection with ambitious enthusiasm: to edit and publish a newspaper—his dreams did not go beyond that; to devote it to Bartley's interest in the political life on which Bartley often hinted he might enter— that would be the sweetest privilege of realized success. Bird already wrote paragraphs for the Free Press, and Bartley let him make up a column of news from the city exchanges, which was partly written and partly selected.

Bartley came to the office rather late on Monday morning, bringing with him the papers from Saturday night's mail, which had lain unopened over Sunday, and went directly into his own room, without looking into the printing-office. He felt feverish and irritable, and he resolved to fill up with selections and let his editorial paragraphing go, or get Bird to do it. He was tired of the work, and sick of Equity: Marcia's face seemed to look sadly in upon his angry discontent, and he no longer wished to go to her for sympathy. His door opened, and without glancing from the newspaper which he held up before him he asked: "What is it, Bird? Do you want copy?"

"Well, no, Mr. Hubbard," answered Bird, "we have copy enough for the force we've got this morning."

"Why, what's up?" demanded Bartley, dropping his paper.

"Lizzie Sawyer has sent word that she is sick, and we haven't heard or seen anything of Hannah Morrison."

"Confound the girls!" said Bartley, "there's always something the matter with them." He rubbed his hand over his forehead, as if to rub out the dull pain there. "Well," he said, "I must go to work myself, then." He rose, and took hold of the lappels of his coat, to pull it off; but something in Bird's look arrested him. "What is it?" he asked.

"Old Morrison was here, just before you came in, and said he wanted to see you. I think he was drunk," said Bird, anxiously. "He said he was coming back again."

"All right; let him come," replied Bartley. "This is a free country—especially in Equity. I suppose he wants Hannah's wages raised, as usual. How much are we behind, on the paper, Henry?"

"We're not a great deal behind, Mr. Hubbard; if we were not so weak-handed."

"Perhaps we can get Hannah back, during the forenoon. At any rate we can ask her honored parent, when he comes."

Where Morrison got his liquor was a question that agitated Equity from time to time, and baffled the officer of the law empowered to see that no strong drink came into the town. Under conditions which made it impossible even in the logging-camps, and rendered the sale of spirits too precarious for the apothecary, who might be supposed to deal in them medicinally, Morrison never failed of his spree when the mysterious mechanism of his appetite enforced it. Probably it was some form of bedevilled cider that supplied the material of his debauch; but even cider was not easily to be had.

Morrison's spree was a movable feast, and recurred at irregular intervals of two, or three, or even six weeks, but it recurred often enough to keep him poor, and his family in a social outlawry against which the kindly instincts of their neighbors struggled in vain. Mrs. Morrison was that pariah who in a village like Equity cuts herself off from hope by taking in washing; and it was a decided rise in the world for Hannah, a wild girl at school, to get a place in the printing-office. Her father had applied for it humbly enough at the tremulous and penitent close of one of his long sprees, and was grateful to Bartley for taking the special interest in her which she reported at home.

But the independence of a drunken shoemaker is proverbial, and Morrison's meek spirit soared into lordly arrogance with his earliest cups. The first warning which the community had of his change of attitude was the conspicuous and even defiant closure of his shop, and the scornful rejection of custom, however urgent or necessitous. All Equity might go in broken shoes, for any patching or half-soling the people got from him. He went about collecting his small dues, and paying up his debts, as long as the money lasted, in token of his resolution not to take any favors from any man thereafter. Then he retired to his house on one of the by-streets, and by degrees drank himself past active offense. It was of course in his defiant humor that he came to visit Bartley, who had learned to expect him whenever Hannah failed to appear promptly at her work. The affair was always easily arranged: Bartley instantly assented, with whatever irony he liked, to Morrison's demands; he refused with overwhelming politeness even to permit him to give himself the trouble to support them by argument; he complimented Hannah inordinately as one of the most gifted and accomplished ladies of his acquaintance, and inquired affectionately after the health of each member of the Morrison family. When Morrison rose to go he always said, in shaking hands: "Well, sir, if there was more like you in Equity a poor man could get along. You're a gentleman, sir." After getting some paces away from the street-door, he stumbled back up the stairs to repeat, "You're a gentleman!" Hannah came during the day, and the wages remained the same: neither of the contracting parties regarded the increase so elaborately agreed upon, and Morrison on becoming sober, gratefully ignored the whole transaction, though by a curious juggle of his brain, he recurred to it in his next spree, and advanced in his new demand from the last rise: his daughter was now nominally in receipt of an income of forty dollars a week, but actually accepted four.

Bartley, on his part, enjoyed the business as an agreeable excitement and a welcome relief from the monotony of his office life. He never hurried Morrison's visits, but amused himself by treating him with the most flattering distinction, and baffling his arrogance by immediate concession. But this morning when Morrison came back, with a front of uncommon fierceness, he merely looked up from his newspapers, to which he had recurred, and said coolly, "Oh, Mr. Morrison! Good-morning. I suppose it's that little advance that you wish to see me about. Take a chair. What is the increase you ask this time? Of course I agree to anything"—

He leaned forward, pencil in hand, to make a note of the figure Morrison should name, when the drunkard approached and struck the table in front of him with his fist, and blazed upon Bartley's face, suddenly uplifted, with his blue crazy eyes.

"No, sir! I wont take a seat, and I don't come on no such business! No, sir!" He struck the table again, and the violence of his blow upset the inkstand. Bartley saved himself by suddenly springing away.

"Hullo, here!" he shouted. "What do you mean by this infernal nonsense?"

"What do *you* mean," retorted the drunkard, "by makin' up to my girl?"

"You're a fool," cried Bartley, "and drunk!"

"I'll show you whether I'm a fool, and I'll show you whether I'm drunk," said Morrison. He opened the door, and beckoned to Bird with an air of mysterious authority. "Young man! Come here!"

Bird was used to the indulgence with which Bartley treated Morrison's tipsy freaks, and supposed that he had been called by his consent to witness another agreement to a rise in Hannah's wages. He came quickly, to help get Morrison out of the way, the sooner, and he was astonished to be met by Bartley with, "I don't want you, Bird."

"All right," answered the boy, and he turned to go out of the door. But Morrison had planted himself against it, and he waved Bird austerely back.

"*I* want you," he said, with drunken impressiveness, "for a witness—wick—witness—while I ask Mr. Hubbard what he means by"—

"Hold your tongue!" cried Bartley. "Get out of this!" He advanced a pace or two towards Morrison, who stood his ground without swerving.

"Now you—you keep quiet, Mr. Hubbard," said Morrison, with a swift drunken change of mood by which he passed from arrogant denunciation to a smooth, patronizing mastery of the situation. "*I* wish this thing all settled amic—ic—amelcabilly."

Bartley broke into a helpless laugh at Morrison's final failure on a word difficult to sober tongues, and the latter went on: "No 'casion for bad feeling on either side. All I want know is, What you mean?"

"Well, go on!" cried Bartley, good-naturedly, and he sat down in his chair, which he tilted back, and clasping his hands behind his head, looked up into Morrison's face. "What do I mean by what?"

Probably Morrison had not expected to be categorical, or to bring anything like a bill of particulars against Bartley, and this demand gave him pause. "What you mean," he said at last, "by always praising her up, so?"

"What I said. She's a very good girl, and a very bright one. You don't deny that?"

"No—no matter what I deny. What—what you lend her all them books for?"

"To improve her mind. You don't object to that? I thought you once thanked me for taking an interest in her."

"Don't you mind what I object to, and what I thank you for," said Morrison, with dignity. "I know what I'm about."

"I begin to doubt. But, get on. I'm in a great hurry this morning," said Bartley.

Morrison seemed to be making a mental examination of his stock of charges, while the strain of keeping his upright position began to tell upon him, and he swayed to and fro against the door.

"What's that word you sent her by my boy, Sat'day night?"

"That she was a smart girl, and would be sure to get on if she was good—or words to that effect. I trust there was no offense in that, Mr. Morrison?"

Morrison surrendered himself to another season of cogitation, in which he probably found his vagueness growing upon him. He ended, by fumbling in all his pockets, and bringing up from the last a crumpled scrap of paper. "What you—what you say to that?"

Bartley took the extended scrap with an easy air. "Miss Morrison's handwriting, I think." He held it up before him, and read aloud, " 'I love my love with an H because he is Handsome.' This appears to be a confidence of Miss Morrison to her Muse. Whom do you think she refers to, Mr. Morrison?"

"What's—what's the first letter your name?" demanded Morrison, with an effort to collect his dispersing severity.

"B," promptly replied Bartley. "Perhaps this concerns you, Henry. Your name begins with an H." He passed the paper up over his head to Bird, who took it silently. "You see," he continued, addressing Bird, but looking at Morrison, as he spoke, "Mr. Morrison wishes to convict me of an attempt upon Miss Hannah's affections. Have you anything else to urge, Mr. Morrison?"

Morrison slid at last from his difficult position into a convenient chair, and struggled to keep himself from doubling forward. "I want know what you mean," he said with dogged iteration.

"I'll show you what I mean," said Bartley with an ugly quiet, while his moustache began to twitch. He sprang to his feet and seized Morrison by the collar, pulling him up out of the chair till he held him clear of the floor, and opened the door with his other hand. "Don't show your face here again—you, or your girl either!" Still holding the man by the collar, he pushed him before him through the office, and gave him a final thrust out of the outer door.

Bartley returned to his room in a white heat: "Miserable tipsy rascal!" he panted. "I wonder who has set him on to this thing."

Bird stood pale and silent, still holding the crumpled scrap of paper in his hand.

"I shouldn't be surprised if that impudent little witch herself had put him up to it. She's capable of it," said Bartley, fumbling aimlessly about on his table, in his wrath, without looking at Bird.

"It's a lie!" said Bird.

Bartley started as if the other had struck him, and as he glared at Bird, the anger went out of his face, for pure amazement. "Are you out of your mind, Henry?" he asked calmly. "Perhaps you're drunk too, this morning? The devil seems to have got into pretty much everybody."

"It's a lie!" repeated the boy, while the tears sprang to his eyes. "She's as good a girl as Marcia Gaylord is, any day!"

"Better go away, Henry," said Bartley with a deadly sort of gentleness.

"I'm going away," answered the boy, his face twisted with weeping. "I've done my last day's work for *you*." He pulled down his shirt sleeves, and buttoned them at the wrists, while the tears ran out over his face: helpless tears, the sign of his womanish tenderness, his womanish weakness.

Bartley continued to glare at him. "Why, I do believe you're in love with her yourself, you little fool!"

"Oh, I've *been* a fool!" cried Bird. "A fool to think as much of you as I always have—a fool to believe that you were a gentleman, and wouldn't take a mean advantage. I was a fool to suppose you wanted to do her any good, when you came praising and flattering her, and turning her head!"

"Well, then," said Bartley with harsh insolence, "don't you be a fool any longer. If you're in love with her, you haven't any quarrel with me, my boy. She flies at higher game than humble newspaper editors. The head of Willett's lumbering gang is your man; and so you may go and tell that old sot, her father. Why, Henry! You don't mean to say you care anything for that girl?"

"And do you mean to say you haven't done everything you could, to turn her head, since she's been in this office? She used to like me well enough at school." All men are blind and jealous children alike, when it comes to question of a woman between them, and this poor boy's passion was turning him into a tiger. "Don't come to *me* with your lies, any more!" Here his rage culminated, and with a blind cry of "Ay!" he struck the paper, which he had kept in his hand into Bartley's face.

The demons, whatever they were, of anger, remorse, pride, shame, were at work in Bartley's heart too, and he returned the blow as instantly as if Bird's touch had set the mechanism of his arm in motion. In contempt of the other's weakness he struck with the flat of his hand; but the blow was enough. Bird fell headlong, and the concussion of his head upon the floor did the rest. He lay senseless.

VII

BARTLEY hung over the boy with such a terror in his soul as he had never had before. He believed that he had killed him, and in this conviction came with the simultaneity of events in dream the sense of all his blame, of which the blow given for a blow seemed the least part. He was not so wrong in that, as he was wrong in what led to it. He did not abhor in himself so much the wretch who had struck his brother down as the light and empty fool who had trifled with that silly hoyden. The follies that seemed so amusing and resultless in their time had ripened to this bitter effect, and he knew that he and not she was mainly culpable. Her self-betrayal, however it came about, was proof that they were more serious with her than with him, and he could not plead to himself even the poor excuse that his fancy had been caught. Amidst the anguish of his self-condemnation, the need to conceal what he had done occurred to him. He had been holding Bird's head in his arms, and imploring him, "Henry! Henry! Wake up!" in a low husky voice; but now he turned to the door and locked it, and the lie by which he should escape sprang to his tongue. "He died in a fit." He almost believed it, as it murmured itself from his lips. There was no mark, no bruise, nothing to show that he had touched the boy. Suddenly he felt the lie choke him. He pulled down the window, to let in the fresh air, and this pure breath of heaven blew into his darkened spirit and lifted there a little the vapors which were thickening in it. The horror of having to tell that lie, even if he should escape by it, all his life long, till he was a gray old man, and to keep the truth forever from his lips, presented itself to him as intolerable slavery. "O, my God!" he spoke aloud, "how can I bear that?" and it was in self-pity that he revolted from it. Few men love the truth for its own sake, and Bartley was not one of these; but he practiced it because his experience had been that lies were difficult to manage, and that they were a burden on the mind. He was not candid; he did not shun concealments and evasions; but positive lies he had kept from, and now he could not trust one to save his life. He unlocked the door, and ran out to find help; he must do that at last; he must do it at any risk; no matter what he said afterwards. When our deeds and motives come to be balanced at the last day, let us hope that mercy and not justice may prevail.

It must have been mercy, that sent the doctor at that moment to the apothecary's on the other side of the street, and enabled Bartley to get him up into his office, without publicity or explanation other than that Henry Bird seemed to be in a fit. The doctor lifted the boy's head, and explored his bosom with his hand.

"Is he—is he dead?" gasped Bartley, and the words came so mechanically from his tongue that he began to believe he had not spoken them, when the doctor answered.

"No! How did this happen? Tell me exactly."

"We had a quarrel. He struck me. I knocked him down." Bartley delivered up the truth, as a prisoner of war—or a captive brigand, perhaps—parts with his weapons one by one.

"Very well," said the doctor. "Get some water."

Bartley poured some out of the pitcher on his table, and the doctor, wetting his handkerchief, drew it again and again over Bird's forehead.

"I never meant to hurt him," said Bartley. "I didn't even intend to strike him when he hit me"—

"Intentions have very little to do with physical effects," replied the doctor sharply. "Henry!"

The boy opened his eyes, and muttering feebly, "My head!" closed them again.

"There's a concussion, here," said the doctor. "We had

better get him home. Drive my sleigh over, will you, from Smith's."

Bartley went out into the glare of the sun, which beat upon him like the eye of the world. But the street was really empty as it often was in the middle of the forenoon, at Equity. The apothecary, who saw him untying the doctor's horse, came to his door, and said jocosely, "Hello, Doc! Who's sick?"

"I am," said Bartley, solemnly, and the apothecary laughed at his readiness. Bartley drove round to the back of the printing-office, where the farmers delivered his wood. "I thought we could get him out better, that way," he explained, and the doctor, who had to befriend a great many concealments in his practice, silently spared Bartley's disingenuousness.

The rush of the cold air, as they drove rapidly down the street, with that limp shape between them, revived the boy, and he opened his eyes, and made an effort to hold himself erect; but he could not, and when they got him into the warm room at home, he fainted again. His mother had met them at the door of her poor little house, without any demonstration of grief or terror: she was far too well acquainted in her widowhood, bereft of all her children but for this son, with sickness and death, to show even surprise, if she felt it. When Bartley broke out into his lamentable confession, "Oh, Mrs. Bird! This is *my* work!" she only wrung her hands and answered, "*Your* work? Oh, Mr. Hubbard, he thought the world of *you!*" and did not ask him how or why he had done it. After they had got Henry on the bed, Bartley was no longer of use, there; but they let him remain, in the corner into which he had shrunk, and from which he watched all that went on, with a dry mouth and faltering breath. It began to appear to him that he was very young to be involved in a misfortune like this; he did not understand why it should have happened to him; but he promised himself that if Henry lived he would try to be a better man in every way.

After he had lost all hope, the time seemed so long, the boy on the bed opened his eyes, once more, and looked round, while Bartley still sat with his face in his hands. "Where—where is Mr. Hubbard?" he faintly asked, with a bewildered look at his mother and the doctor.

Bartley heard the weak voice, and staggered forward, and fell on his knees beside the bed. "Here, here! Here I am, Henry! Oh, Henry, I didn't intend"— He stopped at the word, and hid his face in the coverlet.

The boy lay as if trying to make out what had happened, and the doctor told him that he had fainted. After a time, he put out his hand and laid it on Bartley's head. "Yes; but I don't understand what makes him cry."

They looked at Bartley, who had lifted his head, and he went over the whole affair, except so far as it related to Hannah Morrison: he did not spare himself; he had often found that strenuous self-condemnation moved others to compassion; and besides, it was his nature to seek the relief of full confession. But Henry heard him through with a blank countenance. "Don't you remember?" Bartley implored at last.

"No, I don't remember. I only remember that there seemed to be something the matter with my head, this morning."

"That was the trouble with me, too," said Bartley. "I must have been crazy—I must have been insane—when I struck you. I can't account for it."

"I don't remember it," answered the boy.

"That's all right," said the doctor. "Don't try. I guess you better let him alone, now," he added to Bartley, with such a significant look that the young man retired from the bedside, and stood awkwardly apart. "He'll get along. You needn't be anxious about leaving him. He'll be better alone."

There was no mistaking this hint. "Well, well!" said Bartley humbly, "I'll go. But I'd rather stay and watch with him—I sha'n't eat or sleep till he's on foot again. And I can't leave till you tell me that you forgive me, Mrs. Bird. I never dreamt—I didn't intend"— He could not go on.

"I don't suppose you meant to hurt Henry," said the mother. "You always pretended to be so fond of him, and he thought

the world of you. But I don't see how you could do it. I presume it was all right."

"No, it was all wrong,—or so nearly all wrong that I must ask
your forgiveness on that ground. I loved him—I thought the
world of him, too. I'd ten thousand times rather have hurt
myself," pleaded Bartley. "Don't let me go till you say that
you forgive me."

"I'll see how Henry gets along," said Mrs. Bird. "I don't
know as I could rightly say I forgive you just yet." Doubtless
she was dealing conscientiously with herself and with him.
"I like to be sure of a thing when I say it," she added.

The doctor followed him into the hall, and Bartley could
not help turning to him for consolation. "I think Mrs. Bird is
very unjust, doctor. I've done everything I could—and said
everything—to explain the matter; and I've blamed myself
where I can't feel that I was to blame; and yet you see how she
holds out against me."

"I dare say," answered the doctor dryly, "she'll feel differently, as she says, if the boy gets well."

Bartley dropped his hat to the floor. "Gets well! Why—why
you think he'll get well, *now*, don't you doctor?"

"Oh, yes; I was merely using her words. He'll get well."

"And—and it wont affect his mind, will it? I thought it was
very strange, his not remembering anything about it"—

"That's a very common phenomenon," said the doctor.
"The patient usually forgets everything that occurred for
some little time before the accident in cases of concussion of
the brain." Bartley shuddered at the phrase, but he could not
ask anything further. "What I wanted to say to you," continued the doctor, "was that this may be a long thing, and
there may have to be an inquiry into it. You're lawyer enough
to understand what that means. I should have to testify to what
I know, and I only know what you've told me."

"Why, you don't doubt"—

"No, sir; I've no reason to suppose you haven't told me the
truth, as far as it goes. If you have thought it advisable to keep

anything back from me, you may wish to tell the whole story to an attorney."

"I haven't kept anything back, Doctor Wills," said Bartley. "I've told you everything—everything that concerned the quarrel. That drunken old scoundrel of a Morrison got us into it. He accused me of making love to his daughter; and Henry was jealous—I never knew he cared anything for her. I hated to tell you this before his mother. But this is the whole truth, so help me God."

"I supposed it was something of the kind," replied the doctor. "I'm sorry for you. You can't keep it from having an ugly look if it gets out; and it may have to be made public. I advise you to go and see Squire Gaylord; he's always stood your friend."

"I—I was just going there," said Bartley; and this was true. Through all, he had felt the need of some sort of retrieval; of re-establishing himself in his own esteem, by some signal stroke; and he could think of but one thing. It was not his fault if he believed that this must combine self-sacrifice with safety, and the greatest degree of humiliation with the largest sum of consolation. He was none the less resolved not to spare himself at all in offering to release Marcia from her engagement. The fact that he must now also see her father upon the legal aspect of his case, certainly complicated the affair, and detracted from its heroic quality. He could not tell which to see first, for he naturally wished his action to look as well as possible; and if he went first to Marcia, and she condemned him, he did not know in what figure he should approach her father. If on the other hand, he went first to Squire Gaylord the old lawyer might insist that the engagement was already at an end by Bartley's violent act, and might well refuse to let a man in his position even see his daughter. He lagged heavy-heartedly up the middle of the street, and left the question to solve itself at the last moment. But when he reached Squire Gaylord's gate, it seemed to him that it would be easier to face the father first; and this would be the right way, too.

He turned aside to the little office, and opened the door without knocking, and as he stood with the knob in his hand, trying to habituate his eyes, full of the snow-glare, to the dimmer light within, he heard a rapturous cry of "Why, Bartley!" and he felt Marcia's arms flung round his neck. His burdened heart yearned upon her with a tenderness he had not known before; he realized the preciousness of an embrace that might be the last; but he dared not put down his lips to hers. She pushed back her head in a little wonder, and saw the haggardness of his face, while he discovered her father looking at them. How strong and pure the fire in her must be when her father's presence could not abash her from this betrayal of her love! Bartley sickened, and he felt her arms slip from his neck. "Why—why—what is the matter?"

In spite of some vaguely magnanimous intention to begin at the beginning, and tell the whole affair just as it happened, Bartley found himself wishing to put the best face on it at first, and trust to chances to make it all appear well. He did not speak at once, and Marcia pressed him into a chair, and then like an eager child, who will not let its friend escape, till it has been told what it wishes to know, she set herself on his knee, and put her hand on his shoulder. He looked at her father, not at her, while he spoke hoarsely: "I have had trouble with Henry Bird, Squire Gaylord, and I've come to tell you about it."

The old Squire did not speak, but Marcia repeated in amazement, "With Henry Bird?"

"He struck me"—

"Henry Bird *struck* you!" cried the girl. "I should like to know why Henry Bird struck *you*, when you'd made so much of him, and he's always pretended to be so grateful!"

Bartley still looked at her father. "And I struck him back."

"You did perfectly right, Bartley," exclaimed Marcia, "and I should have despised you if you had let any one run over you. Struck you! I declare"—

He did not heed her, but continued to look at her father—

"I didn't intend to hurt him—I hit him with my open hand —but he fell and struck his head on the floor. I'm afraid it hurt him pretty badly." He felt the pang that thrilled through the girl at his words, and her hand trembled on his shoulder; but she did not take it away.

The old man came forward from the pile of books which he and Marcia had been dusting, and sat down in a chair on the other side of the stove. He pushed back his hat from his forehead, and asked dryly, "What commenced it?"

Bartley hesitated. It was this part of the affair which he would rather have imparted to Marcia after seeing it with her father's eyes or possibly, if her father viewed it favorably, have had him tell her. The old man noticed his reluctance. "Hadn't you better go into the house, Marsh?" She merely gave him a look of utter astonishment for answer, and did not move. He laughed noiselessly, and said to Bartley: "Go on."

"It was that drunken old scoundrel of a Morrison, who began it!" cried Bartley, in angry desperation. Marcia dropped her hand from his shoulder, while her father worked his jaws upon the bit of stick he had picked up from the pile of wood, and put between his teeth. "You know that whenever he gets on a spree he comes to the office and wants Hannah's wages raised."

Marcia sprang to her feet. "Oh, I knew it! I knew it! I told you she would get you into trouble! I told you so!" She stood clinching her hands, and her father bent his keen scrutiny first upon her, and then upon the frowning face with which Bartley regarded her.

"Did he come to have her wages raised to-day?"

"No."

"What did he come for?" He involuntarily assumed the attitude of a lawyer cross-questioning a slippery witness.

"He came for— He came— He accused me of— He said I had—made love to his confounded girl."

Marcia gasped.

"What made him think you had?"

"It wasn't necessary for him to have any reason. He was drunk. I had been kind to the girl, and favored her all I could, because she seemed to be anxious to do her work well; and I praised her for trying."

"Um-umph," commented the squire. "And that made Henry Bird jealous?"

"It seems that he was fond of her. I never dreamed of such a thing, and when I put old Morrison out of the office, and came back he called me a liar, and struck me in the face." He did not lift his eyes to the level of Marcia's, who in her gray dress stood there like a gray shadow, and did not stir or speak.

"And you never had made up to the girl at all?"

"No."

"Kissed her, I suppose, now and then?" suggested the Squire. Bartley did not reply.

"Flattered her up, and told her how much you thought of her, occasionally?"

"I don't see what that has to do with it," said Bartley with a sulky defiance.

"No, I suppose it's what you'd do with most any pretty girl," returned the Squire. He was silent awhile. "And so you knocked Henry down. What happened then?"

"I tried to bring him to, and then I went for the doctor. He revived, and we got him home to his mother's. The doctor says he will get well; but he advised me to come and see you."

"Any witnesses of the assault?"

"No; we were alone in my own room."

"Told any one else about it?"

"I told the doctor and Mrs. Bird. Henry couldn't remember it at all."

"Couldn't remember about Morrison, or what made him mad at you?"

"Nothing."

"And that's all about it?"

"Yes."

The two men had talked across the stove at each other,

practically ignoring the girl, who stood apart from them, gray in the face as her dress, and suppressing a passion which had turned her as rigid as stone.

"Now, Marcia," said her father, kindly, "better go into the house. That's all there is of it."

"No, that isn't all," she answered. "Give me my ring, Bartley. Here's yours." She slipped it off her finger, and put it into his mechanically extended hand.

"Marcia!" he implored, confronting her.

"Give me my ring, please."

He obeyed, and put it into her hand. She slipped it back on the finger from which she had so fondly suffered him to take it yesterday, and replace it with his own.

"I'll go into the house, now, father. Good-by, Bartley." Her eyes were perfectly clear and dry, and her voice controlled; and as he stood passive before her, she took him round the neck, and pressed against his face, once, and twice, and thrice, her own gray face, in which all love and unrelenting and despair were painted. Once and again she held him, and looked him in the eyes, as if to be sure it was he. Then with a last pressure of her face to his, she released him, and passed out of the door. "She's been talking about you, here, all the morning," said the Squire with a sort of quiet absence, as if nothing in particular had happened, and he were commenting on a little fact that might possibly interest Bartley. He ruminated upon the fragment of wood in his mouth a while before he added: "I guess she wont want to talk about you any more. I drew you out a little, on that Hannah Morrison business, because I wanted her to understand just what kind of fellow you were. You see it isn't the trouble you've got into with Henry Bird that's killed her; it's the cause of the trouble. I guess if it had been anything else she'd have stood by you. But you see that's the one thing she couldn't bear, and I'm glad it's happened now instead of afterwards: I guess you're one of that *kind*, Mr. Hubbard."

"Squire Gaylord!" cried Bartley, "upon my sacred word of

honor, there isn't any more of this thing than I've told you. And I think it's pretty hard to be thrown over for—for"—

"Fooling with a pretty girl, when you get a chance and the girl seems to like it? Yes, it *is* rather hard. And I suppose you haven't even seen her since you were engaged to Marcia?"

"Of course not! That is"—

"It's a kind of retroactive legislation on Marcia's part," said the Squire, rubbing his chin, "and that's against one of the first principles of law. But women don't seem to be able to grasp that idea. They're queer about some things. They appear to think they marry a man's whole life—his past as well as his future, and that makes 'em particular. And they distinguish between different kinds of men. You'll find 'em pinning their faith to a fellow who's been through pretty much everything, and swearing by him from the word go; and another chap, who's never *done* any thing very bad, they wont trust half a minute out of their sight. Well, I guess Marcia *is* of rather a jealous disposition," he concluded, as if Bartley had urged this point.

"She's very unjust to me," Bartley began.

"Oh, yes—she's *unjust*," said her father. "I don't deny that. But it wouldn't be any use talking to her. She'd probably turn round with some excuse about what she had suffered, and that would be the end of it. She would say that she couldn't go through it again. Well, it ought to be a comfort to you to think you don't care a great deal about it."

"But I *do* care!" exclaimed Bartley. "I care all the world for it. I"—

"Since when?" interrupted the Squire. "Do you mean to say that you didn't know till you asked her yesterday that Marcia was in love with you?" Bartley was silent. "I guess you knew it as much as a year ago, didn't you? Everybody else did. But you'd just as soon it had been Hannah Morrison or any other pretty girl. *You* didn't care! But Marcia did, you see. She wasn't one of the kind that let any good-looking fellow make love to them. It was because it was *you*; and you knew it.

We're plain men, Mr. Hubbard; and I guess you'll get over this, in time. I shouldn't wonder if you began to mend, right away."

Bartley found himself helpless in the face of this passionless sarcasm. He could have met stormy indignation or any sort of invective in kind; but the contemptuous irony with which his pretensions were treated, the cold scrutiny with which his motives were searched was something he could not meet. He tried to pull himself together for some sort of protest, but he ended by hanging his head in silence. He always believed that Squire Gaylord had liked him, and here he was treating him like his bitterest enemy, and seeming to enjoy his misery. He could not understand it; he thought it extremely unjust, and past all the measure of his offense. This was true, perhaps; but it is doubtful if Bartley would have accepted any suffering no matter how nicely proportioned in punishment of his wrong-doing. He sat hanging his head, and taking his pain in rebellious silence, with a gathering hate in his heart for the old man.

"Mwell!" said the Squire at last, rising from his chair, "I guess I must be going."

Bartley sprang to his feet aghast. "You're not going to leave me in the lurch are you? You're not"—

"Oh, I shall take care of you, young man,—don't be afraid. I've stood your friend, too long, and your name's been mixed up too much with my girl's, for me to let you come to shame openly, if I can help it. I'm going to see Dr. Wills, about you, and I'm going to see Mrs. Bird, and try to patch it up, somehow."

"And—and—where shall I go?" gasped Bartley.

"You might go to the devil, for all I cared for you," said the old man, with the contempt which he no longer cared to make ironical. "But I guess you better go back to your office, and go to work as if nothing had happened—till something does happen. I shall close the paper out as soon as I can. I was thinking of doing that just before you came in. I was thinking of taking you into the law business with me. Marcia and I were talking about it, here. But I guess you wouldn't like the idea, now."

He seemed to get a bitter satisfaction out of these mockeries, from which, indeed, he must have suffered quite as much as Bartley. But he ended, sadly and almost compassionately, with, "Come, come! You must start sometime," and Bartley dragged his leaden weight out of the door. The Squire closed it after him; but he did not accompany him down the street. It was plain he did not wish to be any longer alone with Bartley, and the young man suspected with a sting of shame that he scorned to be seen with him.

VIII

THE MORE Bartley dwelt upon his hard case, during the week that followed, the more it appeared to him that he was punished out of all proportion to his offence. He was in no mood to consider such mercies as that he had been spared from seriously hurting Bird; and that Squire Gaylord and Doctor Wills had united with Henry's mother in saving him from open disgrace. The physician, indeed, had perhaps indulged a professional passion for hushing the matter up, rather than any pity for Bartley. He probably had the scientific way of looking at such questions; and saw much physical cause for moral effects. He refrained, with the physician's reticence, from inquiring into the affair; but he would not have thought Bartley without excuse under the circumstances. In regard to the relative culpability in matters of the kind his knowledge of women enabled him to take much the view of the woman's share that other women take.

But Bartley was ignorant of the doctor's leniency, and associated him with Squire Gaylord in the feeling that made his last week in Equity a period of social outlawry. There were moments in which he could not himself escape the same point of view. He could rebel against the severity of the condemnation he had fallen under in the eyes of Marcia and her father; he could, in the light of example and usage, laugh at the notion of harm in his behavior to Hannah Morrison; yet he found himself looking at it as a treachery to Marcia. Certainly she had no right to question his conduct before his engagement.

Yet if he knew that Marcia loved him, and was waiting with life-and-death anxiety for some word of love from him, it was cruelly false to play with another at the passion which was such a tragedy to her. This was the point that, put aside however often, still presented itself, and its recurrence if he could have known it, was mercy and reprieve from the only source out of which these could come.

Hannah Morrison did not return to the printing-office, and Bird was still sick, though it was now only a question of time when he should be out again. Bartley visited him some hours every day, and sat and suffered under the quiet condemnation of his mother's eyes. She had kept Bartley's secret with the same hardness with which she had refused him her forgiveness, and the village had settled down into an ostensible acceptance of the theory of a faint as the beginning of Bird's sickness, with such other conjectures as the doctor freely permitted each to form. Bartley found his chief consolation in the work which kept him out of the way of a great deal of question. He worked far into the night, as he must, to make up for the force that was withdrawn from the office. At the same time he wrote more than ever in the paper, and he discovered in himself that dual life, of which every one who sins or sorrows is sooner or later aware: that strange separation of the intellectual activity from the suffering of the soul, by which the mind toils on in a sort of ironical indifference to the pangs that wring the heart; the realization that in some ways his brain can get on perfectly well without his conscience.

There was a great deal of sympathy felt for Bartley at this time, and his popularity in Equity was never greater than now when his life there was drawing to a close. The spectacle of his diligence was so impressive that when on the following Sunday the young minister who had succeeded to the pulpit of the orthodox church, preached a sermon on the beauty of industry from the text "Consider the Lilies," there were many who said that they thought of Bartley, the whole while, and one—a lady—asked Mr. Savin if he did not have Mr. Hubbard in mind in the picture he drew of the Heroic Worker. They wished that Bartley could have heard that sermon.

Marcia had gone away early in the week to visit in the town where she used to go to school, and Bartley took her going away as a sign that she wished to put herself wholly beyond his reach, or any danger of relenting at sight of him. He talked with no one about her; and going and coming irregularly to his meals, and keeping himself shut up in his room when he was not at work, he left people very little chance to talk with him. But they conjectured that he and Marcia had an understanding; and some of the ladies used such scant opportunity as he gave them to make sly allusions to her absence and his desolate condition. They were confirmed in their surmise, by the fact known from actual observation, that Bartley had not spoken a word to any other young lady since Marcia went away.

"Look here, my friend," said the philosopher from the logging-camp, when he came in for his paper on the Tuesday afternoon following, "seems to me from what I hear tell around here, you're tryin' to kill yourself on this newspaper. Now it wont do; I tell you it wont do."

Bartley was addressing for the mail the papers which one of the girls was folding. "What are you going to do about it?" he demanded of his sympathizer with whimsical sullenness, and not troubling himself to look up at him.

"Well, I hain't exactly settled, yet," replied the philosopher, who was of a tall, lank figure, and of a mighty brown beard. "But I've been around pretty much everywhere, and I find that about the poorest use you can put a man to is to kill him."

"It depends a good deal on the man," said Bartley. "But that's stale, Kinney. It's the old formula of the anti-capital-punishment fellows. Try something else. They're not talking of hanging me yet." He kept on writing, and the philosopher stood over him with a humorous twinkle of enjoyment at Bartley's readiness.

"Well, I'll allow it's old," he admitted. "So's Homer."

"Yes; but you don't pretend that you wrote Homer."

Kinney laughed mightily; then he leaned forward, and slapped Bartley on the shoulder with his newspaper. "Look here!" he exclaimed, "I *like* you!"

"Oh, try some other tack! Lots of fellows like me." Bartley kept on writing.

"I gave you your paper, didn't I, Kinney?"

"You mean that you want me to get out?" was the response.

"Far be it from me to say so."

This delighted Kinney as much as the last refinement of hospitality would have pleased another man.

"Look here!" he said, "I want you should come out and see our camp. I can't fool away any more time on you here; but I want you should come out and see us. Give you something to write about. Hey?"

"The invitation comes at a time when circumstances over which I have no control oblige me to decline it. I admire your prudence, Kinney."

"No, honest Injian, now," protested Kinney. "Take a day off, and fill up with dead advertisements. That's the way they used to do, out in Alkali City when they got short of help on the Eagle, and we liked it just as well."

"Now you are talking sense," said Bartley looking up at him. "How far is it to your settlement?"

"Two miles, if you're goin'; three and a half, if you ain't."

"When are you coming in again?"

"I'm in, now."

"I can't go with you to-day."

"Well, how'll to-morrow morning suit?"

"To-morrow morning will suit," said Bartley.

"All right. If anybody comes in to see the editor to-morrow morning, Marrilla," said Kinney to the girl, "you tell 'em he's sick, and gone a-loggin', and wont be back till Saturday. Say!" he added, laying his hand on Bartley's shoulder, "you ain't foolin'?"

"If I am," replied Bartley, "just mention it."

"Good!" said Kinney. "To-morrow it is, then."

Bartley finished addressing the newspapers, and then he put

them up in wrappers and packages, for the mail. "You can go, now, Marrilla," he said to the girl. "I'll have some copy for you and Kitty; you'll find it on my table in the morning."

"All right," answered the girl.

Bartley went to his supper, which he ate with more relish than he had felt for his meals since his troubles began, and he took part in the supper-table talk with something of his old audacity. The change interested the lady-boarders and they agreed that he must have had a letter. He returned to his office, and worked till nine o'clock, writing and selecting matter out of his exchanges. He spent most of the time in preparing the funny column, which was a favorite feature in the Free Press. Then he put the copy where the girls would find it in the morning, and leaving the door unlocked, he took his way up the street towards Squire Gaylord's.

He knew that he should find the lawyer in his office, and he opened the office-door without knocking, and went in. He had not met Squire Gaylord since the morning of his dismissal, and the old man had left him for the past eight days without any sign as to what he expected of Bartley, or of what he intended to do in his affair.

They looked at each other, but exchanged no sort of greeting, as Bartley, unbidden, took a chair on the opposite side of the stove; the Squire did not put down the book he had been reading. "I've come to see what you're going to do about the Free Press," said Bartley.

The old man rubbed his bristling jaw, that seemed even lanker than when Bartley saw it last. He waited almost a minute before he said: "I don't know as I've got any call to tell you."

"Then I'll tell you what *I'm* going to do about it," retorted Bartley. "I'm going to leave it. I've done my last day's work on that paper. Do you think," he cried, angrily, "that I'm going to keep on in the dark, and let you consult your pleasure as to my future? No, sir! You don't know your man, quite, Mr. Gaylord."

"You've got over your scare," said the lawyer.

"I've got over my scare," Bartley retorted.

"And you think, because you're not afraid, any longer, that you're out of danger. I know my man as well as you do, I guess."

"If you think I care for the danger, you don't. You may do what you please. Whatever you do, I shall know it isn't out of kindness for me. I didn't believe from the first that the law could touch me, and I wasn't uneasy on that account. But I didn't want to involve myself in a public scandal, for Miss Gaylord's sake. Miss Gaylord has released me from any obligations to her; and now you may go ahead and do what you like." Each of the men knew how much truth there was in this; but for the moment in his anger, Bartley believed himself sincere, and there is no question but his defiance was so. Squire Gaylord made him no answer, and after a minute of expectation Bartley added, "At any rate I've done with the Free Press. I advise you to stop the paper, and hand the office over to Henry Bird, when he gets about. I'm going out to Willett's logging-camp, to-morrow, and I'm coming back to Equity on Saturday. You'll know where to find me till then, and after that you may look me up if you want me."

He rose to go, but stopped with his hand on the door-knob, at a sound, preliminary to speaking, which the old man made in his throat. Bartley stopped, hoping for a farther pretext of quarrel but the lawyer merely asked, "Where's the key?"

"It's in the office-door."

The old man now looked at him as if he no longer saw him, and Bartley went out, baulked of his purpose in part, and in that degree so much the more embittered.

Squire Gaylord remained an hour longer; then he blew out his lamp, and left the little office for the night. A light was burning in the kitchen, and he made his way round to the back door of the house, and let himself in. His wife was there, sitting before the stove, in those last delicious moments before going to bed, when all the house is mellowed to such a warmth that it seems hard to leave it to the cold and dark. In this poor lady, who had so long denied herself spiritual comfort, there was a certain obscure luxury: she liked little dainties of the table; she liked soft warmth, an easy cushion. It was doubtless in the disintegration of the finer qualities of her nature, that as they grew older together, she threw more and more the burden of acute feeling upon the husband to whose doctrine of life she had submitted, but had never been reconciled. Marriage is, with all its disparities a much more equal thing than appears, and the meek little wife, who has all the advantage of public sympathy, knows her power over her oppressor, and at some tender spot in his affections or his nerves can inflict an anguish that will avenge her for years of coarser aggression. Thrown in upon herself in so vital a matter as her religion, Mrs. Gaylord had involuntarily come to live largely for herself, though her talk was always of husband. She gave up for him, as she believed, her soul's salvation, but she held him to account for the uttermost farthing of the price. She padded herself round at every point where she could have suffered through her sensibilities, and lived soft and snug in the shelter of his iron will and indomitable courage. It was not apathy that she had felt when their children died one after another, but an obscure and formless expectation that Mr. Gaylord would suffer enough for both. Marcia was the youngest, and her mother left her training almost wholly to her father; she sometimes said that she never supposed the child would live. She did not actually urge this in excuse, but she had the appearance of doing so; and she held aloof from them both in their mutual relations, with mildly critical reserves. They spoiled each other, as father and daughter are apt to do, when left to themselves. What was good in the child certainly received no harm from his indulgence; and what was naughty was after all not so very naughty. She was passionate, but she was generous; and if she showed a jealous temperament that must hereafter make her unhappy, for the time being it charmed and flattered her father to have her so fond of him that she could not endure any rivalry in his affection. Her education proceeded fitfully. He would not let her be forced to household tasks that she disliked; and as a little girl she went to school chiefly because she liked to go, and not because she would have been obliged to if she had not chosen. When she grew older, she wished to go away to school, and her father allowed her: he had no great respect for boarding-schools, but if Marcia wanted to try it, he was willing to humor the joke. What resulted was a great proficiency in the things that pleased her, and ignorance of the other things. Her father bought her a piano, on which she did not play much, and he bought her whatever dresses she fancied. He never came home from a journey, without bringing her something; and he liked to take her with him, when he went away to other places. She had been several times at Portland, and once at Montreal; he was very proud of her: he could not see that any one was better looking, or dressed any better than his girl.

He came into the kitchen, and sat down with his hat on, and taking his shin between his hands moved uneasily about on his chair.

"What's brought you in so early?" asked his wife.

"Well, I got through," he briefly explained. After a while he said, "Bartley Hubbard's been out there."

"You don't mean't he knew she"—

"No, he didn't know anything about that. He came to tell me he was going away."

"Well, I don't know what you're going to do, Mr. Gaylord," said his wife, shifting the responsibility wholly upon him. " 'D he seem to want to make it up?"

"Mno!" said the Squire, "he was on his high horse. He knows he ain't in any danger, now."

"Ain't you afraid she'll carry on dreadfully, when she finds out 't he's gone for good?" asked Mrs. Gaylord, with a sort of implied satisfaction that the carrying on was not to affect her.

"Myes," said the Squire, "I suppose she'll carry on. But I don't know what to do about it. Sometimes I almost wish I'd tried to make it up between 'em that day; but I thought she'd better see, once for all, what sort of man she was going in for, if she married him. It's too late, now, to do any thing. The fellow came in to-night for a quarrel, and nothing else; I could see that; and I didn't give him any chance."

"You feel sure," asked Mrs. Gaylord impartially, "that Marcia wa'n't too particular?"

"No, Miranda, I don't feel sure of anything, except that it's past your bedtime. You better go. I'll sit up a while, yet. I came in, because I couldn't settle my mind to anything, out there." He took off his hat in token of his intending to spend the rest of the evening at home, and put it on the table at his elbow.

His wife sewed at the mending in her lap, without offering to act upon his suggestion. "It's plain to be seen that she can't get along without him."

"She'll have to, now," replied the Squire.

"I'm afraid," said Mrs. Gaylord softly, "that she'll be down sick. She don't look as if she'd slept any great deal since she's been gone. I d'know as I like very much to see her looking, the way she does. I guess you've got to take her off, somewheres."

"Why, she's just been off, and couldn't stay!"

"That's because she thought he was here, yet. But if he's gone, it wont be the same thing."

"Well, we've got to fight it out, some way," said the Squire. "It wouldn't do to give in to it, now. It always *was* too much of a one-sided thing, at the best; and if we tried now to mend it up, it would be ridiculous. I don't believe he would come back at all, now, and if he did, he wouldn't come back on any equal terms. He'd want to have everything his own way. Mno!" said the Squire, as if confirming himself in a conclusion often reached already in his own mind, "I saw by the way he began to-night that there wa'n't anything to be done with him. It was fight from the word go."

"Well," said Mrs. Gaylord with gentle, skeptical interest in the outcome, "if you've made up your mind to that, I hope you'll be able to carry it through."

"That's what I've made up my mind to," said her husband.

Mrs. Gaylord rolled up the sewing in her work-basket, and packed it away against the side, bracing it with several pairs of newly darned socks and stockings neatly folded one into the other. She took her time for this, and when she rose at last to go out, with her basket in her hand, the door opened in her face, and Marcia entered. Mrs. Gaylord shrank back, and then slipped round behind her daughter and vanished. The girl took no notice of her mother, but went and sat down on her father's knee, throwing her arms round his neck, and dropping her haggard face on his shoulder. She had arrived at home a few hours earlier, having driven over from a station ten miles distant on a road that did not pass near Equity. After giving as much of a shock to her mother's mild nature as it was capable of receiving by her unexpected return, she had gone to her own room and remained ever since without seeing her father. He put up his thin old hand and passed it over her hair, but it was long before either of them spoke.

At last Marcia lifted her head, and looked her father in the face with a smile so pitiful that he could not bear to meet it. "Well, father?" she said.

"Well, Marsh," he answered huskily.

"What do you think of me now?"

"I'm glad to have you back again," he replied.

"You know why I came?"

"Yes, I guess I know."

She put down her head again, and moaned and cried, "Father! Father!" with dry sobs. When she looked up, confronting him with her tearless eyes, "What shall I do? What shall I do?" she demanded desolately.

He tried to clear his throat to speak, but it required more than one effort to bring the words.

"I guess you better go along with me up to Boston. I'm going up the first of the week."

"No," she said quietly.

"The change would do you good. It's a long while since you've been away from home," her father urged.

She looked at him in sad reproach of his uncandor. "You know there's nothing the matter with me, father. You know what the trouble is."

He was silent. He could not face the trouble.

"I've heard people talk of a heartache," she went on. "I never believed there was really such a thing. But I know there is, now. There's a pain here." She pressed her hand against her breast. "It's sore with aching. What shall I do? I shall have to live through it somehow."

"If you don't feel exactly well," said her father, "I guess you better see the doctor."

"What shall I tell him is the matter with me? That I want Bartley Hubbard?" He winced at the words, but she did not. "He knows that already. Everybody in town does. It's never been any secret. I couldn't hide it, from the first day I saw him. I'd just as lief as not they should say as I was dying for him. I shall not care what they say when I'm dead."

"You'd oughtn't—you'd oughtn't to talk that way, Marcia," said her father gently.

"What difference?" she demanded, scornfully.

There was truly no difference, so far as concerned any creed of his, and he was too honest to make further pretence.

"What shall I do?" she went on again. "I've thought of praying; but what would be the use?"

"I've never denied that there was a God, Marcia," said her father.

"Oh, I know. *That* kind of God! Well, well! I know that I talk like a crazy person! Do you suppose it was providential, my being with you in the office that morning when Bartley came in?"

"No," said her father, "I don't. I think it was an accident."

"Mother said it was Providential, my finding him out before it was too late."

"I think it was a good thing. The fellow has the making of a first-class scoundrel in him."

"Do you think he's a scoundrel now?" she asked quietly.

"He hasn't had any great opportunity yet," said the old man, conscientiously sparing him.

"Well, then, I'm sorry I found him out. Yes! If I hadn't, I might have married him, and perhaps if I had died soon I might *never* have found him out. He could have been good to me a year or two, and then if I died, I should have been safe. Yes, I wish he could have deceived me till after we were married. Then I *couldn't* have borne to give him up, may be."

"You *would* have given him up, even then. And that's the only thing that reconciles me to it now. I'm sorry for you, my girl; but you'd have made me sorrier then. Sooner or later he'd have broken your heart."

"He's broken it now," said the girl calmly.

"Oh, no, he hasn't," replied her father with a false cheerfulness that did not deceive her. "You're young, and you'll get over it. I mean to take you away from here, for a while. I mean to take you up to Boston; and on to New York. I shouldn't care if we went as far as Washington. I guess when you've seen a little more of the world you wont think Bartley Hubbard's the only one in it."

She looked at him so intently that he thought she must be pleased at his proposal. "Do you think I could get him back?" she asked.

Her father lost his patience; it was a relief to be angry. "No, I don't think it. I know you couldn't. And you ought to be ashamed of mentioning such a thing!"

"Oh, ashamed! No, I've got past that. I have no shame any more, where he's concerned. Oh, I'd give the world if I could call him back—if I could only undo what I did! I was wild. I wasn't reasonable; I wouldn't listen to him. I drove him away without giving him a chance to say a word! Of course he must hate me, now. What makes you think he wouldn't come back?"

"I know he wouldn't," answered her father, with a sort of groan. "He's going to leave Equity, for one thing, and"—

"Going to leave Equity?" she repeated absently. Then he felt her tremble. "How do you know he's going?" She turned upon her father, and fixed him sternly with her eyes.

"Do you suppose he would stay, after what's happened, any longer than he could help?"

"How do you know he's going?" she repeated.

"He told me."

She stood up. "He told you? When?"

"To-night."

"Why, where—where did you see him?" she whispered.

"In the office."

"Since—since—I came? Bartley been here! And you didn't tell me—you didn't let me know?"

They looked at each other in silence. At last, "When is he going?" she asked.

"To-morrow morning."

She sat down in the chair which her mother had left, and clutched the back of another, on which her fingers opened and closed convulsively, while she caught her breath in irregular gasps. She broke into a low moaning, at last, the expression of abject defeat in the struggle she had waged with herself. Her father watched her with dumb compassion. "Better go to bed, Marcia," he said with the same dry calm as if he had been sending her away after some pleasant evening which she had suffered to run too far into the night.

"Don't you think—don't you think—he'll have to see you again before he goes?" she made out to ask.

"No; he's finished up with me," said the old man.

"Well, then," she cried desperately, "you'll have to go to him, father, and get him to come! I can't help it! I can't give him up! You've got to go to him, now, father—yes, yes, you have! You've got to go and tell him. Go and get him to come, for *mercy's* sake! Tell him that I'm sorry—that I beg his pardon —that I didn't think—I didn't understand—that I know he didn't do anything wrong"— She rose, and placing her hand on her father's shoulder, accented each entreaty with a little push.

He looked up into her face with a haggard smile of sympathy. "You're crazy, Marcia," he said, gently.

"Don't laugh!" she cried. "I'm not crazy, now. But I was,

then—yes, stark, staring crazy. Look here, father! I want to tell you—I want to explain to you!" She dropped upon his knee again, and tremblingly passed her arm round his neck. "You see I had just told him the day before that I shouldn't care for anything that happened before we were engaged; and then at the very first thing I went and threw him off! And I had no right to do it. He knows that, and that's what makes him so hard towards me. But if you go and tell him that I see now I was all wrong, and that I beg his pardon; and then ask him to give me *one* more trial, just one *more*— You can do as much as that for me, can't you?"

"Oh, you poor, crazy girl!" groaned her father. "Don't you see that the trouble is in what the fellow *is*; and not in any particular thing that he's done? He's a scamp, through and through; and he's all the more a scamp when he doesn't know it. He hasn't got the first idea of anything but selfishness."

"No, no! Now, I'll tell you—now, I'll prove it to you. That very Sunday when we were out riding together; and we met her and her mother, and their sleigh upset, and he had to lift her back; and it made me wild to see him, and I wouldn't hardly touch him or speak to him afterwards, he didn't say one angry word to me. He just pulled me up to him, and wouldn't let me be mad; and he said that night he didn't mind it a bit because it showed how much I liked him. Now, doesn't that prove he's good—a good deal better than I am, and that he'll forgive me, if you'll go and ask him? I know he isn't in bed, yet; he always sits up late—he told me so; and you'll find him there in his room. Go straight to his room, father; don't let anybody see you down in the office; I couldn't bear it; and slip out with him as quietly as you can. But, oh do hurry, now! Don't lose another minute"—

A wild joy sprang into her face, as her father rose; a joy that it was terrible to him to see die out of it as he spoke: "I tell you it's no use, Marcia! He wouldn't come if I went to him"—

"Oh, yes—yes he would! I know he would! If "—

"He wouldn't! You're mistaken. I should have to get down

in the dust for nothing. He's a bad fellow, I tell you; and you've got to give him up."

"You hate me!" cried the girl. The old man walked to and fro, clutching his hands. Their lives had always been in such intimate sympathy, his life had so long had her happiness for its sole pleasure, that the pang in her heart racked his with as sharp an agony. "Well, I shall die; and then I hope you will be satisfied."

"Marcia, Marcia!" pleaded her father. "You don't know what you're saying."

"You're letting him go away from me—you're letting me lose him—you're killing me!"

"He wouldn't come, my girl. It would be perfectly useless to go to him. You must—you *must* try to control yourself, Marcia. There's no other way—there's no other hope. You're disgraceful. You ought to be ashamed. You ought to have some pride about you. I don't know what's come over you since you've been with that fellow. You seem to be out of your senses. But try—try, my girl, to get over it. If you fight it, you'll conquer yet. You've got a spirit for anything. And I'll help you, Marcia. I'll take you anywhere. I'll do anything for you"—

"You wouldn't go to him, and ask him to come here, if it would save his life!"

"No," said the old man with a desperate quiet, "I wouldn't."

She stood looking at him, and then she sank suddenly, and straight down, as if she were sinking through the floor. When he lifted her, he saw that she was in a dead faint, and while the swoon lasted would be out of her misery. The sight of this had wrung him so that he had a kind of relief in looking at her lifeless face; and he was slow in laying her down again, like one that fears to wake a sleeping child. Then he went to the foot of the stairs and softly called to his wife: "Miranda! Miranda!"

IX

KINNEY came into town the next morning bright and early, as he phrased it; but he did not stop at the hotel for Bartley till nine o'clock. "Thought I'd give you time for breakfast," he explained, "and so I didn't hurry up any about gettin' in my supplies."

It was a beautiful morning, so blindingly sunny, that Bartley winked as they drove up through the glistening street, and was glad to dip into the gloom of the first woods; it was not cold: the snow felt the warmth, and packed moistly under their runners. The air was perfectly still; at a distance on the mountain sides it sparkled as if full of diamond-dust. Far overhead some crows called. "The sun's getting high," said Bartley, with the light sigh of one to whom the thought of spring brings no hope.

"Well, I shouldn't begin to plough for corn just yet," replied Kinney. "It's curious," he went on, "to see how anxious we are to have a thing over, it don't much matter what it is, whether it's summer or winter. I suppose we'd feel different if we wa'n't sure there was going to be another of 'em. I guess that's one reason why the Lord concluded not to keep us clearly posted on the question of another life. If it wa'n't for the uncertainty of the thing, there are a lot of fellows like you that wouldn't stand it here a minute. Why if we had a dead sure thing of over-the-river—good climate, plenty to eat and wear, and not much to do—I don't believe any of us would keep Darling Minnie waiting, well, a *great* while. But you see the thing's all on paper, and that makes us cautious, and willing to hang on here a while longer. Looks splendid on the map: streets regularly laid out; public squares; band-stands; churches; solid blocks of houses with all the modern improvements; but you can't tell whether there's any town there till you're on the ground; and then if you don't like it, there's no way of gettin' back to the States."

He turned round upon Bartley, and opened his mouth wide to imply that this was pleasantry.

"Do you throw your philosophy in, all under the same price, Kinney?" asked the young fellow.

"Well, yes; I never charge anything over," said Kinney. "You see I have a good deal of time to think when I'm around by myself all day, and the philosophy don't cost *me* anything, and the fellows like it. Roughing it the way they do, they can stand most anything. Hey?" He now not only opened his mouth upon Bartley, but thrust him in the side with his elbow; and then laughed noisily.

Kinney was the cook. He had been over pretty nearly the whole uninhabitable globe, starting as a gaunt and awkward boy from the Maine woods, and keeping until he came back to them in late middle-life the same gross and ridiculous optimism. He had been at sea, and had been shipwrecked on several islands in the Pacific; he had passed a rainy season at Panama, and a yellow-fever season at Vera Cruz, and had been carried far into the interior of Peru by a tidal wave during an earthquake season; he was in the Border Ruffian War of Kansas, and he clung to California till prosperity deserted her after the completion of the Pacific road. Wherever he went he carried or found adversity; but with a heart fed on the metaphysics of Horace Greeley, and buoyed up by a few wildly interpreted maxims of Emerson, he had always believed in other men, and their fitness for the terrestrial millennium which was never more than ten days or ten miles off. It is not necessary to say that he had continued as poor as he began, and that he was never able to contribute to those railroads, mills, elevators, towns, cities which were sure to be built, sir, sure to be built, wherever he went. When he came home at last to the woods some hundreds of miles north of Equity, he found that some one had realized his early dream of a summer hotel on the shore of the beautiful lake there; and he unenviously settled down to admire the landlord's thrift, and to act as guide and cook for parties of young ladies and gentlemen who started from the hotel to camp in the woods. This brought him into the society of cultivated people, for which he had a real passion. He had always had a few thoughts rattling round in his skull, and he liked to make sure of them in talk with those who had enjoyed greater advantages than himself. He never begrudged them their luck; he simply and sweetly admired them; he made studies of their several characters and was never tired of analyzing them to their advantage to the next summer's parties. Late in the fall, he went in, as it is called, with a camp of loggers, among whom he rarely failed to find some remarkable men. But he confessed that he did not enjoy the steady three or four months in the winter-woods, with no coming out at all till spring; and he had been glad of this chance in a logging-camp near Equity, in which he had been offered the cook's place by the owner, who had tested his fare in the northern woods the summer before. Its proximity to the village allowed him to loaf in upon civilization at least once a week, and he spent the greater part of his time at the Free Press office on publication-day. He had always sought the society of newspaper men, and wherever he could, he had given them his. He was not long in discovering that Bartley was smart as a steel-trap; and by an early and natural transition from calling the young-lady compositors by their pet names, and patting them on their shoulders, he had arrived at a like affectionate intimacy with Bartley.

As they worked deep into the woods on their way to the camp, the road dwindled to a well-worn track between the stumps and bushes. The ground was rough, and they constantly plunged down the slopes of little hills, and climbed the sides of the little valleys, and from time to time they had

to turn out for teams drawing logs to the mills in Equity, each
with its equipage of four or five wild young fellows who saluted
Kinney with an ironical cheer or jovial taunt, in passing.

"They're all just so," he explained, with pride, when the
last party had passed. "They're gentlemen, every one of 'em—
perfect gentlemen."

They came at last to a wider clearing than any they had yet
passed through, and here on a level of the hillside stretched
the camp: a long, low structure of logs, with the roof broken
at one point by a stove pipe, and the walls irregularly pierced
by small windows; around it crouched and burrowed in the
drift the sheds that served as stables and storehouses. The sun
shone and shone with dazzling brightness upon the opening,
and the sound of distant shouts, and the rhythmical stroke of
axes came to it out of the forest; but the camp was deserted,
and in the stillness Kinney's voice seemed strange and alien.
"Walk in, walk in!" he said hospitably. "I've got to look after
my horse."

But Bartley remained at the door, blinking in the sunshine,
and harking to the near silence that sang in his ears. A curious
feeling possessed him: sickness of himself as of some one
else; a longing, consciously helpless, to be something different;
a sense of captivity to habits and thoughts and hopes that cen-
tred in himself, and served him alone.

"Terribly peaceful around here," said Kinney, coming back
to him, and joining him in a survey of the landscape, with his
hands on his hips, and a stem of timothy projecting from his
lips.

"Yes, terribly," assented Bartley.

"But it *aint* a bad way for a man to live, as long as he's young;
or ain't got anybody that wants his company more than his
room. Be the place for you."

"On which ground?" Bartley asked dryly, without taking his
eyes from a distant peak that showed through the notch in the
forest.

Kinney laughed in as unselfish enjoyment as if he had made
the turn himself. "Well that ain't exactly what I meant to

say: what I meant was that any man engaged in intellectual pursuits wants to come out and commune with nature, every little while."

"You call the Equity Free Press intellectual pursuits?" demanded Bartley with scorn. "I suppose it is," he added. "Well, here I am—right on the commune. But nature's such a big thing, I think it takes two to commune with her."

"Well, a girl's a help," assented Kinney.

"I wasn't thinking of a girl, exactly," said Bartley, with a little sadness. "I mean that if you're not in first-rate spiritual condition, you're apt to get floored, if you undertake to commune with nature."

"I guess that's about so. If a man's got anything on his mind a big railroad depot's the place for *him*. But you're run down. You ought to come out here, and take a hand, and be a man amongst men." Kinney talked partly for quantity, and partly for pure, indefinite good feeling.

Bartley turned toward the door. "What have you got inside, here?"

Kinney flung the door open, and followed his guest within. The first two thirds of the cabin was used as a dormitory, and the sides were furnished with rough bunks, from the ground to the roof. The round, unhewn logs showed their form everywhere; the crevices were caulked with moss; and the walls were warm and tight. It was dark, between the bunks, but beyond it was lighter, and Bartley could see at the further end a vast cooking-stove, and three long tables with benches at their sides. A huge coffee-pot stood on the top of the stove, and various pots and kettles surrounded it.

"Come into the dining-room and sit down in the parlor," said Kinney, drawing off his coat, as he walked forward. "Take the sofa," he added, indicating a movable bench. He hung his coat on a peg, and rolled up his shirt-sleeves, and began to whistle cheerily, like a man who enjoys his work, as he threw open the stove-door, and poked in some sticks of fuel. A brooding warmth filled the place, and the wood made a pleasant crackling as it took fire.

"Here's my desk," said Kinney, pointing to a barrel that supported a broad smooth board top. "This is where I compose my favorite works." He turned round, and cut out of a mighty mass of dough in a tin trough, a portion which he threw down on his table, and attacked with a rolling-pin. "That means pie, Mr. Hubbard," he explained, "and pie means meat-pie—or squash-pie, at a pinch. To-day's pie-baking day. But you needn't be troubled on that account. So's to-morrow and so was yesterday. Pie twenty-one times a week, is the word; and don't you forget it. They say old Agassiz," Kinney went on, in that easy familiar fondness with which our people like to speak of greatness that impresses their imagination, "they say old Agassiz recommended fish as the best food for the brain. Well, I don't suppose but what it is. But I don't know but what pie is more stimulating to the fancy. I *never* saw anything like meat-pie to make ye dream."

"Yes," said Bartley, nodding gloomily, "I've tried it."

Kinney laughed. "Well, I guess folks of sedentary pursuits, like you and me, don't need it; but these fellows that stamp round in the snow all day, they want something to keep their imagination goin'. And I guess pie does it. Anyway they can't seem to get enough of it. Ever try apples when you was at work? They say old Greeley kep' his desk full of 'em; kep' munchin' away, all the while, when he was writin' his editorials. And one of them German poets—I don't know but what it was old Gutty himself—kept *rotten* ones in *his* drawer; liked the smell of 'em. Well, there's a good deal of apple in meat-pie. May be it's the apple that does it. *I* don't know. But I guess if your pursuits are sedentary you better take the apple separate."

Bartley did not say anything; but he kept a lazily interested eye on Kinney as he rolled out his pie-crust, fitted it into his tins, filled these from a jar of mince-meat, covered them with a sheet of dough pierced in herring-bone pattern, and marshalled them at one side ready for the oven.

"If fish *is* any better for the brain," Kinney proceeded, "they can't complain of any want of it, at least in the salted form. They get fish-balls three times a week for breakfast, as reg'lar as Sunday, Tuesday and Thursday comes round. And Fridays I make up a sort of chowder for the Kanucks; they're Catholics, you know, and I don't believe in interferin' with *any* man's religion, it don't matter what it is."

"You ought to be a deacon in the First Church at Equity," said Bartley.

"Is that so? Why?" asked Kinney.

"Oh, they don't believe in interfering with any man's religion either."

"Well," said Kinney thoughtfully, pausing with the rolling-pin in his hand, "there's such a thing as being *too* liberal, I suppose."

"The world's tried the other thing a good while," said Bartley, with cynical amusement.

It seemed to chill the flow of the good fellow's optimism, so that he assented with but lukewarm satisfaction, "Well, that's so, too," and he made up the rest of his pies in silence.

"Well!" he exclaimed, at last, as if shaking himself out of an unpleasant revery, "I guess we shall get along, somehow. Do you like pork and beans?"

"Yes, I do," said Bartley.

"We're goin' to have 'em for dinner. You can hit beans, any meal you drop in on us: beans twenty-one times a week, just like pie. Set 'em in to warm," he said, taking up a capacious earthen pot, near the stove, and putting it into the oven. "I been pretty much everywheres, and I don't know as I found anything for a stand-by that come up to beans. I'm goin' to give 'em potatoes and cabbage to-day—kind of a boiled-dinner day—but you'll see there aint one in ten'll touch 'em to what there will these old residenters. Potatoes and cabbage'll do for a kind of a delicacy—sort of a side-dish—on-*tree*, you know—but give 'em beans for a steady diet. Why off there in Chili, even, the people regularly live on beans—not exactly like ours; broad and flat; but they're beans. Wa'n't there some those ancients—old Horace, or Virgil, maybe—rung in something about beans in some their poems?"

"I don't remember anything of the kind," said Bartley, languidly.

"Well, I don't know as *I* can. I just have a dim recollection of language thrown out at the object—as old Matthew Arnold says. But it might have been something in Emerson."

Bartley laughed. "I didn't suppose you were such a reader, Kinney."

"Oh, I nibble round wherever I can get a chance. Mostly in the newspapers, you know. I don't get any time for books, as a general rule. But there's pretty much everything in the papers. I should call beans a brain-food."

"I guess you call anything a brain-food that you happen to like, don't you, Kinney?"

"No, sir," said Kinney, soberly, "but I like to see the philosophy of a thing when I get a chance. Now, there's tea, for example," he said, pointing to the great tin-pot on the stove.

"Coffee, you mean," said Bartley.

"No, sir, I mean tea. That's tea; and I give it to 'em three times a day, good and strong—molasses in it, and no milk. That's a brain-food, if ever there was one. Sets 'em up, right on end, every time. Clears their heads, and keeps the cold out."

"I should think you were running a seminary for young ladies, instead of a logging-camp," said Bartley.

"No, but look at it: I'm in earnest about tea. You look at the tea-drinkers and the coffee-drinkers, all the world over! Look at 'em in our own country! All the Northern people and all the go-ahead people drink tea. The Pennsylvanians and the Southerners drink coffee. Why, our New England folks don't even know how to *make* coffee, so it's fit to drink! And it's just so, all over Europe. The Russians drink tea, and they'd e't up those coffee-drinkin' Turks long ago, if the tea-drinkin' English hadn't kept 'em from it. Go anywhere's you like, in the North, and you find 'em drinkin' tea. The Swedes and Norwegians in Aroostook county drink it; and they drink it at home."

"Well, what do you think of the French and Germans? They

drink coffee, and they're pretty smart, active people too."

"French and Germans drink coffee?"

"Yes."

Kinney stopped short in his heated career of generalization, and scratched his shaggy head. "Well," he said finally, "I guess they're a kind of a missing link, as old Darwin says." He joined Bartley in his laugh cordially, and looked up at the round clock nailed to a log. "It's about time I set my tables, anyway. Well," he asked, apparently to keep the conversation from flagging, while he went about this work, "how is the good old Free Press getting along?"

"It's going to get along without me, from this out," said Bartley. "This is my last week in Equity."

"No!" retorted Kinney, in tremendous astonishment.

"Yes; I'm off at the end of the week. Squire Gaylord takes the paper back, for the committee; and I suppose Henry Bird will run it for a while; or perhaps they'll stop it altogether. It's been a losing business for the committee."

"Why, I thought you'd bought it of 'em."

"Well, that's what I expected to do; but the office hasn't made any money. All that I've saved is in my colt and cutter."

"That sorrel?"

Bartley nodded. "I'm going away about as poor as I came. I couldn't go much poorer."

"Well!" said Kinney in the exhaustion of adequate language. He went on laying the plates and knives and forks, in silence. These were of undisguised steel; the dishes and the drinking-mugs were of that dense and heavy make, which the keepers of cheap restaurants use to protect themselves against breakage, and which their servants chip to the quick at every edge. Kinney laid bread and crackers by each plate, and on each he placed a vast slab of cold corned-beef. Then he lifted the lid of the pot in which the cabbage and potatoes were boiling together, and pricked them with a fork. He dished up the beans in a succession of deep tins, and set them at intervals along the tables, and began to talk again.

"Well, now, I'm sorry. I'd just begun to feel real well acquainted with you. Tell you the truth, I didn't take much of a fancy, to *you*, first off."

"Is that so?" asked Bartley, not much disturbed by the confession.

"Yes, sir. Well, come to boil it down," said Kinney, with the frankness of the analytical mind that disdains to spare itself in the pursuit of truth, "I didn't like your good clothes. I don't suppose I ever had a suit of clothes to fit me. Feel kind of ashamed, you know, when I go into the store, and take the first thing the Jew wants to put off onto me. Now, I suppose you go to Macullar and Parker's in Boston, and you get what *you* want."

"No; I have my measure at a tailor's," said Bartley, with ill-concealed pride in the fact.

"You don't say so!" exclaimed Kinney. "Well!" he said, as if he might as well swallow this pill, too, while he was about it. "Well, what's the use? I never was the figure for clothes, anyway. Long, gangling boy to start with, and a lean, stoop-shouldered man. I found out sometime ago that a fellow wa'n't necessarily a bad fellow because he had money; or a good fellow because he hadn't. But I hadn't quite got over hating a man because he had style. Well, I suppose it was a kind of a *survival*, as old Tylor calls it. But I tell you, I sniffed round you a good while before I made up my mind to swallow you. And that turnout of yours, it kind of staggered me, after I got over the clothes. Why it wa'n't so much the colt—any man likes to ride after a sorrel colt; and it wa'n't so much the cutter: it was the red linin' with pinked edges that you had to your robe; and it was the red ribbon you had tied round the waist of your whip. When I see that ribbon on that whip, dumn you, I wanted to kill you." Bartley broke out into a laugh, but Kinney went on soberly. "But thinks I to myself: 'Here! Now you stop right here! You wait! You give the fellow a chance for his life. Let him have a chance to show whether that whip-ribbon goes all through him, first. If it does, kill him cheerfully; but

STERTOROUS

give him a chance *first*.' Well, sir, I gave you the chance, and you showed that you deserved it. I guess you taught me a lesson. When I see you at work, pegging away, hard at something or other, every time I went into your office, up and coming with everybody, and just as ready to pass the time of day with me, as the biggest bug in town, thinks I: 'You'd have made a great mistake to kill that fellow, Kinney!' And I just made up my mind to like you."

"Thanks," said Bartley with ironical gratitude.

Kinney did not speak at once. He whistled thoughtfully through his teeth, and said: "I'll tell you what: if you're going away *very* poor, I know a wealthy chap you can raise a loan out of."

Bartley thought seriously, for a moment. "If your friend offers me twenty dollars, I'm not too well dressed to take it."

"All right," said Kinney. He now dished up the cabbage and potatoes; and throwing a fresh handful of tea into the pot, and filling it up with water, he took down a tin horn, with which he went to the door, and sounded a long, stertorous note.

X

"Guess it was the clothes, again," said Kinney, as he began to wash his tins and dishes after the dinner was over, and the men had gone back to their work. "I could see 'em eyein' you over, when they first came in, and I could see that they didn't exactly like the looks of 'em. It would wear off in time, but it *takes* time for it to wear off; and it had to go pretty rusty, for a start-off. Well, I don't know as it makes much difference to you, does it?"

"Oh, I thought we got along very well," said Bartley with a careless yawn. "There wasn't much chance to get acquainted." Some of the loggers were as handsome and well-made as he, and were of as good origin and traditions, though he had some advantages of training. But his two-button cutaway, his well-fitting trowsers, his scarf with a pin in it, had been too much for these young fellows in their long stoga boots and flannel shirts. They looked at him askance, and dispatched their meal with more than their wonted swiftness, and were off again into the woods without any demonstrations of satisfaction in Bartley's presence.

He had perceived their grudge for he had felt it in his time. But it did not displease him; he had none of the pain with which Kinney, who had so long bragged of him to the loggers, saw that his guest was a failure. "I guess they'll come out all right in the end," he said. In this warm atmosphere, after the gross and heavy dinner he had eaten he yawned again and again. He folded his overcoat into a pillow for his bench, and lay down, and lazily watched Kinney about his work. Presently he saw Kinney seated on a block of wood beside the stove, with his elbow propped in one hand, and holding a magazine, out of which he was reading; he wore spectacles, which gave him a fresh and interesting touch of grotesqueness. Bartley found that an empty barrel had been placed on each side of him, evidently to keep him from rolling off his bench.

"Hello!" he said. "Much obliged to you, Kinney. I haven't been taken such good care of since I can remember. Been asleep, haven't I?"

"About an hour," said Kinney, with a glance at the clock, and ignoring his agency in Bartley's comfort.

"Food for the brain!" said Bartley, sitting up. "I should think so. I've dreamt a perfect New American Cyclopedia and a pronouncing gazetteer, thrown in."

"Is *that* so?" said Kinney, as if pleased with the suggestive character of his cookery, now established by eminent experiment.

Bartley yawned a yawn of satisfied sleepiness, and rubbed his hand over his face.

"I suppose," he said, "if I'm going to write anything about Camp Kinney, I had better see all there is to see."

"Well, yes, I presume you had," said Kinney. "We'll go over to where they're cuttin', pretty soon, and you can see all there is in an hour. But I presume you'll *want* to see it so as to ring in some description, hey? Well, that's all right. But what you going to do with it, when you've done it, now you're out of the Free Press?"

"Oh, I shouldn't have printed it in the Free Press, anyway. Coals to Newcastle, you know. I'll tell you what I think I'll do, Kinney: I'll get my outlines, and then you post me with a lot of facts—queer characters, accidents, romantic incidents, snowings-up, threatened starvation, adventures with wild animals —and I can make something worth while; get out two or three columns, so they can print it in their Sunday edition. And then I'll take it up to Boston, with me, and seek my fortune with it."

"Well, sir, I'll do it," said Kinney, fired with the poetry of the idea. "I'll post you! Dumn 'f I don't wish *I* could write! Well, I *did* used to scribble once for an agricultural paper; but I don't call that writin'. I've set down, well, I guess as much as sixty times, to try to write out what I know about loggin' "—

"Hold on!" cried Bartley, whipping out his note-book. "That's first-rate. That'll do for the first line in the head: *What I Know about Logging*: large caps. Well!"

Kinney shut his magazine, and took his knee between his hands, closing one of his eyes in order to sharpen his recollection. He poured forth a stream of reminiscence, mingled observation, and personal experience. Bartley followed him with his pencil, jotting down points, striking in sub-head lines, and now and then interrupting him with cries of "Good!" "Capital!" "It's a perfect mine—it's a mint!" "By Jove!" he exclaimed, "I'll make *six* columns of this! I'll offer it to one of the magazines, and it'll come out illustrated! Go on, Kinney."

"Hark!" said Kinney, craning his neck forward to listen. "I thought I heard sleigh-bells. But I guess it wasn't. Well, sir, as I was sayin', they fetched that fellow into camp with both feet frozen to the knees— Dumn 'f it *wa'n't* bells!" He unlimbered himself, and hurried to the door at the other end of the cabin, which he opened, letting in a clear block of the afternoon sunshine, and a gush of sleigh-bell music, shot with men's voices, and the cries and laughter of women.

"Well, sir," said Kinney, coming back, and making haste to roll down his sleeves and put on his coat. "*Here's* a nuisance! A whole party of folks—two sleigh-loads—right *on* us. I don't know who they *be*, or where they're from. But I know where I wish they *was*. Well, of course, it's natural they should want to see a loggin' camp," added Kinney, taking himself to task for his inhospitable mind, "and there ain't any harm in it. But I wish they'd give a fellow a *little* notice!"

The voices and bells drew nearer, but Kinney seemed resolved to observe the decorum of not going to the door till some one knocked.

"Kinney! Kinney! Hello, Kinney!" shouted a man's voice,

as the bells hushed before the door, and broke into a musical clash, when one of the horses tossed his head.

"Well, sir," said Kinney, rising, "I guess it's old Willett himself. He's the owner: lives up to Portland, and been threatening to come down here all winter, with a party of friends. You just stay still," he added; and he paid himself the deference that every true American owes himself in his dealings with his employer: he went to the door very deliberately, and made no haste on account of the repeated cries of "Kinney! Kinney!" in which others of the party outside now joined.

When he opened the door again, the first voice saluted him with a roar of laughter: "Why, Kinney! I began to think you were dead!"

"No, sir," Bartley heard Kinney reply, "it takes more to kill me than you'd suppose." But now he stepped outside, and the talk became unintelligible. Finally, Bartley heard what was imaginably Mr. Willett's voice saying "Well, let's go in and have a look at it now," and with much outcry and laughter the ladies were invisibly helped to dismount, and presently the whole party came stamping and rustling in.

Bartley's blood tingled. He liked this, and he stood quite self-possessed, with his thumbs in his waistcoat pockets and his elbows dropped, while Mr. Willett advanced in a friendly way: "Ah, Mr. Hubbard! Kinney told us you were in here, and asked me to introduce myself while he looked after the horses. My name's Willett. These are my daughters: this is Mrs. Macallister of Montreal, Mrs. Witherby of Boston; Miss Witherby, and Mr. Witherby. *You* ought to know each other: Mr. Hubbard is the editor of the Equity Free Press; Mr. Witherby of the Boston Events, Mr. Hubbard. Oh! And *Mr.* Macallister."

Bartley bowed to the Willett and Witherby ladies, and shook hands with Mr. Witherby, a large, solemn man, with a purse-mouth and tight rings of white hair who treated him with the pomp inevitable to the owner of a city newspaper in meeting a country editor.

At the mention of his name Mr. Macallister, a slight little straight man in a long ulster and a seal-skin cap, tiddled farcically forward on his toes, and giving Bartley his hand said, "Ah, haow d'e-do, *haow* d'e-do!"

Mrs. Macallister fixed upon him the eye of the flirt who knows her man. She was of the dark-eyed English type; her eyes were very large and full, and her smooth black hair was drawn flatly backward, and fastened in a knot just under her dashing fur cap. She wore a fur sack, and she was equipped against the cold as exquisitely as her Southern sisters defend themselves from the summer. Bits of warm color, in ribbon and scarf flashed out here and there; when she flung open her sack, she showed herself much more lavishly buttoned and bugled and bangled than the Americans. She sat down on the movable bench which Bartley had vacated, and crossed her feet, very small and saucy even in their arctics, on a stick of firewood, and cast up her neat profile, and rapidly made eyes at every part of the interior. "Why, it's delicious, you know. I never saw anything so comfortable. I want to spend the rest of me life here, you know." She spoke very far down in her throat, and with a rising inflection in each sentence. "I'm going to have a quarrel with you, Mr. Willett, for not telling me what a delightful surprise you had for us here. Oh, but I'd no idea of it, I assure you!"

"Well, I'm glad you like it, Mrs. Macallister," said Mr. Willett with the clumsiness of American middle-age when summoned to say something gallant. "If I'd told you what a surprise I had for you, it wouldn't have been one."

"Oh, it's no good you're trying to get out of it *that* way," retorted the beauty. "There he comes now! I'm really in love with him, you know," she said, as Kinney opened the door, and came hulking forward.

Nobody said anything, at once, but Bartley laughed finally and ventured, "Well, I'll propose for you to Kinney."

"Oh, I dare say!" cried the beauty with a lively effect of wit. "Mr. Kinney, I've fallen in love with your camp, d'ye know," she added, as Kinney drew near, "and I'm beggin' Mr. Willett to let me come and live here among you."

"Well, ma'am," said Kinney, a little abashed at this proposition, "you couldn't do a better thing for your health, I *guess*."

The proprietor of the Boston Events turned about, and began to look over the arrangements of the interior; the other ladies went with him, conversing in low tones. "These must be the places where the men sleep," they said, gazing at the bunks.

"We must get Kinney to explain things to us," said Mr. Willett a little restlessly.

Mrs. Macallister jumped briskly to her feet. "Oh, yes, do, Mr. Willett, make him explain everything! I've been tryin' to coax it out of him, but he's *such* a tease!"

Kinney looked very sheepish, in this character, and Mrs. Macallister hooked Bartley to her side for the tour of the interior. "I can't let you away from me, Mr. Hubbard; your friend's so satirical, I'm afraid of him. Only fancy, Mr. Willett! He's been talkin' to *me* about brain-foods! I know he's makin' fun of me; and it isn't kind, is it, Mr. Hubbard?"

She did not give the least notice to the things that the others looked at, or to Kinney's modest lecture upon the manners and customs of the loggers. She kept a little apart with Bartley, and plied him with bravadoes, with pouts, with little cries of surprise. In the midst of these he heard Mr. Willett saying, "You ought to get some one to come and write about this for your paper, Witherby." But Mrs. Macallister was also saying something, with a significant turn of her floating eyes, and the thing that concerned Bartley, if he were to make his way among the newspapers, in Boston, slipped from his grasp like the idea which we try to seize in a dream. She made sure of him for the drive to the place which they visited to see the men felling the trees, by inviting him to a seat at her side in the sleigh; this crowded the others, but she insisted, and they all gave way, as people must to the caprices of a pretty woman. Her coquetries united British wilfulness to American nonchalance, and seemed to have been graduated to the appreciation of garrison and St. Lawrence River steamboat and watering-place society. The Willett ladies had already found it necessary to explain to the Witherby ladies that they had met her the summer before at the seaside; and that she had stopped at Portland on her way to England; they did not know her very well, but some friends of theirs did; and their father had asked her to come with them to the camp: they added that the Canadian ladies seemed to expect the gentlemen to be a great deal more attentive than ours were. They had known as little what to do with Mr. Macallister's small-talk and compliments, as his wife's audacities, but they did not view Bartley's responsiveness with pleasure. If Mrs. Macallister's arts were not subtle, as Bartley, even in the intoxication of her preference, could not keep from seeing, still in his mood it was consoling, to be singled out by her: it meant that even in a logging-camp he was recognizable by any person of fashion as a good-looking, well-dressed man of the world. It embittered him the more against Marcia, while in some sort it vindicated him to himself.

The early winter sunset was beginning to tinge the snow with crimson, when the party started back to camp, where Kinney was to give them supper; he had it greatly on his conscience that they should have a good time, and he promoted it as far as hot mince-pie and newly-fried dough-nuts would go. He also opened a few canned goods, as he called some very exclusive sardines and peaches, and he made an entirely fresh pot of tea, and a pan of soda-biscuit. Mrs. Macallister made remarks across her plate which were for Bartley alone; and Kinney who was seriously waiting upon his guests, refused to respond to Bartley's joking reference to himself of some questions and comments of hers.

After supper, when the loggers had withdrawn to the other end of the long hut, she called out to Kinney, "Oh, *do* tell them to smoke: we shall not mind it at all, I assure you. Can't some of them do something? Sing or dance?"

Kinney unbent a little, at this. "There's a first-class clog-dancer, among them; but he's a little stuck-up, and I don't know as you could get him to dance," he said in a low tone.

"What a bloated aristocrat!" cried the lady. "Then the only thing is for us to dance first. Can they play?"

"One of 'em can whistle like a bird—he can whistle like a

whole band," answered Kinney, warming. "And of course the Kanucks can fiddle."

"And what are Kanucks? Is *that* what you call us Canadians?"

"Well, ma'am, it aint quite the thing to do," said Kinney, penitently.

"It isn't at *all* the thing to do! Which are the Kanucks?"

She rose, and went forward with Kinney, in her spoiled way, and addressed a swarthy, gleaming-eyed young logger in French. He answered with a smile that showed all his white teeth, and turned to one of his comrades; then the two rose, and got violins out of the bunks, and came forward. Others of their race joined them, but the Yankees hung gloomily back; they clearly did not like these liberties, this patronage.

"I shall have your clog-dancer on his feet yet, Mr. Kinney," said Mrs. Macallister, as she came back to her place.

The Canadians began to play and sing those gay, gay airs of old France, which they have kept unsaddened through all the dark events that have changed the popular mood of the mother-country. They have matched words to them in celebration of their life on the great rivers and in the vast forests of the North, and in these blithe barcaroles and hunting songs breathes the joyous spirit of a France that knows neither doubt nor care; France untouched by Revolution or Napoleonic wars: some of the airs still keep the very words that came overseas with them two hundred years ago. The transition to the dance was quick and inevitable; a dozen slim young fellows were gliding about behind the players, pounding the hard earthen floor, and singing in time. "Oh, come, come!" cried the beauty, rising and stamping impatiently with her little foot, "suppose we dance, too."

She pulled Bartley forward, by the hand; her husband followed with the taller Miss Willett; two of the Canadians, at the instance of Mrs. Macallister came forward and politely asked the honor of the other young ladies' hands in the dance; their temper was infectious, and the cotillion was in full life before their partners had time to wonder at their consent. Mrs. Macallister could sing some of the Canadian songs; her voice, clear and fresh, rang through those of the men, while in at the window thrown open for air, came the wild cries of the forest: the wail of a catamount, and the solemn hooting of a distant owl.

"Isn't it jolly good fun?" she demanded, when the figure was finished; and now Kinney went up to the first-class clog-dancer, and prevailed with him to show his skill. He seemed to comply on condition that the whistler should furnish the music: he came forward, with a bashful hauteur, bridling stiffly like a girl, and struck into the laborious and monotonous jig which is perhaps our national dance; he was exquisitely shaped, and as he danced, he suppled more and more, while the whistler warbled a wilder and swifter strain, and kept time with his hands. There was something that stirred the blood in the fury of the strain and dance: when it was done, Mrs. Macallister caught off her cap and ran round the spectators to make them pay; she excused no one, and she gave the money to Kinney telling him to get his loggers something to keep the cold out. "I should say whiskey, if I were in the Canadian bush," she suggested.

"Well *I* guess we sha'n't say anything of that sort in *this* camp," said Kinney.

She turned upon Bartley, "I know Mr. Hubbard is dying to do something. Do something, Mr. Hubbard!" Bartley looked up in surprise at this interpretation of his tacit wish to distinguish himself before her. "Come, sing us some of your student songs." Bartley's vanity had confided the fact of his college training to her, and he was really thinking just then that he would like to give them a serio-comic song, for which he had been famous with his class. He borrowed the violin of a Kanuck, and sitting down strummed upon it banjo-wise. The song was one of those which is partly spoken and acted; he really did it very well; but the Willett and Witherby ladies did not seem to understand it, quite; and the gentlemen looked

as if they thought this very undignified business for an educated American.

Mrs. Macallister feigned a yawn, and put up her hand to
hide it. "*Oh*, what a styupid song!" she said. She sprang to her
feet, and began to put on her wraps. The others were glad of
this signal to go, and followed her example. "Good-bye!" she
cried, giving her hand to Kinney. "*I* don't think your ideas
are ridiculous. I think there's no end of good sense in them,
I assure you. I hope you wont leave off that regard for the
brain in your cooking. Good-bye!" She waved her hand to the
Americans, and then to the Kanucks, as she passed out between
their respectfully parted ranks. "Adieu, messieurs!" She merely
nodded to Bartley; the others parted from him coldly, as he
fancied, and it seemed to him that he had been made responsible for that woman's coquetries, when he was conscious, all
the time of having forborne even to meet them half way. But
this was not so much to his credit as he imagined. The flirt
can only practice her audacities safely by grace of those upon
whom she uses them, and if men really met them half way
there could be no such thing as flirting.

XI

THE LOGGERS pulled off their boots and got into their bunks, where some of them lay and smoked, while others fell asleep directly.

Bartley made some indirect approaches to Kinney for sympathy in the snub which he had received, and which rankled in his mind with unabated keenness.

But Kinney did not respond. "Your bed's ready," he said. "You can turn in whenever you like."

"What's the matter?" asked Bartley.

"Nothing's the matter, if you say so," answered Kinney going about some preparations for the morning's breakfast.

Bartley looked at his resentful back. He saw that he was hurt, and he surmised that Kinney suspected him of making fun of his eccentricities to Mrs. Macallister. He *had* laughed at Kinney, and tried to amuse her with him; but he could not have made this appear as harmless as it was. He rose from the bench on which he had been sitting, and shut with a click the pen-knife with which he had been cutting a pattern on its edge. "I shall have to say good-night to you, I believe," he said going to the peg on which Kinney had hung his hat and overcoat. He had them on, and was buttoning the coat in an angry tremor before Kinney looked up and realized what his guest was about.

"Why, what—why, where—you goin'?" he faltered in dismay.

"To Equity," said Bartley, feeling in his coat-pockets for his gloves, and drawing them on, without looking at Kinney, whose great hands were in a pan of dough.

"Why—why—no, you ain't!" he protested, with a revulsion of feeling that swept away all his resentment, and left him nothing but remorse for his inhospitality.

"No?" said Bartley, putting up the collar of the first ulster worn by a native in that region.

"Why, look here!" cried Kinney, pulling his hands out of the dough, and making a fruitless effort to cleanse them upon each other. "I don't want you to go, this way."

"Don't you? I'm sorry to disoblige you; but I'm going," said Bartley.

Kinney tried to laugh. "Why, Hubbard—why, Bartley—why, Bart!" he exclaimed. "What's the matter with you? I ain't mad!"

"You have an unfortunate manner, then. Good-night." He strode out between the bunks full of snoring loggers. Kinney hurried after him, imploring and protesting in a low voice, trying to get before him, and longing to lay his floury paws upon him and detain him by main force, but even in his distress, respecting Bartley's overcoat too much to touch it.

He followed him out into the freezing air in his shirt-sleeves, and besought him not to be such a fool. "It makes me feel like the devil!" he exclaimed, pitifully. "You come back, now, half a minute, and I'll make it all right with you. I know I can; you're a gentleman; and you'll understand. *Do* come back! I shall never get over it, if you don't!"

"I'm sorry," said Bartley, "but I'm not going back. Good-night."

"Oh, good Lordy!" lamented Kinney. "What am I goin' to do? Why, man! It's a good three mile and more to Equity and the woods is full of catamounts. I tell ye 'tain't safe for ye." He kept following Bartley down the path to the road.

"I'll risk it," said Bartley.

Kinney had left the door of the camp open, and the yells and curses of the awakened sleepers recalled him to himself.

"Well, well! If you will *go*," he groaned in despair, "here's that money." He plunged his doughy hand into his pocket,

hypercritical omnipotence

and pulled out a roll of bills. "Here it is. I hain't time to count it; but it'll be all right, anyhow"—

Bartley did not even turn his head to look round at him.

"Keep your money!" he said, as he plunged forward through the snow. "I wouldn't touch a cent of it to save your life."

"All right," said Kinney, in hapless contrition, and he returned to shut himself in with the reproaches of the loggers and the upbraiding of his own heart.

Bartley dashed along the road in a fury that kept him unconscious of the intense cold; and he passed half the night when he was once more in his own room, packing up his effects against his departure next day. When all was done he went to bed half wishing that he might never rise from it again. It was not that he cared for Kinney; that fool's sulking was only the climax of a long series of injuries of which he was the victim at the hands of a hypercritical omnipotence.

Despite his conviction that it was useless to struggle longer against such injustice, he lived through the night, and came down late to breakfast, which he found stale, and without the compensating advantage of finding himself alone at the table. Some ladies had lingered there to clear up on the best authority the distracting rumors concerning him which they had heard the day before. Was it true that he had intended to spend the rest of the winter in logging; and *was* it true that he was going to give up the Free Press; and was it *true* that Henry Bird was going to be the editor? Bartley gave a sarcastic confirmation to all these reports; and went out to the printing office to gather up some things of his. He found Henry Bird there, looking pale and sick, but at work and seemingly in authority. This was what Bartley had always intended when he should go out, but he did not like it, and he resented some small changes that had already been made in the editor's room, in tacit recognition of his purpose not to occupy it again.

Bird greeted him stiffly, the printer-girls briefly nodded to him, suppressing some little hysterical titters, and tacitly let him feel that he was no longer master there. While he was in the composing-room, Hannah Morrison came in, apparently from some errand outside, and catching sight of him, stared, and pertly passed him in silence.

On his inkstand he found a letter from Squire Gaylord, briefly auditing his last account, and enclosing the balance due him. From this the old lawyer with the careful smallness of a village business man had deducted various little sums for things that Bartley had never expected to pay for. With a like thriftiness the landlord, when Bartley asked for his bill, had charged certain items that had not appeared in the bills before: Bartley felt that the charges were trumped up; but he was powerless to dispute them; besides he hoped to sell the landlord his colt and cutter, and he did not care to prejudice that matter. Some bills from storekeepers, which he thought he had paid, were handed to him by the landlord, and each of the churches had sent in a little account for pew rent for the past eighteen months: he had always believed himself dead headed at church. He outlawed the latter by tearing them to pieces in the landlord's presence, and dropping the fragments into a spittoon. It seemed to him that every soul in Equity was making a clutch at the rapidly diminishing sum of money which Squire Gaylord had enclosed to him, and which was all he had in the world. On the other hand, his popularity in the village seemed to have vanished over night. He had sometimes fancied a general and rebellious grief when it should become known that he was going away; but instead there was an acquiescence amounting to airiness. He wondered if anything about his affairs with Henry Bird and Hannah Morrison had leaked out. But he did not care. He only wished to shake the snow of Equity off his feet as soon as possible.

After dinner, when the boarders had gone out, and the loafers had not yet gathered in, he offered the landlord his colt and cutter. Bartley knew that the landlord wanted the colt; but now the latter said: "I don't know as I care to buy any hosses, right in the winter this way."

"All right," answered Bartley. "Just have the colt put into the cutter."

Andy Morrison brought it round. The boy looked at Bartley's set face with a sort of awe-stricken affection: his adoration for the young man survived all that he had heard said against him at home during the series of family quarrels that had ensued upon his father's interview with him; he longed to testify somehow his unabated loyalty, but he could not think of anything to do, much less to say.

Bartley pitched his valise into the cutter, and then as Andy left the horse's head to give him a hand with his trunk, offered him a dollar. "I don't want anything," said the boy, shyly refusing the money out of pure affection.

But Bartley mistook his motive, and thought it sulky resentment. "Oh, very well," he said. "Take hold."

The landlord came out. "Hold on a minute," he said. "Where you goin' to take the cars?"

"At the Junction," answered Bartley. "I know a man there that will buy the colt. What is it you want?"

The landlord stepped back a few paces, and surveyed the establishment: "I should like to ride after that hoss," he said, "if you ain't in any great of a hurry."

"Get in," said Bartley, and the landlord took the reins. From time to time, as he drove, he rose up and looked over the dashboard to study the gait of the horse. "I've noticed he strikes, some, when he first comes out in the spring."

"Yes," Bartley assented.

"Pulls consid'able."

"He pulls."

The landlord rose again, and scrutinized the horse's legs. "I don't know as I ever noticed 't he'd capped his hock before."

"Didn't you?"

"Done it kickin', nights, I guess."

"I guess so."

The landlord drew the whip lightly across the colt's rear: he shrank together, and made a little spring forward, but behaved perfectly well. "I don't know as I should always be sure he wouldn't kick in the daytime."

"No," said Bartley, "you never can be sure of anything."

They drove along in silence. At last the landlord said, "Well, he ain't so fast, as I *supposed*."

"He's not so fast a horse as some," answered Bartley.

The landlord leaned over sidewise for an inspection of the colt's action forward. "Hain't never thought he had a splint on that forrad off leg?"

"A splint? Perhaps he has a splint."

They returned to the hotel, and both alighted.

"Skittish devil," remarked the landlord, as the colt quivered under the hand he laid upon him.

"He's skittish," said Bartley.

The landlord retired as far back as the door, and regarded the colt critically. "Well, I s'pose you've always used him too well ever to winded him, but dumn 'f he don't *blow* like it."

"Look here, Simpson," said Bartley, very quietly. "You know this horse as well as I do, and you know there isn't an out about him. You want to buy him because you always have. Now make me an offer."

"Well," groaned the landlord, "what'll you take for the whole rig, just as it stands: colt, cutter, leathers and robe."

"Two hundred dollars," promptly replied Bartley.

"I'll give ye seventy-five," returned the landlord with equal promptness.

"Andy, take hold of the end of that trunk, will you." The landlord allowed them to put the trunk into the cutter. Bartley got in, too, and shifting the baggage to one side folded the robe around him from his middle down, and took his seat. "This colt can road you right along all day inside of five minutes, and he can trot inside of two-thirty, every time; and you know it as well as I do."

"Well," said the landlord, "make it an even hundred." Bartley leaned forward and gathered up the reins. "Let go his head, Andy," he quietly commanded.

"Make it one and a quarter," cried the landlord, not seeing that his chance was past. "What do you say."

What Bartley said as he touched the colt with the whip the

landlord never knew. He stood watching the cutter's swift disappearance up the road, in a sort of stupid expectation of its return. When he realized that Bartley's departure was final, he said under his breath: "Sold, ye dumned old fool, and serve ye right," and went in-doors with a feeling of admiration for colt and man that bordered on reverence.

XII

THIS LAST DROP of the local meanness filled Bartley's bitter cup. As he passed the house at the end of the street, he seemed to drain it all. He knew that the old lawyer was there sitting by the office stove, drawing his hand across his chin, and Bartley hoped that he was still as miserable as he had looked when he last saw him; but he did not know that by the window in the house which he would not even look at, Marcia sat, self-prisoned in her room, with her eyes upon the road, famishing for the thousandth part of a chance to see him pass. She saw him now, for the instant of his coming and going; with eyes trained to take in every point, she saw the preparation which seemed like final departure, and with a gasp of "Bartley!" as if she were trying to call after him, she sank back into her chair, and shut her eyes.

He drove on, plunging into the deep hollow beyond the house, and keeping for several miles the road they had taken on that Sunday together; but he did not make the turn that brought them back to the village again. The pale sunset was slanting over the snow when he reached the Junction, for he had slackened his colt's pace, after he had put ten miles behind him; not choosing to reach a prospective purchaser with his horse all blown and bathed with sweat. He wished to be able to say, "Look at him! He's come fifteen miles since three o'clock, and he's as keen as when he started."

This was true, when, having left his baggage at the Junction, he drove another mile into the country to see the farmer of the gentleman who had his summer house here, and who had once bantered Bartley to sell him his colt. The farmer was away, and would not be at home till the up-train from Boston was in. Bartley looked at his watch, and saw that to wait would lose him the six o'clock down-train: there would be no other till eleven o'clock. But it was worth while: the gentleman had said, "When you want the money for that colt, bring him over any time; my farmer will have it ready for you." He waited for the up-train, but when the farmer arrived, he was full of all sorts of scruples and reluctances. He said he should not like to buy it till he had heard from Mr. Farnham; he ended by offering Bartley eighty dollars for the colt on his own account: he did not want the cutter. "You write to Mr. Farnham," said Bartley, "that you tried that plan with me, and it wouldn't work; he's lost the colt." He made this brave show of indifference, but he was disheartened, and having carried the farmer home from the Junction for the convenience of talking over the trade with him, he drove back again through the early nightfall in sullen desperation.

The weather had softened and was threatening rain or snow; the dark was closing in spiritlessly; the colt, shortening from a trot into a short, springy jolt, dropped into a walk, at last, as if he were tired, and gave Bartley time enough on his way back to the Junction for reflection upon the disaster into which his life had fallen. These passages of utter despair are commoner to the young than they are to those whom years have experienced in the impermanence of any fate, good, bad, or indifferent, unless, perhaps, the last may seem rather constant. Taken in reference to all that had been ten days ago, the present ruin was incredible, and had nothing reasonable in proof of its existence. Then he was prosperously placed and in the way to better himself indefinitely. Now, he was here in the dark, with fifteen dollars in his pocket, and an unsalable horse on his hands; outcast, deserted, homeless, hopeless: and by whose fault? He owned even then that he had committed some follies; but in his sense of Marcia's all-giving love he had risen for once in his life to a conception of self-devotion, and in taking herself from him as she did she had taken from him the highest incentive he had ever known, and had checked him in his first feeble impulse to do and be all in all for another. It was she who had ruined him.

As he jumped out of the cutter at the Junction, the station-master stopped with a cluster of parti-colored signal lanterns in his hand and cast their light over the sorrel. "Nice colt you got there."

"Yes," said Bartley blanketing the horse, "do you know anybody who wants to buy?"

"Whose is he?" asked the man.

"He's mine!" shouted Bartley. "Do you think I stole him?"

"*I* don't know where you got him," said the man, walking off, and making a soft play of red and green lights on the snow beyond the narrow platform.

Bartley went into the great ugly barn of a station, trembling, and sat down in one of the gouged and whittled armchairs near the stove. A pomp of time-tables, and luminous advertisements of Western railroads and their land-grants decorated the wooden walls of the gentlemen's waiting room which had been sanded to keep the gentlemen from writing and sketching upon them. This was the more judicious because the ladies' room, in the absence of tourist travel, was locked in winter, and they were obliged to share the gentlemen's. In summer, the junction was a busy place, but after the snow fell and until the snow thawed, it was a desolation relieved only by the arrival of the sparsely-peopled through trains from the north and east; and by such local travellers as wished to take trains not stopping at their own stations. These broke in upon the solitude of the joint stationmaster and baggage-man and switch-tender with just sufficient frequency to keep him in a state of uncharitable irritation and unrest. To-night Bartley was the sole intruder, and he sat by the stove wrapped in a cloud of rebellious memories, when one side of a colloquy without made itself heard.

"What?"

Some question was repeated.

"No, it went down half an hour ago."

An inaudible question followed.

"Next down train at eleven."

There was now a faintly audible lament or appeal.

"Guess you'll have to come earlier next time. Most folks doos that wants to take it."

Bartley now heard the despairing moan of a woman; he had already divined the sex of the futile questioner whom the stationmaster was bullying; but he had divined it without compassion, and if he had not himself been a sufferer from the man's insolence he might even have felt a ferocious satisfaction in it. In a word he was at his lowest and worst when the door opened, and the woman came in, with a movement at once bewildered and daring, which gave him the impression of a despair as complete and final as his own. He doggedly kept his place; she did not seem to care for him, but in the uncertain light of the lamp above them she drew near the stove, and putting one hand to her pocket as if to find her handkerchief, she flung aside her veil with her other, and showed her tear-stained face.

He was on his feet, somehow. "Marcia!"

"Oh!—Bartley!"—

He had seized her by the arm, to make sure that she was there in verity of flesh and blood, and not by some trick of his own senses, as a cold chill running over him had made him afraid. At the touch their passion ignored all that they had made each other suffer; her head was on his breast, his embrace was round her; it was a moment of delirious bliss that intervened between the sorrows that had been, and the reasons that must come.

"What—what are you doing here, Marcia?" he asked at last. They sank on the benching that ran round the wall; he held her hands fast in one of his, and kept his other arm about her as they sat side by side.

"I don't know—I"— She seemed to rouse herself by an effort from her rapture. "I was going to see Netty Spaulding. And I saw you driving past our house; and I thought you were coming here; and I couldn't bear—I couldn't bear to let you go away without telling you that I was wrong; and asking—asking you to forgive me. I thought you would do it—I thought you would know that I had behaved that way because I—I—cared so much for you— I thought—I was afraid you had gone on the other train"— She trembled and sank back in his embrace from which she had lifted herself a little.

"How did you get here?" asked Bartley, as if willing to give himself all the proofs he could of the everyday reality of her presence.

"Andy Morrison brought me. Father sent him from the hotel. I didn't care what you would say to me. I wanted to tell you that I was wrong, and not let you go away feeling that—that—you were all to blame. I thought when I had done that you might drive me away—or laugh at me, or anything you pleased, if only you would let me take back"—

"Yes," he answered dreamily. All that wicked hardness was breaking up within him; he felt it melting drop by drop in his heart. This poor love-tossed soul, this frantic, unguided, reckless girl, was an angel of mercy to him, and in her folly and error a messenger of heavenly peace and hope. "I am a bad fellow, Marcia," he faltered. "You ought to know that. You did right to give me up. I made love to Hannah Morrison; I never promised to marry her, but I made her think that I was fond of her."

"I don't care for that," replied the girl. "I told you when we were first engaged that I would never think of anything that had gone before that; and then when I would not listen to a word from you that day, I broke my promise."

"When I struck Henry Bird, because he was jealous of me, I was as guilty as if I had killed him."

"If you had killed him, I was bound to you by my word. Your striking him was part of the same thing—part of what I had promised I never would care for." A gush of tears came into his eyes, and she saw them. "Oh, poor Bartley! Poor Bartley!" She took his head between her hands and pressed it hard against her heart, and then wrapped her arms tight about him, and softly bemoaned him.

They drew a little apart, when the man came in with his lantern, and set it down to mend the fire. But as a railroad employé he was far too familiar with the love that vaunts itself on all railroad trains to feel that he was an intruder. He scarcely looked at them, and went out, when he had mended the fire, and left it purring.

"Where is Andy Morrison?" asked Bartley. "Has he gone back?"

"No; he is at the hotel over there. I told him to wait till I found out when the train went north."

"So you inquired when it went to Boston," said Bartley with a touch of his old raillery. "Come," he added, taking her hand under his arm. He led her out of the room to where his cutter stood outside.

She was astonished to find the colt there. "I wonder I didn't see it. But if I had I should have thought that you had sold it and gone away; Andy told me you were coming here to sell the colt. When the man told me the express was gone, I knew you were on it."

They found the boy stolidly waiting for Marcia on the verandah of the hotel, stamping first upon one foot and then the other, and hugging himself in his greatcoat, as the coming snowfall blew its first flakes in his face.

"Is that you, Andy?" asked Bartley.

"Yes, sir," answered the boy without surprise at finding him with Marcia.

"Well, here! Just take hold of the colt's head a minute." As the boy obeyed, Bartley threw the reins on the dashboard, and leaped out of the cutter, and went within. He returned after a brief absence, followed by the landlord.

"Well, it ain't more'n a mile 'n' a half if it's that. You just keep straight along this street, and take your first turn to the left, and you're right at the house; it's the first house on the left hand side."

"Thanks," returned Bartley. "Andy: you tell the Squire that you left Marcia with me, and I said I would see about her getting back. You needn't hurry."

"All right," said the boy and he disappeared round the corner of the house, to get his horse from the barn.

"Well, I'll be all ready by the time you're here," said the landlord still holding the hall door ajar. "Luck *to* you!" he shouted, shutting it.

Marcia locked both her hands through Bartley's arm, and leaned her head on his shoulder. Neither spoke for some minutes. Then he asked, "Marcia, do you know where you are?"

"With you," she answered in a voice of utter peace.

"Do you know where we are going?" he asked, leaning over to kiss her cold, pure cheek.

"No," she answered in as perfect content as before.

"We are going to get married."

He felt her grow tense in her clasp upon his arm, and hold there rigidly for a moment, while the swift thoughts whirled through her mind. Then as if the struggle had ended, she silently relaxed, and leaned more heavily against him.

"There's still time to go back, Marcia," he said, "if you wish. That turn to the right, yonder, will take us to Equity, and you can be at home in two hours." She quivered. "I'm a poor man—I suppose you know that; I've only got fifteen dollars in the world, and the colt here. I know I can get on; I'm not afraid for myself; but if you would rather wait; if you're not perfectly certain of yourself— Remember, it's going to be a struggle; we're going to have some hard times"—

"You forgive me?" she huskily asked, for all answer, without moving her head from where it lay.

"Yes, Marcia."

"Then—hurry."

The minister was an old man, and he seemed quite dazed

at the suddenness of their demand for his services. But he gathered himself together, and contrived to make them man and wife, and to give them his marriage-certificate.

"It seems as if there were something else," he said, absently, as he handed the paper to Bartley.

"Perhaps it's this," said Bartley, giving him a five-dollar note in return.

"Ah, perhaps," he replied, in unabated perplexity. He bade them serve God, and let them out into the snowy night, through which they drove back to the hotel.

The landlord had kindled a fire on the hearth of the Franklin stove in his parlor, and the blazing hickory snapped in electrical sympathy with the storm when they shut themselves into the bright room, and Bartley took Marcia fondly into his arms.

"Wife!"

"Husband!"

They sat down before the fire, hand in hand, and talked of the light things that swim to the top, and eddy round and round on the surface of our deepest moods. They made merry over the old minister's perturbation, which Bartley found endlessly amusing. Then he noticed that the dress Marcia had on was the one she had worn to the Sociable in Lower Equity, and she said, yes, she had put it on because he once said he liked it. He asked her when, and she said O, she knew; but if he could not remember, she was not going to tell him. Then she wanted to know if he recognized her by the dress before she lifted her veil in the station.

"No," he said, with a teasing laugh, "I wasn't thinking of you."

"Oh, Bartley!" she joyfully reproached him. "You must have been!"

"Yes, I was! I was so mad at you, that I was glad to have that brute of a station-master bullying *some* woman!"

"Bartley!"

He sat holding her hand. "Marcia," he said gravely, "we

must write to your father at once, and tell him. I want to begin life in the right way, and I think it's only fair to him."

She was enraptured at his magnanimity. "Bartley! That's *like* you! Poor father! I declare—Bartley, I'm afraid I had forgotten him! It's dreadful; but—*you* put everything else out of my head. I do believe I've died and come to life somewhere else!"

"Well, *I* haven't," said Bartley, "and I guess you'd better write to your father. *You'd* better write; at present he and I are not on speaking terms. Here!" he took out his note-book, and gave her his stylographic pen after striking the fist that held it upon his other fist, in the fashion of the amateurs of that reluctant instrument, in order to bring down the ink.

"Oh, what's that?" she asked.

"It's a new kind of pen. I got it for a notice in the Free Press."

"Is Henry Bird going to edit the paper?"

"I don't know, and I don't care," answered Bartley. "I'll go out and get an envelope and ask the landlord what's the quickest way to get the letter to your father."

He took up his hat, but she laid her hand on his arm. "Oh, send for him!" she said.

"Are you afraid I sha'n't come back?" he demanded, with a laughing kiss. "I want to see him about something else, too."

"Well, don't be gone long." They parted with an embrace that would have fortified older married people for a year's separation. When Bartley came back, she handed him the leaf she had torn out of his book, and sat down beside him while he read it, with her arm over his shoulder.

"Dear father," the letter ran, "Bartley and I are married. We were married an hour ago, just across the New Hampshire line, by the Rev. Mr. Jessup. Bartley wants I should let you know the very first thing. I am going to Boston with Bartley to-night, and as soon as we get settled there, I will write again. I want you should forgive us both; but if you wont forgive Bartley, you mustn't me. You were mistaken about Bartley, and I was right. Bartley has told me everything and I am perfectly satisfied. Love to mother.

"Marcia.

"P.S. I *did* intend to visit Netty Spaulding. But I saw Bartley driving past on his way to the Junction, and I determined to see him if I could before he started for Boston, and tell him I was all wrong, no matter what he said or did afterwards. I ought to have told you I meant to see Bartley; but then you would not have let me come, and if I had not come I should have died."

"There's a good deal of Bartley in it," said the young man with a laugh.

"You don't like it!"

"Yes, I do; it's all right. Did you use to take the prize for composition at boarding-school?"

"Why, I think it's a very good letter for when I'm in such an excited state."

"It's beautiful," cried Bartley, laughing more and more. The tears started to her eyes.

"Marcia," said her husband fondly, "what a child you are! If ever I do anything to betray your trust in me"—

There came a shuffling of feet outside the door, a clinking of glass and crockery, and a jarring sort of blow, as if some one were trying to rap on the panel with the edge of a heavy laden waiter. Bartley threw the door open and found the landlord there, red and smiling with the waiter in his hand. "I thought I'd bring your supper in here, you know," he explained confidentially, "so's't you could have it a little more snug. And my wife she kind o' got wind o' what was goin' on—women will, you know," he said with a wink—"and she's sent ye in some hot biscuit and a little jell, and some of her cake." He set the waiter down on the table, and stood admiring its mystery of napkinned dishes. "She guessed you wouldn't object to some cold chicken, and she's put a little of that on. Sha'n't cost ye any more," he hastened to assure them. "Now, this is your room till the train comes, and there ain't agoin' anybody come in here. So you can make yourselves at home. And *I* hope you'll enjoy your supper, as much as we did our'n the night *we* was married. There! I guess I'll let the lady fix the table; she looks as if she knowed how."

He got himself out of the room again, and then Marcia, who had made him some embarrassed thanks, burst out in praise of his pleasantness.

"Well, he ought to be pleasant," said Bartley, "he's just beaten me on a horse-trade. I've sold him the colt."

"Sold him the colt!" cried Marcia, tragically dropping the napkin she had lifted from the plate of cold chicken.

"Well, we couldn't very well have taken him to Boston with us. And we couldn't have got there without selling him. You know you haven't married a millionaire, Marcia."

"How much did you get for the colt?"

"Oh, I didn't do so badly. I got a hundred and fifty for him."

"And you had fifteen besides."

"That was before we were married. I gave the minister five for you—I think you are worth it. I wanted to give fifteen."

"Well, then, you have a hundred and sixty now. Isn't that a great deal?"

"An everlasting lot," said Bartley with an impatient laugh. "Don't let the supper cool, Marcia!"

She silently set out the feast, but regarded it ruefully. "You oughtn't to have ordered so much, Bartley," she said. "You couldn't afford it."

"I can afford anything when I'm hungry. Besides I only ordered the oysters and coffee; all the rest is conscience money —or sentiment—from the landlord. Come, come! Cheer up, now! We sha'n't starve to-night, anyhow."

"Well, I know father will help us."

"We sha'n't count on him," said Bartley. "Now, *drop* it!" He put his arm round her shoulders and pressed her against him till she raised her face for his kiss.

"Well, I *will!*" she said, and the shadow lifted itself from their wedding feast, and they sat down and made merry as if they had all the money in the world to spend. They laughed and joked; they praised the things they liked, and made fun of the others.

"How strange! How perfectly impossible it all seems! Why last night I was taking supper at Kinney's logging-camp, and hating you at every mouthful with all my might. Everything seemed against me, and I was feeling ugly, and flirting like mad with a fool from Montreal: she had come out there from Portland for a frolic with the owner's party. You made me do it, Marcia!" he cried jestingly. "And remember that if you want me to be good, you must be kind. The other thing seems to make me worse and worse."

"I will—I will, Bartley," she said humbly, "I will try to be kind and patient with you. I will indeed."

He threw back his head and laughed and laughed. "Poor—poor old Kinney! He's the cook, you know, and he thought I'd been making fun of him to that woman, and he behaved so, after they were gone, that I started home in a rage; and he followed me out with his hands all covered with dough, and wanted to stop me, but he couldn't for fear of spoiling my clothes"— He lost himself in another paroxysm.

Marcia smiled a little. Then, "What sort of a looking person was she?" she tremulously asked.

Bartley stopped abruptly: "Not one ten thousandth part as good-looking, nor one millionth part as bright as Marcia Hubbard!" He caught her and smothered her against his breast.

"I don't care! I don't care!" she cried. "I was to blame more than you, if you flirted with her, and it serves me right. Yes, I will never say anything to you for anything that happened after I behaved so to you!"

"There wasn't anything else happened!" cried Bartley. "And the Montreal woman snubbed me soundly before she was done with me."

"Snubbed you!" exclaimed Marcia, with illogical indignation. This delighted Bartley so much that it was long before he left off laughing over her.

Then they sat down and were silent till she said, "And did you leave him in a temper?"

"Who? Kinney? In a perfect devil of a temper. I wouldn't even borrow some money he wanted to lend me."

"Write to him, Bartley!" said his wife, seriously. "I love you so I can't bear to have anybody bad friends with you!"

XIII

THE WHOLE THING was so crazy, as Bartley said, that it made
no difference if they kept up the expense a few days longer.
He took a hack from the depot, when they arrived in Boston,
and drove to the Revere House, instead of going up in the
horse-car. He entered his name on the register with a flourish,
"Bartley J. Hubbard and Wife, *Boston,*" and asked for a room
and fire, with laconic gruffness; but the clerk knew him at once
for a country person, and when the call-boy followed him into
the parlor where Marcia sat in the tremor into which she now
fell whenever Bartley was out of her sight, the boy discerned
her provinciality at a glance, and made free to say that he
guessed they had better let him take their things up to their
room, and come up themselves after the porter had got their
fire going.

"All right," said Bartley, with hauteur; and he added for
no reason, "Be quick about it."

"Yes, sir," said the boy.

"What time is supper—dinner, I mean?"

"It's ready now, sir."

"Good. Take up the things. Come just as you are, Marcia.
Let him take your cap—no, keep it on; a good many of them
come down in their bonnets."

Marcia put off her sack, and gloves, and hastily repaired the
ravages of travel as best she could. She would have liked to go
to her room just long enough to brush her hair a little, and the
fur cap made her head hot; but she was suddenly afraid of

doing something that would seem countrified, in Bartley's eyes; and she promptly obeyed: they had come from Portland in a parlor car, and she had been able to make a traveler's toilet before they reached Boston.

She had been at Portland several times with her father; but he stopped at a second-class hotel where he had always put up when alone, and she was new to the vastness of hotel mirrors and chandeliers, the glossy paint, the frescoing, the fluted pillars, the tessellated marble pavements upon which she stepped when she left the brussels carpeting of the parlors. She clung to Bartley's arm, silently praying that she might not do anything to mortify him, and admiring everything he did without question. He made a halt as they entered the glittering dining-room, and stood frowning till the head waiter ran respectfully up to them, and ushered them with sweeping bows to a table which they had to themselves. Bartley ordered their dinner with nonchalant ease, beginning with soup and going to black coffee with dazzling intelligence. While their waiter was gone with their order, he beckoned with one finger to another, and sent him out for a paper, which he unfolded and spread on the table, taking a toothpick into his mouth, and running the sheet over with his eye. "I just want to see what's going on to-night," he said without looking at Marcia.

She made a little murmur of acquiescence in her throat, but she could not speak for strangeness. She began to steal little timid glances about, and to notice the people at the other tables. In her heart she did not find the ladies so very well dressed, as she had expected the Boston ladies to be; and there was no gentleman there to compare with Bartley either in style or looks. She let her eyes finally dwell on him, wishing that he would put his paper away and say something; but afraid to ask, lest it should not be quite right: all the other gentlemen were reading papers. She was feeling lonesome and homesick, when he suddenly glanced at her and said, "How pretty you look, Marsh!"

"Do I?" she asked with a little, grateful throb, while her eyes joyfully suffused themselves.

"Pretty as a pink," he returned. "Gay—isn't it?" he continued, with a wink that took her again into his confidence, from which his study of the newspaper had seemed to exclude her. "I'll tell you what I'm going to do: I'm going to take you to the Museum, after dinner, and let you see Boucicault in the 'Colleen Bawn.'" He swept his paper off the table, and unfolded his napkin in his lap, and leaning back in his chair, began to tell her about the play. "We can walk: it's only just round the corner," he said at the end.

Marcia crept into the shelter of his talk—he sometimes spoke rather loud—and was submissively silent. When they got into their own room, which had gilt lambrequin frames, and a chandelier of three burners, and a marble mantel and marble-topped table, and washstand, and Bartley turned up the flaring gas, she quite broke down, and cried on his breast, to make sure that she had got him all back again.

"Why Marcia!" he said. "I know just how you feel. Don't you suppose I understand as well as you do that we're a country couple? But I'm not going to give myself away; and you mustn't, either. There wasn't a woman in that room that could compare with you—*dress* or looks!"

"You were splendid!" she whispered, "and just like the rest; and that made me feel somehow as if I had lost you."

"I know—I saw just how you felt; but I wasn't going to say anything for fear you'd give way right there. Come! There's plenty of time before the play begins. I call this *nice!* Old fashioned, rather, in the decorations," he said, "but pretty good for its time."

He had pulled up two armchairs in front of the glowing grate of anthracite; as he spoke, he cast his eyes about the room, and she followed his glance obediently. He had kept her hand in his, and now he held her slim finger-tips in the fist which he rested on his knee. "No; I'll tell you what, Marcia: if you want to get on in a city, there's no use being afraid of people. No use being afraid of *anything*, so long as we're good to each other. And you've got to believe in me, right along. Don't you let anything get you on the wrong track. I believe that as long as you have faith in me, I shall deserve it; and when you don't"—

"Oh, Bartley, you know I didn't doubt you! I just got to thinking, and I was a little worked up! I suppose I'm excited."

"I know it! I know it!" cried her husband. "Don't you suppose I understand *you?*"

They talked a long time together, and made each other loving promises of patience. They confessed their faults, and pledged each other that they would try hard to overcome them. They wished to be good; they both felt they had much to retrieve; but they had no concealments and they knew that was the best way to begin the future, of which they did their best to conceive seriously. Bartley told her his plans about getting some newspaper work till he could complete his law-studies. He meant to settle down to practice in Boston. "You have to wait longer for it than you would in a country-place; but when you get it it's worth while." He asked Marcia whether she would look up his friend Halleck if she were in his place; but he did not give her time to decide: "I guess I wont do it. Not just yet, at any rate. He might suppose that I wanted something of him. I'll call on him when I don't need his help."

Perhaps, if they had not planned to go to the theatre they would have stayed where they were; for they were tired, and it was very cosy. But when they were once in the street, they were glad they had come out. Bowdoin Square and Court street, and Tremont Row were a glitter of gas-lights, and the shops with their placarded bargains dazzled Marcia. "Is it one of the principal streets?" she asked Bartley.

He gave the laugh of a veteran habitué of Boston. "Tremont Row? No! Wait till I show you Washington street to-morrow! There's the Museum," he said, pointing to the long row of globed lights on the façade of the building. "Here we are in Scollay's Square. There's Hanover street; there's Cornhill; Court crooks down that way; here's Pemberton Square." His familiarity with these names estranged him to her again; she clung the closer to his arm, and caught her breath nervously as they turned in with the crowd that was climbing the stairs to the box-office of the theatre. Bartley left her a moment while he pushed his way up to the little window and bought the tickets. "First-rate seats," he said, coming back to her, and taking her hand under his arm again, "and a great piece of luck. They were just returned for sale by the man in front of me, or I should have had to take something way up in the gallery. There's a regular jam. These are right in the centre of the parquet." Marcia did not know what the parquet was; she heard its name with the certainty that but for Bartley she should not be equal to it. All her village pride was quelled; she had only enough self-control to act upon Bartley's instructions not to give herself away by any conviction of rusticity. They passed in through the long colonnaded vestibule, with its paintings and plaster casts and rows of birds and animals in glass cases on either side and she gave scarcely a glance at any of those objects endeared by association if not by intrinsic beauty to the Boston play-goer: Gulliver, with the Lilliputians swarming upon him; the painty-necked ostriches and pelicans; the mummied mermaid under a glass-bell; the governors' portraits; the stuffed elephant; Washington crossing the Delaware; Cleopatra applying the Asp; Sir William Pepperell, at full length on canvas and the pagan months and seasons in plaster,—if all these are indeed the subjects—were dim phantasmagoria, amid which she and Bartley moved scarcely more real. The usher in his dress coat, ran up the aisle to take their checks, and led them down to their seats; half a dozen elegant people stood to let them in to their places; the theatre was filled with faces: at Portland where she saw "The Lady of Lyons" with her father, three quarters of the house was empty. Bartley only had time to lean over and whisper, "The place is packed with Beacon street swells. It's a regular field night," when the bell tinkled and the curtain rose.

As the play went on the rich jacqueminot red flamed into her cheeks, and burnt there, a steady blaze, to the end. The people about her laughed and clapped, and at times they seemed to be crying. But Marcia sat through every part as stoical as a savage, and, except for the flaming color in her cheeks, making no sign of interest or intelligence. Bartley talked of the play all the way home, but she said nothing, and in their own room he asked: "Didn't you really like it? Were you disappointed? I haven't been able to get a word out of you about it. Didn't you like Boucicault?"

"I didn't know which he was," she answered with impassioned exultation. "I didn't care for him. I only thought of that poor girl, and her husband who despised her"—

She stopped. Bartley looked at her a moment, and then caught her to him and fell a laughing over her, till it seemed as if he never would end. "And you thought—you thought," he cried, trying to get his breath, "you thought you were Eily, and I was Hardress Cregan! Oh, I see, I see!" He went on making a mock and a burlesque of her tragical hallucination till she laughed with him at last.

When he put his hand up to turn out the gas, he began his joking afresh: "The real thing for Hardress to do," he said, fumbling for the key, "is to *blow* it out. That's what Hardress usually does when he comes up from the rural districts with Eily on their bridal tour. That finishes off Eily, without troubling Danny Mann. The only drawback is that it finishes off Hardress, too: they're *both* found suffocated in the morning."

XIV

THE NEXT DAY after breakfast, while they stood together before the parlor fire, Bartley proposed one plan after another for spending the day. Marcia rejected them all, with perfectly recovered self-composure. "Then what *shall* we do?" he asked, at last.

"Oh, I don't know," she answered rather absently. She added, after an interval, smoothing the warm front of her dress, and putting her foot on the fender, "What did those theatre-tickets cost?"

"Two dollars," he replied carelessly. "Why?"

Marcia gasped. "Two dollars! Oh, Bartley, we couldn't afford it!"

"It seems we did."

"And here—how much are we paying here?"

"That room with fire," said Bartley, stretching himself, "is seven dollars a day"—

"We must not stay another instant," said Marcia, all a woman's terror of spending money on anything but dress, all a wife's conservative instinct, rising within her. "How much have you got left?"

Bartley took out his pocket-book, and counted over the bills in it. "A hundred and twenty dollars."

"Why, what has become of it all? We had a hundred and sixty!"

"Well, our railroad tickets were nineteen, the sleeping car was three, the parlor car was three, the theatre was two, the hack was fifty cents; and we'll have to put down the other two and a half to refreshments."

Marcia listened in dismay. At the end she drew a long breath. "Well, we must go away from here, as soon as possible—*that* I know. We'll go out and find some boarding place. That's the first thing."

"Oh, now, Marcia, you're not going to be so severe as that, are you?" pleaded Bartley. "A few dollars, more or less, are not going to keep us out of the poorhouse. I just want to stay here three days: that will leave us a clean hundred, and we can start fair"—

He was half joking, but she was wholly serious. "No, Bartley! Not another hour—not another minute! Come!" She took his arm, and bent it up into a crook, in which she put her hand and pulled him toward the door. "Well, after all," he said, "it will be some fun looking up a room." There was no one else in the parlor; in going to the door they took some waltzing steps together.

While she dressed to go out, he looked up places where rooms were let with or without board, in the newspaper. "There don't seem to be a great many," he said meditatively, bending over the open sheet. But he cut out half a dozen advertisements with his editorial scissors, and they started upon their search.

They climbed those pleasant old up-hill streets that converge to the State-house, and looked into the houses on the quiet Places that stretch from one thoroughfare to another. They had decided that they would be content with two small rooms, one for a chamber, and the other for a parlor, where they could have a fire. They found exactly what they wanted in the first house at which they applied, one flight up, with sunny windows, looking down the street; but it made Marcia's blood run cold, when the landlady said that the price was thirty dollars a week. At another place, the rooms were only twenty; the position was quite as good, and the carpet and furniture prettier.

This was still too dear, but it seemed comparatively reasonable till it appeared that this was the price without board. "I think we should prefer rooms with board, shouldn't we?" asked Bartley with a sly look at Marcia.

The prices were of all degrees of exorbitance, and they varied for no reason, from house to house; one landlady had been accustomed to take more and another less, but never little enough for Marcia, who overruled Bartley again and again when he wished to close with some small abatement of terms. She declared now that they must put up with one room, and they must not care what floor it was on. But the cheapest room with board was fourteen dollars a week, and Marcia had fixed her ideal at ten: even that was too high, for them.

"The best way will be to go back to the Revere House at seven dollars a day," said Bartley; he had lately been leaving the transaction of the business entirely to Marcia, who had rapidly acquired alertness and decision in it.

She could not respond to his joke. "What is there left?" she asked.

"There isn't anything left," he said; "we've got to the end."

They stood on the edge of the pavement, and looked up and down the street, and then by a common impulse they looked at the house opposite, where a placard in the window advertised "Apartments to let—to Gentlemen only."

"It would be of no use asking there," murmured Marcia with sad abstraction.

"Well, let's go over and try," said her husband. "They can't do more than turn us out of doors."

"I know it wont be of any use," Marcia sighed, as people do when they hope to gain something by forbidding themselves hope. But she helplessly followed, and stood at the foot of the doorsteps while he ran up and rang.

It was apparently the woman of the house who came to the door, and shrewdly scanned them.

"I see you have apartments to let," said Bartley.

"Well, yes," admitted the woman, as if she considered it useless to deny it, "I *have*."

"I should like to look at them," returned Bartley with

promptness. "Come, Marcia!" and re-inforced by her he invaded the premises before the landlady had time to repel him. "I'll tell you what we want," he continued, turning into the little reception-room at the side of the door, "and if you haven't got it, there's no need to trouble you: we want a fair-sized room, anywhere between the cellar-floor and the roof, with a bed and a stove and a table in it, that sha'n't cost us more than ten dollars a week with board."

"Set down," said the landlady, herself setting the example, by sinking into the rocking-chair behind her, and beginning to rock, while she made a brief study of the intruders. "Want it for yourselves?"

"Yes," said Bartley.

"Well," returned the landlady, "I always *have* p'ferred single gentlemen."

"I inferred as much from a remark which you made in your front-window," said Bartley, indicating the placard.

The landlady smiled. They were certainly a very pretty-appearing young couple, and the gentleman was evidently up and coming. Mrs. Nash liked Bartley, as most people of her grade did, at once. "It's always b'en my exper'ence," she explained with the lazily rhythmical drawl, in which most half-bred New Englanders speak, "that I seemed to get along *ruther* better with gentlemen. They give less trouble as a general *rule*," she added, with a glance at Marcia, as if she did not deny that there were exceptions, and Marcia might be a striking one.

Bartley seized his advantage. "Well, my wife hasn't been married long enough to be unreasonable. I guess you'd get along."

They both laughed, and Marcia, blushing, joined them. "Well, I *thought* when you first come up the steps you hadn't been married, well, not a *great* while," said the landlady.

"No," said Bartley. "It seems a good while to my wife; but we were only married day before yesterday."

"The land!" cried Mrs. Nash.

"Bartley!" whispered Marcia, in soft upbraiding.

"What? Well, say last week, then. We were married last week, and we've come to Boston to seek our fortune."

His wit overjoyed Mrs. Nash. "You'll find Boston an awful hard place to get along," she said, shaking her head with a warning smile.

"I shouldn't think so, by the price Boston people ask for their rooms," returned Bartley. "If I had rooms to let I should get along pretty easily."

This again delighted the landlady. "I guess you aint goin' to get out of spirits, anyway," she said. "Well," she continued, "I *have* got a room 't I guess would suit you. Unexpectedly vacated." She seemed to recur to the language of an advertisement in these words, which she pronounced as if reading them. "It's pretty high up," she said with another warning shake of the head.

"Stairs to get to it?" asked Bartley.

"Plenty of *stairs*."

"Well, I like when a place is pretty high up to have plenty of stairs to get to it. I guess we'll see it, Marcia." He rose.

"Well, I'll just go up and see if it's *fit* to be seen, first," said the landlady.

"Oh, Bartley!" said Marcia, when she had left them alone, "how *could* you joke so, about our just being married!"

"Well, I saw she wanted awfully to ask. And anybody can tell it by looking at us, anyway. We can't keep that to ourselves, any more than we can our greenness. Besides, it's money in our pockets: she'll take something off our board for it, you'll see. Now, will you manage the bargaining from this on? I stepped forward because the rooms were for gentlemen only."

"I guess I'd better," said Marcia.

"All right; then I'll take a back seat, from this out."

"Oh, I do *hope* it wont be too much!" sighed the young wife. "I'm so *tired*, looking."

"You can come right along up," the landlady called down through the oval spire formed by the ascending handrail of the stairs. They found her in a broad low room whose ceiling sloped with the roof, and had the pleasant irregularity of the angles and recessions of two dormer windows. The room was clean and cosy; there was a table, and a stove that could be used open or shut; Marcia squeezed Bartley's arm to signify that it would do, perfectly, if only the price would suit.

The landlady stood in the middle of the floor and lectured: "Now, there! I get five dollas a week for this room; and I gen'ly let it to two gentlemen. It's just been vacated by two gentlemen, unexpectedly; but it's had to get gentlemen at this time the yea; and that's the reason I thought of takin' you. As I *say*, I don't much like ladies for inmates, and so I put in the window for gentlemen only. But it's no use bein' too particular; I can't have the room layin' empty on my hands. If it suits you, you can have it for four dollas. It's high up, and there's no use tryin' to deny it. But there ain't such anotha' view as them windes commands, anywheres. You can see the harbor, and pretty much the whole coast."

"Anything extra for the view?" said Bartley, glancing out.

"No, I throw that in."

"Does the price include gas and fire?" asked Marcia, sharpened as to all details by previous interviews.

"It includes the gas, but it don't include the fire," said the landlady, firmly. "And it's pretty low, at that, as you've found out, I guess."

"Yes, it *is* low," said Marcia. "Bartley, I think we'd better take it." She looked at him timidly, as if she were afraid he might not think it good enough; she did not think it good enough for him, but she felt that they must make their money go as far as possible.

"All *right!*" he said. "Then it's a bargain."

"And how much more will the board be?"

"Well, the'e," the landlady said, with candor; "I don't know as I can meet your views. I don't neve give boad. But there's plenty of houses, right on the street here, where you can get dayboard from four dollars a week, up."

"Oh, dear!" sighed Marcia; "and that would make it twelve dollars!"

"Why the dear suz, child!" exclaimed the landlady, "you didn't expect to get it for less?"

"We must," said Marcia.

"Then you'll have to go to a mechanics' boardin' house."

"I suppose we shall," she returned dejectedly. Bartley whistled.

"Look here," said the landlady, "ain't you from Down East, some'eres?"

Marcia started, as if the woman had recognized them. "Yes," she said.

"Well, now," said Mrs. Nash, "I'm from down Maine way, myself, and I'll tell you what I should do, if I was in your *place*. You don't want much of anything for breakfast or tea; you can boil you an egg on the stove here, and you can make your own tea or coffee; and if I was you, I'd go out for my dinners to an eatin' house. I heard some my lodgers tellin' how they done. Well, I heard the very gentlemen that occupied this room sayin' how they used to go to an eatin' house, and one'd order one thing and another another, and then they'd halve it between 'em, and make out a first rate meal, for about a quarter apiece. Plenty of places now where they give you a cut o' lamb or rib-beef for a shillin', and they bring you bread and butter and potato with it; an' it's always enough for two. That's what they *said*. I haint never tried it myself; but as long as you hain't got but yourselves to care for there aint any reason why *you* shouldn't."

They looked at each other.

"Well," added the landlady for a final touch, "*say* fire. That stove wont burn a great deal, anyway."

"All right," said Bartley, "we'll take the room—for a month, at least."

Mrs. Nash looked a little embarrassed. If she had made some concession to the liking she had conceived for this pretty young couple, she could not risk everything. "I always have to get the first week in advance,—where there aint no reference," she suggested.

"Of course," said Bartley, as he took out his pocket-book,

which he had a boyish satisfaction in letting her see was well-filled. "Now, Marcia," he continued, looking at his watch, "I'll just run over to the hotel, and give up our room before they get us in for dinner."

Marcia accepted Mrs. Nash's invitation to come and sit with her till the chill was off the room; and she borrowed a pen and paper of her to write home. The note she sent was brief: she was not going to seem to ask anything of her father. But she was going to do what was right; she told him where she was, and she sent her love to her mother. She would not speak of her things; he might send them or not, as he chose; but she knew he would. This was the spirit of her letter; and her training had not taught her to soften and sweeten her phrase; but no doubt the old man who was like her, would understand that she felt no compunction for what she had done, and that she loved him though she still defied him.

Bartley did not ask her what her letter was when she demanded a stamp of him, on his return; but he knew. He inquired of Mrs. Nash where these cheap eating houses were to be found, and he posted the letter in the first box they came to, merely saying, "I hope you haven't been asking any favors, Marsh?"

"No, indeed!"

"Because I couldn't stand that."

Marcia had never dined in a restaurant, and she was somewhat bewildered by the one into which they turned. There was a great show of roast and steak and fish, and game and squash and cranberry pie in the window, and at the door a tack was driven through a mass of bills-of-fare, two of which Bartley plucked off as they entered, with a knowing air and then threw on the floor when he found the same thing on the table. The table had a marble top, and a silver-plated castor in the centre. The plates were laid, with a coarse red doyly in a cocked-hat on each, and a thinly plated knife and fork crossed beneath it; the plates were thick and heavy; the handle as well as the blade of the knife was metal and silvered. Besides the castor, there was a bottle of Leicestershire sauce on the table, and salt in what Marcia thought a pepper-box; the marble was of an unctuous translucence, in places, and showed the course of the cleansing napkin on its smeared surface. The place was hot, and full of confused smells of cooking; all the tables were crowded, so that they found places with difficulty, and pale, plain girls, of the Provincial and Irish-American type, in fashionable bangs and pull-backs, went about taking the orders which they wailed out towards a semi-circular hole opening upon a counter at the further end of the room; there they received the dishes ordered, and hurried with them to the customers, before whom they laid them with a noisy clacking of the heavy crockery. A great many of the people seemed to be taking hulled-corn and milk; baked beans formed another favorite dish, and squash-pie was in large request. Marcia was not critical; roast-turkey for Bartley and stewed chicken for herself with cranberry-pie for both seemed to her a very good and sufficient dinner, and better than they ought to have had. She asked Bartley if this were anything like Parker's; he had always talked to her about Parker's.

"Well, Marcia," he said, folding up his doyly, which does not betray use like the indiscreet white napkin, "I'll just take you round and show you the *outside* of Parker's; and some day we'll go there and get dinner."

He not only showed her Parker's but the City Hall; they walked down School street, and through Washington as far as Boylston; and Bartley pointed out the Old South, and brought Marcia home by the Common, where they stopped to see the boys coasting under the care of the police between two long lines of spectators. "The State House," said Bartley, with easy command of the facts, and pointing in the several directions; "Beacon street; Public Garden; Back Bay." She came home to Mrs. Nash joyfully admiring the city, but admiring still more her husband's masterly knowledge of it.

Mrs. Nash was one of those people who partake intimately of the importance of the place in which they live; to whom it is sufficient splendor and prosperity to be a Bostonian or New Yorker or Chicagoan, and who experience a delicious self-flattery in the celebration of the municipal grandeur. In his degree, Bartley was of this sort, and he exchanged compliments of Boston with Mrs. Nash till they grew into warm favor with each other.

After a while he said he must go up stairs and do some writing; and then he casually dropped the fact that he was an editor, and that he had come to Boston to get an engagement on a newspaper; he implied that he had come to take one.

"Well," said Mrs. Nash, smoothing the back of the cat which she had in her lap, "I guess there ain't anything like our Boston papers. And they say this new one—the Daily Events—is goin' to take the lead. You acquainted any with our Boston editors?"

Bartley hemmed. "Well,—I know the proprietor of the Events."

"Oh, yes: Mr. Witherby. Well, they say he's got the money. I hear my lodgers talkin' about that paper consid'able. I hain't never seen it."

Bartley now went up stairs; he had an idea in his head. Marcia remained with Mrs. Nash a few moments. "He's been in Boston before," she said with proud satisfaction; "he visited here when he was in college."

"Gaw, is he college-bred?" cried Mrs. Nash. "Well, I thought he looked 'most too wide awake for that. He ain't a bit offish. He seems *re'l* practical. What you hurryin' off so, for?" she asked, as Marcia rose, and stood poised on the threshold, in act to follow her husband. "Why don't you set here with me, while he's at his writin'? You'll just keep talkin' to him and takin' his mind off, the whole while. You stay here!" she commanded hospitably. "You'll just be in the way, up there."

This was a novel conception to Marcia; but its good sense struck her. "Well, I will," she said. "I'll run up a minute to leave my things and then I'll come back."

She found Bartley dragging the table, on which he had already laid out his writing materials, into a good light, and she threw her arms round his neck, as if they had been a great while parted. "Come up to kiss me good luck?" he asked, finding her lips.

"Yes, and to tell you how splendid you are, going right to work this way," she answered fondly.

"Oh, I don't believe in losing time; and I've got to strike while the iron's hot, if I'm going to write out that logging-camp business. I'll take it over to that Events man, and hit him with it while it's fresh in his mind."

"Yes," said Marcia. "Are you going to write that out?"

"Why, I told you I was. Any objections?" He did not pay much attention to her and he asked his question jokingly, as he went on making his preparations.

"It's hard for me to realize that people can care for such things. I thought perhaps you'd begin with something else," she suggested, hanging up her sack and hat in the closet.

"No, that's the very thing to begin with," he answered carelessly. "What are you going to do? Want that book to read that I bought on the cars?"

"No, I'm going down to sit with Mrs. Nash, while you're writing."

"Well, that's a good idea."

"You can call me when you're done."

"Done!" cried Bartley. "I shan't be done till this time to-morrow. I'm going to make a lot about it."

"Oh!" said his wife. "Well, I suppose the more there is the more you will get for it. Shall you put in about those people coming to see the camp?"

"Yes, I think I can work that in so that old Witherby will like it. Something about a distinguished Boston newspaper proprietor and his refined and elegant ladies, as a sort of contrast to the rude life of the loggers."

"I thought you didn't admire them a great deal."

"Well, I didn't much. But I can work them up."

Marcia was quite ready to go; Bartley had seated himself at his table; but she still hovered about.

"And are you—shall you—put that Montreal woman in?"

"Yes, get it all in. She'll work up, first-rate."

Marcia was silent. Then she said:

"I shouldn't think you'd put her in if she was so silly and disagreeable."

Bartley turned round, and saw the look on her face that he could not mistake. He rose, and took her by the chin. "Look here, Marsh!" he said, "didn't you promise me you'd stop that?"

"Yes," she murmured, while the color flamed into her cheeks.

"And will you?"

"I *did* try"—

He looked sharply into her eyes. "Confound the Montreal woman! I wont put in a word about her. There!" He kissed Marcia, and held her in his arms, and soothed her as if she had been a jealous child.

"Oh, Bartley! Oh, Bartley!" she cried, "I love you so!"

"I think it's a remark you made before," he said, and with a final kiss and laugh, he pushed her out of the door; and she ran down stairs to Mrs. Nash again.

"Your husband ever write poetry, any?" enquired the landlady.

"No," returned Marcia; "he used to, in college. But he says it don't pay."

"One my lodgers—well she was a lady; you can't seem to get gentlemen oftentimes in the summer season, for *love* or money, and I was puttin' up with her,—breakin' joints,—as you may say, for the time *bein'*—*she* wrote poetry; 'n' I guess she found it pretty poor pickin'. Used to write for the weekly papers, she said, 'n' the child'n's magazines. Well, she couldn't get more'n a doll' or two, 'n' I dunno but what less, for a piece as long as that." Mrs. Nash held her hands about a foot apart. "Used to show 'em to me, and tell me about 'em. I declare, I used to pity her. I used tell her I ruther break stone for *my* livin'."

Marcia sat talking more than an hour to Mrs. Nash, informing herself upon the history of Mrs. Nash's past and present lodgers; and about the ways of the city, and the prices of provisions and dress-goods. The dearness of everything alarmed and even shocked her; but she came back to her faith in Bartley's ability to meet and overcome all difficulties. She grew drowsy in the close air which Mrs. Nash loved, after all her fatigues and excitements, and she said she guessed she would go up and see how Bartley was getting on. But when she stole into the room, and saw him busily writing, she said, "Now I wont speak a word, Bartley," and coiled herself down under a shawl on the bed, near enough to put her hand on his shoulder if she wished, and fell asleep.

XV

It took Bartley two days to write out his account of the logging camp. He worked it up to the best of his ability, giving all the facts that he had got out of Kinney, and relieving these with what he considered picturesque touches. He had the newspaper instinct, and he divined that his readers would not care for his picturesqueness without his facts. He therefore subordinated this, and he tried to give his description of the loggers a politico-economical interest, dwelling upon the variety of nationalities engaged in the industry, and the changes it had undergone in what he called its *personnel*; he enlarged upon its present character and its future development, in relation to what he styled in a line of small capitals, with an early use of the favorite newspaper possessive,

COLUMBIA'S MORIBUND SHIP-BUILDING.

And he interspersed his text plentifully with exclamatory headings intended to catch the eye with startling fragments of narration and statement such as,

THE PINE TREE STATE'S STORIED STAPLE,
MORE THAN A MILLION OF MONEY,
UNBROKEN WILDERNESS,
WILD CATS, LYNXES AND BEARS,
BITTEN OFF,

BOTH LEGS FROZEN TO THE KNEES,
CANADIAN SONGS,
JOY UNCONFINED,
THE LAMPLIGHT ON THEIR SWARTHY FACES.

He spent a final forenoon in polishing his article up and stuffing it full of telling points. But after dinner on this last day he took leave of Marcia with more trepidation than he was willing to show, or knew how to conceal. Her devout faith in his success seemed to unnerve him, and he begged her not to believe in it so much.

He seized what courage he had left in both hands, and found himself, after the usual reluctance of the people in the business-office, face to face with Mr. Witherby in his private room. Mr. Witherby had lately dismissed his managing-editor for his neglect of the true interests of the paper as represented by the counting-room, and was managing the Events himself. He sat before a table strewn with newspapers and manuscripts, and as he looked up, Bartley saw that he did not recognize him.

"How do you do, Mr. Witherby? I had the pleasure of meeting you the other day in Maine—at Mr. Willett's logging-camp. Hubbard is my name; remember me as editor of the Equity Free Press."

"Oh, yes," said Mr. Witherby, rising and standing at his desk, as a sort of compromise between asking his visitor to sit down and telling him to go away. He shook hands in a loose way, and added, "I presume you would like to exchange. But the fact is our list is so large already, that we can't extend it, just now; we can't"—

Bartley smiled. "I don't want any exchange, Mr. Witherby. I'm out of the Free Press."

"Oh!" said the city journalist, with relief. He added, in a leading tone: "Then"—

"I've come to offer you an article—an account of lumbering in our State. It's a little sketch that I've prepared from what I saw in Mr. Willett's camp, and some facts and statistics I've picked up. I thought it might make an attractive feature of your Sunday edition."

"The Events," said Mr. Witherby, solemnly, "does not publish a Sunday edition."

"Of course not," answered Bartley, inwardly cursing his blunder, "I mean your Saturday evening supplement." He handed him his manuscript.

Mr. Witherby looked at it with the worry of a dull man who has assumed unintelligible duties. He had let the other papers "get ahead of him" on several important enterprises lately, and he would have been glad to retrieve himself; but he could not be sure that this was an enterprise. He began by saying that their last Saturday Supplement was just out, and the next was full; and ended by declaring with stupid pomp, that the Events preferred to send its own reporters to write up those matters. Then he hemmed, and looked at Bartley, and he would really have been glad to have him argue him out of this position; but Bartley could not divine what was in his mind. The cold fit which sooner or later comes to every form of authorship, seized him. He said awkwardly he was very sorry, and putting his manuscript back in his pocket, he went out, feeling curiously light-headed as if his rebuff had been a stunning blow. The affair was so quickly over that he might well have believed it had not happened. But he was sickeningly disappointed; he had counted upon the sale of his article to the Events; his hope had been founded upon actual knowledge of the proprietor's intention, and although he had rebuked Marcia's overweening confidence, he had expected that Witherby would jump at it. But Witherby had not even looked at it.

Bartley walked a long time in the cold winter sunshine. He would have liked to go back to his lodging, and hide his face in Marcia's hands, and let her pity him, but he could not bear the thought of her disappointment, and he kept walking. At last he regained courage enough to go to the editor of the paper for which he used to correspond in the summer, and which had always printed his letters. This editor was busy, too, but he apparently felt some obligations to civility with Bartley, and though he kept glancing over his exchanges as they talked, he now and then glanced at Bartley also. He said that he should be glad to print the sketch, but that they never paid for outside material, and he advised Bartley to go with it to the Events, or to the Daily Chronicle-Abstract; the Abstract and the Brief Chronicle had lately consolidated, and they were showing a good deal of enterprise. Bartley said nothing to betray that he had already been at the Events office, and upon this friendly editor's invitation to drop in again, sometime, he went away considerably re-inspirited. "If you should happen to go to the Chronicle-Abstract folks," the editor called after him, "you can tell 'em I suggested your coming."

The managing editor of the Chronicle-Abstract was reading a manuscript, and he did not desist from his work on Bartley's appearance which he gave no sign of welcoming. But he had a whimsical, shrewd, kind face, and Bartley felt that he should get on with him, though he did not rise and though he let Bartley stand.

"Yes," he said. "Lumbering, hey? Well, there's some interest in that, just now, on account of this talk about the decay of our ship-building interests. Anything on that point?"

"That's the very point I touch on first," said Bartley.

The editor stopped turning over his manuscript.

"Let's see," he said, holding out his hand for Bartley's article. He looked at the first head-line, "What I know about Logging," and smiled, "Old, but good." Then he glanced at the other headings, and ran his eye down the long strips on which Bartley had written; nibbled at the text here and there a little; returned to the first paragraph, and read that through; looked back at something else, and then read the close. "I guess you can leave it," he said, laying the manuscript on the table.

"No, I guess not," said Bartley, with equal coolness, gathering it up.

The editor looked fairly at him for the first time, and smiled.

Evidently, he liked this. "What's the reason? Any particular hurry?"

"I happen to know that the Events is going to send a man down east to write up this very subject. And I don't propose to leave this article here till they steal my thunder, and then have it thrown back on my hands not worth the paper it's written on."

The editor tilted himself back in his chair, and braced his knees against his table. "Well, I guess you're right," he said. "What do you want for it?"

This was a terrible question. Bartley knew nothing about the prices that city papers paid; he feared to ask too much, but he also feared to cheapen his wares by asking too little. "Twenty-five dollars," he said, huskily.

"Let's look at it," said the editor, reaching out his hand for the manuscript again. "Sit down." He pushed a chair towards Bartley with his foot, having first swept a pile of newspapers from it to the floor. He now read the article more fully, and then looked up at Bartley, who sat still, trying to hide his anxiety. "You're not quite a new hand at the bellows, are you?"

"I've edited a country paper."

"Yes? Where?"

"Down in Maine."

The editor bent forward and took out a long narrow blank-book. "I guess we shall want your article. What name?"

"Bartley J. Hubbard." It sounded in his ears like some other's name.

"Going to be in Boston some time?"

"All the time," said Bartley, struggling to appear nonchalant. The revulsion from the despair into which he had fallen after his interview with Witherby was still very great. The order on the counting-room which the editor had given him shook in his hand. He saw his way before him clearly now; he wished to propose some other things that he would like to write; but he was saved from this folly for the time by the editor's saying, in a tone of dismissal:

"Better come in, to-morrow, and see a proof. We shall put you into the Wednesday supplement."

"Thanks," said Bartley. "Good day."

The editor did not hear him, or did not think it necessary to respond from behind the newspaper which he had lifted up between them, and Bartley went out. He did not stop to cash his order; he made boyish haste to show it to Marcia, as something more authentic than the money itself, and more sacred. As he hurried homeward he figured Marcia's ecstasy in his thought. He saw himself flying up the stairs to their attic three steps at a bound, and bursting into the room, where she sat, eager and anxious, and flinging the order into her lap; and then when she had read it with rapture at the sum, and pride in the smartness with which he had managed the whole affair, he saw himself catching her up and dancing about the floor with her. He thought how fond of her he was, and he wondered that he could ever have been cold or lukewarm.

She was standing at the window of Mrs. Nash's little reception-room when he reached the house. It was not to be as he had planned, but he threw her a kiss, glad of the impatience which would not let her wait till he could find her in their own room, and he had the precious order in his hand to dazzle her eyes as soon as he should enter. But as he sprang into the hall, his foot struck against a trunk, and some boxes.

"Hello!" he cried, "your things have come!"

Marcia lingered within the door of the room; she seemed afraid to come out. "Yes," she said faintly. "Father brought them. He has just been here."

He seemed there still, and the vision unnerved her as if Bartley and he had been confronted there in reality. Her husband had left her hardly a quarter of an hour when a hack drove up to the door and her father alighted. She let him in herself, before he could ring, and waited tremulously for what he should do or say. But he merely took her hand, and stooping over gave her the chary kiss with which he used to greet her at home when he returned from an absence.

She flung her arms round his neck: "Oh, father!"

"Well, well! There, there!" he said, and then he went into the reception-room with her; and there was nothing in his manner to betray that anything unusual had happened since they last met. He kept his hat on, as his fashion was, and he kept on his overcoat, below which the skirts of his dresscoat hung an inch or two; he looked old and weary and shabby.

"I can't leave Bartley, father!" she began hysterically.

"I haven't come to separate you from your husband, Marcia. What made you think so? It's your place to stay with him."

"He's out, now," she answered, in an incoherent hopefulness. "He's just gone. Will you wait and see him, father?"

"No, I guess I can't wait," said the old man. "It wouldn't do any good for us to meet now."

"Do you think he coaxed me away? He didn't. He took pity on me—he forgave me. And I didn't mean to deceive you when I left home, father. But I couldn't help trying to see Bartley again."

"I believe you, Marcia. I understand. The thing had to be. Let me see your marriage certificate." She ran up to her room and fetched it. Her father read it carefully. "Yes, that is all right," he said, and returned it to her. He added, after an absent pause: "I have brought your things, Marcia. Your mother packed all she could think of."

"How *is* mother?" asked Marcia, as if this had first reminded her of her mother.

"She is usually well," replied her father.

"Wont you—wont you come up and see our room, father?" Marcia asked after the interval following this feint of interest in her mother.

"No," said the old man rising restlessly from his chair, and buttoning at his coat, which was already buttoned. "I guess I sha'n't have time. I guess I must be going."

Marcia put herself between him and the door. "Wont you let me tell you about it, father?"

"About what?"

"How—I came to go off with Bartley. I want you should know!"

"I guess I know all I want to know about it, Marcia. I accept the facts. I told you how I felt. What you've done hasn't changed me towards you. I understand you better than you understand yourself; and I can't say that I'm surprised. Now I want you should make the best of it."

"You don't forgive Bartley!" she cried passionately. "Then I don't want you should forgive me!"

"Where did you pick up this nonsense about forgiving?" said her father knitting his shaggy brows. "A man does this thing or that, and the consequence follows. I couldn't forgive Bartley so that he could escape any consequence of what he's done; and you're not afraid I shall hurt him?"

"Stay and see him!" she pleaded. "He is so kind to me! He works night and day, and he has just gone out to sell something he has written for the papers."

"I never said he was lazy," returned her father. "Do you want any money, Marcia?"

"No, we have plenty. And Bartley is earning it all the time. I *wish* you would stay and see him!"

"No, I'm glad he didn't happen to be in," said the Squire. "I sha'n't wait for him to come back. It wouldn't do any good, just yet, Marcia; it would only do harm. Bartley and I haven't had time to change our minds about each other yet. But I'll say a good word for him to you. You're his wife; and it's your part to help him, not to hinder him. You can make him worse by being a fool; but you needn't be a fool. Don't worry him about other women; don't be jealous. He's your husband, now; and the worst thing you can do is to doubt him."

"I wont, father, I wont indeed! I will be good, and I will try to be sensible. Oh, I *wish* Bartley could know how you feel!"

"Don't tell him from *me*," said her father. "And don't keep making promises and breaking them. I'll help the man in with your things."

He went out, and came in again with one end of a trunk, as if he had been giving the man a hand with it into the house at home, and she suffered him as passively as she had suffered him to do her such services all her life. Then he took her hand laxly in his, and stooped down for another chary kiss. "Good-bye, Marcia."

"Why, father, are you going to *leave* me?" she faltered.

He smiled in melancholy irony at the bewilderment, the childish forgetfulness of the circumstances which her words expressed. "Oh, no! I'm going to take you with me."

His sarcasm restored her to a sense of what she had said, and she ruefully laughed at herself through her tears. "What am I talking about? Give my love to mother! When will you come again?" she asked, clinging about him, almost in the old playful way.

"When you want me," said the Squire, freeing himself.

"I'll write!" she cried after him, as he went down the steps; and if there had been at any moment a consciousness of her cruelty to him in her heart, she lost it, when he drove away, in her anxious waiting for Bartley's return. It seemed to her, that though her father had refused to see him his visit was of happy augury for future kindness between them, and she was proudly eager to tell Bartley what good advice her father had given her. But the sight of her husband suddenly turned these thoughts to fear. She trembled, and all that she could say was, "I know father will be all right, Bartley."

"How?" he retorted savagely. "By the way he abused me to you? Where is he?"

"He's gone—gone back."

"I don't care where he's gone, so he's gone. Did he come to take you home with him? Why didn't you go?—Oh, Marcia!" The brutal words had hardly escaped him, when he ran to her as if he would arrest them before their sense should pierce her heart.

She thrust him back with a stiffly extended arm, "Keep away! Don't touch me!" She walked by him up the stairs without looking round at him, and he heard her close their door and lock it.

XVI

BARTLEY stood for a moment, and then went out and wandered aimlessly about till night-fall. He went out shocked and frightened at what he had done, and ready for any reparation. But this mood wore away, and he came back sullenly determined to let her make the advances toward reconciliation, if there was to be one. Her love had already made his peace, and she met him in the dimly lighted little hall with a kiss of silent penitence and forgiveness. She had on her hat and shawl, as if she had been waiting for him to come and take her out to tea; and on their way to the restaurant, she asked him of his adventure among the newspapers. He told her briefly, and when they sat down at their table he took out the precious order and showed it to her. But its magic was gone; it was only an order for twenty-five dollars, now; and two hours ago it had been success, rapture, a common hope and a common joy. They scarcely spoke of it, but talked soberly of indifferent things.

She could not recur to her father's visit at once, and he would not be the first to mention it. He did nothing to betray his knowledge of her intention, as she approached the subject through those feints that women use, and when they stood again in their little attic room she was obliged to be explicit.

"What hurt me, Bartley," she said, "was that you should think for an instant that I would let father ask me to leave you, or that he would ask such a thing. He only came to tell me to be good to you, and help you, and trust you; and not worry you with my silliness and—and—jealousy. And I don't ever

167

mean to. And I know he will be good friends with you yet. He praised you for working so hard;"—she pushed it a little beyond the bare fact;—"he always did that; and I know he's only waiting for a good chance to make it up with you."

She lifted her eyes, glistening with tears, and it touched his peculiar sense of humor to find her offering him reparation, when he had felt himself so outrageously to blame; but he would not be outdone in magnanimity, if it came to that.

"It's all right, Marsh. I was a furious idiot, or I should have let you explain at once. But you see I had only one thought in my mind, and that was my luck, which I wanted to share with you; and when your father seemed to have come in between us again—"

"Oh, yes, yes!" she answered. "I understand." And she clung to him in the joy of this perfect intelligence, which she was sure could never be obscured again.

When Bartley's article came out, she read it with a fond admiration which all her praises seemed to leave unsaid. She bought a scrap-book, and pasted the article into it, and said that she was going to keep everything he wrote.

"What are you going to write the next thing?" she asked.

"Well, that's what I don't know," he answered. "I can't find another subject like that, so easily."

"Why, if people care to read about a logging-camp, I should think they would read about almost anything. Nothing could be too common for them. You might even write about the trouble of getting cheap enough rooms in Boston."

"Marcia," cried Bartley, "you're a treasure! I'll write about that very thing! I know the Chronicle-Abstract will be glad to get it."

She thought he was joking till he came to her after a while for some figures which he did not remember. He had the true newspaper instinct, and went to work with a motive that was as different as possible from the literary motive. He wrote for the effect which he was to make, and not from any artistic pleasure in the treatment. He did not attempt to give it form, to imagine a young couple like himself and Marcia coming down from the country to place themselves in the city; he made no effort to throw about it the poetry of their ignorance and their poverty, or the pathetic humor of their dismay at the disproportion of the prices to their means. He set about getting all the facts he could, and he priced a great many lodgings in different parts of the city; then he went to a number of real-estate agents, and, giving himself out as a reporter of the Chronicle-Abstract, he interviewed them as to house-rents, past and present. Upon these bottom facts, as he called them, he based a "spicy" sketch, which had also largely the character of an *exposé*. There is nothing the public enjoys so much as an *exposé*; it seems to be made in the reader's own interest; it somehow constitutes him a party to the attack upon the abuse, and its effectiveness redounds to the credit of all the newspaper's subscribers. After a week's stay in Boston, Bartley was able to assume the feelings of a native who sees his city falling into decay through the rapacity of its landladies. In the heading of ten or fifteen lines which he gave his sketch, the greater number were devoted to this feature of it; though the space actually allotted to it in the text was comparatively small. He called his report "Boston's Boarding-Houses," and he spent a paragraph upon the relation of boarding-houses to civilization, before detailing his own experience and observation. This part had many of those strokes of crude picturesqueness and humor which he knew how to give, and was really entertaining; but it was when he came to contrast the rates of house-rent and the cost of provisions with the landladies'

"PERPENDICULAR PRICES"

that Bartley showed all the virtue of a born reporter. The sentences were vivid and telling; the *ensemble* was very alarming; and the conclusion was inevitable that, unless this abuse could somehow be reached, we should lose a large and valuable portion of our population; especially those young married people of small means with whom the city's future prosperity so largely rested, and who must drift away to find homes in rival communities if the present exorbitant demands were maintained.

As Bartley had foretold, he had not the least trouble in selling this sketch to the Chronicle-Abstract. The editor probably understood its essential cheapness perfectly well; but he also saw how thoroughly readable it was. He did not grumble at the increased price which Bartley put upon his work; it was still very far from dear; and he liked the young Downeaster's enterprise. He gave him as cordial a welcome as an overworked man may venture to offer when Bartley came in with his copy, and he felt like doing him a pleasure. Some things out of the logging-camp sketch had been copied, and people had spoken to the editor about it, which was a still better sign that it was a hit.

"Don't you want to come round to our club to-night?" asked the editor, as he handed Bartley the order for his money across the table. "We have a bad dinner, and we try to have a good time. We're all newspaper men together."

"Why, thank you," said Bartley, "I guess I should like to go."

"Well, come round at half-past five, and go with me."

Bartley walked homeward rather soberly. He had meant, if he sold this article, to make amends for the disappointment they had both suffered before, and to have a commemorative supper with Marcia at Parker's; he had ignored a little hint of hers about his never having taken her there yet, because he was waiting for this chance to do it in style. He resolved that, if she did not seem to like his going to the club, he would go back and withdraw his acceptance. But when he told her he had been invited,—he thought he would put the fact in this tentative way,—she said: "I hope you accepted!"

"Would you have liked me to?" he asked, with relief.

"Why, of course! It's a great honor. You'll get acquainted with all those editors, and perhaps some of them will want to give you a regular place."

A salaried employment was their common ideal of a provision for their future.

"Well, that's what I was thinking myself," said Bartley.

"Go and accept at once," she pursued.

"Oh, that isn't necessary. If I get round there by half-past five, I can go," he answered.

His lurking regret ceased when he came into the reception-room, where the members of the club were constantly arriving, and putting off their hats and overcoats, and then falling into groups for talk. His friend of the Chronicle-Abstract introduced him lavishly, as our American custom is. Bartley had a little strangeness, but no bashfulness, and, with his essentially slight opinion of people, he was promptly at his ease. These men liked his handsome face, his winning voice, the good-fellowship of his instant readiness to joke; he could see that they liked him, and that his friend Ricker was proud of the impression he made; before the evening was over he kept himself with difficulty from patronizing Ricker a little.

The club has grown into something much more splendid and expensive; but it was then content with a dinner certainly as bad as Ricker promised, but fabulously modest in price, at an old-fashioned hotel, whose site was long ago devoured by a dry-goods palace. The drink was commonly water or beer; occasionally, if a great actor or other distinguished guest honored the board, some spendthrift ordered champagne. But no one thought fit to go to this ruinous extreme for Bartley. Ricker offered him his choice of beer or claret, and Bartley temperately preferred water to either; he could see that this raised him in Ricker's esteem.

No company of men can fail to have a good time at a public dinner, and the good time began at once with these journalists, whose overworked week ended in this Saturday-evening jollity. They were mostly young men, who found sufficient compensation in the excitement and adventure of their underpaid labors, and in the vague hope of advancement; there were grizzled beards among them, for whom neither the novelty nor the expectation continued, but who loved the life for its own sake, and would hardly have exchanged it for prosperity. Here and there was an old fellow, for whom probably all illusion was gone; but he was proud of his vocation, proud even of the changes that left him somewhat superannuated in his tastes and methods. None, indeed, who have ever known it, can wholly forget the generous rage with which journalism inspires its followers. To each of those young men, beginning the strangely fascinating life as reporters and correspondents, his paper was as dear as his king once was to a French noble; to serve it night and day, to wear himself out for its sake, to merge himself in its glory, and to live in its triumphs without personal recognition from the public, was the loyal devotion which each expected his sovereign newspaper to accept as its simple right. They went and came, with the prompt and passive obedience of soldiers, wherever they were sent, and they struggled each to "get in ahead" of all the others with the individual zeal of heroes. They expanded to the utmost limits of occasion, and they submitted with an anguish that was silent to the editorial excision, compression, and mutilation of reports that were vitally dear to them. What becomes of these ardent young spirits, the inner history of journalism in any great city might pathetically show; but the outside world only knows them in the fine frenzy of interviewing, or of recording the midnight ravages of what they call the devouring element, or of working up horrible murders or tragical accidents, or of tracking criminals who have baffled all the detectives. Hearing their talk, Bartley began to realize that journalism might be a very different thing from what he had imagined it in a country printing-office, and that it might not be altogether wise to consider it merely as a stepping-stone to the law.

With the American eagerness to recognize talent, numbers of good fellows spoke to him about his logging sketch; even those who had not read it seemed to know about it as a hit. They were delighted to be able to say, "Ricker tells me that you offered it to old Witherby, and he wouldn't look at it!" He found that this fact, which he had doubtfully confided to

Ricker, was not offensive to some of the Events people who were there; one of them got him aside, and darkly owned to him that Witherby was doing everything that any one man could to kill the Events, and that in fact the counting-room was running the paper.

All the club united in abusing the dinner, which in his rustic ignorance Bartley had not found so infamous; but they ate it with perfect appetite and with mounting good spirits. The president brewed punch in a great bowl before him, and, rising with a glass of it in his hand, opened a free parliament of speaking, story-telling, and singing. Whoever recollected a song or a story that he liked called upon the owner of it to sing it or tell it; and it appeared not to matter how old the fun or the music was: the company was resolved to be happy; it roared and clapped till the glasses rang. "You will like this song," Bartley's neighbors to right and left of him prophesied: or, "Just listen to this story of Mason's,—it's capital,"—as one or another rose in response to a general clamor. When they went back to the reception-room they carried the punch-bowl with them, and there, amid a thick cloud of smoke, two clever amateurs took their places at the piano, and sang and played to their hearts' content, while the rest, glass in hand, talked and laughed, or listened, as they chose. Bartley had not been called upon, but he was burning to try that song in which he had failed so dismally in the logging-camp. When the pianist rose at last, he slipped down into the chair, and, striking the chords of the accompaniment, he gave his piece with brilliant audacity. The room silenced itself, and then burst into a roar of applause, and cries of "Encore!" There could be no doubt of the success.

"Look here, Ricker," said a leading man, at the end of the repetition, "your friend must be one of us!"—and, rapping on the table, he proposed Bartley's name.

In that simple time the club voted *viva voce* on proposed members, and Bartley found himself elected by acclamation, and in the act of paying over his initiation fee to the treasurer, before he had well realized the honor done him. Everybody near him shook his hand, and offered to be of service to him. Much of this cordiality was merely collective good-feeling; something of it might justly be attributed to the punch; but the greater part was honest. In this civilization of ours, grotesque and unequal and imperfect as it is in many things, we are bound together in a brotherly sympathy unknown to any other. We new men have all had our hard rubs, but we do not so much remember them in soreness or resentment as in the wish to help forward any other who is presently feeling them. If he will but help himself too, a hundred hands are stretched out to him.

Bartley had kept his head clear of the punch, but he left the club drunk with joy and pride, and so impatient to be with Marcia and tell her of his triumphs, that he could hardly wait to read the proof of his boarding-house article, which Ricker had put in hand at once for the Sunday edition. He found Marcia sitting up for him, and she listened with a shining face while he hastily ran over the most flattering facts of the evening. She was not so much surprised at the honors done him as he had expected: but she was happier, and she made him repeat it all and give her the last details. He was afraid she would ask him what his initiation had cost; but she seemed to have no idea that it had cost anything, and though it had swept away a third of the money he had received for his sketch, he still resolved that she should have that supper at Parker's.

"I consider my future made," he said aloud, at the end of his swift cogitation on this point.

"Oh, yes!" she responded, rapturously. "We needn't have a moment's anxiety. But we must be very saving still till you get a place."

"Oh, certainly," said Bartley.

XVII

DURING several months that followed, Bartley's work consisted of interviewing, of special reporting in all its branches, of correspondence by mail and telegraph from points to which he was sent; his leisure he spent in studying subjects which could be treated like that of the boarding-houses. Marcia entered into his affairs with the keen half-intelligence which characterizes a woman's participation in business; whatever could be divined, she was quickly mistress of; she vividly sympathized with his difficulties and his triumphs; she failed to follow him in matters of political detail or of general effect; she could not be dispassionate or impartial; his relation to any enterprise was always more important than anything else about it. On some of his missions he took her with him, and then they made it a pleasure excursion; and if they came home late with the material still unwritten, she helped him with his notes, wrote from his dictation, and enabled him to give a fuller report than his rivals. She caught up with amusing aptness the technical terms of the profession, and was voluble about getting in ahead of the Events and the other papers, and she was indignant if any part of his report was cut out or garbled, or any feature was spoiled.

He made a "card" of grouping and treating with picturesque freshness the spring openings of the milliners and dry-goods people; and when he brought his article to Ricker, the editor ran it over, and said,

"Guess you took your wife with you, Hubbard."

"Yes, I did," Bartley owned. He was always proud of her

looks, and it flattered him that Ricker should see the evidences of her feminine taste and knowledge in his account of the bonnets and dress-goods. "You don't suppose I could get at all these things by inspiration, do you?"

Marcia was already known to some of his friends whom he had introduced to her in casual encounters. They were mostly unmarried, or, if married, they lived at a distance, and they did not visit the Hubbards at their lodgings. Marcia was a little shy, and did not quite know whether they ought to call without being asked, or whether she ought to ask them; besides, Mrs. Nash's reception-room was not always at her disposal, and she would not have liked to take them all the way up to her own room. Her social life was, therefore, confined to the public places where she met these friends of her husband's. They sometimes happened together at a restaurant, or saw one another between the acts at the theatre, or on coming out of a concert. Marcia was not so much admired for her conversation by her acquaintance, as for her beauty and her style; a rustic reluctance still lingered in her; she was thin and dry in her talk with any one but Bartley, and she could not help letting even men perceive that she was uneasy when they interested him in matters foreign to her.

Bartley did not see why they could not have some of these fellows up in their room for tea; but Marcia told him it was impossible. In fact, although she willingly lived this irregular life with him, she was at heart not at all a Bohemian. She did not like being in lodgings or dining at restaurants; on their horse-car excursions into the suburbs, when the spring opened, she was always choosing this or that little house as the place where she would like to live, and wondering if it were within their means. She said she would gladly do the work herself; she hated to be idle so much as she now must. The city's novelty wore off for her sooner than for him: the concerts, the lectures, the theatres, had already lost their zest for her, and she went because he wished her to go, or in order to be able to help him with what he was always writing about such things.

As the spring advanced, Bartley conceived the plan of a local study, something in the manner of the boarding-house article, but on a much vaster scale: he proposed to Ricker a timely series on the easily accessible hot-weather resorts, to be called "Boston's Breathing-Places," and to relate mainly to the sea-side hotels and their surroundings. His idea was encouraged, and he took Marcia with him on most of his expeditions for its realization. These were largely made before the regular season had well begun; but the boats were already running, and the hotels were open, and they were treated with the hospitality which a knowledge of Bartley's mission must invoke. As he said, it was a matter of business, give and take on both sides, and the landlords took more than they gave in any such trade.

On her part, Marcia regarded dead-heading as a just and legitimate privilege of the press, if not one of its chief attributes; and these passes on boats and trains, this system of paying hotel bills by the presentation of a card, constituted distinguished and honorable recognition from the public. To her simple experience, when Bartley told how magnificently the reporters had been accommodated, at some civic or commercial or professional banquet, with a table of their own, where they were served with all the wines and courses, he seemed to have been one of the principal guests, and her fear was that his head should be turned by his honors. But, at the bottom of her heart, though she enjoyed the brilliancy of his present life, she did not think his occupation comparable to the law in dignity. Bartley called himself a journalist, now, but his newspaper connection still identified him in her mind with those country editors of whom she had always heard her father speak with such contempt: men dedicated to poverty and the despite of the local notables who used them. She could not shake off the old feeling of degradation, even when she heard Bartley and some of his fellow-journalists talking in their boastfulest vein of the sovereign character of journalism; and she secretly resolved never to relinquish her purpose of having him a lawyer. Till he was fairly this, in regular and prosperous practice, she knew that she should not have shown her father that she was right in marrying Bartley.

In the meantime their life went ignorantly on in the obscure channels where their isolation from society kept it longer than was natural. Three or four months after they came to Boston, they were still country people, with scarcely any knowledge of the distinctions and differences so important to the various worlds of any city. So far from knowing that they must not walk in the Common, they used to sit down on a bench there, in the pleasant weather, and watch the opening of the spring, among the lovers whose passion had a publicity that neither surprised nor shocked them. After they were a little more enlightened, they resorted to the Public Garden, where they admired the bridge, and the rock-work, and the statues. Bartley, who was already beginning to get up a taste for art, boldly stopped and praised the Venus, in the presence of the gardeners planting tulip-bulbs.

They went sometimes to the Museum of Fine Arts, where they found a pleasure in the worst things which the best never afterward gave them; and where she became as hungry and tired as if it were the Vatican. They had a pride in taking books out of the Public Library, where they walked about on tiptoe with bated breath; and they thought it a divine treat to hear the great organ play at noon. As they sat there in the Music Hall, and let the mighty instrument bellow over their strong young nerves, Bartley whispered Marcia the jokes he had heard about the organ; and then, upon the wave of aristocratic sensation from this experience, they went out and dined at Copeland's, or Weber's, or Fera's, or even at Parker's: they had long since forsaken the humble restaurant with its doilies and its ponderous crockery, and they had so mastered the art of ordering that they could manage a dinner as cheaply at these finer places as anywhere, especially if Marcia pretended not to care much for her half of the portion, and connived at its transfer to Bartley's plate.

In his hours of leisure, they were so perpetually together that it became a joke with the men who knew them to say, when asked if Bartley were married, "Very *much* married." It was not wholly their inseparableness that gave the impression of this extreme conjugality; as I said, Marcia's uneasiness when others interested Bartley in things alien to her, made itself felt even by these men. She struggled against it because she did not wish to put him to shame before them, and often with an aching sense of desolation she sent him off with them to talk apart, or left him with them if they met on the street, and walked home alone rather than let any one say that she kept her husband tied to her apron-strings. His club, after the first sense of its splendor and usefulness wore away, was an ordeal; she had failed to conceal that she thought the initiation and annual fees extravagant. She knew no other bliss like having Bartley sit down in their own room with her; it did not matter whether they talked; if he were busy, she would as lief sit and sew, or sit and silently look at him as he wrote. In these moments she liked to feign that she had lost him, that they had never been married, and then come back with a rush of joy to the reality. But on his club nights she heroically sent him off, and spent the evening with Mrs. Nash. Sometimes she went out by day with the landlady, who had a passion for auctions and cemeteries, and who led Marcia to an intimate acquaintance with such pleasures. At Mount Auburn, Marcia liked the marble lambs, and the emblematic hands pointing upward with the dexter finger, and the infants carved in stone, and the angels with folded wings and lifted eyes, better than the casts which Bartley said were from the antique, in the Museum. On this side her mind was as wholly dormant as that of Mrs. Nash herself. She always came home feeling as if she had not seen Bartley for a year, and fearful that something had happened to him. The hardest thing about their irregular life was that he must sometimes be gone two or three days at a time, when he could not take her with him. Then it seemed to her that she could not draw a full breath in his absence;

and once he found her almost wild on his return: she had begun to fancy that he was never coming back again. He laughed at her when she betrayed her secret, but she was not ashamed; and when he asked her, "Well, what if I hadn't come back?" she answered passionately, "It wouldn't have made much difference to me: I should not have lived."

The uncertainty of his income was another cause of anguish to her. At times he earned forty or fifty dollars a week: oftener he earned ten; there was now and then a week when everything that he put his hand to failed, and he earned nothing at all. Then Marcia despaired; her frugality became a mania, and they had quarrels about what she called his extravagance. She imbittered his daily bread by blaming him for what he spent on it; she wore her oldest dresses, and would have had him go shabby in token of their adversity. Her economies were frantic child's-play,—methodless, inexperienced, fitful: and they were apt to be followed by remorse in which she abetted him in some wanton excess.

The future of any heroic action is difficult to manage; and the sublime sacrifice of her pride and all the conventional proprieties which Marcia had made in giving herself to Bartley was inevitably tried by the same sordid tests that every married life is put to.

That salaried place which he was always seeking on the staff of some newspaper, proved not so easy to get as he had imagined in the flush of his first successes. Ricker willingly included him among the Chronicle-Abstract's own correspondents and special reporters; and he held the same off-and-on relation to several other papers; but he remained without a more definite position. He earned perhaps more money than a salary would have given him, and in their way of living he and Marcia laid up something out of what he earned. But it did not seem to her that he exerted himself to get a salaried place; she was sure that, if so many others who could not write half so well had places, he might get one if he only kept trying. Bartley laughed at these business-turns of Marcia's, as he called them; but sometimes they enraged him, and he had days of sullen resentment when he resisted all her advances toward reconciliation. But he kept hard at work, and he always owned at last how disinterested her most ridiculous alarm had been.

Once, when they had been talking as usual about that permanent place on some newspaper, she said,

"But I should only want that to be temporary, if you got it. I want you should go on with the law, Bartley! I've been thinking about that. I don't want you should always be a journalist."

Bartley smiled.

"What could I do for a living, I should like to know, while I was studying law?"

"You could do some newspaper work,—enough to support us,—while you were studying. You said when we first came to Boston that you should settle down to the law."

"I hadn't got my eyes open, then. I've got a good deal longer row to hoe than I supposed, before I can settle down to the law."

"Father said you didn't need to study but a little more."

"Not if I were going into the practice at Equity. But it's a very different thing, I can tell you, in Boston; I should have to go in for a course in the Harvard Law School, just for a little start-off."

Marcia was silenced, but she asked, after a moment:

"Then you're going to give up the law, altogether?"

"I don't know what I'm going to do; I'm going to do the best I can for the present, and trust to luck. I don't like special reporting, for a finality; but I shouldn't like shystering, either."

"What's shystering?" asked Marcia.

"It's pettifogging in the city courts. Wait till I can get my basis,—till I have a fixed amount of money for a fixed amount of work,—and then I'll talk to you about taking up the law again. I'm willing to do it whenever it seems the right thing. I guess I should like it, though I don't see why it's any better than journalism, and I don't believe it has any more prizes."

"But you've been a long time trying to get your basis on a newspaper," she reasoned. "Why don't you try to get it in some other way? Why don't you try to get a clerk's place with some lawyer?"

"Well, suppose I was willing to starve along in that way, how should I go about to get such a place?" demanded Bartley, with impatience.

"Why don't you go to that Mr. Halleck you visited here? You used to tell me he was going to be a lawyer."

"Well, if you remember so distinctly what I said about going into the law when I first came to Boston," said her husband, angrily, "perhaps you'll remember that I said I shouldn't go to Halleck until I didn't need his help. I shall not go to him for *his* help."

Marcia gave way to spiteful tears.

"It seems as you were ashamed to let them know that you were in town. Are you afraid I shall want to get acquainted with them? Do you suppose I shall want to go to their parties, and disgrace you?"

Bartley took his cigar out of his mouth, and looked blackly at her.

"So, that's what you've been thinking, is it?"

She threw herself upon his neck.

"No! no, it isn't!" she cried, hysterically. "You know that I never thought it till this instant; you know I didn't think it at all; I just *said* it. My nerves are all gone; I don't know *what* I'm saying half the time, and you're as strict with me as if I were as well as ever! I may as well take off my things,—I'm not well enough to go with you, to-day, Bartley."

She had been dressing while they talked for an entertainment which Bartley was going to report for the Chronicle-Abstract, and now she made a feint of wishing to remove her hat. He would not let her. He said that if she did not go, he should not; he reproached her with not wishing to go with him any more; he coaxed her laughingly and fondly.

"It's only because I'm not so strong, now," she said, in a

whisper that ended in a kiss on his cheek. "You must walk very slowly, and not hurry me."

The entertainment was to be given in aid of the Indigent Children's Surf-Bathing Society, and it was at the end of June, rather late in the season. But the Society itself was an afterthought, not conceived till a great many people had left town on whose assistance such a charity must largely depend. Strenuous appeals had been made, however: it was represented that ten thousand poor children could be transported to Nantasket Beach, and there, as one of the ladies on the committee said, bathed, clam-baked, and lemonaded three times during the summer at a cost so small that it was a saving to spend the money. Class Day falling about the same time, many exiles at Newport and on the North Shore came up and down; and the affair promised to be one of social distinction, if not pecuniary success. The entertainment was to be varied: a distinguished poet was to read an old poem of his, and a distinguished poetess was to read a new poem of hers; some professional people were to follow with comic singing; an elocutionist was to give impressions of noted public speakers; and a number of vocal and instrumental amateurs were to contribute their talent.

Bartley had instructions from Ricker to see that his report was very full socially. "We want something lively, and, at the same time, nice and tasteful, about the whole thing, and I guess you're the man to do it. Get Mrs. Hubbard to go with you, and keep you from making a fool of yourself about the costumes." He gave Bartley two tickets. "Mighty hard to get, I can tell you, for *love* or money,—especially love," he said; and Bartley made much of this difficulty in impressing Marcia's imagination with the uncommon character of the occasion. She had put on a new dress which she had just finished for herself, and which was a marvel not only of cheapness, but of elegance; she had plagiarized the idea from the costume of a lady with whom she stopped to look in at a milliner's window where she formed the notion of her bonnet. But Marcia had imagined the things anew in relation to herself, and made them her own; when Bartley first saw her in them, though he had witnessed their growth from the germ, he said that he was afraid of her, she was so splendid, and he did not quite know whether he felt acquainted. When they were seated at the concert, and had time to look about them, he whispered, "Well, Marsh, I don't see anything here that comes near you in style," and she flung a little corner of her drapery out over his hand so that she could squeeze it: she was quite happy again.

After the concert, Bartley left her for a moment, and went up to a group of the committee near the platform, to get some points for his report. He spoke to one of the gentlemen, note-book and pencil in hand, and the gentleman referred him to one of the ladies of the committee, who, after a moment of hesitation, demanded in a rich tone of injury and surprise, "Why! Isn't this Mr. Hubbard?" and, indignantly answering herself, "Of *course* it is!" gave her hand with a sort of dramatic cordiality, and flooded him with questions: "When did you come to Boston? Are you at the Hallecks'? Did you come— Or no, you're *not* Harvard. You're not *living* in Boston? And what in the world are *you* getting items for? Mr. Hubbard, Mr. Atherton."

She introduced him in a breathless climax to the gentleman to whom he had first spoken, and who had listened to her attack on Bartley with a smile which he was at no trouble to hide from her. "Which question are you going to answer first, Mr. Hubbard?" he asked quietly, while his eyes searched Bartley's for an instant with inquiry which was at once kind and keen. His face had the distinction which comes of being clean-shaven in our bearded times.

"Oh, the last," said Bartley. "I'm reporting the concert for the Chronicle-Abstract, and I want to interview some one in authority about it."

"Then interview *me*, Mr. Hubbard," cried the young lady. "*I'm* in authority about this affair,—it's my own invention, as the White Knight says,—and then I'll interview you afterward.

MRS. KINGSBERRY

And you've gone into journalism, like all the Harvard men!
So glad it's you, for you can be a perfect godsend to the cause
if you will. The entertainment hasn't given us all the money
we shall want, by any means, and we shall need all the help
the press can give us. Ask me any questions you please, Mr.
Hubbard: there isn't a soul here that I wouldn't sacrifice to the
last personal particular if the press will only do its duty in return. You've no idea how we've been working during the last
fortnight since this Old Man of the Sea-Bathing sprang upon
us. I was sitting quietly at home, thinking of anything else in
the world, I can assure you, when this atrocious idea occurred
to me." She ran on to give a full sketch of the inception and
history of the scheme up to the present time. Suddenly she
arrested herself and Bartley's flying pencil: "Why, you're not
putting all that nonsense down?"

"Certainly I am," said Bartley, while Mr. Atherton, with a
laugh, turned and walked away to talk with some other ladies.
"It's the very thing I want. I shall get in ahead of all the other
papers on this; they haven't had anything like it, yet."

She looked at him for a moment in horror. Then:

"Well, go on; I would do anything for the cause!" she cried.

"Tell me who's been here, then," said Bartley.

She recoiled a little.

"I don't like giving names."

"But I can't say who the people were unless you do."

"That's true," said the young lady thoughtfully. She prided
herself on her thoughtfulness, which sometimes came before
and sometimes after the fact. "You're not obliged to say who
told you?"

"Of course not."

She ran over a list of historical and distinguished names, and
he slyly asked if this and that lady were not dressed so and so,
and worked in the costumes from her unconsciously elaborate
answers; she was afterward astonished that he should have
known what people had on. Lastly he asked what the committee expected to do next, and was enabled to enrich his re-

port with many authoritative expressions and intimations. The lady became all zeal in these confidences to the public; at last, she told everything she knew, and a great deal that she merely hoped.

"And now come into the committee-room and have a cup of coffee; I know you must be faint with all this talking," she concluded. "I want to ask you something about yourself." She was not older than Bartley, but she addressed him with the freedom we use in encouraging younger people.

"Thank you," he said coolly; "I can't very well. I must go back to my wife, and hurry up this report."

"Oh, is Mrs. Hubbard here?" asked the young lady, with well-controlled surprise. "Present me to her!" she cried, with that fearlessness of social consequences for which she was noted; she believed there were ways of getting rid of undesirable people without treating them rudely.

The audience had got out of the hall, and Marcia stood alone near one of the doors waiting for Bartley. He glanced proudly toward her, and said: "I shall be very glad."

Miss Kingsbury drifted by his side across the intervening space, and was ready to take Marcia impressively by the hand when she reached her; she had promptly decided her to be very beautiful and elegantly simple in dress, but she found her smaller than she had looked at a distance. Miss Kingsbury was herself rather large,—sometimes, she thought, rather too large: certainly too large if she had not had such perfect command of every inch of herself. In complexion she was richly blonde, with beautiful fair hair roughed over her forehead, as if by a breeze, and apt to escape in sunny tendrils over the peachy tints of her temples. Her features were massive rather than fine; and though she thoroughly admired her chin and respected her mouth, she had doubts about her nose which she frankly referred to friends for solution: had it not *too* much of a knob at the end? She seemed to tower over Marcia as she took her hand at Bartley's introduction, and expressed her pleasure at meeting her.

"I don't know why it need be such a surprise to find one's gentlemen friends married, but it always is, somehow. I don't think Mr. Hubbard would have known me if I hadn't insisted upon his recognizing me; I can't blame him: it's three years since we met. Do you help him with his reports? I know you do! You *must* make him lenient to our entertainment,—the cause is so good! How long have you been in Boston? Though I don't know why I should ask that,—you may have always been in Boston! One used to know everybody; but the place *is* so large, now. I should like to come and see you; but I'm going out of town to-morrow, for the summer. I'm not really here now, except *ex officio*; I ought to have been away weeks ago, but this Indigent Surf-Bathing has kept me. You've no idea what such an undertaking is. But you *must* let me have your address, and as soon as I get back to town in the fall, I shall insist upon looking you up. *Good*-bye! I must run away now, and leave you; there are a thousand things for me to look after yet to-day."

She took Marcia again by the hand, and superadded some bows and nods and smiles of parting, after she released her, but she did not ask her to come into the committee-room and have some coffee; and Bartley took his wife's hand under his arm and went out of the hall.

"Well," he said, with a man's simple pleasure in Miss Kingsbury's friendliness to his wife, "that's the girl I used to tell you about,—the rich one with the money in her own right, whom I met at the Hallecks'. She seemed to think you were about the thing, Marsh! I saw her eyes open as she came up, and I felt awfully proud of you: you never looked half so well. But why didn't you *say* something?"

"She didn't give me any chance," said Marcia, "and I had nothing to say, any way. I thought she was very disagreeable."

"Disagreeable!" repeated Bartley, in amaze.

Miss Kingsbury went back to the committee-room, where one of the amateurs had been lecturing upon her.

"Clara Kingsbury can say and do, from the best heart in the

world, more offensive things in ten minutes than malice could invent in a week. Somebody ought to go out and drag her away from that reporter by main force. But I presume it's too late already; she's had time to destroy us all. You'll see that there wont be a shred left of us in *his* paper, at any rate. Really, I wonder that, in a city full of nervous and exasperated people like Boston, Clara Kingsbury has been suffered to live. She throws her whole soul into everything she undertakes, and she has gone so *en masse* into this Indigent Bathing, and splashed about in it so, that *I* can't understand how we got anybody to come to-day. Why, I haven't the least doubt that she's offered that poor man a ticket to go down to Nantasket and bathe with the other Indigents; she's treated *me* as if I ought to be personally surf-bathed for the last fortnight; and if there's any chance for us left by her tactlessness, you may be sure she's gone at it with her conscience, and simply swept it off the face of the earth.''

XVIII

ONE HOT DAY in August, when Bartley had been doing nothing for a week, and Marcia was gloomily forecasting the future, when they would have to begin living upon the money they had put into the savings-bank, she reverted to the question of his taking up the law again. She was apt to recur to this in any moment of discouragement, and she urged him now to give up his newspaper work, with that wearisome persistence with which women can torment the men they love.

"My newspaper work seems to have given me up, my dear," said Bartley. "It's like asking a fellow not to marry a girl that wont have him." He laughed and then whistled; and Marcia burst into fretful, futile tears, which he did not attempt to assuage.

They had been all summer in town; the country would have been no change to them; and they knew nothing of the sea-side, except the crowded, noisy, expensive resorts near the city. Bartley wished her to go to one of these for a week or two, at any rate, but she would not; and in fact neither of them had the born citizen's conception of the value of a summer vacation. But they had found their attic intolerable; and, the single gentlemen having given up their rooms by this time, Mrs. Nash let Marcia have one lower down, where they sat looking out on the hot street.

"Well," cried Marcia at last, "you don't care for my feelings, or you would take up the law again."

Her husband rose with a sigh that was half a curse, and went out. After what she had said, he would not give her the satisfaction of knowing what he meant to do; but he had it in his head to go to that Mr. Atherton to whom Miss Kingsbury had introduced him, and ask his advice; he had found out that Mr. Atherton was a lawyer, and he believed that he would tell him what to do. He could at least give him some authoritative discouragement which he might use in these discussions with Marcia.

Mr. Atherton had his office in the Events building, and Bartley was on his way thither when he met Ricker.

"Seen Witherby?" asked his friend. "He was round looking for you."

"What does Witherby want with me?" asked Bartley, with a certain resentment.

"Wants to give you the managing-editorship of the Events," said Ricker, jocosely.

"Pshaw! Well, he knows where to find me, if he wants me very badly."

"Perhaps he doesn't," suggested Ricker. "In that case, you'd better look him up."

"Why, you don't advise"—

"Oh, *I* don't advise anything! But if *he* can let by-gones be by-gones, I guess *you* can afford to! I don't know just what he wants with you, but if he offers you anything like a basis, you'd better take it."

Bartley's basis had come to be a sort of by-word between them; Ricker usually met him with some such demand as, "Well, what about the basis?" or "How's your poor basis?" Bartley's ardor for a salaried position amused him, and he often tried to argue him out of it. "You're much better off as a free lance. You make as much money as most of the fellows in places, and you lead a pleasanter life. If you were on any one paper, you'd have to be on duty about fifteen hours out of the twenty-four; you'd be out every night till three or four o'clock; you'd have to do fires, and murders, and all sorts of police business; and now you work mostly on fancy jobs: something you suggest yourself, or something you're specially asked to do. That's a kind of a compliment, and it gives you scope."

Nevertheless, if Bartley had his heart set upon a basis, Ricker wanted him to have it. "Of course," he said, "I was only joking about the basis. But if Witherby should have something permanent to offer, don't quarrel with your bread and butter, and don't hold yourself *too* cheap. Witherby's going to get all he can, for as little as he can, every time."

Ricker was a newspaper man in every breath. His great interest in life was the Chronicle-Abstract, which paid him poorly and worked him hard. To get in ahead of the other papers was the object for which he toiled with unremitting zeal; but after that he liked to see a good fellow prosper, and he had for Bartley that feeling of comradery which comes out among journalists when their rivalries are off. He would hate to lose Bartley from the Chronicle-Abstract; if Witherby meant business, Bartley and he might be excoriating each other before a week passed, in sarcastic references to "our esteemed contemporary of the Events," and "our esteemed contemporary of the Chronicle-Abstract"; but he heartily wished him luck, and hoped it might be some sort of inside work.

When Ricker left him, Bartley hesitated. He was half minded to go home and wait for Witherby to look him up, as the most dignified and perhaps the most prudent course. But he was curious and impatient, and he was afraid of letting the chance, whatever it might be, slip through his fingers. He suddenly resolved upon a little ruse, which would still oblige Witherby to make the advance, and yet would risk nothing by delay. He mounted to Witherby's room in the Events building, and pushed open the door. Then he drew back embarrassed, as if he had made a mistake.

"Excuse me," he said, "isn't Mr. Atherton's office on this floor?"

Witherby looked up from the papers on his desk, and cleared his throat. When he overreached himself he was apt to hold any party to the transaction accountable for his error. Ever since he refused Bartley's paper on the logging-camp, he had accused him in his heart of fraud because he had sold the rejected sketch to another paper, and anticipated Witherby's tardy enterprise in the same direction. Each little success that Bartley made added to Witherby's dislike; and whilst Bartley had written for all the other papers, he had never got any work from the Events. Witherby had the guilty sense of having hated him as he looked up, and Bartley on his part was uneasily sensible of some mocking paragraphs of a more or less personal cast, which he had written in the Chronicle-Abstract, about the enterprise of the Events.

"Mr. Atherton is on the floor above," said Witherby. "But I'm very glad you happened to look in, Mr. Hubbard. I—I was just thinking about you. Ah—wont you take a chair?"

"Thanks," said Bartley, non-committally; but he sat down in the chair which the other rose to offer him.

Witherby fumbled about among the things on his desk before he resumed his own seat.

"I hope you have been well since I saw you?"

"Oh, yes, I'm always well. How have you been?"

Bartley wondered whither this exchange of civilities tended; but he believed he could keep it up as long as old Witherby could.

"Why, I have not been very well," said Witherby, getting into his chair and taking up a paper-weight to help him in talk. "The fact is, I find that I have been working too hard. I have undertaken to manage the editorial department of the Events in addition to looking after its business, and the care has been too great. It has told upon me. I flatter myself that I have not allowed either department to suffer"—

He referred this point so directly to him that Bartley made a murmur of assent, and Witherby resumed.

"But the care has told upon me. I am not so well as I could wish. I need rest, and I need help," he added.

Bartley had by this time made up his mind that, if Witherby had anything to say to him, he should say it unaided.

Witherby put down the paper-weight, and gave his attention for a moment to a paper-cutter.

"I don't know whether you have heard that Mr. Clayton is going to leave us?"

"No," Bartley said, "I hadn't heard that."

"Yes, he is going to leave us. Mr. Clayton and I have not agreed upon some points, and we have both judged it best that we should part." Witherby paused again, and changed the positions of his inkstand and mucilage-bottle. "Mr. Clayton has failed me, as I may say, at the last moment, and we have been compelled to part. I found Mr. Clayton—unpractical."

He looked again at Bartley, who said,

"Yes?"

"Yes. I found Mr. Clayton so much at variance in his views with—with my own views—that I could do nothing with him. He has used language to me which I am sure he will regret. But that is neither here nor there; he is going. I have had my eye on you, Mr. Hubbard, ever since you came to Boston, and have watched your career with interest. But I thought of Mr. Clayton, in the first instance, because he was already attached to the Events, and I wished to promote him. Office during good behavior, and promotion in the direct line: I'm *that* much of a civil-service reformer," said Witherby.

"Certainly," said Bartley.

"But, of course, my idea in starting the Events was to make money."

"Of course."

"I hold that the first duty of a public journal is to make money for the owner; all the rest follows naturally."

"You're quite right, Mr. Witherby," said Bartley. "Unless it makes money, there can be no enterprise about it, no independence,—nothing. That was the way I did with my little paper down in Maine. The first thing—I told the committee when I took hold of the paper—is to keep it from losing money; the next is to make money with it. First peaceable, then pure: that's what I told them."

"Precisely so!" Witherby was now so much at his ease with

Bartley that he left off tormenting the things on his desk, and used his hands in gesticulating.

"Look at the churches themselves! No church can do any good till it's on a paying basis. As long as a church is in debt, it can't secure the best talent for the pulpit or the choir, and the members go about feeling discouraged and out of heart. It's just so with a newspaper. I say that a paper does no good till it pays; it has no influence, its motives are always suspected, and you've got to make it pay by hook or by crook before you can hope to—to—forward any good cause by it. That's what *I* say. Of course," he added, in a large, smooth way, "I'm not going to contend that a newspaper should be run *solely* in the interest of the counting-room. Not at all! But I do contend that when the counting-room protests against a certain course the editorial-room is taking, it ought to be respectfully listened to. There are always two sides to every question. Suppose all the newspapers pitch in—as they sometimes do—and denounce a certain public enterprise: a projected scheme of railroad legislation, or a peculiar system of banking, or a coöperative mining interest, and the counting-room sends up word that the company advertises heavily with us; shall *we* go and join indiscriminately in that hue and cry, or shall we give our friends the benefit of the doubt?"

"Give them the benefit of the doubt," answered Bartley. "That's what I say."

"And so would any other practical man!" said Witherby. "And that's just where Mr. Clayton and I differed. Well, I needn't allude to him any more," he added, leniently. "What I wish to say is this, Mr. Hubbard: I am overworked, and I feel the need of some sort of relief. I know that I have started the Events in the right line at last,—the only line in which it can be made a great, useful, and respectable journal, efficient in every good cause,—and what I want now is some sort of assistant in the management who shall be in full sympathy with my own ideas. I don't want a mere slave,—a tool; but I do want an independent, right-minded man, who shall be with me for the success of the paper the whole time and every time, and shall not be continually setting up his will against mine on all sorts of *doctrinaire* points. That was the trouble with Mr. Clayton. I have nothing against Mr. Clayton personally; he is an excellent young man in very many respects; but he was all wrong about journalism, all wrong, Mr. Hubbard. I talked with him a great deal, and tried to make him see where his interest lay. He had been on the paper as a reporter from the start, and I wished very much to promote him to this position; which he could have made the best position in the country. The Events is an evening paper; there is no night-work; and the whole thing is already thoroughly systematized. Mr. Clayton had plenty of talent, and all he had to do was to step in under my direction and put his hand on the helm. But, no! I should have been glad to keep him in a subordinate capacity; but I had to let him go. He said that he would not report the conflagration of a peanut-stand for a paper conducted on the principles I had developed to him. Now, that is no way to talk. It's absurd."

"Perfectly." Bartley laughed his rich, caressing laugh, in which there was the insinuation of all worldly-wise contempt for Clayton and all worldly-wise sympathy with Witherby. It made Witherby feel good, better, perhaps, than he had felt at any time since his talk with Clayton.

"Well, now, what do you say, Mr. Hubbard? Can't we make some arrangement with you?" he asked, with a burst of frankness.

"I guess you can," said Bartley. The fact that Witherby needed him was so plain that he did not care to practice any finesse about the matter.

"What are your present engagements?"

"I haven't any."

"Then you can take hold at once?"

"Yes."

"That's good."

Witherby now entered at large into the nature of the position which he offered Bartley. They talked a long time, and in becoming better acquainted with each other's views, as they called them, they became better friends. Bartley began to respect Witherby's business ideas, and Witherby, in recognizing all the admirable qualities of this clear-sighted and level-headed young man, began to feel that he had secretly liked him from the first, and had only waited a suitable occasion to unmask his affection. It was arranged that Bartley should come on as Witherby's assistant, and should do whatever he was asked to do in the management of the paper; he was to write on topics as they occurred to him, or as they were suggested to him. "I don't say whether this will lead to anything more, Mr. Hubbard, or not; but I do say that you will be in the direct line of promotion."

"Yes, I understand that," said Bartley.

"And now as to terms," continued Witherby, a little tremulously.

"And now as to terms," repeated Bartley to himself; but he said nothing aloud. He felt that Witherby had cut out a great deal of work for him, and work of a kind that he could not easily find another man both willing and able to do. He resolved that he would have all that his service was worth.

"What should you think of twenty dollars a week?" asked Witherby.

"I shouldn't think it was enough," said Bartley, amazed at his own audacity, but enjoying it, and thinking how he had left Marcia with the intention of offering himself to Mr. Atherton as a clerk for ten dollars a week. "There is a great deal of labor in what you propose, and you command my whole time. You would not like to have me do any work outside of the Events."

"No," Witherby assented. "Would twenty-five be nearer the mark?" he inquired soberly.

"It would be nearer, certainly," said Bartley. "But I guess you had better make it thirty." He kept a quiet face, but his heart throbbed.

"Well, say thirty, then," replied Witherby, so promptly that Bartley perceived with a pang that he might as easily have got forty from him. But it was now too late, and a salary of fifteen hundred a year passed the wildest hopes he had cherished half an hour before.

"All right," he said quietly. "I suppose you want me to take hold at once?"

"Yes, on Monday. Oh, by the way," said Witherby, "there is one little piece of outside work which I should like you to finish up for us; and we'll agree upon something extra for it, if you wish. I mean our 'Solid Men' series. I don't know whether you've noticed the series in the Events?"

"Yes," said Bartley, "I have."

"Well, then, you know what they are. They consist of interviews—guarded and inoffensive as respects the sanctity of private life—with our leading manufacturers and merchant princes at their places of business and their residences, and include a description of these, and some account of the lives of the different subjects."

"Yes, I have seen them," said Bartley. "I've noticed the general plan."

"You know that Mr. Clayton has been doing them. He made them a popular feature. The parties themselves were very much pleased with them."

"Oh, people are always tickled to be interviewed," said Bartley. "I know they put on airs about it, and go round complaining to each other about the violation of confidence, and so on; but they all like it. You know I reported that Indigent Surf-Bathing entertainment, in June, for the Chronicle-Abstract. I knew the lady who got it up, and I interviewed her after the entertainment."

"Miss Kingsbury?"

"Yes." Witherby made an inarticulate murmur of respect for Bartley in his throat, and involuntarily changed toward him, but not so subtly that Bartley's finer instinct did not take note of the change. "She was a fresh subject, and she told me everything. Of course I printed it all. She was awfully shocked —or pretended to be—and wrote me a very Oh-dear-how-could-you note about it. But I went round to the office the next day, and I found that nearly every lady mentioned in the interview had ordered half a dozen copies of that issue sent to her sea-side address, and the office had been full of Beacon-street swells the whole morning buying Chronicle-Abstracts—'the one with the report of the concert in it.' " These low views of high society, coupled with an apparent familiarity with it, modified Witherby more and more. He began to see that he had got a prize. "The way to do with such fellows as your 'Solid Men,' " continued Bartley, "is to submit a proof to 'em. They never know exactly what to do about it, and so you print the inter-view with their approval, and make 'em *particeps criminis.* I'll finish up the series for you, and I wont make any very heavy extra charge."

"I should wish to pay you whatever the work was worth," said Witherby, not to be outdone in nobleness.

"All right; we sha'n't quarrel about that, at any rate."

Bartley was getting toward the door, for he was eager to be gone now to Marcia, but Witherby followed him up as if willing to detain him.

"My wife," he said, "knows Miss Kingsbury. They have been on the same charities together."

"I met her a good while ago, when I was visiting a chum of mine at his father's house here. I didn't suppose she'd know me; but she did at once, and began to ask me if I was at the Hallecks',—as if I had never gone away."

"Mr. Ezra B. Halleck?" inquired Witherby reverently. "Leather trade?"

"Yes," said Bartley. "I believe his first name was Ezra. Ben Halleck was my friend. Do you know the family?" asked Bartley.

"Yes, we have met them—in society. I hope you're pleasantly situated where you are, Mr. Hubbard? Should be glad to have you call at the house."

"Thank you," said Bartley; "my wife will be glad to have Mrs. Witherby call."

"Oh!" cried Witherby. "I didn't know you were married! That's good! There's nothing like marriage, Mr. Hubbard, to keep a man going in the right direction. But you've begun pretty young."

"Nothing like taking a thing in time," answered Bartley. "But I haven't been married a great while; and I'm not so young as I look. Well, good-afternoon, Mr. Witherby."

"*What* did you say was your address?" asked Witherby, taking out his note-book. "My wife will certainly call. She's down at Nantasket now, but she'll be up the first part of September, and then she'll call. *Good*-afternoon."

They shook hands at last, and Bartley ran home to Marcia. He burst into the room with a glowing face.

"Well, Marcia," he shouted, "I've got my basis!"

"Hush! No! Don't be so loud! You haven't!" she answered, springing to her feet. "I don't believe it! How hot you are!"

"I've been running almost—all the way from the Events office. I've got a place on the Events,—assistant managing-editor,—thirty dollars a week," he panted.

"I knew you would succeed yet—I knew you would, if I could only have a little patience. I've been scolding myself ever since you went. I thought you were going to do something desperate, and I had driven you to it. But Bartley, Bartley! It can't be true, is it? Here, here! Do take this fan. Or no, I'll fan you, if you'll let me sit on your knee! O poor thing, how hot you are! But I thought you wouldn't write for the Events; I thought you hated that old Witherby, who acted so ugly to you when you first came."

"Oh, Witherby is a pretty good old fellow," said Bartley, who had begun to get his breath again. He gave her a full history of the affair, and they rejoiced together over it, and were as happy as if Bartley had been celebrating a high and honorable good fortune. She was too ignorant to feel the disgrace, if there were any, in the compact which Bartley had closed, and he had no principles, no traditions by which to perceive it. To them it meant unlimited prosperity; it meant provision for the future, which was to bring a new responsibility and a new care.

"We will take the parlor with the alcove, now," said Bartley. "Don't excite yourself," he added, with tender warning.

"No, no," she said, pillowing her head on his shoulder, and shedding peaceful tears.

"It doesn't seem as if we should ever quarrel again, does it?"

"No, no! We never shall," she murmured. "It has always come from my worrying you about the law, and I shall never do that any more. If you like journalism better, I shall not urge you any more to leave it, now you've got your basis."

"But I'm going on with the law, now, for that very reason. I shall read law all my leisure time. I feel independent, and I shall not be anxious about the time I give, because I shall know that I can afford it."

"Well, only you mustn't overdo." She put her lips against his cheek. "You're more to me than anything you can do for me."

"Oh, Marcia!"

XIX

Now that Bartley had got his basis, and had no favors to ask of any one, he was curious to see his friend Halleck again; but when, in the course of the "Solid Men Series," he went to interview the "Nestor of the Leather Interest," as he meant to call the elder Halleck, he resolved to let him make all the advances. On a legitimate business errand it should not matter to him whether Mr. Halleck welcomed him or not. The old man did not wait for Bartley to explain why he came; he was so simply glad to see him that Bartley felt a little ashamed to confess that he had been eight months in Boston without making himself known. He answered all the personal questions with which Mr. Halleck plied him; and in his turn he inquired after his college friend.

"Ben is in Europe," said his father. "He has been there all summer; but we expect him home about the middle of September. He's been a good while settling down," continued the old man, with an unconscious sigh. "He talked of the law at first, and then he went into business with me; but he didn't seem to find his calling in it; and now he's taken up the law again. He's been in the law school at Cambridge, and he's going back there for a year or two longer. I thought you used to talk of the law yourself when you were with us, Mr. Hubbard."

"Yes, I did," Bartley assented. "And I haven't given up the notion yet. I've read a good deal of law already; but when I came up to Boston, I had to go into newspaper work till I could see my way out of the woods."

"Well," said Mr. Halleck, "that's right. And you say you like the arrangement you've made with Mr. Witherby?"

"It's ideal—for me," answered Bartley.

"Well, that's good," said the old man. "And you've come to interview me. Well, that's all right. I'm not much used to being in print, but I shall be glad to tell you all I know about leather."

"You may depend upon my not asking anything that will be disagreeable to you, Mr. Halleck," said Bartley, touched by the old man's trusting friendliness. When his inquisition ended, he slipped his note-book back into his pocket, and said with a smile:

"We usually say something about the victim's private residence, but I guess I'll spare you that, Mr. Halleck."

"Why, we live in the old place, and I don't suppose there is much to say. We are plain people, and we don't like to change. When I built there, thirty years ago, Rumford street was one of the most desirable streets in Boston. There was no Back Bay, then, you know, and we thought we were doing something very fashionable. But fashion has drifted away, and left us high and dry enough on Rumford street; though we don't mind it. We keep the old house and the old garden pretty much as you saw them. You can say whatever you think best. There's a good deal of talk about the intrusiveness of the newspapers; all I know is that they've never intruded upon me. We shall not be afraid that you will abuse our house, Mr. Hubbard, because we expect you to come there again. When shall it be? Mrs. Halleck and I have been at home all summer; we find it the most comfortable place; and we shall be very glad if you'll drop in any evening and take tea with us. We keep the old hours; we've never taken kindly to the late dinners. The girls are off at the mountains, and you'd see nobody but Mrs. Halleck. Come this evening!" cried the old man, with mounting cordiality.

His warmth, as he put his hand on Bartley's shoulder, made the young man blush again for the reserve with which he had been treating his own affairs. He stammered out, hoping that the other would see the relevancy of the statement:

"Why, the fact is, Mr. Halleck, I—I'm married."

"Married!" said Mr. Halleck. "Why didn't you tell me before? Of course we want Mrs. Hubbard, too. Where are you living? We wont stand upon ceremony among old friends. Mrs. Halleck will come with the carriage and fetch Mrs. Hubbard, and your wife must take that for a call. Why, you don't know how glad we shall be to have you both! I wish Ben was married. You'll come?"

"Of course we will," said Bartley. "But you mustn't let Mrs. Halleck send for us; we can walk perfectly well."

"*You* can walk if you want, but Mrs. Hubbard shall ride," said the old man.

When Bartley reported this to Marcia,

"Bartley!" she cried. "In her carriage? I'm afraid!"

"Nonsense! She'll be a great deal more afraid than you are. She's the bashfulest old lady you ever saw. All that I hope is that you wont overpower her."

"Bartley, hush! Shall I wear my silk, or"—

"Oh, wear the silk, by all means. Crush them at a blow!"

Rumford street is one of those old-fashioned thoroughfares at the west end of Boston, which are now almost wholly abandoned to boarding-houses of the poorer class. Yet they are charming streets, quiet, clean, and respectable, and worthy still to be the homes, as they once were, of solid citizens. The red brick houses, with their swell fronts, looking in perspective like a succession of round towers, are reached by broad granite steps, and their doors are deeply sunken within the wagon-roofs of white-painted Roman arches. Over the door there is sometimes the bow of a fine transom, and the parlor windows on the first floor of the swell front have the same azure gleam as those of the beautiful old houses which front the Common on Beacon street.

When her husband bought his lot there, Mrs. Halleck could hardly believe that a house on Rumford street was not too fine for her. They had come to the city simple and good young village people, and simple and good they had remained, through the advancing years which had so wonderfully—Mrs. Halleck hoped, with a trembling heart, not wickedly—prospered them. They were of faithful stock, and they had been true to their traditions in every way. One of these was constancy to the orthodox religious belief in which their young hearts had united, and which had blessed all their life; though their charity now abounded perhaps more than their faith. They still believed that for themselves there was no spiritual safety except in their church; but since their younger children had left it, they were forced tacitly to own that this might not be so in all cases. Their last endeavor for the church in Ben's case was to send him to the college where he and Bartley met; and this was such a failure on the main point, that it left them remorsefully indulgent. He had submitted, and had foregone his boyish dreams of Harvard, where all his mates were going; but the sacrifice seemed to have put him at odds with life. The years which had proved the old people mistaken would not come back upon their recognition of their error. He returned to the associations from which they had exiled him too much estranged to resume them, and they saw, with the unavailing regrets which visit fathers and mothers in such cases, that the young know their own world better than their elders can know it, and have a right to be in it and of it, superior to any theory of their advantage which their elders can form. Ben was not the fellow to complain; in fact, after he came home from college, he was allowed to shape his life according to his own rather fitful liking. His father was glad now to content him in anything he could, it was so very little that Ben asked. If he had suffered it, perhaps his family would have spoiled him.

The Halleck girls went early in July to the Profile House, where they had spent their summers for many years; but the old people preferred to stay at home, and only left their large, comfortable house for short absences. Their ways of life had been fixed in other times, and Mrs. Halleck liked better than mountain or sea the high-walled garden that stretched back of their house to the next street. They had bought through to this street when they built, but they had never sold the lot that fronted on it. They laid it out in box-bordered beds, and there were clumps of hollyhocks, sunflowers, lilies, and phlox in different corners; grapes covered the trellised walls; there were some pear-trees that bore blossoms and sometimes ripened their fruit beside the walk. Mrs. Halleck used to work in the garden; her husband seldom descended into it, but he liked to sit on the iron-railed balcony overlooking it from the back parlor.

As for the interior of the house, it had been furnished, once for all, in the worst style of that most tasteless period of household art which prevailed from 1840 to 1870; and it would be impossible to say which was most hideous, the carpets or the chandeliers, the curtains or the chairs and sofas; crude colors, lumpish and meaningless forms, abounded in a rich and horrible discord. The old people thought it all beautiful, and those daughters who had come into the new house as little girls revered it; but Ben and his youngest sister, who had been born in the house, used the right of children of their parents' declining years to laugh at it. Yet they laughed with a sort of filial tenderness.

"I suppose you know how frightful you have everything about you, Olive?" said Clara Kingsbury, one day after the Eastlake movement began, as she took a comprehensive survey of the Halleck drawing-room through her *pince-nez*.

"Certainly," answered the youngest Miss Halleck. "It's a perfect chamber of horrors. But I like it, because everything's so exquisitely in keeping."

"Really, I feel as if I had seen it all for the first time," said Miss Kingsbury. "I don't believe I ever realized it before."

She and Olive Halleck were great friends, though Clara was fashionable and Olive was not.

"It would all have been different," Ben used to say, in whimsical sarcasm of what he had once believed, "if I had gone to Harvard. Then the fellows in my class would have come to the house with me, and we should have got into the right set naturally. Now, we're outside of everything, and it makes me mad, because we've got money enough to be inside, and there's nothing to prevent it. Of course, I'm not going to say that leather is quite as blameless as cotton, socially, but taken in the wholesale form it isn't so very malodorous; and it's quite as good as other things that are accepted."

"It's not the leather, Ben," answered Olive, "and it's not your not going to Harvard altogether, though that has something to do with it. The trouble's in me. I was at school with all those girls Clara goes with, and I could have been in that set if I'd wanted; but I didn't really want to. I saw, at a very tender age, that it was going to be more trouble than it was worth, and I just quietly kept out of it. Of course, I couldn't have gone to Papanti's without a fuss, but mother would have let me go if I had made the fuss; and I could be hand and glove with those girls now, if I tried. They come here whenever I ask them; and when I meet them on charities, I'm awfully popular. No, if I'm not fashionable, it's my own fault. But what difference does it make to you, Ben? You dont want to marry any of those girls as long as your heart's set on that unknown charmer of yours." Ben had once seen his charmer in the street of a little Down-East town, where he met her walking with some other boarding-school girls; in a freak, with his fellow-students, he had bribed the village photographer to let him have the picture of this young lady, which he had sent home to Olive, marked, "My Lost Love."

"No, I don't want to marry anybody," said Ben. "But I hate to live in a town where I'm not first chop in everything."

"Pshaw!" cried his sister, "I guess it doesn't trouble you much."

"Well, I don't know that it does," he admitted.

Mrs. Halleck's black coachman drove her to Mrs. Nash's door on Canary Place, where she alighted and rang with as great perturbation as if it had been a palace, and these poor young people to whom she was going to be kind were princes. It was sufficient that they were strangers; but Marcia's anxiety, evident even to meekness like Mrs. Halleck's, restored her somewhat to her self-possession; and the thought that Bartley, in spite of his personal splendor, was a friend of Ben's, was a help, and she got home with her guests without great chasms in the conversation, though she never ceased to twist the window-tassel in her embarrassment.

Mr. Halleck came to her rescue at her own door, and let them in. He shook hands with Bartley again, and viewed Marcia with a fatherly friendliness that took away half her awe of the ugly magnificence of the interior. But still she admired that Bartley could be so much at his ease. He pointed to a stick at the foot of the hat-rack, and said, "How much that looks like Halleck!" which made the old man laugh, and clap him on the shoulder, and cry: "So it does! so it does! Recognized it, did you? Well, we shall soon have him with us again, now. Seems a long time to us since he went."

"Still limps a little?" asked Bartley.

"Yes, I guess he'll never quite get over that."

"I don't believe I should like him to," said Bartley. "He wouldn't seem natural without a cane in his hand, or hanging by the crook over his left elbow, while he stood and talked."

The old man clapped Bartley on the shoulder again, and laughed again at the image suggested.

"That's so! that's so! You're right, I *guess!*"

As soon as Marcia could lay off her things in the gorgeous chamber to which Mrs. Halleck had shown her, they went out to tea in the dining-room overlooking the garden.

"Seems natural, don't it?" asked the old man, as Bartley turned to one of the windows.

"Not changed a bit, except that I was here in winter, and I hadn't a chance to see how pretty your garden was."

"It *is* pretty, isn't it?" said the old man. "Mother—Mrs. Halleck, I mean—looks after it. She keeps it about right. Here's Cyrus!" he said, as the serving-man came into the room with something from the kitchen in his hands. "You remember Cyrus, I guess, Mr. Hubbard?"

"Oh, yes!" said Bartley, and when Cyrus had set down his dish, Bartley shook hands with the New Hampshire exemplar of freedom and equality; he was no longer so young as to wish to mark a social difference between himself and the inside man who had served Mr. Halleck with unimpaired self-respect for twenty-five years.

There was a vacant place at table, and Mr. Halleck said he hoped it would be taken by a friend of theirs. He explained that the possible guest was his lawyer, whose office Ben was going into after he left the law school; and presently Mr. Atherton came. Bartley was prepared to be introduced anew, but he was flattered and the Hallecks were pleased to find that he and Mr. Atherton were already acquainted; the latter was so friendly that Bartley was confirmed in his belief that you could not make an interview too strong, for he had celebrated Mr. Atherton among the other people present at the Indigent Surf-Bathing entertainment.

Mr. Atherton was put next to Marcia, and after a while he began to talk with her, feeling with a tacit skill for her highest note, and striking that with kindly perseverance. It was not a very high note, and it was not always a certain sound. She could not be sure that he was really interested in the simple matters he had set her to talking about, and from time to time she was afraid that Bartley did not like it; she would not have liked him to talk so long or so freely with a lady. But she found herself talking on, about boarding, and her own preference for keeping house; about Equity, and what sort of place it was, and how far from Crawford's; about Boston, and what she had seen and done there since she had come in the winter. Most of her remarks began or ended with Mr. Hubbard; many of her opinions, especially in matters of taste, were frank repetitions of what Mr. Hubbard thought; her conversation had the charm and pathos of that of the young wife who devotedly loves her husband, who lives in him and for him, tests everything by him, refers everything to him. She had a good mind, though it was as bare as it could well be of most of the things that the ladies of Mr. Atherton's world put into their minds.

Mrs. Halleck made from time to time a little murmur of satisfaction in Marcia's loyalty, and then sank back into the meek silence which she only emerged from to propose more tea to some one, or to direct Cyrus about offering this dish or that.

After they rose, she took Marcia about and showed her the house, ending with the room which Bartley had had when he visited there. They sat down in this room and had a long chat, and when they came back to the parlor they found Mr. Atherton already gone. Marcia inferred the early habits of the household from the departure of this older friend, but Bartley was in no hurry; he was enjoying himself, and he could not see that Mr. Halleck seemed at all sleepy.

Mrs. Halleck wished to send them home in her carriage, but they would not hear of this; they would far rather walk, and when they had been followed to the door, and bidden to mind the steps as they went down, the wide open night did not seem too large for their content in themselves and each other.

"Did you have a nice time?" asked Bartley, though he knew he need not.

"The best time I ever had in the world!" cried Marcia.

They discussed the whole affair; the two old people; Mr. Atherton, and how pleasant he was; the house and its splendors, which they did not know were hideous.

"Bartley," said Marcia at last, "I *told* Mrs. Halleck."

"Did you?" he returned, in trepidation; but after a while he laughed. "Well, all right, if you wanted to."

"Yes, I did; and you can't think how kind she was. She says we must have a house of our own somewhere, and she's going round with me in her carriage to help me to find one."

"Well," said Bartley, and he fetched a sigh, half of pride, half of dismay.

"Yes, I long to go to housekeeping. We can afford it now.

She says we can get a cheap little house, or half a house, up at the South End, and it wont cost us any more than to board, hardly; and that's what I think, too."

"Go ahead, if you can find the house. I don't object to my own fireside. And I suppose we must."

"Yes, we must. Aint you glad of it?"

They were in the shadow of a tall house, and he dropped his face toward the face she lifted to his, and gave her a silent kiss that made her heart leap toward him.

XX

WITH the other news that Halleck's mother gave him on his return, she told him of the chance that had brought his old college comrade to them again, and how Bartley was now married, and was just settled in the little house she had helped his wife to find.

"He has married a very pretty girl," she said.

"Oh, I dare say!" answered her son. "He isn't the fellow to have married a plain girl."

"Your father and I have been to call upon them in their new house, and they seem very happy together. Mr. Hubbard wants you should come to see them. He talks a great deal about you."

"I'll look them up in good time," said the young man. "Hubbard's ardor to see me will keep."

That evening Mr. Atherton came to tea, and Halleck walked home with him to his lodgings, which were over the hill, and beyond the Public Garden.

"Yes, it's very pleasant, getting back," he said, as they sauntered down the Common side of Beacon street, "and the old town is picturesque after the best they can do across the water."

He halted his friend, and brought himself to a rest on his cane, for a look over the hollow of the Common and the level of the Garden, where the late September dark was keenly spangled with lamps. " 'My heart leaps up,' and so forth, when I see that. Now that Athens and Florence and Edinburgh are past, I don't think there is any place quite so well worth being born in as Boston." He moved forward again, gently surging with his limp, in a way that had its charm for those that loved him. "It's more authentic and individual, more municipal, after the old pattern, than any other modern city. It gives its stamp, it characterizes. The Boston Irishman, the Boston Jew, is a quite different Irishman or Jew from those of other places. Even Boston provinciality is a precious testimony to the authoritative personality of the city. Cosmopolitanism is a modern vice, and we're antique, we're classic, in the other thing. Yes, I'd rather be a Bostonian, at odds with Boston, than one of the curled darlings of any other community."

A friend knows how to allow for mere quantity in your talk, and only replies to the quality; separates your earnest from your whimsicality, and accounts for some whimsicality in your earnest.

"I didn't know but you might have got that bee out of your bonnet on the other side," said Atherton.

"No, sir; we change our skies but not our bees. What should I amount to without my grievance? You wouldn't have known me. This talk to-night about Hubbard has set my bee to buzzing with uncommon liveliness; and the thought of the law school next week does nothing to allay him. The law school isn't Harvard; I realize that more and more, though I have tried to fancy that it was. No, sir, my wrongs are irreparable. I had the making of a real Harvard man in me, and of a Unitarian, nicely balanced between radicalism and amateur episcopacy. Now, I am an orthodox ruin, and the undutiful step-son of a Down-East *alma mater*. I belong nowhere; I'm at odds. Is Hubbard's wife really handsome, or is she only country-pretty?"

"She's beautiful,—I assure you, she's beautiful," said Atherton, with such earnestness that Halleck laughed.

"Well, that's right, as my father says. How's she beautiful?"

"That's difficult to tell. It's rather a superb sort of style; and —What did you really use to think of your friend?" Atherton broke off to ask.

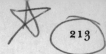

"Who? Hubbard?"

"Yes."

"He was a poor, cheap sort of a creature. Deplorably smart, and regrettably handsome. A fellow that assimilated everything to a certain extent, and nothing thoroughly. A fellow with no more moral nature than a base-ball. The sort of chap you'd expect to find, the next time you met him, in Congress or the house of correction."

"Yes, that accounts for it," said Atherton, thoughtfully.

"Accounts for what?"

"The sort of look she had. A look as if she were naturally above him, and had somehow fascinated herself with him, and were worshiping him in some sort of illusion."

"Doesn't that sound a little like refining upon the facts? Recollect, I've never seen her, and I don't say you're wrong."

"I'm not sure I'm not, though. I talked with her, and found her nothing more than honest and sensible and good; simple in her traditions, of course, and countrified yet, in her ideas, with a tendency to the intensely practical. I don't see why she mightn't very well be his wife. I suppose every woman hoodwinks herself about her husband in some degree."

"Yes; and we always like to fancy something pathetic in the fate of pretty girls that other fellows marry. I notice that we don't sorrow much over the plain ones. How's the divine Clara?"

"I believe she's well," said Atherton. "I haven't seen her, all summer. She's been at Beverly."

"Why, I should have supposed she would have come up and surf-bathed those indigent children with her own hand. She's equal to it. What made her falter in well-doing?"

"I don't know that we can properly call it faltering. There was a deficit in the appropriation necessary, and she made it up herself. After that, she consulted me seriously as to whether she ought not to stay in town and superintend the execution of the plan. But I told her she might fitly delegate that. She was all the more anxious to perform her whole duty, because she confessed that indigent children were personally unpleasant to her."

Halleck burst out laughing.

"That's like Clara! How charming women are! They're charming even in their goodness! I wonder the novelists don't take a hint from that fact, and stop giving us those scaly heroines they've been running lately. Why, a real woman can make righteousness delicious and virtue piquant. I like them for that!"

"Do you?" asked Atherton, laughing in his turn at the single-minded confession. He was some years older than his friend.

They had got down to Charles street, and Halleck took out his watch at the corner lamp.

"It isn't at all late yet; only half-past eight. The days are getting shorter."

"Well?"

"Suppose we go and call on Hubbard now? He's right up here on Clover street."

"I don't know," said Atherton. "It would do for you; you're an old friend. But for me,—wouldn't it be rather unceremonious?"

"Oh, come along! They'll not be punctilious. They'll like our dropping in, and I shall have Hubbard off my conscience. I must go to see him sooner or later, for decency's sake."

Atherton suffered himself to be led away.

"I suppose you wont stay long?"

"Oh, no; I shall cut it very short," said Halleck.

And they climbed the narrow little street where Marcia had at last found a house, after searching the South End quite to the Highlands, and ransacking Charlestown and Cambridge-port. These points all seemed to her terribly remote from where Bartley must be at work during the day, and she must be alone without the sight of him from morning till night. The accessibility of Canary Place had spoiled her for distances; she wanted Bartley at home for their one-o'clock dinner; she wanted to have him within easy call at all times; and she was glad when none of those far-off places yielded quite what they desired in a house. They took the house on Clover street, though it was a little dearer than they expected, for two years, and they furnished it, as far as they could, out of the three or four hundred dollars they had saved, including the remaining hundred from the colt and cutter, kept sacredly intact by Marcia. When you entered, the narrow staircase cramped you into the little parlor opening out of the hall; and back of the parlor was the dining-room. Overhead were two chambers, and overhead again were two chambers more; in the basement was the kitchen. The house seemed absurdly large to people who had been living for the last seven months in one room, and the view of the Back Bay from the little bow-window of the front chamber added all outdoors to their superfluous space.

Bartley came himself to answer Halleck's ring, and they met at once with such a "Why, Halleck!" and "How do you do, Hubbard?" as restored something of their old college comradery. Bartley welcomed Mr. Atherton under the gas-light he had turned up, and then they huddled into the little parlor, where Bartley introduced his old friend to his wife. Marcia wore a sort of dark robe, trimmed with bows of crimson ribbon, which she had made herself, and in which she looked a Roman patrician in an avatar of Boston domesticity; and Bartley was rather proud to see his friend so visibly dazzled by her beauty. It quite abashed Halleck, who limped helplessly about, after his cane had been taken from him, before he sat down, while Marcia, from the vantage of the sofa and the covert of her talk with Atherton, was content that Halleck should be plain and awkward, with close-cut drab hair and a dull complexion. She would not have liked even a man who knew Bartley before she did to be very handsome.

Halleck and Bartley had some talk about college days, from which their eyes wandered at times; and then Marcia excused herself to Atherton and went out, re-appearing after an interval at the sliding doors, which she rolled open between the parlor and dining-room. A table set for supper stood behind her, and, as she leaned a little forward, with her hands each on a leaf of the door, she said, with shy pride, "Bartley, I thought the gentlemen would like to join you," and he answered, "Of course they would," and led the way out, refusing to hear any demur. His heart swelled with satisfaction in Marcia; it was something like, having fellows drop in upon you, and be asked out to supper in this easy way. It made Bartley feel good, and he would have liked to give Marcia a hug on the spot. He could not help pressing her foot under the table, and exchanging a quiver of the eyelashes with her, as he lifted the lid of the white tureen, and looked at her across the glitter of their new crockery and cutlery. They made the jokes of the season about the oyster being promptly on hand for the first of the R months, and Bartley explained that he was sometimes kept at the Events office rather late, and that then Marcia waited supper for him, and always gave him an oyster stew, which she made herself. She could not stop him, and the guests praised the oysters, and then they praised the dining-room and the parlor. And when they rose from the table Bartley said, "Now we must show you the house," and persisted, against her deprecations, in making her lead the way. She was, in fact, willing enough to show it; her taste had made their money go to the utmost in furnishing it; and, though most people were then still in the period of green reps and tan terry, and of dull black-walnut movables, she had everywhere bestowed little touches that told. She had covered the marble parlor-mantel with cloth and fringed it, and she had set on it two vases in the Pompeiian colors then liked; her carpet was of wood colors and a moss pattern; she had done what could be done with folding carpet chairs to give the little room a specious air of luxury; the center-table was heaped with her sewing and Bartley's newspapers.

"We've just moved in, and we haven't furnished *all* the rooms yet," she said of two empty ones which Bartley perversely flung open.

"And I don't know that we shall. The house is much too big

for us; but we thought we'd better take it," he added, as if it were a castle for vastness.

Halleck and Atherton were silent for some moments after they came away, and then:

"*I* don't believe he whips her," suggested the latter.

"No, I guess he's fond of her," said Halleck, gravely.

"Did you see how careful he was of her, coming up and down stairs? That was very pretty; and it was pretty to see them both so ready to show off their young housekeeping to us."

"Yes, it improves a man to get married," said Halleck, with a long, stifled sigh. "It's improved the most selfish hound I ever knew."

XXI

The two elder Miss Hallecks were so much older than Olive, the youngest, that they seemed to be of a sort of intermediary generation between her and her parents, though Olive herself was well out of her teens, and was the senior of her brother Ben by two or three years. The elder sisters were always together, and they adhered in common to the religion of their father and mother. The defection of their brother was passive, but Olive, having conscientiously adopted an alien faith, was not a person to let others imagine her ashamed of it, and her Unitarianism was outspoken. In her turn she formed a kind of party with Ben inside the family, and would have led him on in her own excesses of independence if his somewhat melancholy indifferentism had consented. It was only in his absence that she had been with her sisters during their summer sojourn in the White Mountains; when they returned home, she vigorously went her way, and left them to go theirs. She was fond of them in her defiant fashion; but in such a matter as calling on Mrs. Hubbard, she chose not to be mixed up with her family, or in any way to countenance her family's prepossessions. Her sisters paid their visit together, and she waited for Clara Kingsbury to come up from the sea-side. Then she went with her to call upon Marcia, sitting observant and noncommittal while Clara swooped through the little house, up stairs and down, clamoring over its prettiness, and admiring the art with which so few dollars could be made to go so far. "Think of finding such a bower on Clover street!" She made Marcia give her the cost of everything; and her heart swelled with pride in her sex when she heard that Marcia had put down all the carpets herself. "I wanted to make them up," Marcia explained, "but Mr. Hubbard wouldn't let me,—it cost so little at the store."

"Wouldn't let you!" cried Miss Kingsbury. "I should hope as much, indeed! Why, my child, you're a Roman matron!"

She came away in agony lest Marcia might think she meant her nose. She drove early the next morning to tell Olive Halleck that she had spent a sleepless night from this cause, and to ask her what she *should* do. "Do you think she will be hurt, Olive? Tell me what led up to it? How did I behave before that? The context is everything in such cases."

"Oh, you went about praising everything, and screaming and shouting, and my-dearing and my-childing her, and patronizing"—

"There, there! say no more! That's sufficient! I see,— I see it all! I've done the very most offensive thing I could, when I meant to be the most appreciative."

"These country people don't like to be appreciated down to the quick, in that way," said Olive. "I should think Mrs. Hubbard was rather a proud person."

"I know! I know!" moaned Miss Kingsbury. "It was ghastly."

"*I* don't suppose she's ashamed of her nose"—

"Olive!" cried her friend, "be still! Why, I can't *bear* it! why, you wretched thing!"

"I dare say all the ladies in Equity make up their own carpets, and put them down, and she thought you were laughing at her."

"*Will* you be still, Olive Halleck?" Miss Kingsbury was now a large blonde mass of suffering. "Oh, dear, dear! What shall I do? It was sacrilege—yes, it was nothing less than sacrilege—to go on as I did. And I meant so well; I did so admire, and respect, and revere her!" Olive burst out laughing. "You wicked girl!" whimpered Clara. "Should you—should you write to her?"

"And tell her you didn't mean her nose? Oh, by all means,

Clara,—by all means! Quite an inspiration. Why not make her an evening party?"

"Olive," said Clara, with guilty meekness, "I have been thinking of that."

"*No*, Clara! Not seriously!" cried Olive, sobered at the idea.

"Yes, seriously. Would it be so very bad? Only just a *little* party," she pleaded. "Half a dozen people or so; just to show them that I really feel—friendly. I know that he's told her all about meeting me here, and I'm not going to have her think I want to drop him because he's married, and lives in a little house on Clover street."

"Noble Clara! So you wish to bring them out in Boston society? What will you do with them after you've got them there?" Miss Kingsbury fidgeted in her chair a little. "Now look me in the eye, Clara! Whom were you going to ask to meet them? Your unfashionable friends, the Hallecks?"

"My friends, the Hallecks, of course."

"And Mr. Atherton, your legal adviser?"

"I had thought of asking Mr. Atherton. You needn't say what he is, if you please, Olive; you know that there's no one I prize so much."

"Very good. And Mr. Cameron?"

"He has got back,—yes. He's very nice."

"A Cambridge tutor; young and of recent attachment to the college, with no local affiliations, yet. What ladies?"

"Miss Strong is a nice girl; she is studying at the Conservatory."

"Yes. Poverty-stricken votary of Miss Kingsbury. Well?"

"Miss Clancy."

"Unfashionable elderly sister of fashionable artist. Yes?"

"The Brayhems."

"Young radical clergyman, and his wife, without a congregation, and hoping for a pulpit in Billerica. Parlor lectures on German literature in the meantime. Well?"

"And Mrs. Savage, I thought."

"Well-preserved young widow of uncertain antecedents

tending to grassiness; outdoor *protégée* of the hostess. Yes, Clara, go on and give your party. It will be *perfectly safe!* But do you think it will *deceive* anybody?"

"Now, Olive Halleck!" cried Clara, "I am not going to have you talking to me in that way! You have no right to do it, and you have no business to do it," she added, trying to pluck up a spirit. "Is there anybody that I value more than I do you and your sisters, and Ben?"

"No. But you don't value us *just in that way*, and you know it. Don't you be a humbug, Clara. Now go on with your excuses."

"I'm not making excuses! Isn't Mr. Atherton in the most fashionable society?"

"Yes. Why don't you ask some other fashionable people?"

"Olive, this is all nonsense,—perfect nonsense! I can invite any one I like to meet any one I like, and if I choose to show Mr. Hubbard's wife a little attention, I can do it, can't I?"

"Oh, of course!"

"And what would be the use of inviting fashionable people —as you call them—to meet them? It would just embarrass them all round."

"Perfectly correct, Miss Kingsbury. All that I want you to do is to face the facts of the case. I want you to realize that, in showing Mr. Hubbard's wife this little attention, you're not doing it because you scorn to drop an old friend, and want to do him the highest honor; but because you think you can palm off your second-class acquaintance on them for first-class, and try to make up in that way for telling her she had a hooked nose!"

"You *know* that I didn't tell her she had a hooked nose."

"You told her that she was a Roman matron,—it's the same thing," said Olive.

Miss Kingsbury bit her lip and tried to look a dignified resentment. She ended by saying, with feeble spite, "I shall have the little evening for all you say. I suppose you wont refuse to come because I don't ask the whole Blue Book to meet them."

"Of course we shall come! I wouldn't miss it for anything. I always like to see how you manage your pieces of social duplicity, Clara. But you needn't expect that I will be a party to the swindle. No, Clara! I shall go to these poor young people and tell them plainly, 'This is not the *best* society; Miss Kingsbury keeps that for' "—

"Olive! I think I never saw even you in such a teasing humor." The tears came into Clara's large, tender blue eyes, and she continued, with an appeal that had no effect, "I'm sure I don't see why you should make it a question of anything of the sort. It's simply a wish to—to have a little company of no particular kind, for no partic— Because I want to."

"Oh, that's it, is it? Then I highly approve of it," said Olive. "When is it to be?"

"I sha'n't tell you, now! You may wait till I'm ready," pouted Clara, as she rose to go.

"Don't go away thinking I'm enough to provoke a saint because *you've* got mad at me, Clara!"

"Mad? You know I'm not mad! But I think you might be a *little* sympathetic *some*times, Olive!" said her friend, kissing her.

"Not in cases of social duplicity, Clara. My wrath is all that saves you. If you were not afraid of me, you would have been a lost worldling long ago."

"I know you always really love me," said Miss Kingsbury, tenderly.

"No, I don't," retorted her friend, promptly. "Not when you're humbugging. Don't expect it, for you wont get it." She followed Clara with a triumphant laugh as she went out of the door; and except for this parting taunt, Clara might have given up her scheme. She first ordered her *coupé* driven home, in fact, and then lowered the window to countermand the direction, and drove to Bartley's door on Clover street.

It was a very handsome equipage, and was in keeping with all the outward belongings of Miss Kingsbury, who mingled a sense of duty and a love of luxury in her life in very exact proportions. When her *coupé* was not standing before some of the wretchedest doors in the city, it was waiting at the finest; and Clara's days were divided between the extremes of squalor and of fashion.

She was the only child of parents who had early left her an orphan. Her father, who was much her mother's senior, was an old friend of Olive's father, and had made him his executor and the guardian of his daughter. Mr. Halleck had taken her into his own family, and, in the conscientious pursuance of what he believed would have been her father's preference, he gave her worldly advantages which he would not have desired for one of his own children. But the friendship that grew up between Clara and Olive was too strong for him in some things, and the girls went to the same fashionable school together.

When his ward came of age, he made over to her the fortune, increased by his careful management, which her father had left her, and advised her to put her affairs in the hands of Mr. Atherton. She had shown a quite ungirlish eagerness to manage them for herself. In the midst of her profusion she had odd accesses of stinginess, in which she fancied herself coming to poverty; and her guardian judged it best that she should have a lawyer who could tell her at any moment just where she stood. She hesitated, but she did as he advised; and having once intrusted her property to Atherton's care, she added her conscience and her reason in large degree, and obeyed him with embarrassing promptness in matters that did not interfere with her pleasures. Her pleasures were of various kinds. She chose to buy herself a fine house, and, having furnished it luxuriously, and unearthed a cousin of her father's in Vermont and brought her to Boston to matronize her, she kept house on a magnificent scale, pinching, however, at certain points with unexpected meanness. When she was alone, her table was of a Spartan austerity; she exacted a great deal from her servants, and paid them as small wages as she could. After that, she did not mind lavishing money upon them in kindness. A seamstress whom she had once employed fell sick, and Miss

Kingsbury sent her to the Bahamas and kept her there till she was well, and then made her a guest in her house till the girl could get back her work. She watched her cook through the measles, caring for her like a mother; and, as Olive Halleck said, she was always portioning or burying the sisters of her second-girls. She was in all sorts of charities, but she was apt to cut her charities off with her pleasures at any moment, if she felt poor. She was fond of dress, and went a great deal into society: she suspected men generally of wishing to marry her for her money, but with those whom she did not think capable of aspiring to her hand, she was generously helpful with her riches. She liked to patronize; she had long supported an unpromising painter at Rome, and she gave orders to desperate artists at home.

The world had pretty well hardened one half of her heart, but the other half was still soft and loving, and into this side of her mixed nature she cowered when she believed she had committed some blunder or crime, and came whimpering to Olive Halleck for punishment. She made Olive her discipline partly in her lack of some fixed religion. She had not yet found a religion that exactly suited her, though she had many times believed herself about to be anchored in some faith forever.

She was almost sorry that she had put her resolution in effect when she rang at the door, and Marcia herself answered the bell, in place of the one servant, who was at that moment hanging out the wash. It seemed wicked to pretend to be showing this pretty creature a social attention, when she meant to palm off a hollow imitation of society upon her. Why should she not ask the very superfinest of her friends to meet such a brilliant beauty? It would serve Olive Halleck right if she should do this, and leave the Hallecks out, and Marcia would certainly be a sensation. She half-believed that she meant to do it when she quitted the house with Marcia's promise that she would bring her husband to tea on Wednesday evening, at eight; and she drove away so far penitent that she resolved at least to make her company distinguished, if not fashionable.

She said to herself that she would make it fashionable yet, if she chose, and as a first move in this direction she easily secured Mr. Atherton: he had no engagements, so few people had got back to town. She called upon Mrs. Witherby, needlessly reminding her of the charity committees they had served on together; and then she went home and actually sent out notes to the plainest daughter and the maiden aunt of two of the most high-born families of her acquaintance. She added to her list an artist and his wife ("Now I shall *have* to let him paint me!" she reflected), a young author whose book had made talk, a teacher of Italian, with whom she was pretending to read Dante, and a musical composer.

Olive came late, as if to get a whole effect of the affair at once; and her smile revealed Clara's failure to her, if she had not realized it before. She read there that the aristocratic and æsthetic additions which she had made to the guests Olive originally divined had not availed; the party remained a humbug. It had seemed absurd to invite anybody to meet two such little, unknown people as the Hubbards; and then, to avoid marking them as the subjects of the festivity by the precedence to be observed in going out to supper, she resolved to have tea served in the drawing-room, and to make it literally tea, with bread and butter, and some thin, ascetic cake.

However sharp he was in business, Mr. Witherby was socially a dull man; and his wife and daughter seemed to partake of his qualities by affinition and heredity. They tried to make something of Marcia, but they failed through their want of art. Mrs. Witherby, finding the wife of her husband's assistant in Miss Kingsbury's house, conceived an awe of her, which Marcia would not have known how to abate if she had imagined it; and in a little while the Witherby family segregated themselves among the photograph albums and the bric-a-brac, from which Clara seemed to herself to be fruitlessly detaching them the whole evening. The plainest daughter and the maiden aunt of the patrician families talked to each other with unavailing intervals of the painter and the author. The radical clergyman and his wife were in danger of a conjugal devotion which society does not favor; the unfashionable sister of the fashionable artist conversed with the young Harvard tutor and the Japanese law-student, whom he had asked leave to bring with him, and whose small, mouse-like eyes continually twinkled away in pursuit of the blonde beauty of his hostess. The widow was winningly attentive, with a tendency to be confidential, to everybody. The Italian could not disabuse himself of the notion that he was expected to be light and cheerful, and when the pupil of the Conservatory sang, he abandoned himself to his error, and clapped and cried bravo with unseemly vivacity. But he was restored to reason when the composer sat down at the piano and played, amid the hush that falls on society at such times, something from Beethoven, and again something of his own, which was so like Beethoven that Beethoven himself would not have known the difference.

Mr. Atherton and Halleck moved about among the sufferers, and did their best to second Clara's efforts for their relief; but it was useless. In the desperation which owns defeat, she resolved to devote herself for the rest of the evening to trying to make at least the Hubbards have a good time; and then, upon the dangerous theory, of which young and pretty hostesses cannot be too wary, that a wife is necessarily flattered by attentions to her husband, she devoted herself exclusively to Bartley, to whom she talked long and with a reckless liveliness of the events of his former stay in Boston. Their laughter and scraps of their reminiscences reached Marcia where she sat in a feint of listening to Ben Halleck's perfunctory account of his college days with her husband, till she could bear it no longer. She rose abruptly, and, going to him, she said that it was time to say good-night.

"Oh, so soon!" cried Clara, mystified and a little scared at the look she saw on Marcia's face. "Good-night," she added, coldly.

The assembly hailed this first token of its disintegration with relief; it became a little livelier; there was a fleeting moment in which it seemed as if it might yet enjoy itself; but its chance passed; it crumbled rapidly away, and Clara was left looking humbly into Olive Halleck's pitiless eyes.

"Thank you for a *delightful* evening, Miss Kingsbury! Congratulate you!" she mocked, with an unsparing laugh. "Such a success! But why didn't you give them something to eat, Clara? Those poor Hubbards have a one-o'clock dinner, and I famished for them. I wasn't hungry myself,—*we* have a two-o'clock dinner!"

XXII

BARTLEY came home elate from Miss Kingsbury's entertainment. It was something like the social success which he used to picture to himself. He had been flattered by the attention specially paid him, and he did not detect the imposition. He was half-starved, but he meant to have up some cold meat and bottled beer, and talk it all over with Marcia.

She did not seem inclined to talk it over on their way home, and when they entered their own door, she pushed in and ran upstairs.

"Why, where are you going, Marcia?" he called after her.

"To bed!" she replied, closing the door after her with a crash of unmistakable significance.

Bartley stood a moment in the fury that tempted him to pursue her with a taunt, and then leave her to work herself out of the transport of senseless jealousy she had wrought herself into. But he set his teeth, and, full of inward cursing, he followed her upstairs with a slow, dogged step. He took her in his arms without a word, and held her fast, while his anger changed to pity, and then to laughing. When it came to that, she put up her arms, which she had kept rigidly at her side, and laid them round his neck, and began softly to cry on his breast.

"Oh, I'm not myself at all, any more!" she moaned penitently.

"Then this is very improper—for me," said Bartley.

The helpless laughter broke through her lamentation, but

she cried a little more to keep herself in countenance.

"But I guess, from a previous acquaintance with the party's character, that it's really all you, Marcia. I don't blame you. Miss Kingsbury's hospitality has left me as hollow as if I'd had nothing to eat for a week; and I know you're perishing from inanition. Hence these tears."

It delighted her to have him make fun of Miss Kingsbury's tea, and she lifted her head to let him see that she was laughing for pleasure now, before she turned away to dry her eyes.

"Oh, poor fellow!" she cried, "I did pity you so when I saw those mean little slices of bread and butter coming round!"

"Yes," said Bartley, "I felt sorry myself. But don't speak of them any more, dearest."

"And I suppose," pursued Marcia, "that all the time she was talking to you there, you were simply ravening."

"I was casting lots in my own mind to see which of the company I should devour first."

His drollery appeared to Marcia the finest that ever was; she laughed and laughed again; when he made fun of the elderly aristocrat's conjecturable toughness, she implored him to stop if he did not want to kill her. Marcia was not in the state in which woman best convinces her enemies of her fitness for empire, but she was charming in her silly happiness, and Bartley felt very glad that he had not yielded to his first impulse to deal savagely with her.

"Come," he said, "let us go out somewhere, and get some oysters."

She began at once to take out her ear-rings and loosen her hair.

"No, I'll get something here in the house; I'm not very hungry. But *you* go, Bartley, and have a good supper, or you'll be sick to-morrow, and not fit to work. Go," she added to his hesitating image in the glass, "I insist upon it. I wont *have* you stay."

His reflected face approached from behind; she turned hers a little, and their mirrored lips met over her shoulder. "Oh, how *sweet* you are, Bartley!" she murmured.

"Yes, you will always find me obedient when commanded to go out and repair my wasted tissue."

"I don't mean *that*, dear," she said softly. "I mean—your not quarreling with me when I'm unreasonable. Why can't we always do so?"

"Well, you see," said Bartley, "it throws the whole burden on the fellow in his senses. It doesn't require any great degree of self-sacrifice to fly off at a tangent, but it's rather a maddening spectacle to the party that holds on."

"Now I will show you," said Marcia, "that I can be reasonable, too: I shall let you go alone to make our party call on Miss Kingsbury." She looked at him heroically.

"Marcia," said Bartley, "you're such a reasonable person when you're the most unreasonable, that I wonder I *ever* quarrel with you. I rather think I'll let *you* call on Miss Kingsbury alone. I shall suffer agonies of suspicion, but it will prove that I have perfect confidence in you." He threw her a kiss from the door, and ran down the stairs. When he returned, an hour later, he found her waiting up for him.

"Why, Marcia!" he exclaimed.

"Oh! I just wanted to say that we will both go to call on her *very soon*. If I sent you, she might think I was mad, and I wont give her that satisfaction."

"Noble girl!" cried Bartley, with irony that pleased her better than praise. Women like to be understood, even when they try not to be understood.

When Marcia went with Bartley to call, Miss Kingsbury received her with careful, perhaps anxious, politeness, but made no further effort to take her up. Some of the people whom Marcia met at Miss Kingsbury's called; and the Witherbys came, father, mother, and daughter together; but between the evident fact that the Hubbards were poor, and the other evident fact that they moved in the best society, the Witherbys did not quite know what to do about them. They asked them to dinner, and Bartley went alone; Marcia was not well enough to go.

He was very kind and tractable, now, and went whenever she bade him go without her, though tea at the Hallecks was getting to be an old story with him, and it was generally tea at the Hallecks to which she sent him. The Halleck ladies came faithfully to see her, and she got on very well with the two older sisters, who gave her all the kindness they could spare from their charities, and seemed pleased to have her so pretty and conjugal, though these things were far from them. But she was afraid of Olive at first, and disliked her as a friend of Miss Kingsbury. This rather attracted the odd girl. What she called Marcia's snubs enabled her to declare in her favor with a sense of disinterestedness, and to indulge her repugnance for Bartley with a good heart. She resented his odious good looks, and held it a shame that her mother should promote his visible tendency to stoutness by giving him such nice things for tea.

"Now, I like Mr. Hubbard," said her mother, placidly. "It's very kind of him to come to such plain folks as we are, whenever we ask him; now that his wife can't come, I know he does it because he likes us."

"Oh, he comes for the eating," said Olive, scornfully. Then another phase of her mother's remark struck her: "Why, mother!" she cried, "I do believe you think Bartley Hubbard's a distinguished man, somehow!"

"Your father says it's very unusual for such a young man to be in a place like his. Mr. Witherby really leaves everything to him, he says."

"Well, I think he'd better not, then! The Events has got to be perfectly horrid, of late. It's full of murders and all uncleanness."

"That seems to be the way with the papers, nowadays. Your father hears that the Events is making money."

"Why, mother! What a corrupt old thing you are! I believe you've been bought up by that disgusting interview with father. Nestor of the Leather Interest! Father ought to have turned him out of doors. Well, this family is getting a little *too* good, for me! And Ben's almost as bad as any of you, of late,—

I haven't a bit of influence with him any more. He seems determined to be friendlier with that *person* than ever; he's always trying to do him good,—I can see it, and it makes me sick. One thing I know: I'm going to stop Mr. Hubbard's calling me Olive. Impudent!"

Mrs. Halleck shifted her ground with the pretense which women use, even amongst themselves, of having remained steadfast.

"He is a very good husband."

"Oh, because he likes to be!" retorted her daughter. "Nothing is easier than to be a good husband."

"Ah, my dear," said Mrs. Halleck, "wait till you have tried."

This made Olive laugh; but she answered with an argument that always had weight with her mother:

"Ben doesn't think he's a good husband."

"What makes you think so, Olive?" asked her mother.

"I know he dislikes him intensely."

"Why, you just said yourself, dear, that he was friendlier with him than ever."

"Oh, that's nothing. The more he disliked him, the kinder he would be to him."

"That's true," sighed her mother. "Did he ever say anything to you about him?"

"No," cried Olive shortly; "he never speaks of people he doesn't like."

The mother returned, with logical severity, "All that doesn't prove that Ben thinks he isn't a good husband."

"He dislikes him. Do you believe a bad man can be a good husband, then?"

"No," Mrs. Halleck admitted, as if confronted with indisputable proof of Bartley's wickedness.

In the meantime the peace between Bartley and Marcia continued unbroken, and these days of waiting, of suffering, of hoping and dreading, were the happiest of their lives. He did his best to be patient with her caprices and fretfulness, and he was at least manfully comforting and helpful, and instant in atonement for every failure. She said a thousand times that she should die without him; and when her time came, he thought that she was going to die before he could tell her of his sorrow for all that he had ever done to grieve her. He did not tell her, though she lived to give him the chance; but he took her and her baby both into his arms, with tears of as much fondness as ever a man shed. He even began his confession; but she said, "Hush! you never did a wrong thing yet that I didn't drive you to." Pale and faint, she smiled joyfully upon him, and put her hand on his head when he hid his face against hers on the pillow, and put her lips against his cheeks. His heart was full; he was grateful for the mercy that had spared him; he was so strong in his silent repentance that he felt like a good man.

"Bartley," she said, "I'm going to ask a great favor of you."

"There's nothing that I can do that *I* shall think a favor, darling!" he cried, lifting his face to look into hers.

"Write for mother to come. I want her!"

"Why, of course."

Marcia continued to look at him, and kept the quivering hold she had laid of his hand when he raised his head.

"Was that all?"

She was silent, and he added,

"I will ask your father to come with her."

She hid her face for the space of one sob.

"I wanted you to offer."

"Why, of course! of course!" he replied.

She did not acknowledge his magnanimity directly, but she lifted the coverlet and showed him the little head on her arm, and the little creased and crumpled face.

"Pretty?" she asked. "Bring me the letter before you send it."

"Yes, that is just right,—perfect!" she sighed, when he came back and read the letter to her, and she fell away to happy sleep.

Her father answered that he would come with her mother

as soon as he got the better of a cold he had taken. It was now well into the winter, and the journey must have seemed more formidable in Equity than in Boston. But Bartley was not impatient of his father-in-law's delay, and he set himself cheerfully about consoling Marcia for it. She stole her white, thin hand into his, and now and then gave it a little pressure to accent the points she made in talking.

"Father was the first one I thought of—after you, Bartley. It seems to me as if baby came half to show me how unfeeling I had been to him. Of course I'm not sorry I ran away and asked you to take me back, for I couldn't have had you if I hadn't done it; but I never realized before how cruel it was to father. He always made such a pet of me; and I know that he thought he was acting for the best."

"I knew that *you* were," said Bartley, fervently.

"What sweet things you always say to me!" she murmured. "But don't you see, Bartley, that I didn't think enough of him? That's what baby seems to have come to teach me." She pulled a little away on the pillow, so as to fix him more earnestly with her eyes. "If baby should behave so to *you* when she grew up, I should hate her."

He laughed, and said,

"Well, perhaps your mother hates you."

"No, they don't—either of them," said Marcia with a sigh. "And I behaved very stiffly and coldly with him when he came up to see me,—more than I had any need to. I did it for your sake; but he didn't mean any harm to you,—he just wanted to make sure that I was safe and well."

"Oh, that's all right, Marsh."

"Yes, I know. But what if he had died!"

"Well, he didn't die," said Bartley, with a smile. "And you've corresponded with them regularly, ever since, and you know they've been getting along all right. And it's going to be altogether different from this out," he added, leaning back, a little weary with a matter in which he could not be expected to take a very cordial interest.

"Truly?" she asked, with one of the eagerest of those hand-pressures.

"It wont be my fault if it isn't," he replied, with a yawn.

"How good you are, Bartley!" she said, with an admiring look, as if it was the goodness of God she was praising.

Bartley released himself, and went to the new crib, in which the baby lay, and with his hands in his pockets stood looking down at it with a curious smile.

"Is it pretty?" she asked, envious of his bird's-eye view of the baby.

"Not definitively so," he answered. "I dare say she will smooth out in time; but she seems to be considerably puckered yet."

"Well," returned Marcia, with forced resignation, "I shouldn't let any one else say so."

Her husband set up a soft, low, thoughtful whistle.

"I'll tell you what, Marcia," he said, presently. "Suppose we name this baby after your father?"

She lifted herself on her elbow, and stared at him as if he must be making fun of her.

"Why, how could we?" she demanded. Squire Gaylord's parents had called his name Flavius Josephus, in a superstition once cherished by old-fashioned people, that the Jewish historian was somehow a sacred writer.

"We can't name her Josephus, but we can call her Flavia," said Bartley. "And if she makes up her mind to turn out a blonde, the name will just fit. Flavia,—it's a very pretty name." He looked at his wife, who suddenly turned her face down on the pillow.

"Bartley Hubbard," she cried, "you're the best man in the world!"

"Oh, no! Only the second-best," suggested Bartley.

In these days they took their fill of the delight of young fatherhood and motherhood. After its morning bath Bartley was called in, and allowed to revere the baby's mottled and dimpled back as it lay face downward on the nurse's lap, feebly wiggling its arms and legs, and responding with ineffectual little sighs and gurgles to her acceptable rubbings with warm flannel. When it was fully dressed, and its long clothes pulled snugly down, and its limp person stiffened into something tenable, he was suffered to take it into his arms, and to walk the room with it. After all, there is not much that a man can actually do with a small baby, either for its pleasure or his own, and Bartley's usefulness had its strict limitations. He was perhaps most beneficial when he put the child in its mother's arms, and sat down beside the bed, and quietly talked, while Marcia occasionally put up a slender hand and smoothed its golden-brown hair, bending her neck over to look at it where it lay, with the action of a mother bird. They examined with minute interest the details of the curious little creature: its tiny finger-nails, fine and sharp, and its small queer fist doubled so tight, and closing on one's finger like a canary's claw on a perch; the absurdity of its foot, the absurdity of its toes, the ridiculous inadequacy of its legs and arms to the work ordinarily expected of legs and arms, made them laugh. They could not tell yet whether its eyes would be black, like Marcia's, or blue, like Bartley's; those long lashes had the sweep of hers, but its mop of hair, which made it look so odd and old, was more like his in color.

"She will be a dark-eyed blonde," Bartley decided.

"Is that nice?" asked Marcia.

"With the telescope sight, they're warranted to kill at five hundred yards."

"Oh, for shame, Bartley! To talk of baby's ever killing!"

"Why, that's what they all come to. It's what you came to yourself."

"Yes, I know. But it's quite another thing with baby." She began to mumble it with her lips, and to talk baby-talk to it. In their common interest in this puppet they already called each other papa and mamma.

Squire Gaylord came alone, and when Marcia greeted him with "Why, father! Where's mother?" he asked, "Did you expect her? Well, I guess your mother's feeling rather too old for such long winter journeys. You know she don't go out a great deal. *I* guess she expects your family down there in the summer."

The old man was considerably abashed by the baby when it was put into his arms, and being required to guess its name, he naturally failed.

"Flavia!" cried Marcia, joyfully. "Bartley named it after you."

This embarrassed the Squire still more.

"Is that so?" he asked, rather sheepishly. "Well, it's quite a compliment."

Marcia repeated this to her husband as evidence that her father was all right now. Bartley and the Squire were in fact very civil to each other; and Bartley paid the old man many marked attentions. He took him to the top of the State House, and walked him all about the city, to show him its points of interest, and introduced him to such of his friends as they met, though the Squire's dress-coat, whether fully revealed by the removal of his surtout, or betraying itself below the skirt of the latter, was a trial to a fellow of Bartley's style. He went with his father-in-law to see Mr. Warren in "Jefferson Scattering Batkins," and the Squire grimly appreciated the burlesque of the member from Cranberry Center; but he was otherwise not a very amusable person, and off his own ground he was not conversable; while he refused to betray his impressions of many things that Bartley expected to astonish him. The Events editorial rooms had no apparent effect upon him, though they were as different from most editorial dens as tapestry carpets, black-walnut desks, and swivel chairs could make them. Mr. Witherby covered him with urbanities and praises of Bartley that ought to have delighted him as a father-in-law; but apparently the great man of the Events was but a strange variety of the type with which he was familiar in the despised country editors. He got on better with Mr. Atherton, who was of a man's profession. The Squire wore his hat throughout their interview, and everywhere except at table and in bed; and as soon as he rose from either, he put it on.

Bartley tried to impress him with such novel traits of cosmopolitan life as a *table d'hôte* dinner at a French restaurant; but the Squire sat through the courses as if his barbarous old appetite had satisfied itself in that manner all his life. After that, Bartley practically gave him up; he pleaded his newspaper work, and left the Squire to pass the time as he could in the little house on Clover street, where he sat half a day at a stretch in the parlor with his hat on, reading the newspapers, his legs sprawled out toward the grate. In this way he probably reconstructed for himself some image of his wonted life in his office at home, and was for the time at peace; but otherwise he was very restless, except when he was with Marcia. He was as fond of her in his way as he had ever been, and though he apparently cared nothing for the baby, he enjoyed Marcia's pride in it; and he bore to have it thrust upon him with the surly mildness of an old dog receiving children's caresses. He listened with the same patience to all her celebrations of Bartley, which were often tedious enough, for she bragged of him constantly, of his smartness and goodness, and of the great success that had crowned the merit of both in him.

Mr. Halleck had called upon the Squire the morning after his arrival, and brought Marcia a note from his wife, offering to have her father stay with them if she found herself too much crowded at this eventful time.

"There! That is just the sort of people the Hallecks are!" she cried, showing the letter to her father. "And to think of our not going near them for months and months after we came to Boston, for fear they were stuck up! But Bartley is always just so proud. Now you must go right in, father, and not keep Mr. Halleck waiting. Give me your hat, or you'll be sure to wear it in the parlor." She made him stoop down to let her brush his coat-collar a little. "There! Now you look something like."

Squire Gaylord had never received a visit except on business in his life, and such a thing as one man calling socially upon another, as women did, was unknown to the civilization of Equity. But, as he reported to Marcia, he got along with Mr. Halleck; and he got along with the whole family when he went with Bartley to tea, upon the invitation Mr. Halleck made him that morning. Probably it appeared to him an objectless hospitality; but he spent as pleasant an evening as he could hope to spend with his hat off and in a frock-coat, which he wore as a more ceremonious garment than the dress-coat of his every-day life. He seemed to take a special liking to Olive Halleck, whose habit of speaking her mind with vigor and directness struck him as commendable. It was Olive who made the time pass for him; and as the occasion was not one for personal sarcasm or question of the Christian religion, her task in keeping the old pagan out of rather abysmal silences must have had its difficulties.

"What did you talk about?" asked Marcia, requiring an account of his enjoyment from him the next morning, after Bartley had gone down to his work.

"Mostly about you, I guess," said the Squire, with a laugh. "There was a large, sandy-haired young woman there"—

"Miss Kingsbury," said Marcia, with vindictive promptness. Her eyes kindled, and she began to grow rigid under the coverlet. "Whom did *she* talk with?"

"Well, she talked a little with me; but she talked most of the time to the young man. She engaged to him?"

"No," said Marcia, relaxing. "She's a great friend of the whole family. I don't know what they meant by telling you it was to be just a family party, when they were going to have strangers in," she pouted.

"Perhaps they didn't count her."

"No."

But Marcia's pleasure in the affair was tainted, and she began to talk of other things.

Her father staid nearly a week, and they all found it rather a long week. After showing him her baby, and satisfying herself that he and Bartley were on good terms again, there was not much left for Marcia. Bartley had been banished to the spare room by the presence of the nurse; and he gave up his bed there to the Squire, and slept on a cot in the unfurnished attic room; the cook, and a small girl got in to help, had the other. The house that had once seemed so vast was full to bursting.

"I never knew how little it was till I saw your father coming down-stairs," said Bartley. "He's too tall for it. When he sits on the sofa, and stretches out his legs, his boots touch the mop-board on the other side of the room. Fact!"

"He wont stay over Sunday," began Marcia, with a rueful smile.

"Why, Marcia, you don't think I want him to go!"

"No; you're as good as can be about it. But I hope he wont stay over Sunday."

"Haven't you enjoyed his visit?" asked Bartley.

"Oh, yes, I've enjoyed it." The tears came into her eyes. "I've made it all up with father; and he doesn't feel hard to me. But, Bartley— Sit down, dear, here on the bed." She took his hand and gently pulled him down. "I see more and more that father and mother can never be what they used to be to me,— that you're all the world to me. Yes, my life is broken off from theirs forever. Could anything break it off from yours? You'll always be patient with me, wont you? And remember that I'd always rather be good when I'm behaving the worst?"

He rose, and went over to the crib, and kissed the head of their little girl.

"Ask Flavia," he said, from the door.

"Bartley!" she cried, in utter fondness, as he vanished from her happy eyes.

The next morning they heard the Squire moving about in his room, and he was late in coming down to breakfast, at which he was ordinarily so prompt.

"He's packing," said Marcia, sadly. "It's dreadful to be willing to have him go."

Bartley went out and met him at his door, bag in hand.

"Hollo!" he cried, and made a decent show of surprise and regret.

"Myes!" said the old man, as they went down-stairs. "I've made out a visit. But I'm an old fellow, and I aint easy away from home. I shall tell Mis' Gaylord how you're gettin' along, and she'll be pleased to hear it. Yes, she'll be pleased to hear it. I guess I shall get off on the ten-o'clock train."

The conversation between Bartley and his father-in-law was perfunctory. Men who have dealt so plainly with each other do not assume the conventional urbanities in their intercourse without effort. They had both been growing more impatient of the restraint; they could not have kept it up much longer.

"Well, I suppose it's natural you should want to be home again, but I can't understand how any one can want to go back to Equity when he has the privilege of staying in Boston."

"Boston will do for a young man," said the Squire, "but I'm too old for it. The city cramps me: it's too tight a fit; and yet I can't seem to find myself in it."

He suffered from the loss of identity which is a common affliction with country people coming to town. The feeling that they are of no special interest to any of the thousands they meet bewilders and harasses them; after the searching neighborhood of village life, the fact that nobody would meddle in their most intimate affairs if they could, is a vague distress. The Squire not only experienced this, but, after reigning so long as the censor of morals and religion in Equity, it was a deprivation for him to pass a whole week without saying a bitter thing to any one. He was tired of the civilities that smoothed him down on every side.

"Well, if you must go," said Bartley, "I'll order a hack."

"I guess I can walk to the depot," returned the old man.

"Oh, no, you can't."

Bartley drove to the station with him, and they bade each other adieu with a hand-shake. They were no longer enemies, but they liked each other less than ever.

"See you in Equity next summer, I suppose," suggested the Squire.

"So Marcia says," replied Bartley. "Well, take care of yourself.—You confounded tight-fisted old woodchuck!" he added, under his breath, for the Squire had allowed him to pay the hack-fare.

He walked home, composing variations on his parting malison, to find that the Squire had profited by his brief absence in ordering the hack to leave with Marcia a silver cup, knife, fork, and spoon, which Olive Halleck had helped him choose, for the baby. In the cup was a check for five hundred dollars. The Squire was embarrassed in presenting the gifts, and when Marcia turned upon him with: "Now, look here, father, what do you mean?" he was at a loss how to explain.

"Well, it's what I always meant to do for you."

"Baby's things are all right," said Marcia. "But I'm not going to let Bartley take any money from you unless you think as well of him as I do, and say so, right out."

The Squire laughed.

"You couldn't quite expect me to do that, could you?"

"No, of course not. But what I mean is, do you think *now* that I did right to marry him?"

"Oh, *you're* all right, Marcia. I'm glad you're getting along so well."

"No, no! Is Bartley all right?"

The Squire laughed again, and rubbed his chin in enjoyment of her persistence.

"You can't expect me to own up to everything all at once."

"So you see, Bartley," said Marcia, in repeating these words to him, "it was quite a concession."

"Well, I don't know about the concession, but I guess there's no doubt about the check," replied Bartley, jocosely.

"Oh, don't say that, dear," protested his wife. "I think father was pleased with his visit every way. I know he's been anxious about me all the time; and yet it was a good deal for him to do, after what he had said, to come down here and as much as take it all back. Can't you look at it from his side?"

"Oh, I dare say it was a dose," Bartley admitted. The money had set several things in a better light. "If all the people that have abused me would take it back as handsomely as your father has,"—he held the check up,—"why, I wish there were twice as many of them."

She laughed for pleasure in his joke.

"I think father was impressed by everything about us,—beginning with baby," she said, proudly.

"Well, he kept his impressions to himself," said Bartley.

"Oh, that's nothing but his way. He never was demonstrative,—like me."

"No, he has his emotions under control—not to say under lock and key—not to add, in irons."

Bartley went on to give some instances of the Squire's fortitude when apparently tempted to express pleasure or interest in his Boston experiences.

They both undeniably felt freer now that he was gone. Bartley staid longer than he ought from his work, in tacit celebration of the Squire's departure, and they were very merry together; but, when he left her, Marcia called for her baby, and, gathering it close to her heart, sighed over it, "Poor father! poor father!"

XXIII

WHEN the spring opened, Bartley pushed Flavia about the sunny pavements in a baby-carriage, while Marcia paced alongside, looking in under the calash top from time to time, arranging the bright afghan, and twitching the little one's lace hood into place. They never noticed that other perambulators were pushed by Irish nurse-girls, or French *bonnes*; they had paid somewhat more than they ought for theirs, and they were proud of it merely as a piece of property. It was rather Bartley's ideal, as it is that of most young American fathers, to go out with his wife and baby in that way; he liked to have his friends see him; and he went out every afternoon he could spare. When he could not go, Marcia went alone. Mrs. Halleck had given her a key to the garden, and on pleasant mornings she always found some of the family there, when she pushed the perambulator up the path, to let the baby sleep in the warmth and silence of the sheltered place. She chatted with Olive or the elder sisters, while Mrs. Halleck drove Cyrus on to the work of tying up the vines and trimming the shrubs, with the pitiless rigor of women when they get a man about some outdoor labor. Sometimes, Ben Halleck was briefly of the party; and one morning when Marcia opened the gate, she found him there alone with Cyrus, who was busy at some belated tasks of horticulture. The young man turned at the unlocking of the gate, and saw Marcia lifting the front wheels of the perambulator to get it over the steps of the pavement outside. He limped hastily down the walk to help her, but she had the carriage in the path before he could reach her, and he had nothing to do but to walk back at its side, as she propelled it toward the house. "You see what a useless creature a cripple is," he said.

Marcia did not seem to have heard him. "Is your mother at home?" she asked.

"I think she is," said Halleck. "Cyrus, go in and tell mother that Mrs. Hubbard is here, wont you?"

Cyrus went, after a moment of self-respectful delay, and Marcia sat down on a bench under a pear-tree beside the walk. Its narrow young leaves and blossoms sprinkled her with shade shot with vivid sunshine, and in her light dress, she looked like a bright, fresh figure from some painter's study of spring. She breathed quickly from her exertion, and her cheeks had a rich, dewy bloom. She had pulled the perambulator round so that she might see her baby while she waited, and she looked at the baby now, and not at Halleck, as she said:

"It is quite hot in the sun to-day."

She had a way of closing her lips, after speaking, in that sweet smile of hers, and then of glancing sidelong at the person to whom she spoke.

"I suppose it is," said Halleck, who remained on foot. "But I haven't been out yet. I gave myself a day off from the law-school, and I hadn't quite decided what to do with it."

Marcia leaned forward, and brushed a tendril of the baby's hair out of its eye.

"She's the greatest little sleeper that ever was when she gets into her carriage," she half mused, leaning back with her hands folded in her lap, and setting her head on one side for the effect of the baby without the stray ringlet. "She's getting so fat," she said, proudly.

Halleck smiled.

"Do you find it makes a difference in pushing her carriage, from day to day?"

Marcia took his question in earnest, as she must take anything but the most obvious pleasantry concerning her baby.

"The carriage runs very easily; we picked out the lightest one we could, and I never have any trouble with it, except getting up curb-stones and crossing Cambridge street. I don't like to cross Cambridge street; there are always so many horse-cars. But it's all down-hill coming here; that's one good thing."

"That makes it a very bad thing going home, though," said Halleck.

"Oh, I go round by Charles street and come up the hill from the other side; it isn't so steep there."

There was no more to be said upon this point, and in the lapse of their talk, Halleck broke off some boughs of the blooming pear, and dropped them on the baby's afghan.

"Your mother wont like your spoiling her pear-tree," said Marcia, seriously.

"She will when she knows that I did it for Miss Hubbard."

"Miss Hubbard!" repeated the young mother, and she laughed in fond derision. "How funny to hear *you* saying that! I thought you hated babies."

Halleck looked at her with strong self-disgust, and he dropped the bough which he had in his hand upon the ground. There is something in a young man's ideal of women, at once passionate and ascetic, so fine that any words are too gross for it. The event which intensified the interest of his mother and sisters in Marcia, had abashed Halleck; when she came so proudly to show her baby to them all, it seemed to him like a mockery of his pity for her captivity to the love that profaned her. He went out of the room in angry impatience, which he could hardly hide when one of his sisters tried to make him take the baby. Little by little his compassion adjusted itself to the new conditions; it accepted the child as an element of her misery in the future, when she must realize the hideous deformity of her marriage. His prophetic sense of this, and of her inaccessibility to human help here and hereafter, made him sometimes afraid of her; but all the more severely he exacted of his ideal of her that she should not fall beneath the tragic dignity of her fate through any levity of her own. Now, at her innocent laugh, a subtle irreverence, which he was not able to exorcise, infused itself into his sense of her.

He stood looking at her, after he dropped the pear-bough, and seeing her mere beauty as he had never seen it before. The bees hummed in the blossoms, which gave out a dull, sweet smell; the sunshine had the luxurious, enervating warmth of spring. He started suddenly from his revery: Marcia had said something.

"I beg your pardon?" he queried.

"Oh, nothing. I asked if you knew where I went to church yesterday?"

Halleck flushed, ashamed of the wrong his thoughts, or rather his emotions, had done.

"No, I don't," he answered.

"I was at your church."

"I ought to have been there myself," he returned, gravely, "and then I should have known."

She took his self-reproach literally.

"You couldn't have seen me. I was sitting pretty far back, and I went out before any of your family saw me. Don't you go there?"

"Not always, I'm sorry to say. Or, rather, I'm sorry not to be sorry. What church do you generally go to?"

"Oh, I don't know. Sometimes to one, and sometimes to another. Bartley used to report the sermons and we went round to all the churches then. That is the way I did at home, and it came natural to me. But I don't like it very well. I want Flavia should belong to some particular church."

"There are enough to choose from," said Halleck, with pensive sarcasm.

"Yes, that's the difficulty. But I shall make up my mind to one of them, and then I shall always keep to it. What I mean is that I should like to find out where most of the good people belong, and then have her be with them," pursued Marcia. "I think it's best to belong to some church, don't you?"

There was something so bare, so spiritually poverty-stricken in these confessions and questions, that Halleck found nothing to say to them.

He was troubled, moreover, as to what the truth was in his own mind. He answered, with a sort of mechanical adhesion to the teachings of his youth: "I should be a recreant not to think so. But I'm not sure that I know what you mean by belonging to some church," he added. "I suppose you would want to believe in the creed of the church, whichever it was."

"I don't know that I should be particular," said Marcia, with perfect honesty.

Halleck laughed sadly.

"I'm afraid *they* would, then, unless you joined the Broad Church."

"What is that?"

He explained as well as he could. At the end she repeated, as if she had not followed him very closely:

"I should like her to belong to the church where most of the good people go. I think that would be the right one, if you could only find which it is."

Halleck laughed again.

"I suppose what I say must sound very queer to you; but I've been thinking a good deal about this lately."

"I beg your pardon," said Halleck. "I had no reason to laugh, either on your account or my own. It's a serious subject."

She did not reply, and he asked, as if she had left the subject:

"Do you intend to pass the summer in Boston?"

"No; I'm going down home pretty early, and I wanted to ask your mother what is the best way to put away my winter things."

"You'll find my mother very good authority on such matters," said Halleck. Through an obscure association with moths that corrupt, he added: "She's a good authority on church matters, too."

"I guess I shall talk with her about Flavia," said Marcia.

Cyrus came out of the house.

"Mis' Halleck will be here in a minute. She's got to get red of a lady that's calling, first," he explained.

"I will leave you, then," said Halleck, abruptly.

"Good-by," answered Marcia, tranquilly. The baby stirred; she pushed the carriage to and fro, without glancing after him as he walked away.

His mother came down the steps from the house, and kissed Marcia for welcome, and looked under the carriage-top at the sleeping baby.

"How she *does* sleep!" she whispered.

"Yes," said Marcia, with the proud humility of a mother who cannot deny the merit of her child, "and she sleeps the whole night through. I'm *never* up with her. Bartley says she's a perfect Seven Sleeper. It's a regular joke with him—her sleeping."

"Ben was a good baby for sleeping, too," said Mrs. Halleck, retrospectively emulous. "It's one of the best signs. It shows that the child is strong and healthy."

They went on to talk of their children, and in their community of motherhood, they spoke of the young man as if he were still an infant.

"He has never been a moment's care to me," said Mrs. Halleck. "A well baby will be well even in teething."

"And I had somehow thought of him as sickly!" said Marcia, in self-derision.

Tears of instant intelligence sprang into his mother's eyes.

"And did you suppose he was *always* lame?" she demanded with gentle indignation. "He was the brightest and strongest boy that ever was, till he was twelve years old. That's what makes it so hard to bear; that's what makes me wonder at the way the child bears it! Did you never hear how it happened? One of the big boys, as he called him, tripped him up at school, and he fell on his hip. It kept him in bed for a year, and he's never been the same since; he will always be a cripple," grieved the mother. She wiped her eyes; she never could think of her boy's infirmity without weeping. "And what seemed the worst of all," she continued, "was that the boy who did it, never expressed any regret for it, or acknowledged it by word or deed, though he must have known that Ben knew who hurt him. He's a man, here, now; and sometimes Ben meets him. But Ben always says that he can stand it if the other one can. He was always just so from the first! He wouldn't let us blame the boy; he said that he didn't mean any harm, and that all was fair in play. And now he says he knows the man is sorry, and would own to what he did, if he didn't have to own to what came of it. Ben says that very few of us have the courage to face the consequences of the injuries we do, and that's what makes people seem hard and indifferent when they are really not so. There!" cried Mrs. Halleck. "I don't know as I ought to have told you about it; I know Ben wouldn't like it. But I can't bear to have any one think he was always lame, though I don't know why I shouldn't: I'm prouder of him since it happened than ever I was before. I thought he was here with you," she added abruptly.

"He went out just before you came," said Marcia, nodding toward the gate. She sat listening to Mrs. Halleck's talk about Ben; Mrs. Halleck took herself to task from time to time, but only to go on talking about him again. Sometimes Marcia commented on his characteristics, and compared them with Bartley's, or with Flavia's, according to the period of Ben's life under consideration. At the end Mrs. Halleck said: "I haven't let you get in a word! Now you must talk about *your* baby. Dear little thing! I feel that she's been neglected. But I'm always just so selfish when I get to running on about Ben. They all laugh at me."

"Oh, I like to hear about other children," said Marcia, turning the perambulator round. "I don't think any one can know too much that has the care of children of their own." She added, as if it followed from something they had been saying of vaccination: "Mrs. Halleck, I want to talk with you about getting Flavia christened. You know I never was christened."

"Weren't you?" said Mrs. Halleck, with a dismay which she struggled to conceal.

"No," said Marcia, "father doesn't believe in any of those things, and mother had got to letting them go, because he didn't take any interest in them. They did have the first children christened, but I was the last."

"I didn't speak with your father on the subject," faltered Mrs. Halleck. "I didn't know what his persuasion was."

"Why, father doesn't belong to *any* church! He believes in a God, but he doesn't believe in the Bible." Mrs. Halleck sank down on the garden-seat too much shocked to speak, and Marcia continued: "I don't know whether the Bible is true or not; but I've often wished that I belonged to church."

"You couldn't, unless you believed in the Bible," said Mrs. Halleck.

"Yes, I know that. Perhaps I should, if anybody proved it to me. I presume it could be explained. I never talked much with any one about it. There must be a good many people who don't belong to church, although they believe in the Bible. I should be perfectly willing to try, if I only knew how to begin."

In view of this ruinous open-mindedness, Mrs. Halleck could only say,

"The way to begin is to read it."

"Well, I will try. How do you know, after you've become so that you believe the Bible, whether you're fit to join the church?"

"It's hard to tell you, my dear. You have to feel first that you have a Saviour,—that you've given your whole heart to him,—that he can save you, and that no one else can; that all you can do yourself wont help you. It's an experience."

Marcia looked at her attentively, as if this were all a very hard saying.

"Yes, I've heard of that. Some of the girls had it at school. But I never did. Well," she said at last, "I don't feel so anxious about myself, just at present, as I do about Flavia. I want to do everything I can for Flavia, Mrs. Halleck. I want her to be christened,—I want her to be baptized into some church. I think a good deal about it. I think sometimes, what if she should die, and I hadn't done that for her, when may be it was one of the most important things"—Her voice shook, and she pressed her lips together.

"Of course," said Mrs. Halleck, tenderly. "I think it is the *most* important thing."

"But there are so many churches," Marcia resumed. "And I don't know about any of them. I told Mr. Halleck, just now, that I should like her to belong to the church where the best people go, if I could find it out. Of course, it was a ridiculous way to talk; I knew he thought so. But what I meant was that I wanted she should be with good people all her life; and I didn't care what she believed."

"It's very important to believe the truth, my dear," said Mrs. Halleck.

"But the truth is so hard to be certain of, and you know goodness as soon as you see it. Mrs. Halleck, I'll tell you what I want: I want Flavia should be baptized into your church. Will you let her?"

"*Let* her? Oh, my dear child, we shall be humbly thankful that it has been put into your heart to choose for her what *we* think is the true church," said Mrs. Halleck, fervently.

"I don't know about that," returned Marcia. "I can't tell whether it's the true church or not, and I don't know that I ever could; but I shall be satisfied, if it's made you what you are," she added simply.

Mrs. Halleck did not try to turn away her praise with vain affectations of humility. "We try to do right, Marcia," she said. "Whenever we do it, we must be helped to it by some power outside of ourselves. I can't tell you whether it's our church; I'm not so sure of that as I used to be. I once thought that there could be no real good out of it; but I *can't* think that, any more: Olive and Ben are as good children as ever lived; I *know* they wont be lost; but neither of them belongs to our church."

"Why, what church does he belong to?"

"He doesn't belong to any, my dear," said Mrs. Halleck, sorrowfully.

Marcia looked at her absently.

"I knew Olive was a Unitarian; but I thought—I thought he"—

"No, he doesn't," returned Mrs. Halleck. "It has been a great cross to his father and me. He is a good boy; but we think the *truth* is in our church!"

Marcia was silent a moment. Then she said, decisively:

"Well, I should like Flavia to belong to your church."

"She couldn't belong to it now," Mrs. Halleck explained. "That would have to come later, when she could understand. But she could be christened in it—dear little thing!"

"Well, christened, then. It must be the training he got in it. I've thought a great deal about it, and I think my worst trouble is that I've been left too free in everything. One mustn't be left too free. I've never had any one to control me, and now I can't control myself at the very times when I need to do it the most, with—with—when I'm in danger of vexing—when Bartley and I"—

"Yes," said Mrs. Halleck, sympathetically.

"And Bartley is just so, too. He's always been left to himself. And Flavia will need all the control we can give her—I know she will. And I shall have her christened in your church, and I shall teach her all about it. She shall go to the Sunday-school, and I will go to church, so that she can have an example. I told father I should do it when he was up here, and he said there couldn't be any harm in it. And I've told Bartley, and *he* doesn't care."

They were both far too single-minded and too serious to find anything droll in the terms of the adhesion of Marcia's family to her plan, and Mrs. Halleck entered into its execution with affectionate zeal.

"Ben, dear," she said, tenderly, that evening, when they were all talking it over in family council, "I hope you didn't drop anything, when that poor creature spoke to you about it this morning, that could unsettle her mind in any way?"

"No, mother," said Halleck, gently.

"I was sure you didn't," returned his mother, repentantly.

They had been talking a long time of the matter, and Halleck now left the room.

"Mother! How could you say such a thing to Ben?" cried Olive, in a quiver of indignant sympathy. "Ben say anything to unsettle anybody's religious purposes! He's got more religion now than all the rest of the family put together!"

"Speak for yourself, Olive," said one of the intermediary sisters.

"Why, Olive, I spoke because I thought she seemed to place more importance on Ben's belonging to the church than anything else, and she seemed so surprised when I told her he didn't belong to any."

"I dare say she thinks Ben is good when she compares him with that mass of selfishness of a husband of hers," said Olive. "But I will thank her," she added, hotly, "not to compare Ben with Bartley Hubbard, even to Bartley Hubbard's disadvantage. I don't feel flattered by it."

"Of course, she thinks all the world of her husband," said Mrs. Halleck. "And I know Ben is good; and as you say, he is religious; I feel that, though I don't understand how, exactly. I wouldn't hurt his feelings for the world, Olive, you know well enough. But it was a stumbling-block when I had to tell that poor, pretty young thing that Ben didn't belong to church; and I could see that it puzzled her. I couldn't have believed," continued Mrs. Halleck, "that there was any person in a Christian land, except among the very lowest, that seemed to understand so little about the Christian religion, or any scheme of salvation. Really, she talked to me like a pagan. She sat there much better dressed and better educated than I was; but I felt like a missionary talking to a South Sea Islander."

"I wonder the old Bartlett pear didn't burst into a palm-tree over your heads," said Olive. Mrs. Halleck looked grieved at her levity, and she hastened to add:

"Don't put up your lip, mother. I understood just what you meant, and I can imagine just how shocking Mrs. Hubbard's heathen remarks must have been. We should all be shocked if we knew how many people there are just like her, and we should all try to deny it, and so would they. I guess Christianity is about as uncommon as civilization—and that's *very* uncommon. If her poor, feeble mind was such a chaos, what do you suppose her husband's is?"

This would certainly not have been easy for Mrs. Halleck to say, then, or to say afterward, when Bartley walked up to the font in her church, with Marcia at his side, and Flavia in his arms, and a faintly ironical smile on his face, as if he had never expected to be got in for this, but was going to see it through now. He had, in fact, said, "Well, let's go the whole figure," when Marcia had expressed a preference for having the rite performed in church, instead of in their own house.

He was unquestionably growing stout, and even Mrs. Halleck noticed that his blonde face was unpleasantly red that day. He was, of course, not intemperate. He always had beer with his lunch, which he had begun to take down town, since the warm weather had come on and made the walk up the hill to Clover street irksome: and he drank beer at his dinner—he liked a late dinner, and they dined at six, now—because it washed away the fatigues of the day and freshened you up. He was rather particular about his beer, which he had sent in by the gross—it came cheaper that way; after trying both the Cincinnati and the Milwaukee lagers, and making a cursory test of the Boston brand, he had settled down upon the American Tivoli; it was cheap, and you could drink a couple of bottles without feeling it. Freshened up by his two bottles, he was apt to spend the evening in an amiable drowse and get early to bed, when he did not go out on newspaper duty. He joked about the three fingers of fat on his ribs, and frankly guessed it was the beer that did it; at such times he said that perhaps he should have to cut down on his Tivoli.

Marcia and he had not so much time together as they used to have; she was a great deal taken up with the baby, and he found it dull at home, not doing anything or saying anything; and, when he did not feel sleepy, he sometimes invented work that took him out at night. But he always came upstairs after putting his hat on, and asked Marcia if he could help her about anything.

He usually met other newspaper men on these excursions, and talked newspaper with them, airing his favorite theories. He liked to wander about with reporters who were working up cases; to look in at the police stations, and go to the fires; and he was often able to give the Events men points that had escaped the other reporters. If asked to drink, he always said, "Thanks, no; I don't do anything in that way. But if you'll make it beer, I don't mind." He took nothing but beer when he hurried out of the theatre into one of the neighboring resorts, just as the great platters of stewed kidneys and *lyonnaise* potatoes came steaming up out of the kitchen, prompt to the drop of the curtain on the last act. Here, sometimes, he met a friend, and shared with him his dish of kidneys and his schooner of beer; and he once suffered himself to be lured by the click of the balls into the back room. He believed that he played a very good game of billiards; but he was badly beaten that night. He came home at daylight fifty dollars out. But he had lost like a gentleman in a game with gentlemen; and he never played again.

By day he worked hard, and since his expenses had been increased by Flavia's coming, he had undertaken more work for more pay. He still performed all the routine labor of a managing editor, and he now wrote the literary notices of The Events, and sometimes, especially if there was anything new, the dramatic criticisms; he brought to the latter task all the freshness of a man who, till the year before, had not been half a dozen times inside a theatre.

He attributed the fat on his ribs to the Tivoli; perhaps it was also owing in some degree to a good conscience, which is a much easier thing to keep than people imagine. At any rate, he now led a tranquil, industrious, and regular life, and a life which suited him so well that he was reluctant to interrupt it by the visit to Equity which he and Marcia had talked of in the early spring. He put it off from time to time, and one day, when she was pressing him to fix some date for it, he said:

"Why can't you go, Marcia?"

"Alone?" she faltered.

"Well, no; take the baby, of course. And I'll run down for a day or two when I get a chance."

Marcia seemed in these days to be schooling herself against the impulses that once brought on her quarrels with Bartley.

"A day or two"—she began, and then stopped and added gravely, "I thought you said you were going to have several weeks' vacation."

"Oh, don't tell me what I *said!*" cried Bartley. "That was before I undertook this extra work, or before I knew what a grind it was going to be. Equity is a good deal of a dose for me, anyway. It's all well enough for you, and I guess the change from Boston will do you good, and do the baby good, but *I* shouldn't look forward to three weeks in Equity with unmitigated hilarity."

"I know it will be stupid for you. But you need the rest. And the Hallecks are going to be at North Conway; and they said they would come over," urged Marcia. "I know we should have a good time."

Bartley grinned.

"Is that your idea of a good time, Marsh? Three weeks of Equity, relieved by a visit from such heavy weights as Ben Halleck and his sisters? Not any in mine, thank you."

"How can you—how *dare* you speak so of them!" cried Marcia, lightening upon him. "Such good friends of yours—such good people"—

Her voice shook with indignation and wounded feeling.

Bartley rose and took a turn about the room, pulling down his waistcoat and contemplating its outward slope with a smile.

"Oh, I've got more friends than I can shake a stick at. And with pleasure at the helm, goodness is a drug in the market—if you'll excuse the mixed metaphor. Look here, Marcia," he added, severely. "If you like the Hallecks, all well and good;

I sha'n't interfere with you; but they bore me. I outgrew Ben Halleck years ago. He's duller than death. As for the old people, there's no harm in them,—though *they're* bores, too,—nor in the old girls; but Olive Halleck doesn't treat me decently. I suppose that just suits you: I've noticed that you never like the women that *do* treat me decently."

"They don't treat me decently!" retorted Marcia.

"Oh, Miss Kingsbury treated you very well that night. She couldn't imagine your being jealous of her politeness to me."

Marcia's temper fired at his treacherous recurrence to a grievance which he had once so sacredly and sweetly ignored.

"If you wish to take up by-gones, why don't you go back to Hannah Morrison at once? She treated you even better than Miss Kingsbury."

"I should have been very willing to do that," said Bartley, "but I thought it might remind you of a disagreeable little episode in your own life, when you flung me away, and had to go down on your knees to pick me up again."

These thrusts which they dealt each other in their quarrels, however blind and misdirected, always reached their hearts: it was the wicked will that hurt, rather than the words. Marcia rose, bleeding inwardly, and her husband felt the remorse of a man who gets the best of it in such an encounter.

"Oh, I'm sorry I said that, Marcia! I didn't mean it; indeed I"— She disdained to heed him as she swept out of the room and up the stairs; and his anger flamed out again.

"I give you fair warning," he called after her, "not to try that trick of locking the door, or I will smash it in."

Her answer was to turn the key in the door with a click which he could not fail to hear.

The peace in which they had been living of late was very comfortable to Bartley; he liked it; he hated to have it broken; he was willing to do what he could to restore it at once. If he had no better motive than this, he still had this motive; and he choked down his wrath, and followed Marcia softly upstairs. He intended to reason with her, and he began, "I say, Marsh," as he turned the door-knob. But you cannot reason through a keyhole, and before he knew he found himself saying, "Will you open this?" in a tone whose quiet was deadly. She did not answer; he heard her stop in her movements about the room, and wait, as if she expected him to ask again. He hesitated a moment whether to keep his threat of breaking the door in; but he turned away and went down-stairs, and so into the street. Once outside, he experienced the sense of release that comes to a man from the violation of his better impulses; but he did not know what to do or where to go. He walked rapidly away; but Marcia's eyes and voice seemed to follow him, and plead with him for his forbearance. He answered his conscience, as if it had been some such presence, that he had forborne too much already, and that now he should not humble himself: that he was right and should stand upon his right. There was not much comfort in it, and he had to brace himself again and again with vindictive resolution.

XXIV

———

BARTLEY walked about the streets for a long time, without purpose or direction, brooding fiercely on his wrongs, and reminding himself how Marcia had determined to have him, and had indeed flung herself upon his mercy, with all sorts of good promises; and had then at once taken the whiphand, and goaded and tormented him ever since. All the kindness of their common life counted for nothing in this furious reverie, or rather it was never once thought of; he cursed himself for a fool that he had ever asked her to marry him, and for doubly a fool that he had married her when she had as good as asked him. He was glad, now, that he had taunted her with that; he only regretted that he had told her he was sorry. He was presently aware of being so tired that he could scarcely pull one leg after another; and yet he felt hopelessly wide awake. It was in simple despair of anything else to do that he climbed the stairs to Ricker's lofty perch in the Chronicle-Abstract office. Ricker turned about as he entered, and stared up at him from beneath the green pasteboard visor with which he was shielding his eyes from the gas; his hair, which was of the harshness and color of hay, was stiffly poked up and strewn about on his skull, as if it were some foreign product.

"Hello!" he said. "Going to issue a morning edition of the Events?"

"What makes you think so?"

"Oh, I supposed you evening paper gents went to bed with the hens. What has kept you up, esteemed contemporary?"

He went on working over some dispatches which lay upon his table.

"Don't you want to come out and have some oysters?" asked Bartley.

"Why this princely hospitality? I'll come with you in half a minute," Ricker said, going to the slide that carried up the copy to the composing-room, and thrusting his manuscript into the box.

"Where are you going?" he asked, when they found themselves out in the soft starlit autumnal air; and Bartley answered with the name of an oyster-house, obscure, but of singular excellence.

"Yes, that's the best place," Ricker commented. "What I continually wonder at in you is the rapidity with which you've taken on the city. You were quite in the green wood when you came here, and now you know your Boston like a little man. I suppose it's your newspaper work that's familiarized you with the place. Well, how do you like friend Witherby, as far as you've gone?"

"Oh, we shall get along, I guess," said Bartley. "He still keeps me in the background, and plays at being editor himself, but he pays me pretty well."

"Not too well, I hope."

"I should like to see him try it."

"I shouldn't," said Ricker. "He'd expect certain things of you, if he did. You'll have to look out for Witherby."

"You mean that he's a scamp?"

"No; there isn't a better conscience than Witherby carries in the whole city. He's perfectly honest. He not only believes that he has a right to run the Events in his way, but he sincerely believes that he is right in doing it. There's where he has the advantage of you, if you doubt him. I don't suppose he ever did a wrong thing in his life; he'd persuade himself that the thing was right before he did it."

"That's a common phenomenon, isn't it?" sneered Bartley. "Nobody sins."

"You're right, partly. But some of us sinners have our misgivings, and Witherby never has. You know he offered me your place?"

"No, I didn't," said Bartley, astonished and not pleased.

"I thought he might have told you. He made me inducements; but I was afraid of him: Witherby is the counting-room incarnate. I talked you into him for some place or other; but he didn't seem to wake up to the value of my advice at once. Then I couldn't tell what he was going to offer you."

"Thank you for letting me in for a thing you were afraid of!"

"I didn't believe he would get you under his thumb, as he would me. You've got more backbone than I have. I have to keep out of temptation; you have noticed that I never drink, and I would rather not look upon Witherby when he is red and giveth his color in the cup. I'm sorry if I've let you in for anything that you regret. But Witherby's sincerity makes him dangerous—I own that."

"I think he has some very good ideas about newspapers," said Bartley, rather sulkily.

"Oh, very," assented Ricker. "Some of the very best going. He believes that the press is a great moral engine, and that it ought to be run in the interest of the engineer."

"And I suppose you believe that it ought to be run in the interest of the public?"

"Exactly—after the public has paid."

"Well, I don't; and I never did. A newspaper is a private enterprise."

"It's private property, but it isn't a private enterprise, and in its very nature it can't be. You know I never talk 'journalism' and stuff; it amuses me to hear the young fellows at it, though I think they might be doing something worse than magnifying their office; they might be decrying it. But I've got a few ideas and principles of my own in my back pantaloons-pocket."

"Haul them out," said Bartley.

"I don't know that they're very well formulated," returned Ricker, "and I don't contend that they're very new. But I consider a newspaper a public enterprise, with certain distinct duties to the public. It's sacredly bound not to do anything to deprave or debauch its readers; and it's sacredly bound not to mislead or betray them, not merely as to questions of morals and politics, but as to questions of what we may lump as 'advertising.' Has friend Witherby developed his great ideas of advertisers' rights to you?" Bartley did not answer, and Ricker went on: "Well, then, you can understand my position, when I say it's exactly the contrary."

"You ought to be on a religious newspaper, Ricker," said Bartley, with a scornful laugh.

"Thank you, a secular paper is bad enough for me."

"Well, I don't pretend that I make the Events just what I want," said Bartley. "At present the most I can do is to indulge in a few cheap dreams of what I should do, if I had a paper of my own."

"What are your dreams? Haul out, as you say."

"I should make it pay, to begin with; and I should make it pay by making it such a thorough newspaper, that every class of people *must* have it. I should cater to the lowest class first, and as long as I was poor, I would have the fullest and best reports of every local accident and crime; that would take *all* the rabble. Then, as I could afford it, I'd rise a little, and give first-class non-partisan reports of local political affairs; that would fetch the next largest class, the ward politicians of all parties. I'd lay for the local religious world, after that—religion comes right after politics in the popular mind, and it interests the women like murder: I'd give the minutest religious intelligence, and not only that, but the religious gossip, and the religious scandal. Then I'd go in for fashion and society—that comes next. I'd have the most reliable and thorough-going financial reports that money could buy. When I'd got my local ground perfectly covered, I'd begin to ramify. Every fellow that could spell, in any part of the country, should understand that if he sent me an account of a suicide, or an elopement, or a murder, or an accident, he should be well paid for it; and I'd rise on the same scale through all the departments. I'd add art criticisms, dramatic and sporting news, and book-reviews, more for the looks of the thing than for anything else; they don't any of 'em appeal to a large class. I'd get my paper into such a shape that people of every kind and degree would have to say, no matter what particular objection was made to it, "Yes, that's so; but it's the best *news*paper in the world, *and we can't get along without it.*"

"And then," said Ricker, "you'd begin to clean up, little by little—let up on your murders and scandals, and purge and live cleanly like a gentleman? The trick's been tried before."

They had arrived at the oyster-house, and were sitting at their table, waiting for the oysters to be brought to them. Bartley tilted his chair back. "I don't know about the cleaning up. I should want to keep all my audience. If I cleaned up, the dirty fellows would go off to some one else; and the fellows that pretended to be clean would be disappointed."

"Why don't you get Witherby to put your ideas in force?" asked Ricker, dryly.

Bartley dropped his chair to all fours, and said with a smile, "He belongs to church."

"Ah, he has his limitations. What a pity! He has the money to establish this great moral engine of yours, and you haven't. It's a loss to civilization."

"One thing, I know," said Bartley, with a certain effect of virtue, "nobody should buy or sell me; and the advertising element shouldn't spread beyond the advertising page."

"Isn't that rather high ground?" inquired Ricker.

Bartley did not think it worth while to answer. "I don't believe that a newspaper is obliged to be superior in tone to the community," he said.

"I quite agree with you."

"And if the community is full of vice and crime, a newspaper can't do better than reflect its condition."

"Ah, there I should distinguish, esteemed contemporary. There are several tones in every community, and it will keep any newspaper scratching to rise above the highest. But if it keeps out of the mud at all it can't help rising above the lowest. And no community is full of vice and crime any more than it is full of virtue and good works. Why not let your model newspaper mirror these?"

"They're not snappy."

"No, that's true."

"You must give the people what they want."

"Are you sure of that?"

"Yes, I am."

"Well, it's a beautiful dream," said Ricker, "nourished on a youth sublime. Why do not these lofty imaginings visit us later in life? You make me quite ashamed of my own ideal newspaper. Before you began to talk I had been fancying that the vice of our journalism was its intense localism. I have doubted a good while whether a drunken Irishman who breaks his wife's head, or a child who falls into a tub of hot water, has really established a claim on the public interest. Why should I be told by telegraph how three negroes died on the gallows in North Carolina? Why should an accurate correspondent inform me of the elopement of a married man with his maid-servant in East Machias? Why should I sup on all the horrors of a railroad accident, and have the bleeding fragments hashed up for me at breakfast? Why should my newspaper give a succession of shocks to my nervous system, as I pass from column to column, and poultice me between shocks with the nastiness of a distant or local scandal? You reply, because I like spice. But I don't. I am sick of spice; and I believe that most of our readers are."

"Cater to them with milk-toast, then," said Bartley.

Ricker laughed with him, and they fell to upon their oysters. When they parted, Bartley still found himself wakeful. He knew that he should not sleep if he went home, and he said to himself that he could not walk about all night. He turned into a gayly lighted basement, and asked for something in the way of a night-cap.

The bar-keeper said there was nothing like a hot-scotch to make you sleep; and a small man, with his hat on, who had been talking with the bar-keeper, and coming up to the counter occasionally to eat a bit of cracker or a bit of cheese out of the two bowls full of such fragments that stood at the end of the counter, said that this was so.

It was very cheerful in the bar-room, with the light glittering on the rows of decanters behind the bar-keeper, a large, stout, clean, pale man in his shirt-sleeves, after the manner of his kind; and Bartley made up his mind to stay there till he was drowsy, and to drink as many hot-scotches as were necessary to the result. He had his drink put on a little table and sat down to it easily, stirring it to cool it a little, and feeling its flattery in his brain from the first sip.

The man who was munching cheese and crackers wore a hat rather large for him, pulled down over his eyes. He now said that he did not care if he took a gin-sling, and the bar-keeper promptly set it before him on the counter, and saluted with "Good evening, Colonel," a large man who came in, carrying a small dog in his arms. Bartley recognized him as the manager of a variety combination playing at one of the theatres, and the manager recognized the little man with the gin-sling as Tommy. He did not return the bar-keeper's salutation, but he asked, as he sat down at a table:

"What do I want for supper, Charley?"

The bar-keeper said, oracularly, as he leaned forward to wipe his counter with a napkin:

"Fricasee chicken."

"Fricassee devil," returned the manager. "Get me a Welsh rabbit."

The bar-keeper, unperturbed by this rejection, called into the tube behind him:

"One Welsh rabbit!"

"I want some cold chicken for my dog," said the manager.

"One cold chicken," repeated the bar-keeper, in his tube.

"White meat," said the manager.

"White meat," repeated the bar-keeper.

"I went into the Parker House one night about midnight, and I saw four doctors there eating lobster salad, and deviled crab, and washing it down with champagne; and I made up my mind that the doctors needn't talk to me any more about what was wholesome. I was going in for what was *good*. And there aint anything better for supper than Welsh rabbit in *this* world."

As the manager addressed this philosophy to the company at large, no one commented upon it, which seemed quite the same to the manager, who hitched one elbow over the back of his chair, and caressed with the other hand the dog lying in his lap.

The little man in the large hat continued to walk up and down, leaving his gin-sling on the counter, and drinking it between his visits to the cracker and cheese.

"What's that new piece of yours, Colonel?" he asked, after awhile. "I aint seen it yet."

"Legs, principally," sighed the manager. "That's what the public wants. I give the public what it wants. I don't pretend to be any better than the public. Nor any worse," he added, stroking his dog.

These ideas struck Bartley in their accordance with his own ideas of journalism as he had propounded them to Ricker. He had drunk half of his hot-scotch.

"That's what I say," assented the little man. "All that a theatre has got to do is to keep even with the public."

"That's so, Tommy," said the manager of a school of morals, with wisdom that impressed more and more the manager of a great moral engine.

"The same principle runs through everything," observed Bartley, speaking for the first time.

The drink had stiffened his tongue somewhat, but it did not incommode his utterance; it rather gave dignity to it, and his head was singularly clear. He lifted his empty glass from the table, and, catching the bar-keeper's eye, said, "Do it again." The man brought it back full.

"It runs through the churches as well as the theatres. As long as the public wanted hell-fire, the ministers gave them hell-fire. But you couldn't get hell-fire—not the pure, old-fashioned brimstone article—out of a popular preacher now, for love or money."

The little man said, "I guess you've got about the size of it there;" and the manager laughed.

"It's just so with the newspapers, too," said Bartley. "Some newspapers used to stand out against publishing murders, and personal gossip, and divorce trials. There aint a newspaper that pretends to keep anyways up with the times, now, that don't do it! The public want spice, and they will have it!"

"Well, sir," said the manager, "that's my way of looking at it. I say if the public don't want Shakspere, give 'em burlesque till they're sick of it. I believe in what Grant said: 'The quickest way to get rid of a bad law is to enforce it.' "

"That's so," said the little man, "every time."

He added to the bar-keeper that he guessed he would have some brandy and soda, and Bartley found himself at the bottom of his second tumbler. He ordered it replenished.

The little man seemed to be getting further away. He said, from the distance to which he had withdrawn:

"You want to go to bed with three night-caps on, like an old-clothes-man."

Bartley felt like resenting the freedom, but he was anxious to pour his ideas of journalism into the manager's sympathetic ear, and he began to talk, with an impression that it behooved him to talk fast. His brain was still very clear, but his tongue was getting stiffer. The manager now had his Welsh rabbit before him; but Bartley could not make out how it had got there, nor when. He was talking fast, and he knew by the way everybody was listening, that he was talking well. Sometimes he left his table, glass in hand, and went and laid down the law to the manager, who smilingly assented to all he said. Once he heard a low growling at his feet, and looking down, he saw the dog with his plate of cold chicken, that had also been conjured into the room somehow.

"Look out," said the manager, "he'll nip you in the leg."

"Curse the dog! he seems to be on all sides of you," said Bartley. "I can't stand anywhere."

"Better sit down then," suggested the manager.

"Good idea," said the little man, who was still walking up and down. It appeared as if he had not spoken for several hours; his hat was further over his eyes. Bartley had thought he was gone.

"What business is it of yours?" he demanded fiercely, moving toward the little man.

"Come, none of that," said the bar-keeper, steadily.

Bartley looked at him in amazement.

"Where's your hat?" he asked.

The others laughed; the bar-keeper smiled.

"Are you a married man?"

"Never mind!" said the bar-keeper, severely.

Bartley turned to the little man:

"You married?"

"Not *much*," replied the other. He was now topping off with a whisky-straight.

Bartley referred himself to the manager:

"You?"

"*Pas si bête*," said the manager, who did his own adapting from the French.

"Well, you're scholar, and you're gentleman," said Bartley. The indefinite articles would drop out, in spite of all his efforts to keep them in. " 'N' I want ask you what you do—to—ask—you —what—would—you—do," he repeated with painful exactness, but he failed to make the rest of the sentence perfect, and he pronounced it all in a word, " 'fyourwifelockyouout."

"I'd take a walk," said the manager.

"I'd bu'st the door in," said the little man.

Bartley turned and gazed at him as if the little man were a much more estimable person than he had supposed. He passed his arm through the little man's, which the other had just crooked to lift his whisky to his mouth.

"Look here," said Bartley, "tha's jus' what *I* told her. I want you to go home 'th me; I want t' introduce you to my wife."

"All right," answered the little man. "Don't care if I do." He dropped his tumbler to the floor. "Hang it up, Charley, glass and all. Hang up this gentleman's night-caps—my account. Gentleman asks me home to his house, I'll hang him—I'll get him hung—well, fix it to suit yourself—every time!"

They got themselves out of the door, and the manager said to the bar-keeper, who came round to gather up the fragments of the broken tumbler,

"Think his wife will be glad to see 'em, Charley?"

"Oh, they'll be taken care of before they reach his house."

XXV

When they were once out under the stars, Bartley, who still felt his brain clear, said that he would not take his friend home at once, but would show him where he visited when he first came to Boston. The other agreed to the indulgence of this sentiment, and they set out to find Rumford street together.

"You've heard of old man Halleck—Lestor Neather Interest? Tha's place—there's where I staid. His son's my frien'—damn stuck-up supercilious beast he is, too. *I* do' care f'r him! I'll show you place, so's't you'll know it when you come to it,—'f I can ever find it."

They walked up and down the street, looking, while Bartley poured his sorrows into the ear of his friend, who grew less and less responsive, and at last ceased from his side altogether. Bartley then dimly perceived that he was himself sitting on a doorstep, and that his head was hanging far down between his knees, as if he had been sleeping in that posture.

"Locked out—locked out of my own door, and by my own wife!" He shed tears, and fell asleep again. From time to time he woke, and bewailed himself to Ricker as a poor boy who had fought his own way; he owned that he had made mistakes, as who had not? Again he was trying to convince Squire Gaylord that they ought to issue a daily edition of the Equity Free Press, and at the same time persuading Mr. Halleck to buy the Events for him, and let him put it on a paying basis. He shivered, sighed, hiccupped, and was dozing off again, when Henry Bird knocked him down, and he fell with a cry, which

271

at last brought to the door the uneasy sleeper who had been listening to him within, and trying to realize his presence, catching his voice in waking intervals, doubting it, drowsing when it ceased, and then catching it and losing it again.

"Hallo, here! What do you want? Hubbard! Is it you? What in the world are you doing here?"

"Halleck," said Bartley, who was unsteadily straightening himself upon his feet, "glad to find you at home. Been looking for your house all night. Want to introduce you to partic-ic-ular friend of mine. Mr. Halleck, Mr. —. Curse me if I know your name"—

"Hold on a minute," said Halleck.

He ran into the house for his hat and coat, and came out again, closing the door softly after him. He found Bartley in the grip of a policeman, whom he was asking his name that he might introduce him to his friend Halleck.

"Do you know this man, Mr. Halleck?" asked the police-man.

"Yes—yes, I know him," said Ben, in a low voice. "Let's get him away quietly, please. He's all right. It's the first time I ever saw him so. Will you help me with him up to Johnson's stable? I'll get a carriage there and take him home."

They had begun walking Bartley along between them; he dozed and paid no attention to their talk.

The policeman laughed.

"I was just going to run him in, when you came out. You didn't come a minute too soon."

They got Bartley to the stable, and he slept heavily in one of the chairs in the office, while the hostlers were putting the horses to the carriage. The policeman remained at the office-door, looking in at Bartley, and philosophizing the situation to Halleck.

"Your speakin' about its bein' the first time you ever saw him so made me think 't I rather help take home a regular habitual drunk to his family, any day, than a case like this. They always seem to take it so much harder the first time. Boards with his mother, I presume?"

"He's married," said Halleck, sadly. "He has a house of his own."

"Well!" said the policeman.

Bartley slept all the way to Clover street, and when the carriage stopped at his door, they had difficulty in waking him sufficiently to get him out.

"Don't come in, please," said Halleck, to the policeman, when this was done. "The man will carry you back to your beat. Thank you, ever so much!"

"All right, Mr. Halleck. Don't mention it," said the policeman, and he leaned back in the hack with an air of luxury, as it rumbled softly away.

Halleck remained on the pavement with Bartley falling limply against him in the dim light of the dawn.

"What you want? What you doing with me?" he demanded with sullen stupidity.

"I've got you home, Hubbard. Here we are at your house."

He pulled him across the pavement, to the threshold, and put his hand on the bell, but the door was thrown open before he could ring, and Marcia stood there, with her face white, and her eyes red with watching and crying.

"Oh, Bartley, oh, Bartley!" she sobbed. "Oh, Mr. Halleck, what is it? Is he hurt? I did it—yes, I did it! It's my fault! Oh, will he die? Is he sick?"

"He isn't very well. He'd better go to bed," said Halleck.

"Yes, yes! I will help you upstairs with him."

"Do' need any help," said Bartley, sulkily. "Go upstairs myself."

He actually did so, with the help of the hand-rail, Marcia running before, to open the door, and smooth the pillows which her head had not touched, and Halleck following him to catch him if he should fall. She unlaced his shoes and got them off, while Halleck removed his coat.

"Oh, Bartley, where do you feel badly, dear? Oh, what shall I do?" she moaned, as he tumbled himself on the bed, and lapsed into a drunken stupor.

"Better—better come out, Mrs. Hubbard," said Halleck.

"Better let him alone, now. You only make him worse, talking to him."

Quelled by the mystery of his manner, she followed him out and down the stairs.

"Oh, *do* tell me what it is," she implored, in a low voice, "or I shall go wild! But tell me and I can bear it! I can bear anything if I know what it is!" She came close to him in her entreaty, and fixed her eyes beseechingly on his, while she caught his hand in both of hers. "Is he—is he insane?"

"He isn't quite in his right mind, Mrs. Hubbard," Halleck began, softly releasing himself, and retreating a little from her, but she pursued him, and put her hand on his arm.

"Oh, then go for the doctor—go instantly! Don't lose a minute! I shall not be afraid to stay alone. Or if you think I'd better not, I will go for the doctor myself."

"No, no," said Halleck, smiling, sadly: the case certainly had its ludicrous side. "He doesn't need a doctor. You mustn't think of calling a doctor. Indeed you mustn't. He'll come out all right of himself. If you sent for a doctor, it would make him very angry."

She burst into tears. "Well, I will do what you say," she cried. "It would never have happened, if it hadn't been for me. I want to tell you what I did," she went on wildly. "I want to tell"—

"Please don't tell me anything, Mrs. Hubbard! It will all come right—and very soon. It isn't anything to be alarmed about. He'll be well in a few hours. I—ah— Good-by!" He had found his cane, and he made a limp toward the door, but she swiftly interposed herself.

"Why," she panted in mixed reproach and terror, "you're not going away? You're not going to leave me before Bartley is well? He may get worse—he may die! You mustn't go, Mr. Halleck!"

"Yes, I must,—I can't stay,—I oughtn't to stay—it wont do! He wont get worse, he wont die"— The perspiration broke out on Halleck's face, which he lifted to hers with a distress as great as her own.

She only answered, "I can't let you go. It would kill me. I wonder at your wanting to go."

There was something ghastly comical in it all, and Halleck stood in fear of its absurdity hardly less than of its tragedy. He rapidly revolved in his mind the possibilities of the case. He thought at first that it might be well to call a doctor, and having explained the situation to him, pay him to remain in charge; but he reflected that it would be insulting to ask a doctor to see a man in Hubbard's condition. He took out his watch, and saw that it was six o'clock; and he said desperately: "You can send for me, if you get anxious"—

"I can't let you go!"

"I must really get my breakfast"—

"The girl will get something for you here. Oh, *don't* go away!" Her lip began to quiver again, and her bosom to rise.

He could not bear it. "Mrs. Hubbard, will you believe what I say?"

"Yes," she faltered, reluctantly.

"Well, I tell you that Mr. Hubbard is in no sort of danger; and I know that it would be extremely offensive to him if I staid."

"Then you must go," she answered promptly, and opened the door, which she had closed for fear he might escape. "I will send for a doctor."

"No, *don't* send for a doctor, don't send for anybody; don't speak of the matter to any one: it would be very mortifying to him. It's merely a—a—kind of—seizure, that a great many people—men—are subject to; but he wouldn't like to have it known." He saw that his words were making an impression upon her; perhaps her innocence was beginning to divine the truth. "Will you do what I say?"

"Yes," she murmured.

Her head began to droop, and her face to turn away in a dawning shame too cruel for him to see.

"I—I will come back as soon as I get my breakfast, to make sure that everything is right."

She let him find his own way out, and Halleck issued upon

the street, as miserable as if the disgrace were his own. It was easy enough for him to get back into his own room without alarming the family. He ate his breakfast absently, and then went out while the others were still at table.

"I don't think Ben seems very well," said his mother, anxiously, and she looked to her husband for the denial he always gave.

"Oh, I guess he's all right. What's the matter with him?"

"It's nothing but his ridiculous, romantic way of taking the world to heart," Olive interposed. "You may be sure he's troubled about something that doesn't concern him in the least. It's what comes of the life-long conscientiousness of his parents. If Ben doesn't turn out a philanthropist of the deepest dye yet, you'll have me to thank for it. I see more and more every day that I was providentially born wicked, so as to keep this besottedly righteous family's head above water."

She feigned an angry impatience with the condition of things; but, when her father went out, she joined her mother in earnest conjectures as to what Ben had on his mind.

Halleck wandered about till nearly ten o'clock, and then he went to the little house on Clover street. The servant-girl answered his ring, and when he asked for Mrs. Hubbard, she said that Mr. Hubbard wished to see him, and please would he step upstairs.

He found Bartley seated at the window, with a wet towel round his head and his face pale with headache.

"Well, old man," he said, with an assumption of comradery that was nauseous to Halleck, "you've done the handsome thing by me. I know all about it. I knew something about it all the time." He held out his hand, without rising, and Halleck forced himself to touch it. "I appreciate your delicacy in not telling my wife. Of course you *couldn't* tell," he said, with depraved enjoyment of what he conceived of Halleck's embarrassment. "But I guess she must have smelt a rat. As the fellows say," he added, seeing the disgust that Halleck could not keep out of his face, "I shall make a clean breast of it, as soon as she can bear it. She's pretty high-strung. Lying down, now," he explained. "You see I went out to get something to make me sleep, and the first thing I knew I had got too much. Good thing I turned up on your door-step; might have been waltzing into the police-court about now. How did you happen to hear me?"

Halleck briefly explained, with an air of abhorrence for the facts.

"Yes, I remember most of it," said Bartley. "Well, I want to thank you, Halleck. You've saved me from disgrace—from ruin, for all I know. Whew, how my head aches!" he said, making an appeal to Halleck's pity, with closed eyes. "Halleck," he murmured, feebly, "I wish you would do me a favor."

"Yes? What is it?" asked Halleck, dryly.

"Go round to the Events office and tell old Witherby that I sha'n't be able to put in an appearance to-day. I'm not up to writing a note, even, and he'd feel flattered at your coming personally. It would make it all right for me."

"Of course, I will go," said Halleck.

"Thanks," returned Bartley plaintively, with his eyes closed.

XXVI

BARTLEY would willingly have passed this affair over with Marcia, like some of their quarrels, and allowed a reconciliation to effect itself through mere lapse of time and daily custom. But there were difficulties in the way to such an end; his shameful escapade had given the quarrel a character of its own, which could not be ignored. He must keep his word about making a clean breast of it to Marcia, whether he liked or not; but she facilitated his confession by the meek and dependent fashion in which she hovered about, anxious to do something or anything for him. If, as he suggested to Halleck, she had divined the truth, she evidently did not hold him wholly to blame for what had happened, and he was not without a self-righteous sense of having given her a useful and necessary lesson. He was inclined to a severity to which his rasped and shaken nerves contributed, when he spoke to her that night, as they sat together after tea; she had some sewing in her lap, little mysteries of soft muslin for the baby, which she was edging with lace, and her head drooped over her work, as if she could not confront him with her swollen eyes.

"Look here, Marcia," he said, "do you know what was the matter with me this morning?"

She did not answer in words; her hands quivered a moment; then she caught up the things out of her lap, and sobbed into them. The sight unmanned Bartley; he hated to see any one cry, even his wife, to whose tears he was accustomed. He dropped down beside her on the sofa, and pulled her head over on his shoulder.

"It was my fault, it was my fault, Bartley!" she sobbed. "Oh, how can I ever get over it?"

"Well, don't cry, don't cry! It wasn't altogether your fault," returned Bartley. "We were both to blame."

"No! I began it. If I hadn't broken my promise about speaking of Hannah Morrison, it never would have happened." This was so true that Bartley could not gainsay it. "But I couldn't seem to help it; and you were—you were—so quick with me; you didn't give me time to think; you— But I was the one to blame, I was to blame!"

"Oh, well, never mind about it; don't take on so," coaxed Bartley. "It's all over now, and it can't be helped. And I can promise you," he added, "that it shall never happen again, no matter what you do," and in making this promise, he felt the glow of virtuous performance. "I think we've both had a lesson. I suppose," he continued sadly, as one might from impersonal reflection upon the temptations and depravity of large cities, "that it's *common* enough. I dare say it isn't the first time Ben Halleck has taken a fellow home in a hack." Bartley got so much comfort from the conjecture he had thrown out for Marcia's advantage, that he felt a sort of self-approval in the fact with which he followed it up. "And there's this consolation about it, if there isn't any other: that it wouldn't have happened now, if it had ever happened before."

Marcia lifted her head and looked into his face:

"What—what do you mean, Bartley?"

"I mean that I never was overcome before in my life by—wine." He delicately avoided saying whisky.

"Well?" she demanded.

"Why, don't you see? If I'd had the habit of drinking, I shouldn't have been affected by it."

"I don't understand," she said, anxiously.

"Why, I knew I shouldn't be able to sleep, I was so mad at you"—

"Oh!"

"And I dropped into the hotel bar-room for a night-cap—for something to make me sleep."

"Yes, yes!" she urged, eagerly.

"I took what wouldn't have touched a man that was in the habit of it."

"Poor Bartley!"

"And the first thing I knew I had got too much. I was drunk—wild drunk," he said, with magnanimous frankness.

She had been listening intensely, exculpating him at every point, and now his innocence all flashed upon her.

"I see—I see!" she cried. "And it was because you had never tasted it before"—

"Well, I had tasted it once or twice," interrupted Bartley, with heroic veracity.

"No matter! It was because you had never more than hardly tasted it that a very little overcame you in an instant. I see!" she repeated, contemplating him, in her ecstasy, as the one habitually sober man in a Boston full of inebriates. "And now I shall never regret it; I shall never care for it; I never shall think about it again! Or, yes! I shall always remember it, because it shows—because it *proves*—that you are always strictly temperance. It was worth happening for that. I am *glad* it happened!"

She rose from his side, and took her sewing nearer the lamp, and resumed her work upon it with shining eyes.

Bartley remained in his place on the sofa, feeling, and perhaps looking, rather sheepish. He had made a clean breast of it, and the confession had redounded only too much to his credit. To do him justice, he had not intended to bring the affair to quite such a triumphant conclusion; and perhaps something better than his sense of humor was also touched when he found himself not only exonerated but transformed into an exemplar of abstinence.

"Well," he said, "it isn't exactly a thing to be glad of, but it certainly isn't a thing to worry yourself about. You know the worst of it, and you know the best of it. It never happened before, and it never shall happen again; that's all. Don't lament over it, don't accuse yourself; just let it go, and we'll both see what we can do after this in the way of behaving better."

He rose from the sofa, and began to walk about the room.

"Does your head still ache?" she asked, fondly. "I *wish* I could do something for it!"

"Oh, I shall sleep it off," returned Bartley.

She followed him with her eyes.

"Bartley!"

"Well?"

"Do you suppose—do you believe—that Mr. Halleck—that he was ever"—

"No, Marcia, I don't," said Bartley, stopping. "I *know* he never was. Ben Halleck is slow; but he's good. I couldn't imagine his being drunk any more than I could imagine your being so. I'd willingly sacrifice his reputation to console you," added Bartley, with a comical sense of his own regret that Halleck was not, for the occasion, an habitual drunkard, "but I cannot tell a lie."

He looked at her with a smile, and broke into a sudden laugh.

"No, my dear, the only person I think of just now, as having suffered similarly with myself, is the great and good Andrew Johnson. Did you ever hear of him?"

"Was he the one they impeached?" she faltered, not knowing what Bartley would be at, but smiling faintly in sympathy with his mirth.

"He was the one they impeached. He was the one who was overcome by wine on his inauguration day, because he had never been overcome before. It's a parallel case!"

Bartley got a great deal more enjoyment out of the parallel case than Marcia. The smile faded from her face, and, "Come, come," he coaxed, "be satisfied with Andrew Johnson, and let Halleck go. Ah, Marcia!" he added, seriously, "Ben Halleck is the kind of man you ought to have married! Don't you suppose that I know I'm not good enough for you? I'm pretty good by fits and starts; but he would have been good right straight along. I should never have had to bring *him* home in a hack to you!"

His generous admission had the just effect. "Hush, Bartley!

Don't talk so! You know that you're better for me than the best man in the world, dear, and even if you were not, I should love you the best. Don't talk, please, that way, of any one else, or it will make me hate you!"

He liked that; and after all he was not without an obscure pride in his last night's adventure as a somewhat hazardous but decided assertion of manly supremacy. It was not a thing to be repeated; but for once in a way it was not wholly to be regretted, especially as he was so well out of it.

He pulled up a chair in front of her, and began to joke about the things she had in her lap; and the shameful and sorrowful day ended in the bliss of a more perfect peace between them than they had known since the troubles of their married life began.

"I tell you," said Bartley, "I shall stick to Tivoli after this, religiously."

It was several weeks later that Halleck limped into Atherton's lodgings, and dropped into one of his friend's easy chairs. The room had a bachelor comfort of aspect, and the shaded lamp on the table shed a mellow light on the green leather-covered furniture, wrinkled and creased, and worn full of such hospitable hollows as that which welcomed Halleck. Some packages of law papers were scattered about on the table; but the hour of the night had come when a lawyer permits himself a novel. Atherton looked up from his as Halleck entered, and stretched out a hand, which the latter took on his way to the easy chair across the table.

"How do you do?" said Atherton, after allowing him to sit for a certain time in the frank silence which expressed better than words the familiarity that existed between them in spite of the lawyer's six or seven years of seniority.

Halleck leaned forward and tapped the floor with his stick; then he fell back again, and laid his cane across the arms of his chair, and drew a long breath.

"Atherton," he said, "if you had found a blackguard of your acquaintance drunk on your doorstep early one morning, and had taken him home to his wife, how would you have expected her to treat you the next time you saw her?"

The lawyer was too much used to the statement, direct and hypothetical, of all sorts of cases, to be startled at this. He smiled slightly, and said:

"That would depend a good deal upon the lady."

"Oh, but generalize! From what you know of women as Woman, what should you expect? Shouldn't you expect her to make you pay somehow for your privity to her disgrace, to revenge her misery upon you? Isn't there a theory that women forgive injuries, but never ignominies?"

"That's what the novelists teach, and we bachelors get most of our doctrine about women from them."

He closed his novel on the paper-cutter, and laying the book upon the table, clasped his hands together at the back of his head.

"We don't go to nature for our impressions; but neither do the novelists, for that matter. Now and then, however, in the way of business, I get a glimpse of realities that make me doubt my prophets. Who had this experience?"

"I did."

"I'm sorry for that," said Atherton.

"Yes," returned Halleck, with whimsical melancholy; "I'm not particularly adapted for it. But I don't know that it would be a very pleasant experience for anybody."

He paused drearily, and Atherton said:

"And how did she actually treat you?"

"I hardly know. I hadn't been at the pains to look them up since the thing happened, and I had been carrying their squalid secret round for a fortnight, and suffering from it as if it were all my own."

Atherton smiled at the touch of self-characterization.

"When I met her and her husband and her baby to-day—a family party—well, she made me ashamed of the melodramatic compassion I had been feeling for her: It seemed that I had been going about unnecessarily, not to say impertinently, haggard with the recollection of her face as I saw it when she opened the door for her blackguard and me that morning. She looked as if nothing unusual had happened at our last meeting: I couldn't brace up all at once: I behaved like a sneak, in view of her serenity."

"Perhaps nothing unusual had happened," suggested Atherton.

"No, that theory isn't tenable," said Halleck. "It was the one fact in the blackguard's favor that she had evidently never seen him in that state before, and didn't know what was the matter. She was wild at first; she wanted to send for a doctor. I think towards the last she began to suspect. But I don't know how she looked *then*: I couldn't look at her."

He stopped, as if still in the presence of the pathetic figure, with its sidelong, drooping head.

Atherton respected his silence a moment before he again suggested, as lightly as before:

"Perhaps she is magnanimous."

"No," said Halleck, with the effort of having also given that theory consideration. "She's not magnanimous, poor soul. I fancy she is rather a narrow-minded person, with strict limitations in regard to people who think ill—or too well—of her husband."

"Then perhaps," said Atherton, with the air of having exhausted conjecture, "she's obtuse."

"I have tried to think that too," replied Halleck, "but I can't manage it. No, there are only two ways out of it: the fellow has abused her innocence and made her believe it's a common and venial affair to be brought home in that state, or else she's playing a part. He's capable of telling her that neither you nor I, for example, ever go to bed sober. But she isn't obtuse: I fancy she's only too keen in all the sensibilities that women suffer through; and I'd rather think that he had deluded her in that way than that she was masquerading about it, for she strikes me as an uncommonly truthful person. I suppose you know whom I'm talking about, Atherton?" he said, with a sudden look at his friend's face, across the table.

"Yes, I know," said the lawyer. "I'm sorry it's come to this already. Though I suppose you're not altogether surprised."

"No, something of the kind was to be expected," Halleck sighed, and rolled his cane up and down on the arms of his chair. "I hope we know the worst."

"Perhaps we do. But I recollect a wise remark you made the first time we talked of these people," said Atherton, replying to the mood rather than the speech of his friend. "You suggested that we rather liked to grieve over the pretty girls that other fellows marry, and that we never thought of the plain ones as suffering."

"Oh, I hadn't any data for my pity in this case, then," replied Halleck. "I'm willing to allow that a plain woman would suffer under the same circumstances; and I think I should be capable of pitying her. But I'll confess that the notion of a pretty woman's sorrow is more intolerable; there's no use denying a fact so universally recognized by the male consciousness. I take my share of shame for it. I wonder why it is? Pretty women always seem to appeal to us as more dependent and child-like. I dare say they're not."

"Some of them are quite able to take care of themselves," said Atherton. "I've known striking instances of the kind. How do you know but the object of your superfluous pity was cheerful because fate had delivered her husband, bound forever, into her hand, through this little escapade of his?"

"Isn't that rather a coarse suggestion?" asked Halleck.

"Very likely. I suggest it; I don't assert it. But I fancy that wives sometimes like a permanent grievance that is always at hand, no matter what the mere passing occasion of the particular disagreement is. It seems to me that I have detected obscure appeals to such a weapon in domestic interviews at which I've assisted in the way of business."

"Don't, Atherton!" cried Halleck.

"Don't, how? In this particular case, or in regard to wives generally? We can't do women a greater injustice than not to account for a vast deal of human nature in them. You may be sure that things haven't come to the present pass with those people, without blame on both sides."

"Oh, do you defend a man for such beastliness by that stale old plea of blame on both sides?" demanded Halleck, indignantly.

"No; but I should like to know what she had said or done to provoke it before I excused her altogether."

"You would! Imagine the case reversed!"

"It isn't imaginable."

"You think there is a special code of morals for women; sins and shames for them that are no sins and shames for us!"

"No, I don't think that. I merely suggest that you don't idealize the victim in this instance. I dare say she hasn't suffered half as much as you have. Remember that she's a person of commonplace traditions, and probably took a simple view of the matter, and let it go as something that could not be helped."

"No, that would not do either," said Halleck.

"You're hard to please. Suppose we imagine her proud enough to face you down on the fact for his sake; too proud to revenge her disgrace on you"—

"Oh, you come back to your old plea of magnanimity! Atherton, it makes me sick at heart to think of that poor creature. That look of hers haunts me! I can't get rid of it!"

Atherton sat considering his friend with a curious smile.

"Well, I'm sorry this has happened to *you*, Halleck."

"Oh, why do you say that to me?" demanded Halleck, impatiently. "Am I a nervous woman, that I must be kept from unpleasant sights and disagreeable experiences? If there's anything of the man about me, you insult it! Why not be a little sorry for her?"

"I'm sorry enough for her; but I suspect that so far you have been the principal sufferer. She's simply accepted the fact and survived it."

"So much the worse, so much the worse!" groaned Halleck. "She'd better have died!"

"Well, perhaps. I dare say she thinks it will never happen again, and has dismissed the subject; while you've had it happening ever since, whenever you've thought of her."

Halleck struck the arms of his chair with his clenched hands.

"Confound the fellow! What business has he to come back into my way, and make me think about his wife? Oh, very likely, it's quite as you say! I dare say she's stupidly content with him; that she's forgiven it and forgotten all about it. Probably she's told him how I behaved, and they've laughed over me together. But does that make it any easier to bear?"

"It ought," said Atherton. "What did the husband do when you met them?"

"Everything but tip me the wink—everything but say in so many words: 'You see I've made it all right with her. Don't you wish you knew how?'"

Halleck dropped his head, with a wrathful groan.

"I fancy," said Atherton, thoughtfully, "that if we really knew how, it would surprise us. Married life is as much a mystery to us outsiders as the life to come, almost. The ordinary motives don't seem to count; it's the realm of unreason. If a man only makes his wife suffer enough, she finds out that she loves him so much she *must* forgive him. And then, there's a great deal in their being bound. They can't live together in enmity, and they must live together. I dare say the offense had merely worn itself out between them."

"Oh, I dare say," Halleck assented, wearily. "That isn't my idea of marriage though."

"It's not mine, either," returned Atherton. "The question is whether it isn't often the fact in regard to such people's marriages."

"Then, they are so many hells," cried Halleck, "where self-respect perishes with resentment, and the husband and wife are enslaved to each other. They ought to be broken up!"

"I don't think so," said Atherton, soberly. "The sort of men and women that marriage enslaves would be vastly more wretched and mischievous, if they were set free. I believe that the hell people make for themselves isn't at all a bad place for them. It's the best place for them."

"Oh, I know your doctrine," said Halleck, rising. "It's horrible. How a man with any kindness in his heart can harbor such a cold-blooded philosophy, *I* don't understand. I wish you joy of it. Good-night," he added, gloomily, taking his hat from the table. "It serves me right for coming to you with a matter that I ought to have been man enough to keep to myself."

Atherton followed him toward the door.

"It wont do you any harm to consider your perplexity in the light of my philosophy. An unhappy marriage isn't the only hell, nor the worst."

Halleck turned.

"What could be a worse hell than marriage without love?" he demanded, fiercely.

"Love without marriage," said Atherton.

Halleck looked sharply at his friend. Then he shrugged his shoulders as he turned again and swung out of the door.

"You're too esoteric for me. It's quite time I was gone."

The way through Clover street was not the shortest way home; but he climbed the hill and passed the little house. He wished to rehabilitate in its pathetic beauty the image which his friend's conjectures had jarred, distorted, insulted; and he lingered for a moment before the door where this vision had claimed his pity for anguish that no after serenity could repudiate. The silence in which the house was wrapt was like another fold of the mystery which involved him. The night wind rose in a sudden gust, and made the neighboring lamp flare, and his shadow wavered across the pavement like the figure of a drunken man. This and not that other was the image which he saw.

XXVII

"OF COURSE," said Marcia, when she and Bartley recurred to the subject of her visit to Equity, "I have always felt as if I should like to have you with me, so as to keep people from talking, and show that it's all right between you and father. But if you don't wish to go, I can't ask it."

"I understand what you mean, and I should like to gratify you," said Bartley. "Not that I care a rap what all the people in Equity think. I'll tell you what I'll do: I'll go down there with you and hang round a day or two; and then I'll come after you, when your time's up, and stay a day or two there. I *couldn't* stand three weeks in Equity."

In the end, he behaved very handsomely. He dressed Flavia out to kill, as he said, in lace hoods and embroidered long-clothes, for which he tossed over half the ready-made stock of the great dry-goods stores; and he made Marcia get herself a new suit throughout, with a bonnet to match, which she thought she could not afford; but he said he should manage it somehow. In Equity he spared no pains to deepen the impression of his success in Boston, and he was affable with everybody. He hailed his friends across the street, waving his hand to them, and shouting out a jolly greeting. He visited the hotel office and the stores to meet the loungers there; he stepped into the printing-office and congratulated Henry Bird on having stopped the Free Press and devoted himself to job-work. He said "Hallo, Marilla! Hallo, Hannah!" and he stood a good while beside the latter at her case, joking and laughing.

He had no resentments. He stopped old Morrison on the street and shook hands with him. "Well, Mr. Morrison, do you find it as easy to get Hannah's wages advanced nowadays as you used to?"

As for his relations with Squire Gaylord, he flattened public conjecture out like a pancake, as he told Marcia, by making the old gentleman walk arm-and-arm with him the whole length of the village street the morning after his arrival. "And I never saw your honored father look as if he enjoyed a thing less," added Bartley. "Well, what's the use? He couldn't help himself." They had arrived on Friday evening, and after spending Saturday in this social way, Bartley magnanimously went with Marcia to church. He was in good spirits, and he shook hands, right and left, as he came out of church. In the afternoon he had up the best team from the hotel stable, and took Marcia the Long Drive, which they had taken the day of their engagement. He could not be contented without pushing the perambulator out after tea, and making Marcia walk beside it, to let people see them with the baby.

He went away the next morning on an early train, after a parting which he made very cheery, and a promise to come down again as soon as he could manage it. Marcia watched him drive off toward the station in the hotel barge, and then she went upstairs to their room, where she had been so long a young girl, and where now their child lay sleeping. The little one seemed the least part of all the change that had taken place. In this room she used to sit and think of him; she used to fly up thither when he came unexpectedly, and order her hair or change a ribbon or her dress, that she might please him better; at these windows she used to sit and watch and long for his coming; from these she saw him go by that day when she thought she should see him no more, and took heart of her despair to risk the wild chance that made him hers. There was a deadly, unsympathetic stillness in the room, which seemed to leave to her all the responsibility for what she had done.

The days began to go by in a sunny, still, midsummer monotony. She pushed the baby out in its carriage, and saw the summer boarders walking or driving through the streets; she returned the visits that the neighbors paid her; in-doors she helped her mother about the house-work. An image of her maiden life reinstated itself. At times it seemed almost as if she had dreamed her marriage. When she looked at her baby in these moods, she thought she was dreaming yet. A young wife, suddenly parted for the first time from her husband, in whose intense possession she has lost her individual existence, and devolving upon her old separate personality, must have strong fancies, strange sensations. Marcia's marriage had been full of such shocks and storms as might well have left her dazed in their entire cessation.

"She seems to be pretty well satisfied here," said her father, one evening when she had gone upstairs with her sleeping baby in her arms.

"She seems to be pretty quiet," her mother non-committally assented.

"Myes," snarled the Squire, and he fell into a long revery, while Mrs. Gaylord went on crocheting the baby a bib, and the smell of the petunia-bed under the window came in through the mosquito-netting. "Myes," he resumed, "I guess you're right. I guess it's only quiet. I guess she aint any more likely to be satisfied than the rest of us."

"I don't see why she shouldn't be," said Mrs. Gaylord, resenting the compassion in the Squire's tone with that curious jealousy a wife feels for her husband's indulgence of their daughter. "She's had her way."

"She's had her way, poor girl,—yes. But I don't know as it satisfies people to have their way always."

Doubtless Mrs. Gaylord saw that her husband wished to talk about Marcia, and must be helped to do so by a little perverseness.

"I don't know but what most of folks would say't she'd made out pretty well. I guess she's got a good provider."

"She didn't need any provider," said the Squire haughtily.

"No; but so long as she would have something, it's well enough that she should have a provider." Mrs. Gaylord felt that this was reasoning, and she smoothed out so much of the bib as she had crocheted across her knees with an air of self-content. "You can't have everything in a husband," she added, "and Marcia ought to know that by this time."

"I've no doubt she knows it," said the Squire.

"Why, what makes you think she's disappointed any?" Mrs. Gaylord came plump to the question at last.

"Nothing she ever said," returned her husband promptly. "She'd die first. When I was up there I thought she talked about him too much to be feeling just right about him. It was Bartley this and Bartley that, the whole while. She was always wanting me to say that I thought she had done right to marry him. I *did* sort of say it, at last—to please her—but I kept thinking that if she felt sure of it, she wouldn't want to talk it into me so. Now, she never mentions him at all, if she can help it. She writes to him every day, and she hears from him often enough—postals, mostly—but she don't talk about Bartley. Bartley!" The Squire stretched his lips back from his teeth, and inhaled a long breath, as he rubbed his chin.

"You don't suppose anything's happened since you was up there," said Mrs. Gaylord.

"Nothing but what's happened from the start. *He's* happened. He keeps happening right along, I guess."

Mrs. Gaylord found herself upon the point of experiencing a painful emotion of sympathy, but she saved herself by saying:

"Well, Mr. Gaylord, I don't know as you've got anybody but yourself to thank for it all. You got him here, in the first *place*."

She took one of the kerosene lamps from the table and went upstairs, leaving him to follow at his will.

Marcia sometimes went out to the Squire's office in the morning, carrying her baby with her, and propping her with law-books on a newspaper in the middle of the floor, while she dusted the shelves, or sat down for one of the desultory talks or the satisfactory silences which she had with her father.

He usually found her there when he came up from the post-office, with the morning mail in the top of his hat: the last evening's Events,—which Bartley had said must pass for a letter from him when he did not write,—and a letter or a postal card from him. She read these, and gave her father any news or message that Bartley sent; and then she sat down at his table to answer them. But one morning, after she had been at home nearly a month, she received a letter for which she postponed Bartley's postal. "It's from Olive Halleck!" she said, with a glance at the handwriting on the envelope; and she tore it open, and ran it through. "Yes, and they'll come here, any time I let them know. They've been at Niagara, and they've come down the St. Lawrence to Quebec, and they will be at North Conway the last of next week. Now, father, I want to do something for them!" she cried, feeling an American daughter's right to dispose of her father and all his possessions for the behoof of her friends at any time. "I want they should come to the house."

"Well, I guess there wont be any trouble about that, if you think they can put up with our way of living." He smiled at her over his spectacles.

"Our way of living! Put up with it! I should hope as *much!* They're just the kind of people that will put up with anything, because they've had everything, and because they're all as sweet and good as they can be. You don't know them, father, you don't half know them! Now, just get right away"—she pushed him out of the chair he had taken at the table—"and let me write to Bartley this instant. He's *got* to come when they're here and I'll invite them to come over at once before they get settled at North Conway."

He gave his dry chuckle to see her so fired with pleasure, and he enjoyed the ardor with which she drove him up out of his chair and dashed off her letters. This was her old way; he would have liked the prospect of the Hallecks' coming, because it made his girl so happy, if for nothing else.

"Father, I will tell you about Ben Halleck," she said, pounding her letter to Olive with the thick of her hand to make the envelope stick. "You know that lameness of his?"

"Yes."

"Well, it came from his being thrown down by another boy when he was at school. He knew the boy that did it; and the boy must have known that Mr. Halleck knew it; but he never said a word to show that he was sorry, or did anything to make up for it. He's a man, now, and lives there in Boston, and Ben Halleck often meets him. He says that if the man can stand it *he* can. Don't you think that's grand? When I heard that I made up my mind that I wanted Flavia to belong to Ben Halleck's church—or the church he did belong to; he doesn't belong to any now!"

"He couldn't have got any damages for such a thing anyway," the Squire said.

Marcia paid no heed to this legal opinion of the case. She took off her father's hat to put the letters into it, and replacing it on his head,—"Now, don't you forget them, father," she cried.

She gathered up her baby and hurried into the house, where she began her preparations for her guests.

The elder Miss Hallecks had announced with much love, through Olive, that they should not be able to come to Equity, and Ben was to bring Olive alone. Marcia decided that Ben should have the guest chamber and Olive should have her room; she and Bartley could take the little room in the L, while their guests remained.

But when the Hallecks came, it appeared that Ben had engaged quarters for himself at the hotel, and no expostulation would prevail with him to come to Squire Gaylord's house.

"We have to humor him in such things, Mrs. Hubbard," Olive explained to Marcia's distress. "And most people get on very well without him."

This explanation was, of course, given in Halleck's presence. His sister added, behind his back:

"Ben has a perfectly morbid dread of giving trouble in a house. He wont let us do anything to make him comfortable at home, and the idea that you should attempt it drove him distracted. You *mustn't* mind it. I don't believe he'd have come if his bachelor freedom couldn't have been respected; and we both wanted to come very much."

The Hallecks arrived in the forenoon and Bartley was due in the evening. But during the afternoon Marcia had a telegram, saying that he could not come till two days later, and asking her to postpone the picnic she had planned. The Hallecks were only going to stay three days, and the suspicion that Bartley had delayed in order to leave himself as little time as possible with them, rankled in her heart so that she could not keep it to herself when they met.

"Was that what made you give me such a cool reception?" he asked, with cynical good-nature. "Well, you're mistaken; I don't suppose I mind the Hallecks any more than they do me. I'll tell you why I staid. Some people dropped down on Witherby, who were a little out of his line—fashionable people that he had asked to let him know if they ever came to Boston; and when they did come and let him know he didn't know what to do about it, and he called on me to help him out. I've been almost boarding with Witherby for the last three days; and I've been barouching round all over the moral vine-yard with his friends: out to Mount Auburn and the Washington Elm and Bunker Hill and Brookline and the Art Museum and Lexington; we've been down the harbor, and we haven't left a monumental stone unturned. They were going north, and they came down here with me; and I got them to stop over a day for the picnic."

"You got them to stop over for the picnic? Why, *I* don't want anybody but ourselves, Bartley! This spoils everything."

"The Hallecks are not ourselves," said Bartley. "And these are jolly people; they'll help to make it go off."

"Who are they?" asked Marcia, with provisional self-control.

"Oh, some people that Witherby met in Portland at Willett's, who used to have the logging camp out here."

"That Montreal woman!" cried Marcia, with fatal divination.

Bartley laughed.

"Yes, Mrs. Macallister and her husband. She's a regular case. She'll amuse you."

Marcia's passionate eyes blazed.

"She shall never come to my picnic in the world!"

"No?" Bartley looked at her in a certain way. "She shall come to mine, then. There will be two picnics. The more the merrier."

Marcia gasped, as if she felt the clutch, in which her husband had her, tightening on her heart. She saw that she could only carry her point against him at the cost of disgraceful division before the Hallecks, for which he would not care in the least. She moved her head a little from side to side, like one that breathes a stifling air. "Oh, let her come," she said quietly, at last.

"Now you're talking business," said Bartley. "I haven't forgotten the little snub Mrs. Macallister gave me, and you'll see me pay her off."

Marcia made no answer, but went down stairs to put what face she could upon the matter to Olive, whom she had left alone in the parlor, while she ran up with Bartley immediately upon his arrival to demand an explanation of him. In her wrathful haste she had forgotten to kiss him, and she now remembered that he had not looked at the baby, which she had all the time had in her arms.

The picnic was to be in a pretty glen three or four miles north of the village, where there was shade on a bit of level green, and a spring bubbling out of a fern-hung bluff: from which you looked down the glen over a stretch of the river. Marcia had planned that they were to drive thither in a four-seated carryall, but the addition of Bartley's guests disarranged this.

"There's only one way," said Mrs. Macallister, who had

driven up with her husband from the hotel to the Squire's house in a buggy. "Mr. Halleck tells me he doesn't know how to drive, and me husband doesn't know the way. Mr. Hubbard must get in here with me, and you must take Mr. Macallister in your party." She looked authoritatively at the others.

"First-rate!" cried Bartley, climbing to the seat which Mr. Macallister left vacant. "We'll lead the way."

Those who followed had difficulty in keeping their buggy in sight. Sometimes Bartley stopped long enough for them to come up, and then, after a word or two of gay banter, was off again.

They had taken possession of the picnic grounds, and Mrs. Macallister was disposing shawls for rugs and drapery, while Bartley, who had got the horse out, and tethered where he could graze, was pushing the buggy out of the way by the shafts when the carryall came up.

"Don't we look quite domestic?" she asked of the arriving company, in her neat English tone, and her rising English inflection. "You know I like this," she added, singling Halleck out for her remark, and making it as if it were brilliant. "I like being out of doors, don't you know. But there's one thing I don't like: we weren't able to get a drop of champagne at that ridiculous hotel. They told us they were not allowed to keep 'intoxicating liquors.' Now I call that jolly stupid, you know. I don't know whatever we shall do if you haven't brought something."

"I believe this is a famous spring," said Halleck.

"How droll you are! Spring, indeed!" cried Mrs. Macallister. "Is *that* the way you let your brother make game of people, Miss Halleck?" She directed a good deal of her rattle at Olive; she scarcely spoke to Marcia, but she was nevertheless furtively observant of her. Mr. Macallister had his rattle, too, which after trying it unsatisfactorily upon Marcia he plied almost exclusively for Olive. He made puns; he asked conundrums; he had all the accomplishments which keep people going in a lively, unintellectual, colonial society; and he had the idea that he must pay attentions and promote repartee. His wife and he played into each other's hands in their *jeux d'esprit*; and kept Olive's inquiring Boston mind at work in the vain endeavor to account for and to place them socially. Bartley hung about Mrs. Macallister, and was nearly as obedient as her husband. He felt that the Hallecks disapproved his behavior, and that made him enjoy it; he was almost rudely negligent of Olive.

The composition of the party left Marcia and Halleck necessarily to each other, and she accepted this arrangement in a sort of passive seriousness; but Halleck saw that her thoughts wandered from her talk with him, and that her eyes were always turning with painful anxiety to Bartley. After their lunch, which left them with the whole afternoon before them, Marcia said, in a timid effort to resume her best leadership of the affair:

"Bartley, don't you think they would like to see the view from the Devil's Backbone?"

"Would you like to see the view from the Devil's Backbone?" he asked in turn of Mrs. Macallister.

"And *what* is the Devil's Backbone?" she inquired.

"It's a ridge of rocks on the bluff above here," said Bartley, nodding his head vaguely toward the bank.

"And *how* do you get to it?" asked Mrs. Macallister, pointing her pretty chin at him in lifting her head to look.

"Walk."

"Thanks; then I shall try to be satisfied with me own backbone," said Mrs. Macallister, who had that freedom in alluding to her anatomy which marks the superior civilization of Great Britain and its colonial dependencies.

"Carry you," suggested Bartley.

"I dare say you'd be very sure-footed; but I'd quite enough of donkeys in the hills at home."

Bartley roared with the resolution of a man who will enjoy a joke at his own expense.

Marcia turned away, and referred her invitation with a glance to Olive.

"I don't believe Miss Halleck wants to go," said Mr. Macallister.

"I couldn't," said Olive, regretfully. "I've neither the feet nor the head for climbing over high rocky places."

Marcia was about to sink down on the grass again, from which she had risen in the hopes that her proposition would succeed, when Bartley called out:

"Why don't you show Ben the Devil's Backbone? The view is worth seeing, Halleck."

"Would you like to go?" asked Marcia, listlessly.

"Yes, I should, very much," said Halleck, scrambling to his feet, "if it wont tire you too much?"

"Oh, no," said Marcia, gently, and led the way. She kept ahead of him in the climb, as she easily could, and she answered briefly to all he said. When they arrived at the top, "There is the view," she said coldly. She waved her hand toward the valley; she made a sound in her throat as if she would speak again, but her voice died in one broken sob.

Halleck stood with downcast eyes and trembled. He durst not look at her, not for what he should see in her face, but for what she should see in his: the anguish of intelligence, the helpless pity. He beat the rock at his feet with the ferule of his stick, and could not lift his head again. When he did, she stood turned from him and drying her eyes on her handkerchief. Their looks met, and she trusted her self-betrayal to him without any attempt at excuse or explanation.

"I will send Hubbard up to help you down," said Halleck.

"Well," she answered, sadly.

He clambered down the side of the bluff, and Bartley started to his feet in guilty alarm when he saw him approach. "What's the matter?"

"Nothing. But I think you had better help Mrs. Hubbard down the bluff."

"Oh!" cried Mrs. Macallister, "A panic! How interesting!"

Halleck did not respond. He threw himself on the grass, and left her to change or pursue the subject as she liked. Bartley showed more *savoir-faire* when he came back with Marcia, after an absence long enough to let her remove the traces of her tears.

"Pretty rough on your game foot, Halleck. But Marcia had got it into her head that it wasn't safe to trust you to help her down, even after you had helped her up."

"Ben," said Olive, when they were seated in the train the next day, "why *did* you send Marcia's husband up there to her?" She had the effect of not having rested till she could ask him.

"She was crying," he answered.

"What do you suppose could have been the matter?"

"What you do: she was miserable about his coquetting with that woman."

"Yes. I could see that she hated terribly to have her come; and that she felt put down by her all the time. What kind of person *is* Mrs. Macallister?"

"Oh, a fool," replied Halleck. "All flirts are fools."

"I think she's more wicked than foolish."

"Oh, no, flirts are better than they seem—perhaps because men are better than flirts think. But they make misery just the same."

"Yes," sighed Olive. "Poor Marcia, poor Marcia! But I suppose that if it were not Mrs. Macallister it would be some one else."

"Given Bartley Hubbard,—yes."

"And given Marcia. Well,—I don't like being mixed up with other people's unhappiness, Ben. It's dangerous."

"I don't like it either. But you can't very well keep out of people's unhappiness in this world."

"No," assented Olive, ruefully.

The talk fell, and Halleck attempted to read a newspaper, while Olive looked out of the window. She presently turned to him.

"Did you ever fancy any resemblance between Mrs. Hubbard and the photograph of that girl we used to joke about— your lost love?"

"Yes," said Halleck.

"What's become of it—the photograph? I can't find it any more; I wanted to show it to her, one day."

"I destroyed it. I burnt it the first evening after I had met Mrs. Hubbard. It seemed to me that it wasn't right to keep it."

"Why, you don't think it was *her* photograph!"

"I think it was," said Halleck.

He took up his paper again, and read on till they left the cars.

That evening, when Halleck came to his sister's room to bid her good-night, she threw her arms round his neck, and kissed his plain, common face, in which she saw a heavenly beauty.

"Ben, dear," she said, "if you don't turn out the happiest man in the world, I shall say there's no use in being good!"

"Perhaps you'd better say that after all I wasn't good," he suggested, with a melancholy smile.

"I shall know better," she retorted.

"Why, what's the matter, now?"

"Nothing. I was only thinking. Good-night!"

"Good-night," said Halleck. "You seem to think my room is better than my company, good as I am."

"Yes," she said, laughing, in that breathless way, which means weeping next, with women. Her eyes glistened.

"Well," said Halleck, limping out of the room, "you're quite good-looking with your hair down, Olive."

"All girls are," she answered. She leaned out of her door-way to watch him as he limped down the corridor to his own room. There was something pathetic, something disappointed and weary in the movement of his figure, and when she shut her door, and ran back to her mirror, she could not see the good-looking girl there for her tears.

XXVIII

"HELLO!" said Bartley, one day after the autumn had brought back all the summer wanderers to the city, "I haven't seen you for a month of Sundays." He had Ricker by the hand, and he pulled him into a door-way to be a little out of the rush on the crowded pavement, while they chatted.

"That's because I can't afford to go to the White Mountains, and swell round at the aristocratic summer resorts like some people," returned Ricker. "I'm a horny-handed son of toil, myself."

"Pshaw!" said Bartley. "Who isn't? I've been here hard at it, except for three days at one time and five at another."

"Well, all I can say is that I saw in the Record personals, that Mr. Hubbard, of the Events, was spending the summer months with his father-in-law, Judge Gaylord, among the spurs of the White Mountains. I supposed you wrote it yourself. You're full of ideas about journalism."

"Oh, come! I wouldn't work that joke any more. Look here, Ricker, I'll tell you what I want. I want you to dine with me."

"Dines people!" said Ricker, in an awe-stricken aside.

"No,—I mean business! You've never seen my kid yet, and you've never seen my house. I want you to come. We've all got back, and we're in nice running order. What day are you disengaged?"

"Let me see," said Ricker, thoughtfully. "So many engagements! Wait! I could squeeze your dinner in some time next month, Hubbard."

"All right. But suppose we say next Sunday. Six is the hour."

"Six? Oh, I can't dine in the middle of the forenoon that way! Make it later!"

"Well, we'll say one P.M., then. I know your dinner hour. We shall expect you."

"Better not, till I come." Bartley knew that this was Ricker's way of accepting, and he said nothing, but he answered his next question with easy joviality. "How are you making it with old Witherby?"

"Oh, hand over hand! Witherby and I were formed for each other. By-by!"

"No, hold on! Why don't you come to the club any more?"

"We-e-ll! The club isn't what it used to be," said Bartley, confidentially.

"Why, of course! It isn't just the thing for a gentleman moving in the select circles of Clover street, as you do; but why not come, sometimes, in the character of distinguished guest, and encourage your humble friends? I was talking with a lot of the fellows about you the other night."

"Were they abusing me?"

"They were speaking the truth about you, and I stopped them. I told them that sort of thing wouldn't do. Why, you're getting fat!"

"You're behind the times, Ricker," said Bartley. "I began to get fat six months ago. I don't wonder the Chronicle-Abstract is running down on your hands. Come round and try my Tivoli on Sunday. That's what gives a man girth, my boy." He tapped Ricker lightly on his hollow waistcoat, and left him with a wave of his hand.

Ricker leaned out of the door-way and followed him down the street with a troubled eye. He had taken stock in Bartley, as the saying is, and his heart misgave him that he should lose on the investment; he could not have sold out to any of their friends for twenty cents on the dollar. Nothing that any one could lay his finger on had happened, and yet there had been a general loss of confidence in that particular stock. Ricker himself had lost confidence in it, and when he lightly mentioned that talk at the club, with a lot of the fellows, he had a serious wish to get at Bartley some time, and see what it was that was beginning to make people mistrust him. The fellows who liked him at first and wished him well, and believed in his talent, had mostly dropped him. Bartley's associates were now the most raffish set on the press, or the green hands; and something had brought this to pass in less than two years. Ricker had believed that it was Witherby; at the Club he had contended that it was Bartley's association with Witherby that made people doubtful of him. As for those ideas that Bartley had advanced in their discussion of journalism, he had considered it all mere young man's nonsense that Bartley would outgrow. But now, as he looked at Bartley's back, he had his misgivings; it struck him as the back of a degenerate man, and that increasing bulk seemed not to represent an increase of wholesome substance, but a corky, buoyant tissue, materially responsive to some sort of moral dry-rot.

Bartley pushed on to the Events office in a blithe humor. Witherby had recently advanced his salary; he was giving him fifty dollars a week now; and Bartley had made himself necessary in more ways than one. He was not only readily serviceable, but since he had volunteered to write those advertising articles for an advance of pay, he was in possession of business facts that could be made very uncomfortable to Witherby in the event of a disagreement. Witherby not only paid him well, but treated him well; he even suffered Bartley to bully him a little, and let him foresee the day when he must be recognized as the real editor of the Events.

At home everything went on smoothly. The baby was well and growing fast; she was beginning to explode airy bubbles on her pretty lips that a fond superstition might interpret as papa and mamma. She had passed that stage in which a man regards his child with despair; she had passed out of slippery and evasive doughiness into a firm tangibility that made it some pleasure to hold her.

Bartley liked to take her on his lap, to feel the spring of her little legs, as she tried to rise on her feet; he liked to have her stretch out her arms to him from her mother's embrace. The innocent tenderness which he experienced at these moments, was satisfactory proof to him that he was a very good fellow, if not a good man. When he spent an evening at home, with Flavia in his lap for half an hour after dinner, he felt so domestic that he seemed to himself to be spending all his evenings at home now. Once or twice it had happened, when the housemaid was out, that he went to the door with the baby on his arm, and answered the ring of Olive and Ben Halleck, or of Olive and one or both of the intermediary sisters.

The Hallecks were the only people at all apt to call in the evening, and Bartley ran so little chance of meeting any one else, when he opened the door with Flavia on his arm, that probably he would not have thought it worth while to put her down, even if he had not rather enjoyed meeting them in that domestic phase. He had not only long felt how intensely Olive disliked him, but he had observed that somehow it embarrassed Ben Halleck to see him in his character of devoted young father. At those times he used to rally his old friend upon getting married, and laughed at the confusion to which the joke put him. He said more than once afterward that he did not see what fun Ben Halleck got out of coming there; it must bore even such a dull fellow as he was to sit a whole evening like that and not say twenty words. "Perhaps he's livelier when I'm not here, though," he suggested. "I always did seem to throw a wet blanket on Ben Halleck." He did not at all begrudge Halleck's having a better time in his absence if he could.

One night when the bell rung Bartley rose, and saying, "I wonder which of the tribe it is this time," went to the door. But when he opened it, instead of hearing the well-known voices, Marcia listened through a hesitating silence, which ended in a loud laugh from without, and a cry from her husband of "Well, I swear! Why, you infamous old scoundrel, come in out of the wet!" There ensued, amidst Bartley's voluble greetings, a noise of shy shuffling about in the hall, as of a man not perfectly master of his footing under social pressure, a sound of husky, embarrassed whispering, a dispute about doffing an overcoat, and question as to the disposition of a hat, and then Bartley re-appeared, driving before him the lank, long figure of a man who blinked in the flash of gaslight, as Bartley turned it all up in the chandelier overhead, and rubbed his immense hands in cruel embarrassment at the beauty of Marcia, set like a jewel in the pretty comfort of the little parlor.

"Mr. Kinney, Mrs. Hubbard," said Bartley, and, having accomplished the introduction, he hit Kinney a thwack between the shoulders with the flat of his hand that drove him stumbling across Marcia's foot-stool into the seat on the sofa to which she had pointed him. "You old fool, where did you come from?"

The refined warmth of Bartley's welcome seemed to make Kinney feel at home, in spite of his trepidations at Marcia's presence. He bobbed his head forward, and stretched his mouth wide, in one of his vast, silent laughs. "Better ask where I'm goin' to."

"Well, I'll ask that, if it'll be any accommodation. Where you going?"

"Illinois."

"For a divorce?"

"Try again."

"To get married?"

"Maybe, after I've made my pile." Kinney's eyes wandered about the room, and took in its evidences of prosperity, with simple, unenvious admiration; he ended with a furtive glimpse of Marcia, who seemed to be a climax of good-luck too dazzling for contemplation; he withdrew his glance from her as if hurt by her splendor, and became serious.

"Well, you're the *last* man I ever expected to see again," said Bartley, sitting down with the baby in his lap, and contemplating Kinney with deliberation. Kinney was dressed in

a long frock coat of cheap diagonals, black cassimere pantaloons, a blue neck-tie, and a celluloid collar. He had evidently
had one of his encounters with a cheap clothier, in which the
Jew had triumphed; but he had not yet visited a barber, and
his hair and beard were as shaggy as they were in the logging
camp; his hands and face were as brown as leather. "But I'm
as glad," Bartley added, "as if you had telegraphed you were
coming. Of course, you're going to put up with us." He had
observed Kinney's awe of Marcia, and he added this touch to
let Kinney see that he was master in his house, and lord even
of that radiant presence.

Kinney started in real distress.

"Oh, no! I couldn't do it! I've got all my things round at
the Quincy House."

"Trunk or bag?" asked Bartley.

"Well, it's a bag; but"—

"All right. We'll step round and get it together. I generally
take a little stroll out, after dinner," said Bartley, tranquilly.

Kinney was beginning again when Marcia, who had been
stealing some covert looks at him under her eyelashes, while
she put together the sewing she was at work on, preparatory to
going up-stairs with the baby, joined Bartley in his invitation.

"You wont make us the least trouble, Mr. Kinney," she
said. "The guest-chamber is all ready, and we shall be glad to
have you stay."

Kinney must have felt the note of sincerity in her words. He
hesitated, and Bartley clinched his tacit assent with a quota-
tion:

" 'The chief ornament of a house is the guests who frequent
it.' Who says that?"

Kinney's little blue eyes twinkled.

"Old Emerson."

"Well, I agree with him. We don't care anything about your
company, Kinney; but we want you for decorative purposes."

Kinney opened his mouth for another noiseless laugh, and
said:

"Well, fix it to suit yourselves."

"I'll carry her up for you," said Bartley to Marcia, who was stooping forward to take the baby from him, "if Mr. Kinney will excuse us a moment."

"All right," said Kinney.

Bartley ventured upon this bold move, because he had found that it was always best to have things out with Marcia at once, and if she was going to take his hospitality to Kinney in bad part, he wanted to get through the trouble.

"That was very nice of you, Marcia," he said, when they were in their own room. "My invitation rather slipped out, and I didn't know how you would like it."

"Oh, I'm very glad to have him stay. I never forget about his wanting to lend you money that time," said Marcia, opening the baby's crib.

"You're a mighty good fellow, Marcia!" cried Bartley, kissing her over the top of the baby's head as she took it from him. "And I'm not half good enough for you. You never forget a benefit. Nor an injury, either," he added, with a laugh. "And I'm afraid that I forget one about as easily as the other."

Marcia's eyes suffused themselves at this touch of self-analysis which, coming from Bartley, had its sadness; but she said nothing, and he was eager to escape and get back to their guest. He told her he should go out with Kinney, and that she was not to sit up, for they might be out late.

In his pride, he took Kinney down to the Events office, and unlocked it, and lit the gas, so as to show him the editorial rooms; and then he passed him into one of the theatres, where they saw part of an Offenbach opera; after that they went to the Parker House and had a New York stew. Kinney said he must be off by the Sunday-night train, and Bartley thought it well to concentrate as many dazzling effects upon him as he could in the single evening at his disposal. He only regretted that it was not the club night, for he would have liked to take Kinney round and show him some of the fellows.

"But never mind," he said. "I'm going to have one of them

dine with us to-morrow, and you'll see about the best of the lot."

"Well, sir," observed Kinney, when they had got back into Bartley's parlor, and he was again drinking in its prettiness in the subdued light of the shaded Argand burner. "I hain't seen anything yet that suits me much better than this."

"It isn't bad," said Bartley. He had got up a plate of crackers and two bottles of Tivoli, and was opening the first. He offered the beaded goblet to Kinney.

"Thank you," said Kinney. "Not any. I never do."

Bartley quaffed half of it in tolerant content.

"I *always* do. Find it takes my nerves down at the end of a hard week's work. Well, now, tell me something about yourself. What are you going to do in Illinois?"

"Well, sir, I've got a friend out there that's got a coal mine, and he thinks he can work me in somehow. I guess he can; I've tried pretty much everything. Why don't you come out there and start a newspaper? We've got a town that's bound to grow."

It amused Bartley to hear Kinney bragging already of a town that he had never seen. He winked a good-natured disdain over the rim of the goblet which he tilted on his lips. "And give up my chances here?" he said, as he set the goblet down:

"Well, that's so!" said Kinney, responding to the sense of the wink. "I'll tell you what, Bartley, I didn't know as you'd speak to me when I rung your bell to-night. But thinks I to myself, 'Dumn it! look here! He can't more'n slam the door in your face, anyway. And you've hankered after him so long—go and take your chances, you old buzzard!' And so I got your address at the Events office pretty early this morning; and I went round all day screwing my courage up, as old Macbeth says—or Ritchloo; *I* don't know which it was—and at last I *did* get myself so that I toed the mark like a little man."

Bartley laughed so that he could hardly get the cork out of the second bottle.

"You see," said Kinney, leaning forward, and taking Bartley's plump, soft knee between his thumb and forefinger, "I felt awfully about the way we parted that night. I felt *bad*. I hadn't acted well, just to my own mind; and it cut me to have you refuse my money; it cut me all the worse because I saw that you was partly right; I *hadn't* been quite fair with you. But I always did admire you, and you know it. Some them little things you used to get off in the old Free Press—well, I could see't you was *smart*. And I liked you; and it kind o' hurt me when I thought you'd been makin' fun o' me to that woman. Well, I could see't I was a dumned old fool, afterward. And I always wanted to tell you so. And I always *did* hope that I should be able to offer you that money again, twice over, and get you to take it just to show that you didn't bear malice." Bartley looked up, with quickened interest. "But I can't do it now, sir," added Kinney.

"Why, what's happened?" asked Bartley, in a disappointed tone, pouring out his second glass from his second bottle.

"Well, sir," said Kinney, with a certain reluctance, "I undertook to provision the camp on spec, last winter, and,—well, you know, I always run a little on food for the brain"— Bartley broke into a reminiscent cackle, and Kinney smiled forlornly,—"and thinks I 'Dumn it, I'll give 'em the real thing, every time.' And I got hold of a health-food circular; and I sent on for a half a dozen barrels of their crackers and half a dozen of their flour, and a lot of cracked cocoa, and I put the camp on a health-food basis. I calculated to bring those fellows out in the spring physically vigorous and mentally enlightened. But my goodness! After the first bakin' o' that flour and the first round o' them crackers it was all up! Fellows got so mad that I suppose if I hadn't gone back to doughnuts and sody biscuits and Japan tea, they'd 'a' burnt the camp down. Of course I yielded. But it ruined me, Bartley; it bu'st me."

Bartley dropped his arms upon the table, and, hiding his face upon them, laughed and laughed again.

"Well, sir," said Kinney, with sad satisfaction, "I'm glad to see that you don't need any money from me." He had been taking another survey of the parlor and the dining-room beyond. "I don't know as I ever saw anybody much better fixed. I should say that you was a success; and you deserve it. You're a smart fellow, Bart, and you're a good fellow. You're a generous fellow." Kinney's voice shook with emotion.

Bartley having lifted his wet and flushed face, managed to say: "Oh, there's nothing mean about *me*, Kinney," as he felt blindly for the beer bottles, which he shook in succession with an evident surprise at finding them empty.

"You've acted like a brother to me, Bartley Hubbard," continued Kinney, "and I shan't forget it in a hurry. I guess it would about broke my heart if you hadn't taken it just the way you did to-night. I should like to see the man that didn't use you well; or the woman, either!" said Kinney, with vague defiance. "Though *they* don't seem to have done so bad by you," he added, in recognition of Marcia's merit. "I should say *that* was the biggest part of your luck. She's a lady, sir, every inch of her. Mighty different stripe from that Montreal woman that cut up so that night."

"Oh, Mrs. Macallister wasn't such a scamp, after all," said Bartley, with magnanimity.

"Well, sir, *you* can say so. I ain't going to be too strict with a *girl*; but I like to see a married woman *act* like a married woman. Now, I don't think you'd catch Mrs. Hubbard flirting with a young fellow the way that woman carried on with you, that night?"

Bartley grinned.

"Well, sir, you're getting along, and you're happy."

"Perfect clam," said Bartley.

"Such a position as you've got—such a house, such a wife, *and* such a baby. Well," said Kinney, rising, "it's a little too much for *me*."

"Want to go to bed?" asked Bartley.

"Yes, I guess I better turn in," returned Kinney, despairingly.

"Show you the way."

Bartley tripped upstairs with Kinney's bag, which they had left standing in the hall, while Kinney creaked carefully after him; and so led the way to the guest chamber, and turned up the gaslight, which had been left burning low.

Kinney stood erect, dwarfing the room, and looked round on the pink chintzing and soft carpet and white coverleted bed and lace-hooded dressing-mirror, with meek veneration.

"Well, I swear!"

He said no more, but sat hopelessly down, and began to pull off his boots.

He was in the same humble mood the next morning, when, having got up inordinately early, he was found trying to fix his mind on a newspaper by Bartley, who came down late to the Sunday breakfast, and led his guest into the dining-room. Marcia, in a bewitching morning-gown, was already there, having put the daintier touches to the meal herself, and the baby in a fresh white dress was there, tied into its arm-chair with a napkin, and beating on the table with a spoon. Bartley's nonchalance amidst all this impressed Kinney with yet more poignant sense of his superiority, and almost deprived him of the powers of speech. When, after breakfast, Bartley took him out to Cambridge on the horse-cars, and showed him the College Buildings and Memorial Hall and the Washington Elm and Mount Auburn, Kinney fell into such a cowed and broken condition that something had to be specially done to put him in repair against Ricker's coming to dinner. Marcia luckily thought of asking him if he would like to see her kitchen. In this region Kinney found himself at home, and praised its neat perfection with professional intelligence. Bartley followed them round with Flavia on his arm, and put in a jocose word here and there, when he saw Kinney about to fall a prey to his respect for Marcia, and so kept him going till Ricker rang. He contrived to give Ricker a hint of the sort of man he had on his hands, and by their joint effort they had Kinney talking about himself at dinner before he knew what he was about. He could not help talking well upon this theme, and he had them so vividly interested, as he poured out adventure after adventure in his strange career, that Bartley began to be proud of him.

"Well, sir," said Ricker, when he came to a pause, "you've lived a romance."

"Yes," replied Kinney, looking at Bartley for his approval, "and I've always thought that if I ever got run clean ashore, high and dry, I'd make a stagger to write it out and do something with it. Do you suppose I could?"

"I promise to take it for the Sunday edition of the Chronicle-Abstract, whenever you get it ready," said Ricker.

Bartley laid his hand on his friend's arm.

"It's bought up, old fellow. That narrative—'Confessions of an Average American'—belongs to the Events."

They had their laugh at this, and then Ricker said to Kinney:

"But look here, my friend! What's to prevent our interviewing you on this little personal history of yours, and using your material any way we like? It seems to me that you've put your head in the lion's mouth."

"Oh, I'm amongst gentlemen," said Kinney, with an innocent swagger. "I understand that."

"Well, I don't know about it," said Ricker. "Hubbard, here, is used to all sorts of hard names; but I've never had that epithet applied to me before."

Kinney doubled himself up over the side of his chair in recognition of Ricker's joke; and when Bartley rose and asked him if he would come into the parlor and have a cigar, he said, with a wink, no, he guessed he would stay with the ladies. He waited with great mystery till the folding-doors were closed and Bartley had stopped peeping through the crevice between them, and then he began to disengage from his watch-chain the golden nugget, shaped to a rude sphere, which hung there. This done, he asked if he might put it on the little necklace—a christening gift from Mrs. Halleck—which the baby had on, to see how it looked. It looked very well, like an old Roman *bolla*, though neither Kinney nor Marcia knew it.

"Guess we'll let it stay there," he suggested, timidly.

"Mr. Kinney!" cried Marcia, in amaze, "I can't let you!"

"Oh, *do* now, ma'am!" pleaded the big fellow, simply. "If you knew how much good it does me, you would. Why, it's been like heaven to me to get into such a home as this, for a day; it has indeed."

"Like heaven?" said Marcia, turning pale. "Oh, my!"

"Well, I don't mean any harm. What I mean is, I've knocked about the world so much, and never had any home of my own, that to see folks as happy as you be makes me happier than I've been since I don't know when. Now, you let it stay. It was the first piece of gold I picked up in Californy when I went out there in '50, and it's about the last; I didn't have very good luck. Well, of course! I know I aint fit to give it; but I want to do it. I think Bartley's about the greatest fellow, and he's the best fellow this world can show. That's the way I feel about him. And I want to do it. Sho! the thing wa'n't no use to me!"

Marcia always gave her maid of all work Sunday afternoon, and she would not trespass upon her rule because she had guests that day. Except for the confusion to which Kinney's unexpected gift had put her, she would have waited for him to join the others before she began to clear away the dinner; but now she mechanically began, and Kinney, to whom these domestic occupations were a second nature, joined her in the work, equally absent-minded in the fervor of his petition.

Bartley suddenly flung open the doors. "My dear, Mr. Ricker says he must be go"— He discovered Marcia with the dish of potatoes in her hand, and Kinney in the act of carrying off the platter of turkey. "Look here, Ricker!"

Kinney came to himself, and opening his mouth above the platter, wide enough to swallow the remains of the turkey, slapped his leg with the hand that he released for the purpose, and shouted, "The ruling passion, Bartley, the ruling passion!"

The men roared; but Marcia, even while she took in the situation, did not see anything so ridiculous in it as they. She smiled a little in sympathy with their mirth, and then said, with a look and tone which he had not seen or heard in her since the day of their picnic at Equity, "Come, see what Mr. Kinney has given baby, Bartley."

They sat up talking Kinney over after he was gone; but even at ten o'clock Bartley said he should not go to bed; he felt like writing.

XXIX

BARTLEY lived well, now. He felt that he could afford it, on fifty dollars a week; and yet somehow he had always a sheaf of unpaid bills on hand. Rent was so much, the butcher so much, the grocer so much; these were the great outlays, and he knew just what they were; but the sum total was always much larger than he expected. At a pinch, he borrowed; but he did not let Marcia know of this, for she would have starved herself to pay the debt; what was worse, she would have wished him to starve with her. He kept the purse and he kept the accounts; he was master in his house, and he meant to be so.

The pinch always seemed to come in the matter of clothes, and then Marcia gave up whatever she wanted, and said she must make the old things do. Bartley hated this; in his position he must dress well, and as there was nothing mean about him, he wished Marcia to dress well too. Just at this time he had set his heart on her having a certain sacque which they had noticed in a certain window one day when they were on Washington Street together. He surprised her a week later by bringing the sacque home to her, and he surprised himself with a sealskin cap which he had long coveted: it was coming winter, now, and for half a dozen days of the season he would really need the cap. There would be many days when it would be comfortable, and many others when it would be tolerable; and he looked so handsome in it that Marcia herself could not quite feel that it was an extravagance. She asked him how they could afford both of the things at once, but he answered with easy mystery that he had provided the funds; and she went gaily round with him to call on the Hallecks that evening and show off her sacque. It was so stylish and pretty that it won her a compliment from Ben Halleck, which she noticed because it was the first compliment, or anything like it, that he had ever paid her. She repeated it to Bartley. "He said that I looked like a Hungarian Princess that he saw in Vienna."

"Well, I suppose it has a hussar kind of look, with that fur trimming and that broad braid. Did anybody say anything about my cap?" asked Bartley with burlesque eagerness.

"Oh, poor Bartley!" she cried in laughing triumph. "I don't believe any of them noticed it; and you kept twirling it round in your hands all the time to make them look."

"Yes, I did my level best," said Bartley.

They had a jolly time about that. Marcia was proud of her sacque; when she took it off and held it up by the loop in the neck, so as to realize its prettiness, she said she should make it last three winters at least; and she leaned over and gave Bartley a sweet kiss of gratitude and affection, and told him not to try to make up for it by extra work, but to help her scrimp for it.

"I'd rather do the extra work," he protested. In fact he already had the extra work done. It was something that he felt he had the right to sell outside of the Events, and he carried his manuscript to Ricker and offered it to him for his Sunday edition.

Ricker read the title and ran his eye down the first slip, and then glanced quickly at Hubbard. "You don't mean it?"

"Yes, I do," said Bartley. "Why not?"

"I thought he was going to use the material himself some time."

Bartley laughed. "He use the material! Why he can't write, any more than a hen; he can make tracks on paper, but nobody would print 'em, much less buy 'em. I know him; he's all right. It wouldn't hurt the material for his purpose, any way; and he'll be tickled to death when he sees it, if he ever does.

Look here, Ricker!" added Bartley, with a touch of anger at the hesitation in his friend's face, "if you're going to spring any conscientious scruples on me, I prefer to offer my manuscript elsewhere. I give you the first chance at it; but it needn't go begging. Do you suppose I'd do this if I didn't understand the man and know just how he'd take it?"

"Why, of course, Hubbard! I beg your pardon. If you say it's all right I'm bound to be satisfied. What do you want for it?"

"Fifty dollars."

"That's a good deal, isn't it?"

"Yes, it is. But I can't afford to do a dishonorable thing for less money," said Bartley with a wink.

The next Sunday, when Marcia came home from church, she went into the parlor a moment to speak to Bartley, before she ran upstairs to the baby. He was writing, and she put her left hand on his back while with her right she held her sacque slung over her shoulder by the loop, and leaned forward with a wandering eye on the papers that strewed the table. In that attitude he felt her pause and grow absorbed, and then rigid; her light caress tightened into a grip. "Why how base! How shameful! That man shall never enter my doors again! Why, it's stealing!"

"What's the matter? What are you talking about?" Bartley looked up with a frown of preparation.

"This!" cried Marcia, snatching up the Chronicle-Abstract at which she had been looking. "Haven't you seen it? Here's Mr. Kinney's life all written out! And when he said that he was going to keep it, and write it out himself. That thief has stolen it!"

"Look out how you talk," said Bartley. "Kinney's an old fool, and he never could have written it out in the world"—

"That makes no difference. He said that he told the things because he knew he was among gentlemen. A great gentleman Mr. Ricker is! And I thought he was so nice!" The tears sprang to her eyes, which flashed again. "I want you to break off with him, Bartley; I don't want you to have anything to do with such a *thief!* And I shall be proud to tell everybody that you've broken off with him *because* he was a thief. Oh, Bartley"—

"Hold your tongue!" shouted her husband.

"I *wont* hold my tongue! And if you defend"—

"Don't you say a word against Ricker. It's all right, I tell you. You don't understand such things. You don't know what you're talking about. I—I—I wrote the thing myself."

He could face her, but she could not face him. There was a subsidence in her proud attitude, as if her physical strength had snapped with her breaking spirit.

"There's no theft about it," Bartley went on. "Kinney would never write it out, and if he did, I've put the material in better shape for him here than he could ever have given it. Six weeks from now nobody will remember a word of it; and he could tell the same things right over again, and they would be just as good as new." He went on to argue the point.

She seemed not to have listened to him. When he stopped, she said in a quiet, passionless voice:

"I suppose you wrote it to get money for this sacque."

"Yes; I did," replied Bartley.

She dropped it on the floor at his feet.

"I shall never wear it again," she said in the same tone, and a little sigh escaped her.

"Use your pleasure about that," said Bartley, sitting down to his writing again, as she turned and left the room.

She went upstairs and came down immediately, with the gold nugget, which she had wrenched from the baby's necklace, and laid it on the paper before him.

"Perhaps you would like to spend it for Tivoli beer," she suggested. "Flavia shall not wear it."

"I'll get it fitted on to my watch-chain." Bartley slipped it into his waistcoat pocket.

The sacque still lay on the floor at his feet; he pulled his chair a little forward and put his feet on it. He feigned to write awhile longer, and then he folded up his papers and went out, leaving Marcia to make her Sunday dinner alone. When he came home late at night, he found the sacque where she had dropped it, and with a curse he picked it up and hung it on the hat-rack in the hall.

He slept in the guest-chamber, and at times during the night the child cried in Marcia's room and waked him; and then he thought he heard a sound of sobbing which was not the child's. In the morning, when he came down to breakfast, Marcia met him with swollen eyes.

"Bartley," she said tremulously, "I wish you would tell me how you felt justified in writing out Mr. Kinney's life in that way."

"My dear," said Bartley, with perfect amiability, for he had slept off his anger, and he really felt sorry to see her so unhappy, "I would tell you almost anything you want on any other subject; but I think we had better remand that one to the safety of silence, and go upon the general supposition that I know what I'm about."

"I can't, Bartley!"

"Can't you? Well, that's a pity." He pulled his chair to the breakfast-table. "It seems to me that girl's imagination always fails her on Mondays. Can she never give us anything but hash and corn-bread when she's going to wash? However, the coffee's good. I suppose *you* made it?"

"Bartley!" persisted Marcia, "I want to believe in everything you do—I want to be proud of it"—

"That will be difficult," suggested Bartley, with an air of thoughtful impartiality, "for the wife of a newspaper man."

"No, no! It needn't be! It mustn't be! If you will only tell me"—

She stopped, as if she feared to repeat her offense.

Bartley leaned back in his chair and looked at her intense face with a smile.

"Tell you that in some way I had Kinney's authority to use his facts? Well, I should have done that yesterday if you had let me. In the first place, Kinney's the most helpless ass in the world. He could never have used his own facts. In the second place, there was hardly anything in his rigmarole the other day that he hadn't told me down there in the lumber camp, with full authority to use it in any way I liked; and I don't see how he could revoke that authority. That's the way I reasoned about it."

"I see—I see!" said Marcia, with humble eagerness.

"Well, that's all there is about it. What I've done can't hurt Kinney. If he ever does want to write his old facts out, he'll be glad to take my report of them, and—spoil it," said Bartley, ending with a laugh.

"And if—if there had been anything wrong about it," said Marcia, anxious to justify him to herself, "Mr. Ricker would have told you so when you offered him the article."

"I don't think Mr. Ricker would have ventured on any impertinence with me," said Bartley, with grandeur. But he lapsed into his wonted, easy way of taking everything. "What are you driving at, Marsh? I don't care particularly for what happened yesterday. We've had rows enough before, and I dare say we shall have them again. You gave me a bad quarter of an hour, and you gave yourself"—he looked at her tear-stained eyes—"a bad night, apparently. That's all there is about it."

"Oh, no, that isn't all! It isn't like the other quarrels we've had. When I think how I've felt toward you ever since, it *scares* me. There can't be anything sacred in our marriage unless we trust each other in everything."

"Well, *I* haven't done any of the mistrusting," said Bartley, with humorous lightness. "But isn't sacred rather a strong word to use in regard to our marriage, anyway?"

"Why—why—what do you mean, Bartley? We were married by a minister."

"Well, yes, by what was left of one," said Bartley. "He couldn't seem to shake himself together sufficiently to ask for the proof that we had declared our intention to get married."

Marcia looked mystified.

"Marriage

"Don't you remember his saying there was something else, and my suggesting to him that it was the fee?"

Marcia turned white.

"Father said the certificate was all right"—

"Oh, he asked to see it, did he? He is a prudent old gentleman. Well, it is all right."

"And what difference did it make about our not proving that we had declared our intention?" asked Marcia, as if only partly reassured.

"No difference to us; and only a difference of sixty dollars fine to him, if it was ever found out."

"And you let the poor old man run that risk?"

"Well, you see, it couldn't be helped. We hadn't declared our intention, and the lady seemed very anxious to be married. You needn't be troubled. We are married, right and tight enough; but I don't know that there's anything *sacred* about it."

"No," Marcia wailed out, "it's tainted with fraud from the beginning."

"If you like to say so," Bartley assented, putting his napkin into its ring.

Marcia hid her face in her arms on the table; the baby left off drumming with its spoon, and began to cry.

Witherby was reading the Sunday edition of the Chronicle-Abstract when Bartley got down to the Events office; and he cleared his throat with a premonitory cough as his assistant swung easily into the room. "Good-morning, Mr. Hubbard," he said. "There is quite an interesting article in yesterday's Chronicle-Abstract. Have you seen it?"

"Yes," said Bartley. "What article?"

"This 'Confessions of an Average American.'" Witherby held out the paper, where Bartley's article, vividly head-lined and sub-headed, filled half a page. "What is the reason *we* cannot have something of this kind?"

"Well, I don't know," Bartley began.

"Have you any idea who wrote this?"

"Oh, yes, I wrote it."

Witherby had the task before him of transmuting an expression of rather low cunning into one of wounded confidence, mingled with high-minded surprise. "I thought it had your ear-marks, Mr. Hubbard; but I preferred not to believe it till I heard the fact from your own lips. I suppose that our contract covered such contributions as this."

"I wrote it out of time, and on Sunday night. You pay me by the week, and all that I do throughout the week belongs to you. The next day after that Sunday I did a full day's work on the Events. I don't see what you have to complain of. You told me when I began that you would not expect more than a certain amount of work from me. Have I ever done less?"

"No, but"—

"Haven't I always done more?"

"Yes; I have never complained of the amount of work. But upon this theory of yours, what you did in your summer vacation would not belong to the Events, or what you did on legal holidays."

"I never have any summer vacation or holidays, legal or illegal. Even when I was down at Equity last summer I sent you something for the paper every day."

This was true, and Witherby could not gainsay it. "Very well, sir. If this is to be your interpretation of our understanding for the future, I shall wish to revise our contract," he said, pompously.

"You can tear it up if you like," returned Bartley. "I dare say Ricker would jump at a little study of the true inwardness of counting-room journalism. Unless you insist upon having it for the Events." Bartley gave a chuckle of enjoyment as he sat down at his desk; Witherby rose and stalked away.

He returned in half an hour and said, with an air of frank concession, touched with personal grief: "Mr. Hubbard, I can see how, from your point of view, you were perfectly justifiable in selling your article to the Chronicle-Abstract. My point of view is different, but I shall not insist upon it; and I wish to withdraw—and—and apologize for—any hasty expressions I may have used."

"All right," said Bartley, with a wicked grin. He had triumphed; but his triumph was one to leave some men with an uneasy feeling, and there was not altogether a pleasant taste in Bartley's mouth. After that his position in the Events office was whatever he chose to make it, but he did not abuse his ascendency, and he even made a point of increased deference toward Witherby. Many courtesies passed between them; each took some trouble to show the other that he had no ill feeling.

Three or four weeks later Bartley received a letter with an Illinois postmark which gave him a disagreeable sensation, at first, for he knew it must be from Kinney. But the letter was so amusingly characteristic, so helplessly ill-spelled and ill-constructed, that he could not help laughing. Kinney gave an account of his travels to the mining town, and of his present situation and future prospects; he was full of affectionate messages and inquiries for Bartley's family, and he said he should never forget that Sunday he had passed with them. In a postscript he added: "They copied that String of lies into our paper, here, out of the Chron.-Ab. It was pretty well done, but if your friend Mr. Ricker done it, I'me not goen to Insult him soon again by calling him a gentleman."

This laconic reference to the matter in a postscript was delicious to Bartley; he seemed to hear Kinney saying the words, and imagined his air of ineffective sarcasm. He carried the letter about with him, and the first time he saw Ricker he showed it to him. Ricker read it without appearing greatly diverted; when he came to the postscript he flushed, and demanded, "What have you done about it?"

"Oh, I haven't done anything. It wasn't necessary. You see, now, what Kinney could have done with his facts if we had left them to him. It would have been a wicked waste of material. I thought the sight of some of his literature would help you wash up your uncleanly scruples on that point."

"How long have you had this letter?" pursued Ricker.

"*I* don't know. A week or ten days."

Ricker folded it up and returned it to him. "Mr. Hubbard," he said, "the next time we meet will you do me the favor to cut my acquaintance?"

Bartley stared at him; he thought he must be joking. "Why, Ricker, what's the matter? I didn't suppose you'd care anything about old Kinney. I thought it would amuse you. Why confound it! I'd just as soon write out and tell him that I did the thing." He began to be angry. "But I can cut your acquaintance fast enough, or any man's, if you're really on your ear!"

"I'm on my ear," said Ricker. He left Bartley standing where they had met.

It was peculiarly unfortunate, for Bartley had occasion within that week to ask Ricker's advice, and he was debarred from doing so by this absurd displeasure. Since their recent perfect understanding, Witherby had slighted no opportunity to cement their friendship, and to attach Bartley more and more firmly to the Events. He now offered him some of the Events stock on extremely advantageous terms, with the avowed purpose of attaching him to the paper. There seemed nothing covert in this, and Bartley had never heard any doubts of the prosperity of the Events, but he would have especially liked to have Ricker's mind upon this offer of stock. Witherby had urged him not to pay for the whole outright, but to accept a somewhat lower salary, and trust to his dividends to make up the difference. The shares had paid fifteen per cent. the year before, and Bartley could judge for himself of the present chances from that showing. Witherby advised him to borrow only fifteen hundred dollars on the three thousand of stock which he offered him, and to pay up the balance in three years by dropping five hundred a year from his salary. It was certainly a flattering proposal; and, under his breath, where Bartley still did most of his blaspheming, he cursed Ricker for an old fool; and resolved to close with Witherby on his own responsibility. After he had done so he told Marcia of the step he had taken.

Since their last quarrel there had been an alienation in her behavior toward him, different from any former resentment. She was submissive and quiescent; she looked carefully after his comfort, and was perfect in her housekeeping; but she held aloof from him somehow, and left him to a solitude in her presence, in which he fancied, if he did not divine, her contempt. But in this matter of common interest, something of their community of feeling revived; they met on a lower level, but they met, for the moment, and Marcia joined eagerly in the discussion of ways and means.

The notion of dropping five hundred from his salary delighted her, because they must now cut down their expenses as much; and she had long grieved over their expenses without being able to make Bartley agree to their reduction. She went upstairs at once and gave the little nurse-maid a week's warning; she told the maid-of-all-work that she must take three dollars a week hereafter, instead of four, or else find another place; she mentally forewent new spring dresses for herself and the baby, and arranged to do herself all of the wash she had been putting out; she put a note in the mouth of the can at the back-door, telling the milkman to leave only two quarts in future; and she came radiantly back to tell Bartley that she had saved half of the lost five hundred a year already. But her countenance fell. "Why, where are you to get the other fifteen hundred dollars, Bartley?"

"Oh, I've thought of that," said Bartley, laughing at her swift alternations of triumph and despair. "You trust to me for that."

"You're not—not going to ask father for it?" she faltered.

"Not very much," said Bartley, as he took his hat to go out.

He meant to make a raise out of Ben Halleck, as he phrased it to himself. He knew that Halleck had plenty of money; he could make the stock itself over to him as security; he did not see why Halleck should hesitate. But when he entered Halleck's room, having asked Cyrus to show him directly there, Halleck gave a start which seemed ominous to Bartley. He had scarcely the heart to open his business, and Halleck listened with changing color, and something only too like the embarrassment of a man who intends a refusal. He would not look Bartley in the face, and when Bartley had made an end he sat for a time without speaking. At last he said, with a quick sigh, as if at the close of an internal conflict: "I will lend you the money!"

Bartley's heart gave a bound, and he broke out into an immense laugh of relief, and clapped Halleck on the shoulder. "You looked deucedly as if you *wouldn't*, old man! By George, you had on such a dismal, hang-dog expression that I didn't know but *you'd* come to borrow money of *me*, and I'd made up my mind not to let you have it! But I'm everlastingly obliged to you, Halleck, and I promise you that you won't regret it."

"I shall have to speak to my father about this," said Halleck, responding coldly to Bartley's robust pressure of his hand.

"Of course—of course."

"How soon shall you want the money?"

"Well, the sooner the better, now. Bring the check round,—can't you?—to-morrow night, and take dinner with us, you and Olive; and we'll celebrate a little. I know it will please Marcia when she finds out who my hard-hearted creditor is!"

"Well," assented Halleck, with a smile so ghastly that Bartley noticed it even in his joy.

"Curse me," he said to himself, "if ever I saw a man so ashamed of doing a good action!"

XXX

THE PRESIDENTIAL canvas of the summer which followed upon these events in Bartley's career was not very active. Sometimes, in fact, it languished so much that people almost forgot it, and a good field was afforded the Events for the practice of independent journalism. To hold a course of strict impartiality, and yet come out on the winning side, was a theory of independent journalism which Bartley illustrated with cynical enjoyment. He developed into something rather artistic the gift which he had always shown in his newspaper work for ironical persiflage. Witherby was not a man to feel this burlesque himself; but when it was pointed out to him by others, he came to Bartley in some alarm for its effect upon the fortunes of the paper. "We can't afford, Mr. Hubbard," he said, with virtuous trepidation, "we can't *afford* to make fun of our friends!"

Bartley laughed at Witherby's anxiety. "They're no more our friends than the other fellows are. We are independent journalists; and this way of treating the thing leaves us perfectly free hereafter to claim, just as we choose, that we were in fun or in earnest on any particular question if we're ever attacked. See?"

"I see," said Witherby, with not wholly subdued misgiving. But after due time for conviction no man enjoyed Bartley's irony more than Witherby when once he had mastered an instance of it. Sometimes it happened that Bartley found him chuckling over a perfectly serious paragraph, but he did not mind that; he enjoyed Witherby's mistake even more than his appreciation.

In these days Bartley was in almost uninterrupted good humor, as he had always expected to be when he became fairly prosperous. He was at no time an unamiable fellow, as he saw it; he had his sulks, he had his moments of anger; but generally he felt good, and he had always believed, and he had promised Marcia, that when he got squarely on his legs he should feel good perpetually. This sensation he now agreeably realized; and he was also now in that position in which he had proposed to himself some little moral reforms. He was not much in the habit of taking stock; but no man wholly escapes the contingencies in which he is confronted with himself and sees certain habits, traits, tendencies, which he would like to change for the sake of his peace of mind hereafter. To some souls these contingencies are full of anguish, of remorse for the past, of despair; but Bartley had never yet seen the time when he did not feel himself perfectly able to turn over a new leaf and blot the old one. There were not many things in his life which he really cared to have very different; but there were two or three shady little corners which he always intended to clean up. He had meant some time or other to have a religious belief of some sort, he did not much care what; since Marcia had taken to the Hallecks' church, he did not see why he should not go with her, though he had never yet done so. He was not quite sure whether he was always as candid with her as he might be, or as kind; though he maintained against this question that in all their quarrels it was six of one and half a dozen of the other. He had never been tipsy but once in his life, and he considered that he had repented and atoned for that enough, especially as nothing had ever come of it; but sometimes he thought he might be overdoing the beer; yes, he thought he must cut down on the Tivoli; he was getting ridiculously fat. If ever he met Kinney again he should tell him that it was he and not Ricker who had appropriated his facts; and he intended to make it up with Ricker somehow.

He had not found just the opportunity yet; but in the meantime he did not mind telling the real cause of their alienation to good fellows who could enjoy a joke. He had his following, though so many of his brother journalists had cooled toward him, and those of his following considered him as smart as chain-lightning and bound to rise. These young men and not very wise elders roared over Bartley's frank declaration of the situation between himself and Ricker, and they contended that if Ricker had taken the article for the Chronicle-Abstract he ought to take the consequences. Bartley told them that of course he should explain the facts to Kinney; but that he meant to let Ricker enjoy his virtuous indignation a while. Once, after a confidence of this kind at the club, where Ricker had refused to speak to him, he came away with a curious sense of moral decay. It did not pain him a great deal, but it certainly surprised him that now with all these prosperous conditions, so favorable for cleaning up, he had so little disposition to clean up. He found himself quite willing to let the affair with Ricker go, and he suspected that he had been needlessly virtuous in his intentions concerning church-going and beer. As to Marcia, it appeared to him that he could not treat a woman of her disposition otherwise than as he did. At any rate, if he had not done everything he could to make her happy she seemed to be getting along well enough, and was probably quite as happy as she deserved to be. They were getting on very quietly now; there had been no violent outbreak on her part since the trouble about Kinney, and then she had practically confessed herself in the wrong, as Bartley looked at it. At last, there was now what might be called a perfect business amity between them. If her life with him was no longer an expression of that intense devotion which she used to show him, it was more like what married life generally comes to, and he accepted her tractability and what seemed her common-sense view of their relations as greatly preferable. With his growth in flesh, Bartley liked peace more and more.

Marcia had consented to go down to Equity alone, that summer, for he had convinced her that during a heated political contest it would not do for him to be away from the paper. He promised to go down for her when she wished to come home; and it was easily arranged for her to travel as far as the Junction under Halleck's escort, when he went to join his sisters in the White Mountains. Bartley missed her and the baby at first. But he soon began to adjust himself with resignation to his solitude. They had determined to keep their maid over the summer, for they had so much trouble in replacing her the last time after their return; and Bartley said he should live very economically. It was quiet, and the woman kept the house cool and clean; she was a good cook, and when Bartley brought a man home to dinner she took an interest in serving it well. Bartley let her order the things from the grocer and butcher, for she knew what they were used to getting, and he had heard so much talk from Marcia about bills since he bought that Events stock, that he was sick of the prices of things. There was no extravagance, and yet he seemed to live very much better after Marcia went. There is no doubt but he lived very much more at his ease. One little restriction after another fell away from him; he went and came with absolute freedom, not only without having to account for his movements, but without having a pang for not doing so. He had the sensation of stretching himself after a cramping posture; and he wrote Marcia the cheerfullest letters, charging her not to cut short her visit from anxiety on his account. He said that he was working hard, but hard work evidently agreed with him, for he was never better in his life. In this high content he maintained a feeling of loyalty by going to the Hallecks, where Mrs. Halleck often had him to tea in pity of his loneliness. They were dull company, certainly; but Marcia liked them, and the cooking was always good. Other evenings he went to the theatres, where there were amusing variety bills; and sometimes he passed the night at Nantasket, or took a run for a day to Newport; he always reported these excursions to Marcia, with expressions of regret that Equity was too far away to run down to for a day.

Marcia's letters were longer and more regular than his; but he could have forgiven some want of constancy, for the sake of a less searching anxiety on her part. She was anxious not only for his welfare, which was natural and proper, but she was anxious about the housekeeping and the expenses, things Bartley could not afford to let trouble him, though he did what he could in a general way to quiet her mind. She wrote fully of the visit which Olive Halleck had paid her, but said that they had not gone about much, for Ben Halleck had only been able to come for a day. She was very well, and so was Flavia.

Bartley realized Flavia's existence with an effort, and for the rest this letter bored him. What could he care about Olive Halleck's coming, or Ben Halleck's staying away? All that he asked of Ben Halleck was a little extension of time when his interest fell due. The whole thing was disagreeable; and he resented what he considered Marcia's endeavor to clap the domestic harness on him again. His thoughts wandered to conditions, to contingencies of which a man does not permit himself even to think without a degree of moral disintegration. In these ill-advised reveries he mused upon his life as it might have been if he had never met her, or if they had never met after her dismissal of him. As he recalled the facts, he was at that time in an angry and embittered mood, but he was in a mood of entire acquiescence; and the reconciliation had been of her own seeking. He could not blame her for it; she was very much in love with him, and he had been fond of her. In fact, he was still very fond of her; when he thought of little ways of hers, it filled him with tenderness. He did justice to her fine qualities, too: her generosity, her truthfulness, her entire loyalty to his best interests; he smiled to realize that he himself preferred his second-best interests, and in her absence he remembered that her virtues were tedious and even painful at times. He had his doubts whether there was sufficient compensation in them. He sometimes questioned whether he had not made a great mistake to get married; he expected now to stick it through; but this doubt occurred to him. A moment came in which he asked himself, What if he had never come back to Marcia that night when she locked him out of her room? Might it not have been better for both of them? She would soon have reconciled herself to the irreparable; he even thought of her happy in a second marriage; and the thought did not enrage him; he generously wished Marcia well. He wished—he hardly knew what he wished. He wished nothing at all but to have his wife and child back again as soon as possible; and he put aside with a laugh the fancies which really found no such distinct formulation as I have given them; which were mere vague impulses, arrested mental tendencies, scraps of undirected reverie. Their recurrence had nothing to do with what he felt to be his sane and waking state. But they recurred, and he even amused himself in turning them over.

XXXI

ONE MORNING in September, not long before Marcia returned, Bartley found Witherby at the office waiting for him. Witherby wore a pensive face, which had the effect of being studied. "Good-morning, Mr. Hubbard," he said, and when Bartley answered, "Good-morning," cheerfully ignoring his mood, he added, "What is this I hear, Mr. Hubbard, about a personal misunderstanding between you and Mr. Ricker?"

"I'm sure I don't know," said Bartley; "but I suppose that, if you have heard anything, *you* know."

"I have heard," proceeded Witherby, a little dashed by Bartley's coolness, "that Mr. Ricker accuses you of having used material in that article you sold him which had been intrusted to you under the seal of confidence, and that you had left it to be inferred by the party concerned that Mr. Ricker had written the article himself."

"All right," said Bartley.

"But, Mr. Hubbard," said Witherby, struggling to rise into virtuous supremacy, "what am I to think of such a report?"

"I can't say; unless you should think that it wasn't your affair. That would be the easiest thing."

"But I *can't* think that, Mr. Hubbard! Such a report reflects through you upon the Events; it reflects upon *me!*" Bartley laughed. "I can't approve of such a thing. If you admit the report, it appears to me that you have—a—done a—a—wrong action, Mr. Hubbard."

Bartley turned upon him with a curious look; at the same

time he felt a pang, and there was a touch of real anguish in the sarcasm of his demand, "Have I fallen so low as to be rebuked by *you?*"

"I—I don't know what you mean by such an expression as that, Mr. Hubbard," said Witherby. "I don't know what I've done to forfeit your esteem,—to justify you in using such language to me."

"I don't suppose you really do," said Bartley. "Go on."

"I have nothing more to say, Mr. Hubbard, except—except to add that this has given me a great blow,—a *great* blow. I had begun to have my doubts before as to whether we were quite adapted to each other, and this has—increased them. I pass no judgment upon what you have done, but I will say that it has made me anxious and—a—unrestful. It has made me ask myself whether upon the whole we should not be happier apart. I don't say that we should; but I only feel that nine out of ten business men would consider you, in the position you occupy on the Events,—a—a—dangerous person."

Bartley got up from his desk, and walked toward Witherby, with his hands in his pockets; he halted a few paces from him, and looked down on him with a sinister smile. "I don't think they'd consider *you* a dangerous person in *any* position."

"May be not, may be not," said Witherby, striving to be easy and dignified. In the effort he took up an open paper from the desk before him, and, lifting it between Bartley and himself, feigned to be reading it.

Bartley struck it out of his trembling hands. "You impudent old scoundrel! Do you pretend to be reading when I speak to you? For half a cent"—

Witherby, slipping and sliding in his swivel-chair, contrived to get to his feet. "No violence, Mr. Hubbard, no violence *here!*"

"Violence!" laughed Bartley. "I should have to *touch* you! Come! Don't be afraid! But don't you put on airs of any sort! I understand your game. You want, for some reason, to get rid of me, and you have seized the opportunity with a sharpness that does credit to your cunning. I don't condescend to deny this report,"—speaking in this lofty strain, Bartley had a momentary sensation of its being a despicable slander,—"but I see that, as far as you are concerned, it answers all the purposes of truth. You think that, with the chance of having this thing exploited against me, I wont expose your nefarious practices, and you can get rid of me more safely now than ever you could again. Well, you're right. I dare say you heard of this report a good while ago, and you've waited till you could fill my place without inconvenience to yourself. So I can go at once. Draw your check for all you owe me, and pay me back the money I put into your stock, and I'll clear out at once."

He went about putting together a few personal effects on his desk.

"I must protest against any allusion to nefarious practices, Mr. Hubbard," said Witherby, "and I wish you to understand that I part from you without the slightest ill-feeling. I shall always have a high regard for your ability, and—and—your social qualities."

While he made these expressions he hastened to write two checks.

Bartley, who had paid no attention to what Witherby was saying, came up and took the checks.

"This is all right," he said of one; but, looking at the other, he added, "Fifteen hundred dollars!—where is the dividend?"

"That is not due till the end of the month," said Witherby. "If you withdraw your money now, you lose it."

Bartley looked at the face to which Witherby did his best to give a high judicial expression.

"*You* old thief!" he said good-humoredly, almost affectionately. "I *have* a mind to tweak your nose!"

But he went out of the room without saying or doing anything more. He wondered a little at his own amiability; but, with the decay of whatever was right-principled in him, he was aware of growing more and more incapable of indignation. Now, his flash of rage over, he was not at all discontented.

With these checks in his pocket, with his youth, his health, and his practised hand, he could have faced the world, with a light heart, if he had not also had to face his wife. But when he thought of the inconvenience of explaining to her, of pacifying her anxiety, of clearing up her doubts on a thousand points, and of getting her simply to eat or sleep till he found something else to do, it dismayed him.

"Good Lord!" he said to himself, "I wish I was dead—or some one."

That conclusion made him smile again.

He decided not to write to Marcia of the change in his affairs, but to take the chance of finding something better before she returned. There was very little time for him to turn round, and he was still without a place or any prospect when she came home. It had sufficed with his acquaintance when he said that he had left the Events because he could not get on with Witherby; but he was very much astonished when it seemed to suffice with her.

"Oh, well," she said, "I am glad of it. You will do better by yourself; and I know you can earn just as much by writing on the different papers."

Bartley knew better than this, but he said:

"Yes, I shall not be in a hurry to take another engagement just yet. But, Marsh," he added, "I was afraid you would blame me—think I had been reckless, or at fault"—

"No," she answered, after a little pause, "I shall not do that any more. I have been thinking all these things over, while I was away from you, and I'm going to do differently after this. I shall believe that you've acted for the best,—that you've not meant to do wrong in anything,—and I shall never question you or doubt you any more."

"Isn't that giving me rather too *much* rope?" asked Bartley, with lightness that masked a vague alarm lest the old times of exaction should be coming back with the old times of devotion.

"No; I see where my mistake has always been. I've always asked too much, and expected too much, even when I didn't ask it. Now, I shall be satisfied with what you don't do, as well as what you do."

"I shall try to live up to my privileges," said Bartley, with a sigh of relief. He gave her a kiss, and then he unclasped Kinney's nugget from his watch-chain, and fastened it on the baby's necklace, which lay in a box Marcia had just taken from her trunk. She did not speak; but Bartley felt better to have the thing off him; Marcia's gentleness, the tinge of sadness in her tone, made him long to confess himself wrong in the whole matter, and justly punished by Ricker's contempt and Witherby's dismissal. But he did not believe that he could trust her to forgive him, and he felt himself unable to go through all that without the certainty of her forgiveness.

As she took the things out of her trunk, and laid them away in this drawer and that, she spoke of events in the village, and told who was dead, who was married, and who had gone away.

"I staid longer than I expected—a little, because father seemed to want me to. I don't think mother's so well as she used to be. I—I'm afraid she seems to be failing, somehow."

Her voice dropped to a lower key, and Bartley said:

"I'm sorry to hear that. I guess she isn't failing. But of course she's getting on, and every year makes a difference."

"Yes, that must be it," she answered, looking at a bundle of collars she had in her hand, as if absorbed in the question as to where she should put them.

Before they slept that night she asked:

"Bartley, did you hear about Hannah Morrison?"

"No. What about her?"

"She's gone—gone away. The last time she was seen was in Portland. They don't know what's become of her. They say that Henry Bird is about heart-broken; but everybody knows she never cared for him. I hated to write to you about it."

Bartley experienced so disagreeable a sensation that he was silent for a time. Then he gave a short, bitter laugh.

"Well, that's what it was bound to come to, sooner or later, I suppose. It's a piece of good luck for Bird."

Bartley went about picking up work from one paper and another, but not securing a basis on any. In that curious and unwholesome leniency which corrupt natures manifest, he and Witherby met at their next encounter on quite amicable terms. Bartley reported some meetings for the Events, and experienced no resentment when Witherby at the office introduced him to the gentleman with whom he had replaced him. Of course Bartley expected that Witherby would insinuate things to his disadvantage, but he did not mind that. He heard of something of the sort being done in Ricker's presence, and of Ricker's saying that in any question of honor and veracity between Witherby and Hubbard he should decide for Hubbard. Bartley was not very grateful for this generous defense; he thought that if Ricker had not been such an ass in the first place there would have been no trouble between them, and Witherby would not have had that handle against him.

He was enjoying himself very well, and he felt entitled to the comparative rest which had not been of his seeking. He wished that Halleck would come back, for he would like to ask his leave to put that money into some other enterprise. His credit was good, and he had not touched the money to pay any of his accumulated bills; he would have considered it dishonorable to do so. But it annoyed him to have the money lying idle. In his leisure he studied the stock market, and he believed that he had several points which were infallible. He put a few hundreds—two or three—of Halleck's money into a mining stock which was so low that it *must* rise. In the meantime he tried a new kind of beer—Norwegian beer,—which he found a little lighter even than Tivoli. It was more expensive, but it was *very* light, and it was essential to Bartley to drink the lightest beer he could find.

He staid a good deal at home now, for he had leisure, and it was a much more comfortable place since Marcia had ceased to question or reproach him. She did not interfere with some bachelor habits he had formed, in her absence, of sleeping far into the forenoon; he now occasionally did night-work on some of the morning papers, and the rest was necessary; he had his breakfast whenever he got up, as if he had been at a hotel. He wondered upon what new theory she was really treating him; but he had always been apt to accept what was comfortable in life without much question, and he did not wonder long. He was immensely good-natured now. In his frequent leisure he went out to walk with Marcia and Flavia, and sometimes he took the little girl alone. He even went to church with them one Sunday, and called at the Hallecks as often as Marcia liked. The young ladies had returned, but Ben Halleck was still away. It made Bartley smile to hear his wife talking of Halleck with his mother and sisters, and falling quite into the family way of regarding him as if he were somehow a saint and martyr.

Bartley was still dabbling in stocks with Halleck's money; some of it had lately gone to pay an assessment which had unexpectedly occurred in place of a dividend. He told Marcia that he was holding the money ready to return to Halleck when he came back, or to put it into some other enterprise where it would help to secure Bartley a new basis. They were now together more than they had been since the first days of their married life in Boston; but the perfect intimacy of those days was gone; he had his reserves, and she her preoccupations,— with the house, with the little girl, with her anxiety about her mother. Sometimes they sat a whole evening together, with almost nothing to say to each other, he reading and she sewing. After an evening of this sort, Bartley felt himself worse bored than if Marcia had spent it in taking him to task as she used to do. Once he looked at her over the top of his paper, and distinctly experienced that he was tired of the whole thing.

But the political canvass was growing more interesting now. It was almost the end of October, and the speech-making had become very lively. The Democrats were hopeful and the Republicans resolute, and both parties were active in getting out their whole strength, as the saying is at such times. This was done not only by speech-making, but by long nocturnal

Election

processions of torch-lights; by day as well as by night, drums throbbed and horns brayed, and the feverish excitement spread its contagion through the whole population. But it did not affect Bartley. He had cared nothing about the canvass from the beginning, having an equal contempt for the "bloody shirt" of the Republicans and the reform pretensions of the Democrats. The only thing that he took an interest in was the betting; he laid his wages with so much apparent science and sagacity that he had a certain following of young men who bet as Hubbard did. Hubbard, they believed, had a long head; he disdained bets of hats, and of barrels of apples, and ordeals by wheelbarrows; he would bet only with people who could put up their money, and his followers honored him for it; when asked where he got his money, being out of place, and no longer instant to do work that fell in his way, they answered from a ready faith that he had made a good thing in mining stocks.

In her heart, Marcia probably did not share this faith. But she faithfully forbore to harass Bartley with her doubts, and on those evenings when he found her such dull company she was silent because if she spoke she must express the trouble in her mind. Women are more apt to theorize their husbands than men in their stupid self-absorption ever realize. When a man is married, his wife almost ceases to be exterior to his consciousness; she afflicts or consoles him like a condition of health or sickness; she is literally part of him in a spiritual sense, even when he is rather indifferent to her; but the most devoted wife has always a corner of her soul in which she thinks of her husband as *him*; in which she philosophizes him wholly aloof from herself. In such an obscure fastness of her being, Marcia had meditated a great deal upon Bartley during her absence at Equity,—meditated painfully and, in her sort, prayerfully upon him. She perceived that he was not her young dream of him; and since it appeared to her that she could not forego that dream and live, she could but accuse herself of having somehow had a perverse influence upon him. She knew that she had never reproached him except for his good, but she saw too that she had always made him worse, and not better. She recurred to what he said the first night they arrived in Boston: "I believe that, if you have faith in me, I shall get along; and when you don't, I shall go to the bad." She could reason to no other effect, than that hereafter, no matter what happened, she must show perfect faith in him by perfect patience. It was hard, far harder than she had thought. But she did forbear; she did use patience.

The election day came and went. Bartley remained out until the news of Tilden's success could no longer be doubted, and then came home jubilant. Marcia seemed not to understand. "I didn't know you cared so much for Tilden," she said, quietly. "Mr. Halleck is for Hayes; and Ben Halleck was coming home to vote."

"That's all right: a vote in Massachusetts makes no difference. I'm for Tilden, because I have the most money up on him. The success of that noble old reformer is worth seven hundred dollars to me in bets." Bartley laughed, rubbed her cheeks with his chilly hands, and went down into the cellar for some beer. He could not have slept without that, in his excitement; but he was out very early the next morning, and in the raw damp of the rainy November day he received a more penetrating chill when he saw the bulletins at the newspaper offices intimating that a fair count might give the Republicans enough Southern States to elect Hayes. This appeared to Bartley the most impudent piece of political effrontery in the whole history of the country, and among those who went about denouncing Republican chicanery at the Democratic club-rooms, no one took a loftier tone of moral indignation than he. The thought that he might lose so much of Halleck's money through the machinations of a parcel of carpet-bagging tricksters filled him with a virtue at which he afterward smiled when he found that people were declaring their bets off. "I laid a wager on the popular result, not on the decision of the Returning Boards," he said in reclaiming his money from the referees. He had some difficulty in getting it all back, but he had got it when he walked homeward at night, after having been out all day; and there now ensued in his soul a struggle as to what he should do with this money. He had it all except the three hundred he had ventured on the mining stock, which would eventually be worth everything he had paid for it. After his frightful escape from losing half of it on those bets, he had an intense longing to be rid of it, to give it back to Halleck, who never would ask him for it, and then to go home and tell Marcia everything, and throw himself on her mercy. Better poverty, better disgrace before Halleck and her, better her condemnation, than this life of temptation that he had been leading. He saw how hideous it was in the retrospect, and he shuddered; his good instincts awoke, and put forth their strength, such as it was; tears came into his eyes; he resolved to write to Kinney and exonerate Ricker, he resolved humbly to beg Ricker's pardon. He must leave Boston; but if Marcia would forgive him, he would go back with her to Equity, and take up the study of the law in her father's office again, and fulfil all her wishes. He would have a hard time to overcome the old man's prejudices, but he deserved a hard time, and he knew he should finally succeed. It would be bitter, returning to that stupid little town, and he imagined the intrusive conjecture and sarcastic comment that would attend his return; but he believed that he could live this down, and he trusted himself to laugh it down. He already saw himself there, settled in the Squire's office, reinstated in public opinion, a leading lawyer of the place, with Congress open before him whenever he chose to turn his face that way.

He had thought of going first to Halleck, and returning the money, but he was willing to give himself the encouragement of Marcia's pleasure, of her forgiveness and her praise in an affair that had its difficulties and would require all his manfulness. The maid met him at the door with little Flavia, and told him that Marcia had gone out to the Hallecks', but had left word that she would soon return, and that then they would have supper together. Her absence dashed his warm impulse, but he recovered himself, and took the little one from the maid. He lighted the gas in the parlor, and had a frolic with Flavia in kindling a fire in the grate, and making the room bright and cheerful. He played with the child and made her laugh; he already felt the pleasure of a good conscience, though with a faint nether ache in his heart which was perhaps only his wish to have the disagreeable preliminaries to his better life over as soon as possible. He drew two easy-chairs up at opposite corners of the hearth, and sat down in one, leaving the other for Marcia; he had Flavia standing on his knees, and clinging fast to his fingers, laughing and crowing while he danced her up and down, when he heard the front door open, and Marcia burst into the room.

She ran to him and plucked the child from him, and then went back as far as she could from him in the room, crying, "Give *me* the child!" and facing him with the look he knew. Her eyes were dilated, and her visage white with the transport that had whirled her far beyond the reach of reason. The frail structure of his good resolutions dropped to ruin at the sight, but he mechanically rose and advanced upon her till she forbade him with a muffled shriek of "Don't *touch* me! So!" she went on, gasping and catching her breath, "it was *you!* I might have known it! I might have guessed it from the first! *You!* Was *that* the reason why you didn't care to have me hurry home this summer? Was that—was that"— She choked, and convulsively pressed her face into the neck of the child, which began to cry.

Bartley closed the doors, and then, with his hands in his pockets, confronted her with a smile of wicked coolness.

"Will you be good enough to tell me what you're talking about?"

"Do you pretend that you don't know? I met a woman at the bottom of the street, just now. Do you know who?"

"No; but it's very dramatic. Go on!"

"It was Hannah Morrison! She reeled against me; and when

I—such a fool as I was!—pitied her, because I was on my way home to you, and was thinking about you, and loving you, and was so happy in it, and asked her how she came to that, she *struck* me, and told me to—to—ask my—husband!"

The transport broke in tears; the denunciation had turned to entreaty in everything but words; but Bartley had hardened his heart now past all entreaty. The idiotic penitent that he had been a few moments ago—the soft, well-meaning dolt—was so far from him now as to be scarce within the reach of his contempt. He was going to have this thing over once for all; he would have no mercy upon himself or upon her; the Devil was in him and uppermost in him, and the Devil is fierce and proud, and knows how to make many base emotions feel like a just self-respect.

"And did you believe a woman like that?" he sneered.

"Do I believe a man like this?" she demanded, with a dying flash of her fury. "You—you don't dare to deny it."

"Oh, no, I don't deny it. For one reason it would be of no use. For all practical purposes, I admit it. What then?"

"What then?" she asked bewildered. "Bartley! You don't mean it!"

"Yes, I do. I mean it. I *don't* deny it. What then? What are you going to do about it?" She gazed at him in incredulous horror. "Come! I mean what I say. What will you do?"

"Oh, merciful God! what shall I do?" she prayed aloud.

"That's just what I'm curious to know. When you leaped in here, just now, you must have meant to do something, if I couldn't convince you that the woman was lying. Well, you see that I don't try. I give you leave to believe whatever she said. What then?"

"Bartley!" she besought him in her despair. "Do you drive me from you?"

"Oh, no, certainly not. That isn't my way. You have driven me from you, and I might claim the right to retaliate, but I don't. I've no expectation that you'll go away, and I want to see what else you'll do. You would have me, before we were married; you were tolerably shameless in getting me; when your jealous temper made you throw me away, you couldn't live till you got me back again; you ran after me. Well, I suppose you've learnt wisdom, now. At least you wont try *that* game again. But what *will* you do?"

He looked at her smiling, while he dealt her these stabs one by one.

She set down the child, and went out to the entry where its hat and cloak hung. She had not taken off her own things, and now she began to put on the little one's garments with shaking hands, kneeling before it.

"I will never live with you again, Bartley," she said.

"Very well. I doubt it, as far as you're concerned; but if you go away now, you certainly *wont* live with me again, for I shall not let you come back. Understand that."

Each had most need of the other's mercy, but neither would have mercy.

"It isn't for what you won't deny. I don't believe that. It's for what you've said now."

She could not make the buttons and the button-holes of the child's sack meet with her quivering fingers; he actually stooped down and buttoned the little garment for her as if they had been going to take the child out for a walk between them. She caught it up in her arms, and sobbing "Good-by, Bartley!" ran out of the room.

"Recollect that if you go, you don't come back," he said.

The outer door crashing to behind her was his answer.

He sat down to think, before the fire he had built for her. It was blazing brightly now, and the whole room had a hideous cosiness. He could not think—he must act. He went up to their room, where the gas was burning low, as if she had lighted it and then frugally turned it down as her wont was. He did not know what his purpose was, but it developed itself. He began to pack his things in a traveling-bag which he took out of the closet, and which he had bought for her when she set out for Equity in the summer; it had the perfume of her dresses yet.

When this was finished, he went down-stairs again, and being now strangely hungry, he made a meal of such things as he found set out on the tea-table. Then he went over the papers in his secretary; he burnt some of them, and put others into his bag.

After all this was done he sat down by the fire again, and gave Marcia a quarter of an hour longer in which to return. He did not know whether he was afraid that she would or would not come. But when the time ended, he took up his bag and went out of the house. It began to rain, and he went back for an umbrella; he gave her that one chance more, and he ran up into their room. But she had not come back. He went out again, and hurried away, through the rain, to the Albany Depot, where he bought a ticket for Chicago. There was as yet nothing definite in his purpose, beyond the fact that he was to be rid of her: whether for a long or short time, or forever, he did not yet know; whether he meant ever to communicate with her, or seek or suffer a reconciliation, the locomotive that leaped westward into the dark with him knew as well as he.

Yet all the mute, obscure forces of habit, which are doubtless the strongest forces in human nature, were dragging him back to her. Because their lives had been united so long, it seemed impossible to sever them, though their union had been so full of misery and discord; the custom of marriage was so subtile and so pervasive, that his heart demanded her sympathy for what he was suffering in abandoning her. The solitude into which he had plunged stretched before him so vast, so sterile and hopeless, that he had not the courage to realize it; he insensibly began to give it limits: he would return after so many months, weeks, days.

He passed twenty-four hours on the train, and left it at Cleveland for the half-hour it stopped for supper. But he could not eat; he had to own to himself that he was beaten, and that he must return, or throw himself into the lake. He ran hastily to the baggage-car, and effected the removal of his bag; then he went to the ticket-office and waited at the end of a long queue for his turn at the window. His turn came at last, and he confronted the nervous and impatient ticket-agent, without speaking.

"Well, sir, what do you want?" demanded the agent. Then, with rising temper, "What is it? Are you deaf? Are you dumb? You can't expect to stand there all night!"

The policeman outside the rail laid his hand on Bartley's shoulder:

"Move on, my friend."

He obeyed, and reeled away in a fashion that confirmed the policeman's suspicions. He searched his pockets again and again; but his porte-monnaie was in none of them. It had been stolen, and Halleck's money with the rest. Now he could not return; nothing remained for him but the ruin he had chosen.

XXXII

HALLECK prolonged his summer vacation beyond the end of October. He had been in town from time to time, and then had set off again on some new absence; he was so restless and so far from well during the last of these flying visits, that the old people were glad when he wrote them that he should stay as long as the fine weather continued. He spoke of an interesting man whom he had met at the mountain resort where he was staying—a Spanish-American, attached to one of the legations at Washington, who had a scheme for Americanizing popular education in his own country. "He has made a regular set at me," Halleck wrote, "and if I had not fooled away so much time already on law and on leather, I should like to fool away a little more on such a cause as this."

He did not mention the matter again in his letters; but the first night after his return, when they all sat together in the comfort of having him at home again, he asked his father:

"What would you think of my going to South America?"

The old man started up from the pleasant after-supper drowse into which he was suffering himself to fall, content with Halleck's presence, and willing to leave the talk to the women folk.

"I don't know what you mean, Ben?"

"I suppose it's my having the matter so much in mind that makes me feel as if we had talked it over. I mentioned it in one of my letters."

"Yes," returned his father; "but I presumed you were joking."

Halleck frowned impatiently; he would not meet the gaze of his mother and sisters, but he addressed himself again to his father.

"I don't know that I was in earnest." His mother dropped her eyes to her mending, with a faint sigh of relief. "But I can't say," he added, "that I was joking, exactly. The man himself was very serious about it."

He stopped, apparently to govern an irritable impulse, and then he went on to set the project of his Spanish-American acquaintance before them, explaining it in detail.

At the end:

"That's good," said his father, "but why need *you* have gone, Ben?"

The question seemed to vex Halleck; he did not answer at once. His mother could not bear to see him crossed, and she came to his help against herself and his father, since it was only supposing the case.

"I presume," she said, "that we could have looked at it as a missionary work."

"It isn't a missionary work, mother," answered Halleck, severely, "in any sense that you mean. I should go down there to teach, and I should be paid for it. And I want to say at once that they have no yellow fever nor earthquakes, and that they have not had a revolution for six years. The country's perfectly safe every way, and so wholesome that it will be a good thing for me. But I shouldn't expect to convert anybody."

"Of course not, Ben," said his mother, soothingly.

"I hope you wouldn't object to it if it *were* a missionary work," said one of the elder sisters.

"No, Anna," returned Ben.

"I merely wanted to know," said Anna.

"Then I hope you're satisfied, Anna," Olive cut in. "Ben won't *refuse* to convert the Uruguayans, if they apply in a proper spirit."

"I think Anna had a right to ask," said Miss Louisa, the eldest.

"Oh, undoubtedly, Miss Halleck," said Olive. "I like to see Ben reproved for misbehavior to his mother, myself."

Her father laughed at Olive's prompt defense.

"Well, it's a cause that we've all got to respect; but I don't see why *you* should go, Ben, as I said before. It would do very well for some young fellow who had no settled prospects, but you've got your duties here. I presume you looked at it in that light. As you said in your letter, you've fooled away so much time on leather and law"—

"I shall never amount to anything in the law!" Ben broke out. His mother looked at him in anxiety; his father kept a steady smile on his face; Olive sat alert for any chance that offered to put down her elder sisters, who drew in their breath, and grew silently a little primmer. "I'm not well"—

"Oh, I know you're not, dear," interrupted his mother, glad of another chance to abet him.

"I'm not strong enough to go on with the line of work I've marked out, and I feel that I'm throwing away the feeble powers I have."

His father answered with less surprise than Halleck had evidently expected, for he had thrown out his words with a sort of defiance; probably the old man had watched him closely enough to surmise that it might come to this with him at last. At any rate, he was able to say, without seeming to assent too readily, "Well, well, give up the law, then, and come back into leather, as you call it. Or take up something else. We don't wish to make anything a burden to you; but take up some useful work at home. There are plenty of things to be done."

"Not for me," said Halleck gloomily.

"Oh, yes, there are," said the old man.

"I see you are not willing to have me go," said Halleck, rising in uncontrollable irritation. "But I wish you wouldn't all take this tone with me!"

"We haven't taken any tone with you, Ben," said his mother, with pleading tenderness.

"I think Anna has decidedly taken a tone," said Olive.

Anna did not retort, but "What tone?" demanded Louisa, in her behalf.

"Hush, children," said their mother.

"Well, well," suggested his father to Ben, "think it over, think it over. There's no hurry."

"I've thought it over; there *is* hurry," retorted Halleck. "If I go, I must go at once."

His mother arrested her thread, half drawn through the seam, letting her hand drop, while she glanced at him.

"It isn't so much a question of your giving up the law, Ben, as of your giving up your family and going so far from us all," said his father. "That's what I shouldn't like."

"I don't like that, either. But I can't help it." He added, "Of course, mother, I shall not go without your full and free consent. You and father must settle it between you." He fetched a quick, worried sigh as he put his hand on the door.

"Ben isn't himself at all," said Mrs. Halleck, with tears in her eyes, after he had left the room.

"No," said her husband. "He's restless. He'll get over this idea in a few days." He urged this hope against his wife's despair, and argued himself into low spirits.

"I don't believe but what it *would* be the best thing for his health, may be," said Mrs. Halleck, at the end.

"I've always had my doubts whether he would ever come to anything in the law," said the father.

The elder sisters discussed Halleck's project apart between themselves, as their wont was with any family interest, and they bent over a map of South America, so as to hide what they were doing from their mother.

Olive had left the room by another door, and she intercepted Halleck before he reached his own.

"What is the matter, Ben?" she whispered.

"Nothing," he answered, coldly. But he added, "Come in, Olive."

She followed him, and hovered near after he turned up the gas.

"I can't stand it here,—I must go," he said, turning a dull, weary look upon her.

"Who was at the Elm House that you knew this last time?" she asked, quickly.

"Laura Dixmore isn't driving me away, if you mean that," replied Halleck.

"I *couldn't* believe it was she! I should have despised you if it was. But I shall hate her, whoever it was."

Halleck sat down before his table, and his sister sank upon the corner of a chair near it, and looked wistfully at him.

"I know there is some one!"

"If you think I've been fool enough to offer myself to any one, Olive, you're very much mistaken."

"Oh, it needn't have come to that," said Olive, with indignant pity.

"My life is a failure here," cried Halleck, moving his head uneasily from side to side. "I feel somehow as if I could go out there and pick up the time I've lost. Great Heaven!" he cried, "if I were only running away from some innocent young girl's rejection, what a happy man I should be!"

"It's some horrid married thing, then, that's been flirting with you!"

He gave a forlorn laugh.

"I'd almost confess it to please you, Olive. But I prefer to get out of the matter without lying, if I could. Why need you suppose any reason but the sufficient one I've given?—Don't afflict me! don't imagine things about me, don't make a mystery of me! I've been blunt and awkward, and I've bungled the business with father and mother; but I want to get away because I'm a miserable fraud here, and I think I might rub on a good while there before I found myself out again."

"Ben," demanded Olive, regardless of his words, "what have you been doing?"

"The old story,—nothing."

"Is that true, Ben?"

"You used to be satisfied with asking once, Olive."

"You *haven't* been so wicked, so careless, as to get some poor creature in love with you, and then want to run away from the misery you've made?"

"I suppose if I look it there's no use denying it," said Halleck, letting his sad eyes meet hers, and smiling drearily. "You insist upon having a lady in the case?"

"Yes. But I see you wont tell me anything; and I *wont* afflict you. Only I'm afraid it's just some silly thing that you've got to brooding over, and that you'll let drive you away."

"Well, you have the comfort of reflecting that I can't get away, whatever the pressure is."

"You know better than that, Ben; and so do I. You know that, if you haven't got father and mother's consent already, it's only because you haven't had the heart to ask for it. As far as that's concerned, you're gone already. But I hope you won't go without thinking it over, as father says,—and talking it over. I hate to have you seem unsteady and fickle-minded, when I know you're not; and I'm going to set myself against this project till I know what's driving you from us,—or till I'm sure that it's something worth while. You needn't expect that I shall help to make it easy for you; I shall help to make it hard."

Her loving looks belied her threats; if the others could not resist Ben when any sort of desire showed itself through his habitual listlessness, how could she, who understood him best and sympathized with him most? "There was something I was going to talk to you about, to-night, if you hadn't scared us all with this ridiculous scheme, and ask you whether you couldn't do something." She seemed to suggest the change of interest with the hope of winning his thoughts away from the direction they had taken; but he listened apathetically, and left her to go farther or not, as she chose. "I think," she added abruptly, "that some trouble is hanging over those wretched Hubbards."

"Some new one?" asked Halleck, with sad sarcasm, turning his eyes toward her, as if with the resolution of facing her.

"You know he's left his place on that newspaper."

"Yes, I heard that when I was at home before."

"There are some very disagreeable stories about it. They say he was turned away by Mr. Witherby for behaving badly—for printing something he oughtn't to have done."

"That was to have been expected," said Halleck.

"He hasn't found any other place, and Marcia says he gets very little work to do. He must be running into debt, terribly. I feel very anxious about them. I don't know what they're living on."

"Probably on some money I lent him," said Halleck, quietly. "I lent him fifteen hundred in the spring. It ought to make him quite comfortable for the present."

"Oh, Ben! Why did you lend him money? You might have known he wouldn't do any good with it."

Halleck explained how and why the loan had been made, and added, "If he's supporting his family with it, he's doing some good. I lent it to him for her sake."

Halleck looked hardily into his sister's face, but he dropped his eyes when she answered, simply:

"Yes, of course. But I don't believe she knows anything about it; and I'm glad of it; it would only add to her trouble. She worships you, Ben!"

"Does she?"

"She seems to think you are perfect, and she never comes here but she asks when you're to be home. I suppose she thinks you have a good influence on that miserable husband of hers. He's going from bad to worse, I guess. Father heard that he is betting on the election. That's what he's doing with your money."

"It would be somebody else's money if it wasn't mine," said Halleck. "Bartley Hubbard must live, and he must have the little excitements that make life agreeable."

"Poor thing!" sighed Olive, "I don't know what she would do if she heard that you were going away. To hear her talk, you would think she had been counting the days and hours till you got back. It's ridiculous, the way she goes on with mother; asking everything about you as if she expected to make Bartley Hubbard over again on your pattern. I should hate to have anybody think me such a saint as she does you. But there isn't much danger, thank goodness! I could laugh, sometimes, at the way she questions us all about you, and is so delighted when she finds that you and that wretch have anything in common. But it's all too miserably sad. She certainly *is* the most single-hearted creature alive," continued Olive, reflectively. "Sometimes she *scares* me with her innocence. I don't believe that even her jealousy ever suggested a wicked idea to her: she's furious because she feels the injustice of giving so much more than he does. She hasn't really a thought for anybody else: I do believe that, if she were free to choose from now to doomsday, she would always choose Bartley Hubbard, bad as she knows him to be. And if she were a widow, and anybody else proposed to her, she would be utterly shocked and astonished."

"Very likely," said Halleck, absently.

"I feel very unhappy about her," Olive resumed. "I know that she's anxious and troubled all the time. *Can't* you do something, Ben? Have a talk with that disgusting thing, and see if you can't put him straight again, somehow?"

"No!" exclaimed Halleck, bursting violently from his abstraction. "I shall have nothing to do with them! Let him go his own way and the sooner he goes to the —. I wont interfere, —I can't, I mustn't! I wonder at you, Olive!" He pushed away from the table, and went limping about the room, searching here and there for his hat and stick, which were on the desk where he had put them, in plain view. As he laid hand on them at last, he met his sister's astonished eyes. "If I interfered, I should not interfere because I cared for *him* at all!" he cried.

"Of course not," said Olive. "But I don't see anything to make you *wonder* at me about that."

"It would be because I cared for her"—

"Certainly! You didn't suppose I expected you to interfere from any other motive?"

He stood looking at her in stupefaction, with his hand on his hat and stick, like a man who doubts whether he has heard aright. Presently a shiver passed over him, another light came into his eyes, and he said quietly, "I'm going out to see Atherton."

"To-night?" said his sister, accepting provisionally, as women do, the apparent change of subject. "Don't go to-night, Ben! You're too tired."

"I'm not tired. I intended to see him to-night, at any rate. I want to talk over this South-American scheme with him."

He put on his hat and moved quickly toward the door.

"Ask him about the Hubbards," said Olive. "Perhaps he can tell you something."

"I don't want to know anything. I shall ask him nothing."

She slipped between him and the door.

"Ben, you haven't heard anything against poor Marcia, have you?"

"No!"

"You don't think she's to blame in any way for his going wrong, do you?"

"How could I?"

"Then I don't understand why you wont do anything to help her."

He looked at her again, and opened his lips to speak once, but closed them before he said:

"I've got my own affairs to worry me. Isn't that reason enough for not interfering in theirs?"

"Not for you, Ben."

"Then I don't choose to mix myself up in other people's misery. I don't like it, as you once said."

"But you can't help it sometimes, as *you* said."

"I can this time, Olive. Don't you see"— he began.

"I see there's something you wont tell me. But I shall find it out," she threatened him half playfully.

"I wish you could," he answered. "Then perhaps you'd let me know." She opened the door for him now, and as he passed out he said gently, "I *am* tired, but I sha'n't begin to rest till I have had this talk with Atherton. I'd better go."

"Yes," Olive assented, "you'd better." She added in banter. "You're altogether too mysterious to be of much comfort at home."

The family heard him close the outside door behind him after Olive came back to them, and she explained:

"He's gone out to talk it over with Mr. Atherton."

His father gave a laugh of relief.

"Well, if he leaves it to Atherton, I guess we needn't worry about it."

"The child isn't at all well," said his mother.

XXXIII

HALLECK met Atherton at the door of his room with his hat and coat on.

"Why, Halleck! I was just going to see if you had come home!"

"You needn't now," said Halleck, pushing by him into the room. "I want to see you, Atherton, on business."

Atherton took off his hat and closed the door with one hand, while he slipped the other arm out of his overcoat sleeve.

"Well, to tell the truth, I was going to mingle a little business myself with the pleasure of seeing you."

He turned up the gas in his drop-light, and took the chair from which he had looked across the table at Halleck, when they talked there before.

"It's the old subject," he said, with a sense of repetition in the situation. "I learn from Witherby that Hubbard has taken that money of yours out of the Events, and from what I hear elsewhere he is making ducks and drakes of it on election bets. What shall you do about it?"

"Nothing," said Halleck.

"Oh! Very well," returned Atherton, with the effect of being a little snubbed, but resolved to take his snub professionally. He broke out, however, in friendly exasperation: "Why in the world did you lend the fellow that money?"

Halleck lifted his brooding eyes, and fixed them half pleadingly, half defiantly upon his friend's face.

"I did it for his wife's sake."

"Yes, I know," returned Atherton. "I remember how you felt. I couldn't share your feeling, but I respected it. However, I doubt if your loan was a benefit to either of them. It probably tempted him to count upon money that he hadn't earned, and that's always corrupting."

"Yes," Halleck replied. "But I can't say that, so far as he's concerned, I'm very sorry. I don't suppose it would do her any good if I forced him to disgorge any balance he may have left from his wagers?"

"No, hardly."

"Then I shall let him alone."

The subject was dismissed, and Atherton waited for Halleck to speak of the business on which he had come. But Halleck only played with the paper-cutter which his left hand had found on the table near him, and, with his chin sunk on his breast, seemed lost in an unhappy reverie.

"I hope you won't accuse yourself of doing him an injury," said Atherton, at last, with a smile.

"Injury?" demanded Halleck, quickly. "What injury? How?"

"By lending him that money."

"Oh! I had forgotten that; I wasn't thinking of it," returned Halleck, impatiently. "I was thinking of something different. I'm aware of disliking the man so much that I should be willing to have greater harm than that happen to him—the greatest, for that matter. Though I don't know, after all, that it would be harm. In another life, if there is one, he might start in a new direction; but that isn't imaginable of him here; he can only go from bad to worse; he can only make more and more sorrow and shame. Why shouldn't one wish him dead, when his death could do nothing but good?"

"I suppose you don't expect me to answer such a question seriously."

"But suppose I did?"

"Then I should say that no man ever wished any such good as that, except from the worst motive; and the less one has to do with such questions, even as abstractions, the better."

"You're right," said Halleck. "But why do you call it an abstraction?"

"Because, in your case, nothing else is conceivable."

"I told you I was willing the worst should happen to him."

"And I didn't believe you."

Halleck lay back in his chair, and laughed wearily.

"I wish I could convince somebody of my wickedness. But it seems to be useless to try. I say things that ought to raise the roof, both to you here and to Olive at home, and you tell me you don't believe me, and she tells me that Mrs. Hubbard thinks me a saint. I suppose now, that if I took you by the button-hole and informed you confidentially that I had stopped long enough at 129 Clover street to put a knife into Hubbard in a quiet way, you wouldn't send for a policeman."

"I should send for a doctor," said Atherton.

"Such is the effect of character! And yet, out of the fulness of the heart the mouth speaketh. Out of the heart proceed all those unpleasant things enumerated in Scripture; but if you bottle them up there, and keep your label fresh, it's all that's required of you—by your fellow-beings, at least. What an amusing thing morality would be if it were not—otherwise. Atherton, do you believe that such a man as Christ ever lived?"

"I know you do, Halleck," said Atherton.

"Well, that depends upon what you call *me*. If what I was,—if my well Sunday-schooled youth—is I, I do. But if I, poising dubiously on the momentary present between the past and future, am I—I'm afraid I don't. And yet it seems to me that I have a fairish sort of faith. I know that, if Christ never lived on earth, some One lived who imagined him, and that One must have been a God. The historical fact oughtn't to matter. Christ being imagined, can't you see what a comfort, what a rapture, it must have been to all these poor souls to come into such a presence and be looked through and through? The relief, the rest, the complete exposure of Judgment Day"—

"Every day is Judgment Day," said Atherton.

"Yes, I know your doctrine. But I mean the Last Day. We ought to have something in anticipation of it, here, in our social system. Character is a superstition, a wretched fetish. Once a year wouldn't be too often to seize upon sinners whose blameless life has placed them above suspicion, and turn them inside out before the community, so as to show people how the smoke of the Pit had been quietly blackening their interior. That would destroy character as a cult."

He laughed again.

"Well, this isn't business—though it isn't pleasure, either, exactly. What I came for was to ask you something. I've finished at the law school, and I'm just ready to begin here in the office with you. Don't you think it would be a good time for me to give up the law? Wait a moment!" he said, arresting in Atherton an impulse to speak. "We will take the decent surprise, the friendly demur, the conscientious scruple, for granted. Now, honestly, do you believe I've got the making of a lawyer in me?"

"I don't think you're very well, Halleck," Atherton began.

"Ah, *you're* a lawyer! You won't give me a direct answer!"

"I will if you wish," retorted Atherton.

"Well."

"Do you want to give it up?"

"Yes."

"Then do it. No man ever prospered in it yet who wanted to leave it. And now, since it's come to this, I'll tell you what I really *have* thought all along. I've thought that, if your heart was really set on the law, you would overcome your natural disadvantages for it; but if the time ever came when you were tired of it, your chance was lost: you never would make a lawyer. The question is, whether that time has come."

"It has," said Halleck.

"Then stop, here and now. You've wasted two years' time, but you can't get it back by throwing more after it. I shouldn't be your friend, I shouldn't be an honest man, if I let you go on with me, after this. A bad lawyer is such a very bad thing. This isn't altogether a surprise to me, but it will be a blow to your father," he added, with a questioning look at Halleck, after a moment.

"It might have been, if I hadn't taken the precaution to deaden the place by a heavier blow first."

"Ah! you have spoken to him already?"

"Yes, I've had it out in a sneaking, hypothetical way. But I could see that, so far as the law was concerned, it was enough; it served. Not that he's consented to the other thing; there's where I shall need your help, Atherton. I'll tell you what my plan is." He stated it bluntly at first; and then went over the ground and explained it fully, as he had done at home. Atherton listened without permitting any sign of surprise to escape him; but he listened with increasing gravity, as if he heard something not expressed in Halleck's slow, somewhat nasal monotone, and at the end he said, "I approve of any plan that will take you away for a while. Yes, I'll speak to your father about it."

"If you think you need any conviction, I could use arguments to bring it about in you," said Halleck, in recognition of his friend's ready concurrence.

"No, I don't need any arguments to convince me, I believe," returned Atherton.

"Then I wish you'd say something to bring *me* round! Unless argument is used by somebody, the plan always produces a cold chill in me." Halleck smiled, but Atherton kept a sober face. "I wish my Spanish-American was here! What makes you think it's a good plan? Why should I disappoint my father's hopes again, and wring my mother's heart by proposing to leave them for any such uncertain good as this scheme promises?" He still challenged his friend with a jesting air, but a deeper and stronger feeling of some sort trembled in his voice.

Atherton would not reply to his emotion; he answered, with obvious evasion: "It's a good cause; in some sort—the best sort—it's a missionary work."

"That's what my mother said to me."

"And the change will be good for your health."

"That's what I said to my mother!"

Atherton remained silent, waiting apparently for Halleck to continue, or to end the matter there, as he chose.

It was some moments before Halleck went on: "You would say, wouldn't you, that my first duty was to my own undertakings, and to those who had a right to expect their fulfillment from me? You would say that it was an enormity to tear myself away from the affection that clings to me in that home of mine, yonder, and that nothing but some supreme motive could justify me? And yet you pretend to be satisfied with the reasons I've given you. You're not dealing honestly with me, Atherton!"

"No," said Atherton, keeping the same scrutiny of Halleck's face which he had bent upon him throughout, but seeming now to hear his thoughts rather than his words. "I knew that you would have some supreme motive; and if I have pretended to approve your scheme on the reasons you have given me, I haven't dealt honestly with you. But perhaps a little dishonesty is the best thing under the circumstances. You haven't told me your real motive, and I can't ask it."

"But you imagine it?"

"Yes."

"And what do you imagine? That I have been disappointed in love? That I have been rejected? That the girl who had accepted me has broken her engagement? Something of that sort?" demanded Halleck, scornfully.

Atherton did not answer.

"Oh, how far you are from the truth! How blest and proud and happy I should be if it were the truth!" He looked into his friend's eyes, and added bitterly: "You're not curious, Atherton: you don't ask me what my trouble really is! Do you wish me to tell you what it is without asking?"

Atherton kept turning a pencil end for end between his fingers, while a compassionate smile slightly curved his lips.

"No," he said, finally, "I think you had better not tell me your trouble. I can believe very well, without knowing it, that it's serious"—

"Oh, tragic!" said Halleck, self-contemptuously.

"But I doubt if it would help you to tell it. I've too much

respect for your good sense to suppose that it's an unreality; and I suspect that confession would only weaken you. If you told me, you would feel that you had made me a partner in your responsibility, and you would be tempted to leave the struggle to me. If you're battling with some temptation, some self-betrayal, you must make the fight alone: you would only turn to an ally to be flattered into disbelief of your danger or your culpability."

Halleck assented with a slight nod to each point that the lawyer made.

"You are right," he said, "but a man of your subtlety can't pretend that he doesn't know what the trouble is in such a simple case as mine."

"I don't know anything certainly," returned Atherton, "and, as far as I can, I refuse to imagine anything. If your trouble concerns some one besides yourself,—and no great trouble can concern one man alone,—you've no right to tell it."

"Another Daniel come to judgment!"

"You must trust to your principles, your self-respect, to keep you right"—

Halleck burst into a harsh laugh, and rose from his chair:

"Ah, there you abdicate the judicial function! Principles, self-respect! Against *that*? Don't you suppose I was approached *through* my principles and self-respect? Why, the Devil always takes a man on the very highest plane. *He* knows all about our principles and self-respect, and what they're made of. How the noblest and purest attributes of our nature, with which we trap each other so easily, must amuse him! Pity, rectitude, moral indignation, a blameless life,—he knows that they're all instruments for him! No, sir! No more principles and self-respect for me,—I've had enough of them; there's nothing for me but to *run*, and that's what I'm going to do. But you're quite right about the other thing, Atherton, and I give you a beggar's thanks for telling me that my trouble isn't mine alone, and I've no right to confide it to you. It *is* mine in the sense that no other soul is defiled with the knowledge of it, and I'm glad you saved me from the ghastly profanation, the sacrilege, of telling it. I *was* sneaking round for your sympathy; I *did* want somehow to shift the responsibility onto you; to get you —God help me!—to flatter me out of my wholesome fear and contempt for myself. Well! That's past, now, and— Goodnight!"

He abruptly turned away from Atherton, and swung himself on his cane toward the door.

Atherton took up his hat and coat. "I'll walk home with you," he said.

"All right," returned Halleck, listlessly.

"How soon shall you go?" asked the lawyer, when they were in the street.

"Oh, there's a ship sailing from New York next week," said Halleck, in the same tone of weary indifference. "I shall go in that."

They talked desultorily of other things.

When they came to the foot of Clover Street, Halleck plucked his hand out of Atherton's arm. "I'm going up through here!" he said, with sullen obstinacy.

"Better not," returned his friend, quietly.

"Will it hurt her if I stop to look at the outside of the house where she lives?"

"It will hurt you," said Atherton.

"I don't wish to spare myself!" retorted Halleck. He shook off the touch that Atherton had laid upon his shoulder, and started up the hill; the other overtook him, and, like a man who has attempted to rule a drunkard by thwarting his freak, and then hopes to accomplish his end by humoring it, he passed his arm through Halleck's again, and went with him. But when they came to the house, Halleck did not stop; he did not even look at it; but Atherton felt the deep shudder that passed through him.

In the week that followed, they met daily, and Halleck's broken pride no longer stayed him from the shame of open self-pity and wavering purpose. Atherton found it easier to persuade the clinging reluctance of the father and mother, than to keep Halleck's resolution for him: Halleck could no longer keep it for himself. "Not much like the behavior of people we read of in similar circumstances," he said once. "*They* never falter when they see the path of duty: they push forward without looking to either hand; or else," he added, with a hollow laugh at his own satire, "they turn their backs on it,—like men! Well!"

He grew gaunt and visibly feeble. In this struggle the two men changed places. The plan for Halleck's flight was no longer his own, but Atherton's; and when he did not rebel against it, he only passively acquiesced. The decent pretense of ignorance on Atherton's part necessarily disappeared: in all but words the trouble stood openly confessed between them, and it came to Atherton's saying, in one of Halleck's lapses of purpose, from which it had required all the other's strength to lift him: "Don't come to me any more, Halleck, with the hope that I shall somehow justify your evil against your good. I pitied you at first; but I blame you now."

"You're atrocious," said Halleck, with a puzzled, baffled look. "What do you mean?"

"I mean that you secretly think you have somehow come by your evil virtuously; and you want me to persuade you that it is different from other evils of exactly the same kind,—that it is beautiful and sweet and pitiable, and not ugly as hell and bitter as death, to be torn out of you mercilessly and flung from you with abhorrence. Well, I tell you that you are suffering guiltily, for no man suffers innocently from such a cause. You must *go*, and you can't go too soon. Don't suppose that I find anything noble in your position. I should do you a great wrong if I didn't do all I could to help you realize that you're in disgrace, and that you're only making a choice of shames in running away. Suppose the truth was known,—suppose that those who hold you dear could be persuaded of it,—could you hold up your head?"

"Do I hold up my head as it is?" asked Halleck. "Did you ever see a more abject dog than I am at this moment? Your wounds are faithful, Atherton; but perhaps you might have spared me this last stab. If you want to know, I can assure you that I don't feel any melodramatic vainglory. I know that I'm running away because I'm beaten, but no other man can know the battle I've fought. Don't you suppose I know how hideous this thing is? No one else can know it in all its ugliness!" He covered his face with his hands. "You are right," he said, when he could find his voice. "I suffer guiltily. I must have known it when I seemed to be suffering for pity's sake; I knew it before, and when you said that love without marriage was a worse hell than any marriage without love, you left me without refuge: I had been trying not to face the truth, but I had to face it then. I came away in hell, and I have lived in hell ever since. I tried to think it was a crazy fancy, and put it on my failing health; I used to make believe that some morning I should wake and find the illusion gone. I abhorred it from the beginning as I do now; it has been torment to me; and yet somewhere in my lost soul—the blackest depth, I dare say!—this shame has been so sweet,—it is so sweet,—the one sweetness of life— Ah!" He dashed the weak tears from his eyes, and rose and buttoned his coat about him. "Well, I shall go. And I hope I shall never come back. Though you needn't mention this to my father as an argument for my going when you talk me over with him," he added, with a glimmer of his wonted irony. He waited a moment, and then turned upon his friend, in sad upbraiding: "When I came to you a year and a half ago, after I had taken that ruffian home drunk to her— Why didn't you warn me then, Atherton? Did you see any danger?"

Atherton hesitated: "I knew that, with your habit of suffering for other people, it would make you miserable; but I couldn't have dreamed this would come of it. But you've never been out of your own keeping for a moment. You are responsible, and you are to blame if you are suffering now, and can find no safety for yourself but in running away."

"That's true," said Halleck, very humbly, "and I won't trouble you any more. I can't go on sinning against her belief in me here, and live. I shall go on sinning against it there, as long as I live; but it seems to me the harm will be a little less. Yes, I will go."

But the night before he went, he came to Atherton's lodging to tell him that he should not go; Atherton was not at home, and Halleck was spared this last dishonor. He returned to his father's house through the rain that was beginning to fall lightly, and as he let himself in with his key, Olive's voice said, "It's Ben!" and at the same time she laid her hand upon his arm with a nervous, warning clutch. "Hush! Come in here!" She drew him from the dimly lighted hall into the little reception-room near the door. The gas was burning brighter there, and in the light he saw Marcia, white and still, where she sat holding her baby in her arms. They exchanged no greeting: it was apparent that her being there transcended all usage, and that they need observe none.

"Ben will go home with you," said Olive, soothingly. "Is it raining?" she asked, looking at her brother's coat. "I will get my waterproof."

She left them a moment. "I have been—been walking—walking about," Marcia panted. "It has got so dark—I'm—afraid to go home. I hate to—take you from them—the last—night."

Halleck answered nothing; he sat staring at her till Olive came back with the water-proof and an umbrella. Then, while his sister was putting the water-proof over Marcia's shoulders, he said, "Let me take the little one," and gathered it, with or without her consent, from her arms into his. The baby was sleeping; it nestled warmly against him with a luxurious quiver under the shawl that Olive threw around it. "You can carry the umbrella," he said to Marcia.

They walked fast, when they got out into the rainy dark, and it was hard to shelter Halleck as he limped rapidly on. Marcia ran forward once, to see if her baby were safely kept from the wet, and found that Halleck had its little face pressed close between his neck and cheek. "Don't be afraid," he said. "I'm looking out for it."

His voice sounded broken and strange, and neither of them

spoke again till they came in sight of Marcia's door. Then she tried to stop him. She put her hand on his shoulder.

"Oh, I'm afraid—afraid to go in," she pleaded.

He halted, and they stood confronted in the light of a street lamp; her face was twisted with weeping.

"Why are you afraid?" he demanded harshly.

"We had a quarrel, and I—I ran away—I said that I would never come back. I left him"—

"You must go back to him," said Halleck. "He's your husband!"

He pushed on again, saying over and over, as if the words were some spell in which he found safety, "You must go back, you must go back, you must go back!"

He dragged her with him now, for she hung helpless on his arm, which she had seized, and moaned to herself. At the threshold, "I can't go in!" she broke out. "I'm afraid to go in! What will he say? What will he do? Oh, come in with me! You are good,—and then I shall not be afraid!"

"You must go in alone! No man can be your refuge from your husband! Here!"

He released himself, and, kissing the warm little face of the sleeping child, he pressed it into her arms. His fingers touched hers under the shawl; he tore his hand away with a shiver.

She stood a moment looking at the closed door; then she flung it open, and, pausing as if to gather her strength, vanished into the brightness within.

He turned, and ran crookedly down the street, wavering from side to side in his lameness, and flinging up his arms to save himself from falling as he ran, with a gesture that was like a wild and hopeless appeal.

XXXIV

Marcia pushed into the room where she had left Bartley. She had no escape from her fate; she must meet it, whatever it was. The room was empty, and she began doggedly to search the house for him, upstairs and down, carrying the child with her. She would not have been afraid now to call him; but she had no voice, and she could not ask the servant anything when she looked into the kitchen. She saw the traces of the meal he had made in the dining-room, and when she went a second time to their chamber to lay the little girl down in her crib, she saw the drawers pulled open, and the things as he had tossed them about in packing his bag. She looked at the clock on the mantel—an extravagance of Bartley's, for which she had scolded him—and it was only half-past eight; she had thought it must be midnight.

She sat all night in a chair beside the bed; in the morning she drowsed and dreamed that she was weeping on Bartley's shoulder, and he was joking her and trying to comfort her, as he used to do when they were first married; but it was the little girl, sitting up in her crib, and crying loudly for her breakfast. She put on the child a pretty frock that Bartley liked, and when she had dressed her own tumbled hair she went down-stairs, feigning to herself that they should find him in the parlor. The servant was setting the table for breakfast, and the little one ran forward:

"Baby's chair; mamma's chair; papa's chair!"

"Yes," answered Marcia, so that the servant might hear too. "Papa will soon be home."

She persuaded herself that he had gone as before for the night, and in this pretense she talked with the child at the table, and she put aside some of the breakfast to be kept warm for Bartley. "I don't know just when he may be in," she explained to the girl. The utterance of her pretense that she expected him encouraged her, and she went about her work almost cheerfully.

At dinner she said, "Mr. Hubbard must have been called away, somewhere. We must get his dinner for him when he comes; the things dry up so in the oven."

She put Flavia to bed early, and then trimmed the fire, and made the parlor cozy against Bartley's coming. She did not blame him for staying away the night before; it was a just punishment for her wickedness, and she should tell him so, and tell him that she knew he never was to blame for anything about Hannah Morrison. She enacted over and over in her mind the scenes of their reconciliation. In every step on the pavement he approached the door; at last all the steps died away, and the second night passed.

Her head was light, and her brain confused with loss of sleep. When the child called her from above, and awoke her out of her morning drowse, she went to the kitchen and begged the servant to give the little one its breakfast, saying that she was sick and wanted nothing herself. She did not say anything about Bartley's breakfast and she would not think anything; the girl took the child into the kitchen with her, and kept it there all day.

Olive Halleck came during the forenoon, and Marcia told her that Bartley had been unexpectedly called away.

"To New York," she added, without knowing why.

"Ben sailed from there to-day," said Olive sadly.

"Yes," assented Marcia.

"We want you to come and take tea with us this evening," Olive began.

"Oh, I can't," Marcia broke in. "I mustn't be away when Bartley gets back." The thought was something definite in the sea of uncertainty on which she was cast away; she never afterward lost her hold of it; she confirmed herself in it by other inventions; she pretended that he had told her where he was going, and then that he had written to her. She almost believed these childish fictions as she uttered them. At the same time, in all her longing for his return, she had a sickening fear that when he came back he would keep his parting threat and drive her away; she did not know how he could do it, but this was what she feared.

She seldom left the house, which at first she kept neat and pretty, and then let fall into slatternly neglect. She ceased to care for her dress or the child's; the time came when it seemed as if she could scarcely move in the mystery that beset her life, and she yielded to a deadly lethargy which paralyzed all her faculties but the instinct of concealment.

She repelled the kindly approaches of the Hallecks, sometimes sending word to the door when they came, that she was sick and could not see them; or when she saw any of them, repeating those hopeless lies concerning Bartley's whereabouts, and her expectations of his return.

For the time she was safe against all kindly misgivings; but there were some of Bartley's creditors who grew impatient of his long absence, and refused to be satisfied with her fables. She had a few dollars left from some money that her father had given her at home, and she paid these all out upon the demand of the first-comer. Afterward, as other bills were pressed, she could only answer with incoherent promises and evasions that scarcely served for the moment. The pursuit of these people dismayed her. It was nothing that certain of them refused further credit; she would have known, both for herself and her child, how to go hungry and cold; but there was one of them who threatened her with the law if she did not pay. She did not know what he could do; she had read somewhere that people who did not pay their debts were imprisoned, and if that disgrace were all she would not care. But if the law were enforced against her the truth would come out;

she would be put to shame before the world as a deserted wife; and this when Bartley had *not* deserted her. The pride that had bidden her heart break in secret rather than suffer this shame, even before itself, was baffled; her one blind device had been concealment, and this poor refuge was possible no longer. If all were not to know, some one must know.

The law with which she had been threatened might be instant in its operation; she could not tell. Her mind wavered from fear to fear. Even while the man stood before her, she perceived the necessity that was upon her, and when he left her she would not allow herself a moment's delay.

She reached the Events building, in which Mr. Atherton had his office, just as a lady drove away in her coupé. It was Miss Kingsbury, who made a point of transacting all business matters with her lawyer at his office, and of keeping her social relations with him entirely distinct, as she fancied, by this means. She was only partly successful, but at least she never talked business with him at her house, and doubtless she would not have talked anything else with him at his office, but for that increasing dependence upon him in everything which she certainly would not have permitted herself if she had realized it. As it was, she had now come to him in a state of nervous exaltation, which was not business-like. She had been greatly shocked by Ben Halleck's sudden freak; she had sympathized with his family till she herself felt the need of some sort of condolence, and she had promised herself this consolation from Atherton's habitual serenity. She did not know what to do when he received her with what she considered an impatient manner, and did not seem at all glad to see her. There was no reason why he should be glad to see a lady calling on business and no doubt he often found her troublesome, but he had never shown it before. She felt like crying at first; then she passed through an epoch of resentment, and then through a period of compassion for him. She ended by telling him with dignified severity that she wanted some money: they usually made some jokes about her destitution when she came upon that errand. He looked surprised and vexed, and:

"I have spent what you gave me last month," she explained.

"Then you wish to anticipate the interest on your bonds?"

"Certainly not," said Clara, rather sharply. "I wish to have the interest up to the present time."

"But I told you," said Atherton, and he could not, in spite of himself, help treating her somewhat as a child, "I told you then that I was paying you the interest up to the first of November. There is none due now. Didn't you understand that?"

"No, I didn't understand," answered Clara. She allowed herself to add, "It is very strange!" Atherton struggled with his irritation, and made no reply. "I can't be left without money," she continued. "What am I to do without it?" she demanded with an air of unanswerable argument. "Why, I *must* have it!"

"I felt that I ought to understand you fully," said Atherton, with cold politeness. "It's only necessary to know what sum you require."

Clara flung up her veil and confronted him with an excited face.

"Mr. Atherton, I don't wish a *loan*; I can't *permit* it; and you know that my principles are entirely against anticipating interest."

Atherton, from stooping over his table, pencil in hand, leaned back in his chair, and looked at her with a smile that provoked her:

"Then may I ask what you wish me to do?"

"No! I can't instruct you. My affairs are in your hands. But I must *say*"— She bit her lip, however, and did not say it. On the contrary she asked, rather feebly, "Is there nothing due on anything?"

"I went over it with you, last month," said Atherton patiently, "and explained all the investments. I could sell some stocks, but this election trouble has disordered everything, and I should have to sell at a heavy loss. There are your mortgages and there are your bonds. You can have any amount of money you want, but you will have to borrow it."

"And that you know I wont do. There should always be a sum of money in the bank," said Clara decidedly.

"I do my very best to keep a sum there, knowing your theory; but your practice is against me. You draw too many checks," said Atherton, laughing.

"Very well!" cried the lady, pulling down her veil. "Then I'm to have nothing?"

"You wont allow yourself to have anything," Atherton began. But she interrupted him haughtily.

"It is certainly very odd that my affairs should be in such a state that I can't have all the money of my own that I want, whenever I want it."

Atherton's thin face paled a little more than usual.

"I shall be glad to resign the charge of your affairs, Miss Kingsbury."

"And I shall accept your resignation," cried Clara, magnificently, "whenever you offer it." She swept out of the office, and descended to her coupé like an incensed goddess. She drew the curtains and began to cry. At her door, she bade the servant deny her to everybody, and went to bed, where she was visited a little later by Olive Halleck, whom no ban excluded. Clara lavishly confessed her sin and sorrow. "Why, I *went* there, more than half, to sympathize with him about Ben; I don't need any money, just yet; and the first thing I knew, I was accusing him of neglecting my interests, and I don't know what all! Of course he had to say he wouldn't have anything more to do with them, and I should have despised him if he hadn't. And now I don't care what becomes of the property: it's never been anything but misery to me ever since I had it, and I always knew it would get me into trouble sooner or later." She whirled her face over into her pillow, and sobbed. "But I *didn't* suppose it would ever make me insult and outrage the best friend I ever had,—and the truest man,—and the noblest gentleman! Oh, *what* will he think of me?"

Olive remained sadly quiet, as if but superficially interested in these transports, and Clara lifted her face again to say in her handkerchief:

"It's a shame, Olive, to burden you with all this at a time when you've care enough of your own."

"Oh, I'm rather glad of somebody else's care; it helps to take my mind off," said Olive.

"Then what would you do?" asked Clara, tempted by the apparent sympathy with her in the effect of her naughtiness.

"You might make a party for him, Clara," suggested Olive, with lack-luster irony.

Clara gave way to a loud burst of grief.

"Oh, Olive Halleck! I didn't suppose you could be *so* cruel!"

Olive rose impatiently.

"Then write to him, or go to him and tell him that you're ashamed of yourself, and ask him to take your property back again."

"Never!" cried Clara, who had listened with fascination. "What would he think of me?"

"Why need you care? It's purely a matter of business!"

"Yes."

"And you needn't mind what he thinks."

"Of course," admitted Clara, thoughtfully.

"He will naturally despise you," added Olive, "but I suppose he does that, now."

Clara gave her friend as piercing a glance as her soft blue eyes could emit, and, detecting no sign of jesting in Olive's sober face, she answered haughtily:

"I don't see what right Mr. Atherton has to despise me!"

"Oh, no! He must admire a girl who has behaved to him as you've done."

Clara's hauteur collapsed, and she began to truckle to Olive.

"If he were *merely* a business man, I shouldn't mind it; but knowing him socially, as I do, and as a—friend, and—an acquaintance, that way, I don't see how I can do it."

"I wonder you didn't think of that before you accused him of fraud and peculation, and all those things."

"I *didn't* accuse him of fraud and peculation!" cried Clara, indignantly.

"You said you didn't know what all you'd called him," said Olive with her hand on the door.

Clara followed her down-stairs.

"Well, I shall never do it in the world," she said, with reviving hope in her voice.

"Oh, I don't expect you to go to him this morning," said Olive, dryly. "That would be a little *too* barefaced."

Her friend kissed her.

"Olive Halleck, you're the strangest girl that ever was. I do believe you'd joke at the point of death! But I'm *so* glad you have been perfectly frank with me, and of course it's worth worlds to know that you think I've behaved horridly, and ought to make *some* reparation."

"I'm glad you value my opinion, Clara. And if you come to me for frankness, you can always have all you want; it's a drug in the market with me."

She meagerly returned Clara's embrace, and left her in a reverie of tactless scheming for the restoration of peace with Mr. Atherton.

Marcia came in upon the lawyer before he had thought, after parting with Miss Kingsbury, to tell the clerk in the outer office to deny him; but she was too full of her own trouble to see the reluctance which it taxed all his strength to quell, and she sank into the nearest chair unbidden. At sight of her Atherton became the prey of one of those fantastic repulsions in which men visit upon women the blame of others' thoughts about them: he censured her for Halleck's wrong; but in another instant he recognized his cruelty, and atoned by relenting a little in his intolerance of her presence. She sat gazing at him with a face of blank misery, to which he could not refuse the charity of a prompting question:

"Is there something I can do for you, Mrs. Hubbard?"

"Oh, I don't know,—I don't know!"

She had a folded paper in her hands, which lay helpless in her lap. After a moment she resumed, in a hoarse, low voice:

"They have all begun to come for their money, and this one—this one says he will have the law of me—I don't know what he means—if I don't pay him."

Marcia could not know how hard Atherton found it to govern the professional suspicion which sprung up at the question of money. But he overruled his suspicion by an effort that was another relief to the struggle in which he was wrenching his mind from Miss Kingsbury's outrageous behavior.

"What have you got there?" he asked, gravely, and not unkindly, and being used to prompt the reluctance of lady clients, he put out his hand for the paper she held.

It was the bill of the threatening creditor, for indefinitely repeated dozens of Tivoli beer.

"Why do they come to *you* with this?"

"Mr. Hubbard is away."

"Oh, yes. I heard. When do you expect him home?"

"I don't know."

"Where is he?"

She looked at him piteously without speaking.

Atherton stepped to his door, and gave the order forgotten before. Then he closed the door, and came back to Marcia.

"Don't you know where your husband is, Mrs. Hubbard?"

"Oh, he will come back! He *couldn't* leave me! He's dead,— I know he's dead; but he will come back! He only went away for the night, and something must have happened to him."

The whole tragedy of her life for the past fortnight was expressed in these wild and inconsistent words; she had not been able to reason beyond the pathetic absurdities which they involved; they had the effect of assertions confirmed in the belief by incessant repetition, and doubtless she had said them to herself a thousand times. Atherton read in them, not only the confession of her despair, but a prayer for mercy, which it would have been inhuman to deny, and for the present he left her to such refuge from herself as she had found in them. He said, quietly:

"You had better give me that paper, Mrs. Hubbard," and took the bill from her. "If the others come with their accounts again, you must send them to me. When did you say Mr. Hubbard left home?"

"The night after the election," said Marcia.

"And he didn't say how long he should be gone?" pursued the lawyer, in the feint that she had known he was going.

"No," she answered.

"He took some things with him?"

"Yes."

"Perhaps you could judge how long he meant to be absent from the preparation he made?"

"I've never looked to see. I couldn't!"

Atherton changed the line of his inquiry. "Does any one else know of this?"

"No," said Marcia, quickly, "I told Mrs. Halleck and all of them that he was in New York, and I said that I had heard from him. I came to you because you were a lawyer, and you would not tell what I told you."

"Yes," said Atherton.

"I want it kept a secret. Oh, do you think he's dead?" she implored.

"No," returned Atherton, gravely. "I don't think he's dead."

"Sometimes it seems to me I could bear it better if I knew he was dead. If he isn't dead, he's out of his mind! He's out of his mind, don't you think, and he's wandered off somewhere."

She besought him so pitifully to agree with her, bending forward and trying to read the thoughts in his face, that he could not help saying, "Perhaps."

A gush of grateful tears blinded her, but she choked down her sobs.

"I said things to him that night that were enough to drive him crazy. I was always the one in fault, but he was always the one to make up first, and he never would have gone away from me if he had known what he was doing! But he will come back, I know he will," she said, rising. "And oh, you won't say anything to anybody, will you? And he'll get back before they find out. I will send those men to you, and Bartley will see about it as soon as he comes home"—

"Don't go, Mrs. Hubbard," said the lawyer. "I want to speak with you a little longer." She dropped again in her chair, and looked at him inquiringly. "Have you written to your father about this?"

"Oh, no," she answered quickly, with an effect of shrinking back into herself.

"I think you had better do so. You can't tell when your husband will return, and you can't go on in this way."

"I will never tell *father*," she replied, closing her lips inexorably.

The lawyer forbore to penetrate the family trouble he divined. "Are you all alone in the house?" he asked.

"The girl is there. And the baby."

"That won't do, Mrs. Hubbard," said Atherton, with a compassionate shake of the head. "You can't go on living there alone."

"Oh, yes, I can. I'm not afraid to be alone," she returned with the air of having thought of this.

"But he may be absent some time yet," urged the lawyer; "he may be absent indefinitely. You must go home to your father and wait for him there."

"I can't do that. He must find me here when he comes," she answered firmly.

"But how will you stay?" pleaded Atherton; he had to deal with an unreasonable creature who could not be driven, and he must plead. "You have no money, and how can you live?"

"Oh," replied Marcia, with an air of having thought of this too, "I will take boarders."

Atherton smiled at the hopeless practicality and shook his head; but he did not oppose her directly. "Mrs. Hubbard," he said, earnestly, "you have done well in coming to me, but let me convince you that this is a matter which can't be kept. It must be known. Before you can begin to help yourself, you must let others help you. Either you must go home to your father and let your husband find you there"—

"He must find me here, in our own house"—

"Then you must tell your friends here that you don't know where he is, nor when he will return, and let them advise together as to what can be done. You must tell the Hallecks"—

"I will *never* tell them!" cried Marcia. "Let me go! I can starve there and freeze, and if he finds me dead in the house, none of them shall have the right to blame him,—to say that he left me,—that he deserted his little child! Oh! oh! oh! oh! What shall I do?"

The hapless creature shook with the thick-coming sobs that overpowered her now, and Atherton refrained once more. She did not seem ashamed before him of the sorrows which he felt it a sacrilege to know, and in a blind, instinctive way he perceived that in proportion as he was a stranger it was possible for her to bear her disgrace in his presence. He spoke at last from the hint he found in this fact: "Will you let me mention the matter to Miss Kingsbury?"

She had looked at him with sad intensity in the eyes, as if trying to fathom any nether thought that he might have. It must have seemed to her at first that he was mocking her, but his words brought her the only relief from her self-upbraiding she had known. To suffer kindness from Miss Kingsbury would be in some sort an atonement to Bartley for the wrong her jealousy had done him; it would be self-sacrifice for his sake; it would be expiation. "Yes, tell her," she answered with a promptness whose obscure motive was not illumined by the flash of passionate pride with which she added, "I shall not care for *her*."

She rose again, and Atherton did not detain her; but when she had left him he lost no time in writing to her father the facts of the case as her visit had revealed them. He spoke of her reluctance to have her situation known to her family, but assured the Squire that he need have no anxiety about her for the present. He promised to keep him fully informed in regard to her, and to telegraph the first news of Mr. Hubbard. He left the Squire to form his own conjectures, and to take whatever action he thought best. For his own part, he had no question that Hubbard had abandoned his wife, and had stolen Halleck's money; and the detectives to whom he went were clear that it was a case of European travel.

XXXV

ATHERTON went from the detectives to Miss Kingsbury, and boldly resisted the interdict at her door, sending up his name with the message that he wished to see her immediately on business. She kept him waiting while she made a frightened toilet, and leaving the letter to him which she had begun half finished on her desk, she came down to meet him in a flutter of despondent conjecture. He took her mechanically yielded hand, and seated himself on the sofa beside her. "I sent word that I had come on business," he said, "but it is no affair of yours,"—she hardly knew whether to feel relieved or disappointed,—"except as you make all unhappy people's affairs your own."

"Oh!" she murmured in meek protest, and at the same time she remotely wondered if these affairs were his.

"I came to you for help," he began again, and again she interrupted him in deprecation.

"You are very good, after—after—what I—what happened,—I'm sure." She put up her fan to her lips, and turned her head a little aside. "Of course I shall be glad to help you in anything, Mr. Atherton; you know I always am."

"Yes, and that gave me courage to come to you, even after the way in which we parted this morning. I knew you would not misunderstand me"—

"No," said Clara softly, doing her best to understand him.

"Or think me wanting in delicacy"—

"Oh, no, no!"

"If I believed that we need not have any embarrassment in meeting in behalf of the poor creature who came to see me just after you left me. The fact is," he went on, "I felt a little freer to promise your interest since I had no longer any business relation to you, and could rely on your kindness like—like—any other."

"Yes," assented Clara, faintly; and she forbore to point out to him, as she might fitly have done, that he had never had the right to advise or direct her at which he hinted, except as she expressly conferred it from time to time. "I shall be only too glad"—

"And I will have a statement of your affairs drawn up to-morrow, and sent to you." Her heart sank; she ceased to move the fan which she had been slowly waving back and forth before her face. "I was going to set about it this morning, but Mrs. Hubbard's visit"—

"Mrs. Hubbard!" cried Clara, and a little air of pique qualified her despair.

"Yes; she is in trouble,—the greatest: her husband has deserted her."

"*Oh*, Mr. Atherton!" Clara's mind was now far away from any concern for herself. The woman whose husband has deserted her supremely appeals to all other women. "I can't believe it! What makes you think so?"

"What she concealed, rather than what she told me, I believe," answered Atherton. He ran over the main points of their interview, and summed up his own conjectures. "I know from things Halleck has let drop that they haven't always lived happily together; Hubbard has been speculating with borrowed money, and he's in debt to everybody. She's been alone in her house for a fortnight, and she only came to me because people had begun to press her for money. She's been pretending to the Hallecks that she hears from her husband, and knows where he is."

"Oh, poor, poor thing!" said Clara, too shocked to say more. "Then they don't know?"

"No one knows but ourselves. She came to me because I was a comparative stranger, and it would cost her less to confess her trouble to me than to them, and she allowed me to speak to you for very much the same reason."

"But I know she dislikes me!"

"So much the better! She can't doubt your goodness"—

"Oh!"

"And if she dislikes you, she can keep her pride better with you."

Clara let her eyes fall, and fingered the edges of her fan. There was reason in this, and she did not care that the opportunity of usefulness was personally unflattering, since he thought her capable of rising above the fact. "What do you want me to do?" she asked, lifting her eyes docilely to his.

"You must find some one to stay with her, in her house, till she can be persuaded to leave it, and you must lend her some money till her father can come to her or write to her. I've just written to him, and I've told her to send all her bills to me; but I'm afraid she may be in immediate need."

"Terrible!" sighed Clara, to whom the destitution of an acquaintance was appalling after all her charitable knowledge of want and suffering. "Of course, we mustn't lose a moment," she added; but she lingered in her corner of the sofa to discuss ways and means with him, and to fathom that sad enjoyment which comfortable people find in the contemplation of alien sorrows. It was not her fault if she felt too kindly toward the disaster that had brought Atherton back to her on the old terms; or if she arranged her plans for befriending Marcia in her desolation with too buoyant a cheerfulness. But she took herself to task for the radiant smile she found on her face, when she ran upstairs and looked into her glass to see how she looked in parting with Atherton: she said to herself that he would think her perfectly heartless.

She decided that it would be indecent to drive to Marcia's under the circumstances, and she walked; though with all the time this gave her for reflection she had not wholly banished this smile when she looked into Marcia's woe-begone eyes. But she found herself incapable of the awkwardnesses she had deliberated, and fell back upon the native motherliness of her heart, into which she took Marcia with sympathy that ignored everything but her need of help and pity. Marcia's bruised pride was broken before the goodness of the girl she had hated, and she performed her sacrifice to Bartley's injured memory, not with the haughty self-devotion which she intended should humiliate Miss Kingsbury, but with the prostration of a woman spent with watching and fasting and despair. She held Clara away for a moment of scrutiny, and then submitted to the embrace in which they recognized and confessed all.

It was scarcely necessary for Clara to say that Mr. Atherton had told her; Marcia already knew that; and Clara became a partisan of her theory of Bartley's absence almost without an effort, in spite of the facts that Atherton had suggested to the contrary. "Of *course!* He has wandered off somewhere, and as soon as he comes to his senses he will hurry home. Why I was reading of such a case only the other day,—the case of a minister who wandered off in just the same way, and found himself out in Western New York somewhere, after he had been gone three months."

"Bartley wont be gone three months," protested Marcia.

"Certainly not!" cried Clara, in severe self-rebuke. Then she talked of his return for a while as if it might be expected at any moment. "In the mean time," she added, "you must stay here; you're quite right about that, too, but you mustn't stay here alone: he'd be quite as much shocked at that as if he found you gone when he came back. I'm going to ask you to let my friend Miss Strong stay with you; and she must pay her board; and you must let me lend you all the money you need. And, dear,"—Clara dropped her voice to a lower and gentler note,— "you mustn't try to keep this from your friends. You must let Mr. Atherton write to your father; you must let me tell the Hallecks: they'll be hurt if you don't. You needn't be troubled; of *course* he wandered off in a temporary hallucination, and nobody will think differently."

She adopted the fiction of Bartley's aberration with so much fervor that she even silenced Atherton's injurious theories with it when he came in the evening to learn the result of her intervention. She had forgotten, or she ignored, the facts as he had stated them in the morning; she was now Bartley's valiant champion, as well as the tender protector of Marcia: she was the equal friend of the whole exemplary Hubbard family.

Atherton laughed, and she asked what he was laughing at.

"Oh," he answered, "at something Ben Halleck once said: a real woman can make righteousness delicious and virtue piquant."

Clara reflected. "I don't know whether I like that," she said finally.

"No?" said Atherton. "Why not?"

She was serving him with an after-dinner cup of tea, which she had brought into the drawing-room, and in putting the second lump of sugar into his saucer she paused again, thoughtfully, holding the little cube in the tongs. She was rather elaborately dressed for so simple an occasion, and her silken train coiled itself far out over the mossy depth of the moquette carpet; the pale blue satin of the furniture, and the delicate white and gold of the decorations, became her wonderfully.

"I can't say, exactly. It seems depreciatory, somehow, as a generalization. But a man might say it of the woman he was in love with," she concluded.

"And you wouldn't approve of a man's saying it of the woman his friend was in love with?" pursued Atherton, taking his cup from her.

"If they were very close friends." She did not know why, but she blushed, and then grew a little pale.

"I understand what you mean," he said, "and I shouldn't have liked the speech from another kind of man. But Halleck's innocence characterized it." He stirred his tea, and then let it stand untasted in his abstraction.

"Yes, he is good," sighed Clara. "If he were not so good, it would be hard to forgive him for disappointing all their hopes in the way he's done."

"It's the best thing he could have done," said Atherton gravely, even severely.

"I know you advised it," asserted Clara. "But it's a great blow to them. How strange that Mr. Hubbard should have disappeared the last night Ben was at home! I'm glad that he got away without knowing anything about it."

Atherton drank off his tea, and refused a second cup with a gesture of his hand. "Yes, so am I," he said. "I'm glad of every league of sea he puts behind him." He rose, as if eager to leave the subject.

Clara rose, too, with the patient acquiescence of a woman, and took his hand proffered in parting. They had certainly talked out, but there seemed no reason why he should go. He held her hand, while he asked, "How shall I make my peace with you?"

"My peace? What for?" She flushed joyfully. "I was the one in fault."

He looked at her mystified. "Why, surely, *you* didn't repeat Halleck's remark?"

"Oh!" she cried indignantly, withdrawing her hand. "I meant *this morning*. It doesn't matter," she added. "If you still wish to resign the charge of my affairs, of course I must submit. But I thought—I thought"— She did not go on, she was too deeply hurt. Up to this moment she had imagined that she had befriended Marcia, and taken all that trouble upon herself for goodness' sake; but now she was ready to upbraid him for ingratitude in not seeing that she had done it for his sake. "You can send me the statement, and then—and then—I don't know what I *shall* do! *Why* do you mind what I said? I've often said quite as much before, and you know that I didn't mean it. I want you to take my property back again, and never to mind anything I say: I'm not worth minding." Her intended upbraiding had come to this pitiful effect of self-contempt, and her hand somehow was in his again. "Do take it back!"

"If I do that," said Atherton, gravely, "I must make my conditions," and now they sat down together on the sofa from which he had risen. "I can't be subjected again to your—disappointments,"—he arrested with a motion of his hand the profuse expression of her penitence and good intentions,—"and I've felt for a long time that this was no attitude for your attorney. You ought to have the right to question and censure; but I confess I can't grant you this. I've allowed myself to make your interests too much my own in everything to be able to bear it. I've thought several times that I ought to give up the trust; but it seemed like giving up so much more, that I never had the courage to do it in cold blood. This morning you gave me my chance to do it in hot blood, and if I resume it, I must make my terms."

It seemed a long speech to Clara, who sometimes thought she knew whither it tended, and sometimes not. She said in a low voice, "Yes."

"I must be relieved," continued Atherton, "of the sense I've had that it was indelicate in me to keep it, while I felt as I've grown to feel—toward you." He stopped: "If I take it back, you must come with it!" he suddenly concluded.

The inconsistency of accepting these conditions ought to have struck a woman who had so long imagined herself the chase of fortune-hunters. But Clara apparently found nothing alarming in the demand of a man who openly acted upon his knowledge of what could only have been matter of conjecture to many suitors she had snubbed. She found nothing incongruous in the transaction, and she said, with as tremulous breath and as swift a pulse as if the question had been solely of herself, "I accept—the conditions."

In the long, happy talk that lasted till midnight, they did not fail to recognize that, but for their common pity of Marcia, they might have remained estranged, and they were decently ashamed of their bliss when they thought of misery like hers. When Atherton rose to bid Clara good-night, Marcia was still watching for Bartley, indulging for the last time the folly of waiting for him as if she definitely expected him that night.

Every night since he disappeared, she had kept the lights

burning in the parlor and hall, and drowsed before the fire till
the dawn drove her to a few hours of sleep in bed. But with the
coming of the stranger who was to be her companion, she must
deny herself even this consolation, and openly accept the fact
that she no longer expected Bartley at any given time. She
bitterly rebelled at the loss of her solitude, in which she could
be miserable in whatever way her sorrow prompted, and the
pangs with which she had submitted to Miss Kingsbury's
kindness grew sharper hour by hour till she maddened in a
frenzy of resentment against the cruelty of her expiation. She
longed for the day to come that she might go to her, and take
back her promises and her submission, and fling her insulting
good-will in her face. She said to herself that no one should
enter her door again till Bartley opened it; she would die
there in the house, she and her baby, and as she stood wringing
her hands and moaning over the sleeping little one, a hideous
impulse made her brain reel; she wished to look if Bartley
had left his pistol in its place; a cry for help against herself
broke from her; she dropped upon her knees.

The day came, and the hope and strength which the mere
light so strangely brings to the sick in spirit as well as the sick
in body visited Marcia. She abhorred the temptation of the
night like the remembrance of a wicked dream, and she went
about with a humble and grateful prayer—to something, to
some one—in her heart. Her housewifely pride stirred again:
that girl should not think she was a slattern; and Miss Strong,
when she preceded her small trunk in the course of the forenoon, found the parlor and the guest-chamber, which she was
to have, swept and dusted, and set in perfect order by Marcia's
hands. She had worked with fury, and kept her heart-ache still,
but it began again at sight of the girl. Fortunately, the conservatory pupil had embraced with even more than Miss
Kingsbury's ardor the theory of Bartley's aberration, and she
met Marcia with a sympathy in her voice and eyes that could
only have come from sincere conviction. She was a simple

country thing, who would never be a prima-donna; but the overflowing sentimentality which enabled her to accept herself at the estimate of her enthusiastic fellow-villagers made her of far greater comfort to Marcia than the sublimest musical genius would have done. She worshiped the heroine of so tragic a fact, and her heart began to go out to her in honest helpfulness from the first. She broke in upon the monotony of Marcia's days with the offices and interests of wholesome commonplace, and exorcised the ghostly silence with her first stroke on the piano,—which Bartley had bought on the installment plan and had not yet paid for.

In fine, life adjusted itself with Marcia to the new conditions, as it does with women less wofully widowed by death, who promise themselves reunion with their lost in another world, and suffer through the first weeks and days in the hope that their parting will be for but days or weeks, and then gradually submit to indefinite delay. She prophesied Bartley's return, and fixed it in her own mind for this hour and that. "Now, in the morning, I shall wake and find him standing by the bed. No, at night he will come in and surprise us at dinner." She cheated herself with increasing faith at each renewal of her hopes. When she ceased to formulate them at last, it was because they had served their end, and left her established, if not comforted, in the superstition by which she lived. His return at any hour or any moment was the fetish which she let no misgiving blaspheme; everything in her of woman and of wife consecrated it. She kept the child in continual remembrance of him by talking of him, and by making her recognize the photographs in which Bartley had abundantly perpetuated himself; at night, when she folded the little one's hands for prayer, she made her pray God to take care of poor papa and send him home soon to mamma. She was beginning to canonize him.

Her father came to see her as soon as he thought it best after Atherton's letter; and the old man had to endure talk of Bartley to which all her former praises were as refreshing shadows of defamation. She required him to agree with everything she said, and he could not refuse; she reproached him for being with herself the cause of all Bartley's errors, and he had to bear it without protest. At the end he could say nothing but "Better come home with me, Marcia," and he suffered in meekness the indignation with which she rebuked him: "I will stay in Bartley's house till he comes back to me. If he is dead, I will die here."

The old man had satisfied himself that Bartley had absconded in his own rascally right mind, and he accepted with tacit grimness the theory of the detectives that he had not gone alone to Europe. He paid back the money which Bartley had borrowed from Halleck, and he set himself as patiently as he could to bear with Marcia's obstinacy. It was a mania which must be indulged for the time, and he could only trust to Atherton to keep him advised concerning her. When he offered her money at parting, she hesitated. But she finally took it, saying, "Bartley will pay it back, every cent, as soon as he gets home. And if," she added, "he doesn't get back soon, I will take some other boarders and pay it myself."

He could see that she was offended with him for asking her to go home. But she was his girl; he only pitied her. He shook hands with her as usual, and kissed her with the old stoicism; but his lips, set to fierceness by the life-long habit of sarcasm, trembled as he turned away. She was eager to have him go; for she had given him Miss Strong's room, and had taken the girl into her own, and Bartley would not like it if he came back and found her there.

Bartley's disappearance was scarcely a day's wonder with people outside his own circle in that time of anxiety for a fair count in Louisiana and Florida, and long before the Returning Boards had partly relieved the tension of the public mind by their decision he had quite dropped out of it. The reporters who called at his house to get the bottom facts in the case, adopted Marcia's theory, given them by Miss Strong, and whatever were their own suspicions or convictions, paragraphed

him with merciful brevity as having probably wandered away
during a temporary hallucination. They spoke of the depres-
sion of spirits which many of his friends had observed in him,
and of pecuniary losses as the cause. They mentioned his possible suicide only to give the report the authoritative denial of
his family; and they added, that the case was in the hands of
the detectives, who believed themselves in possession of important clews. The detectives in fact remained constant to
their original theory, that Bartley had gone to Europe, and
they were able to name with reasonable confidence the person
with whom he had eloped. But these were matters hushed up
among the force and the press. In the meantime, Bartley had
been simultaneously seen at Montreal and Cincinnati, at about
the same time that an old friend had caught a glimpse of him
on a train bound westward from Chicago.

So far as the world was concerned, the surmise with which
Marcia saved herself from final despair was the only impression that even vaguely remained of the affair. Her friends, who
had compassionately acquiesced in it at first, waited for the
moment when they could urge her to relinquish it and go
home to her father; but while they waited, she gathered
strength to establish herself immovably in it, and to shape her
life more and more closely about it. She had no idea, no instinct, but to stay where he had left her till he came back. She
opposed this singly and solely against all remonstrance, and
treated every suggestion to the contrary as an instigation to
crime. Her father came from time to time during the winter to
see her, but she would never go home with him even for a
day. She put her plan in force; she took other boarders: other
girl students like Miss Strong, whom her friends brought her
when they found that it was useless to oppose her and so began
to abet her; she worked hard, and she actually supported herself at last in a frugal independence. Her father consulted with
Atherton and the Hallecks; he saw that she was with good
and faithful friends, and he submitted to what he could not
help. When the summer came, he made a last attempt to in-

duce her to go home with him. He told her that her mother wished to see her. She would not understand. "I'll come," she said, "if mother gets seriously sick. But I can't go home for the summer. If I hadn't been at home last summer, *he* would never have got into that way, and *it* would never have happened."

She went home at last, in obedience to a peremptory summons; but her mother was too far gone to know her when she came. Her quiet, narrow life had grown colder and more inward to the end, and it passed without any apparent revival of tenderness for those once dear to her; the funeral publicity that followed seemed a final touch of the fate by which all her preferences had been thwarted in the world.

Marcia stayed only till she could put the house in order after they had laid her mother to rest among the early reddening sumacs under the hot glare of the August sun; and when she came away, she brought her father with her to Boston, where he spent his days as he might, taking long and aimless walks, devouring heaps of newspapers, rusting in idleness, and aging fast, as men do in the irksomeness of disuse.

Halleck's father was beginning to show his age, too; and Halleck's mother lived only in her thoughts of him, and her hopes of his return; but he did not even speak of this in his letters to them. He said very little of himself, and they could merely infer that the experiment to which he had devoted himself was becoming less and less satisfactory. Their sense of this added its pang to their unhappiness in his absence.

One day Marcia said to Olive Halleck:

"Has any one noticed that you are beginning to look like your sisters?"

"*I've* noticed it," answered the girl. "I always *was* an old maid, and now I'm beginning to show it."

Marcia wondered if she had not hurt Olive's feelings; but she would never have known how to excuse herself; and latterly she had been growing more and more like her father in certain traits. Perhaps her passion for Bartley had been the one spring of tenderness in her nature, and, if ever it were spent, she would stiffen into the old man's stern aridity.

XXXVI

IT WAS nearly two years after Atherton's marriage that Halleck one day opened the door of the lawyer's private office, and, turning the key in the lock, limped forward to where the latter was sitting at his desk. Halleck was greatly changed: the full beard that he had grown scarcely hid the savage gauntness of his face; but the change was not so much in lines and contours as in that expression of qualities which we call looks.

"Well, Atherton!"

"Halleck! *You!*"

The friends looked at each other; and Atherton finally broke from his amaze and offered his hand, with an effect, even then, of making conditions. But it was Halleck who was the first to speak again.

"How *is* she? Is she well? Is she still here? Have they heard anything from him yet?"

"No," said Atherton, answering the last question with the same provisional effect as before.

"Then he is *dead*. That's what I knew; that's what I *said!* And here I am. The fight is over, and that's the end of it. I'm beaten."

"You look it," said Atherton, sadly.

"Oh, yes; I look it. That's the reason I can afford to be frank, in coming back to my friends. I knew that with this look in my face I should make my own welcome; and it's cordial even beyond my expectations."

"I'm not glad to see you, Halleck," said Atherton. "For your own sake I wish you were at the other end of the world."

"Oh, I know that. How are my people? Have you seen my father lately? Or my mother? Or—Olive?"

A pathetic tremor shook his voice.

"Why, haven't *you* seen them yet?" demanded Atherton.

Halleck laughed cynically.

"My dear friend, my steamer arrived this morning, and I'm just off the New York train. I've hurried to your office in all the impatience of friendship. I'm very lucky to find you here so late in the day! You can take me home to dinner, and let your domestic happiness preach to me. Come, I rather like the notion of that!"

"Halleck," said Atherton, without heeding his banter, "I wish you would go away again! No one knows you are here, you say, and no one need ever know it."

Halleck set his lips and shook his head, with a mocking smile.

"I'm surprised at you, Atherton, with your knowledge of human nature. I've come to stay; you must know that. You must know that I had gone through everything before I gave up, and that I haven't the strength to begin the struggle over again. I tell you I'm beaten, and I'm glad of it; for there is rest in it. You would waste your breath if you talked to me in the old way; there's nothing in me to appeal to, any more. If I was wrong— But I don't admit, any more, that I was wrong: by heaven, I was *right!*"

"You *are* beaten, Halleck," said Atherton, sorrowfully.

He pushed himself back in his chair, and clasped his hands together behind his head, as his habit was in reasoning with obstinate clients.

"What do you propose to do?"

"I propose to stay."

"What for?"

"What for? Till I can prove that he is dead."

"And then?"

"Then I shall be free to ask her." He added, angrily: "You know what I've come back for; why do you torment me with these questions? I did what I could; I ran away. And the last night I saw her, I thrust her back into that hell she called her home, and I told her that no man could be her refuge from that devil, her husband, when she had begged me in her mortal terror to go in with her and save her from him. *That* was the recollection I had to comfort me when I tried to put her out of my mind,—out of my soul! When I heard that he was gone, I respected her days of mourning. God knows how I endured it, now it's over; but I did endure it. I waited, and here I am. And you ask me to go away again. Ah!" He fetched his breath through his set teeth, and struck his fist on his knee. "He is *dead!* And now, if she will, she can marry me. Don't look at me as if I had killed him! There hasn't been a time in these two infernal years when I wouldn't have given my life to save his— for *her* sake. I know that; and that gives me courage, it gives me hope."

"But if he isn't dead?"

"Then he has abandoned her, and she has the right to be free. She can get a divorce!"

"Oh!" said Atherton, compassionately, "has that poison got into *you*, Halleck? You might ask her, if she were a widow, to marry you; but how will you ask her, if she's still a wife, to get a divorce and then marry you? How will you suggest that to a woman whose constancy to her mistake has made her sacred to you?" Halleck seemed about to answer; but he only panted, dry-lipped and open-mouthed, and Atherton continued: "You would have to corrupt her soul first. I don't know what change you've made in yourself during these two years; you look like a desperate and defeated man, but you don't look like *that*. You don't *look* like one of those scoundrels who lure women from their duty, ruin homes, and destroy society—not in the old libertine fashion in which the seducer had at least the grace to risk his life, but safely, smoothly, under the shelter of our infamous laws. Have you really come back here to give your father's honest name, and the example of a man of your own blameless life, in support of conditions that tempt people to marry with a mental reservation, and that weaken every marriage bond with the guilty hope of escape whenever a fickle mind, or secret lust, or wicked will may dictate? Have you come to join yourself to those miserable specters who go shrinking through the world, afraid of their own past, and anxious to hide it from those they hold dear; or do you propose to defy the world, to help form within it the community of outcasts with whom shame is not shame, nor dishonor dishonor? How will you like the society of those uncertain men, those certain women?"

"You are very eloquent," said Halleck, "but I ask you to observe that these little abstractions don't interest me. I've a concrete purpose, and I can't contemplate the effect of other people's actions upon American civilization. When you ask me to believe that I oughtn't to try to rescue a woman from the misery to which a villain has left her, simply because some justice of the peace consecrated his power over her, I decline to be such a fool. I use my reason, and I see who it was that defiled and destroyed that marriage, and I know that she is as free in the sight of God as if he had never lived. If the world doesn't like my open shame, let it look to its own secret shame— the marriages made and maintained from interest and ambition and vanity and folly. I will take my chance with the men and women who have been honest enough to own their mistake, and to try to repair it, and I will preach by my life that marriage has no sanctity but what love gives it, and that, when love ceases, marriage ceases, before heaven. If the laws have come to recognize that, by whatever fiction, so much the better for the laws!" Halleck rose.

"Well, then," cried Atherton, rising too, "you shall meet me on your own ground! This poor creature is constant in every breath she draws, to the ruffian who has abandoned her. I must believe, since you say it, that you are ready to abet her in getting a divorce, even one of those divorces that are 'obtained without publicity, and for any cause,' "—Halleck winced,— "that you are willing to put your sisters to shame before the world, to break your mother's heart and your father's pride—to insult the ideal of goodness that she herself has formed of you; but how will you begin? The love on her part, at least, hasn't ceased; has the marriage?"

"She shall tell me," answered Halleck. He left Atherton without another word, and in resentment that effaced all friendship between them, though after this parting they still kept up its outward forms, and the Athertons took part in the rejoicings with which the Hallecks celebrated Ben's return. His meeting with the lawyer was the renewal of the old conflict on terms of novel and hopeless degradation. He had mistaken for peace that exhaustion of spirit which comes to a man in battling with his conscience; he had fancied his struggle over, and he was to learn now that its anguish had just begun. In that delusion his love was to have been a law to itself, able to loose and to bind, and potent to beat down all regrets, all doubts, all fears, that questioned it; but the words with which Marcia met him struck his passion dumb.

"Oh, I am so glad you have come back!" she said. "Now I know that we can find him. You were such friends with him, and you understood him so well, that you will know just what to do. Yes, we shall find him now, and we should have found him long ago, if you had been here. Oh, if you had never gone away! But I can never be grateful enough for what you said to me that night when you would not come in with me. The words have rung in my ears ever since; they showed that you had faith in him, more faith than I had, and I've made them my rule and my guide. No one has been my refuge from him, and no one ever shall be. And I thank you—yes, I thank you on my bended knees—for making me go into the house alone; it's my one comfort that I had the strength to come back to him, and let him do anything he would to me, after I had treated him so; but I've never pretended it was my own strength. I have always told everybody that the strength came from you!"

Halleck had brought Olive with him; she and Marcia's father listened to these words with the patience of people who had heard them many times before; but at the end Olive glanced at Halleck's downcast face with fond pride in the satisfaction she imagined they must give him. The old man ruminated upon a bit of broom-straw, and absently let the little girl catch by his hands, as she ran to and fro between him and her mother while her mother talked. Halleck made a formless sound in his throat, for answer, and Marcia went on.

"I've got a new plan now, but it seems as if father took a pleasure in discouraging *all* my plans. I *know* that Bartley's shut up, somewhere, in some asylum, and I want them to send detectives to all the asylums in the United States and in Canada,—you can't tell how far off he would wander in that state, —and inquire if any stray insane person has been brought to them. Doesn't it seem to you as if that would be the right way to find him? I want to talk it all over with you, Mr. Halleck, for I know *you* can sympathize with me; and if need be I will go to the asylums myself; I will walk to them, I will crawl to them on my knees! When I think of him shut up there among those raving maniacs, and used as they use people in some of the asylums—oh, oh, oh, oh!"

She broke out into sobs, and caught her little girl to her breast. The child must have been accustomed to her mother's tears; she twisted her head round, and looked at Halleck with a laughing face.

Marcia dried her eyes, and asked, with quivering lips, "Isn't she like him?"

"Yes," replied Halleck huskily.

"She has his long eyelashes exactly, and his hair and complexion, hasn't she?"

The old man sat chewing his broom-straw in silence; but when Marcia left the room to get Bartley's photograph, so that Halleck might see the child's resemblance to him, her father looked at Halleck from under his beetling brows: "I don't think we need trouble the *asylums* much for Bartley Hubbard. But if it was to search the State's-prisons and the jails, the rum-holes and the gambling-hells, or if it was to dig up the scoundrels who have been hung under assumed names during the last two years, I should have some hopes of identifying him."

Marcia came back, and the old man sat in cast-iron quiet, as if he had never spoken; it was clear that, whatever hate he felt for Bartley, he spared her; and that if he discouraged her plans, as she said, it was because they were infected by the craze in which she canonized Bartley.

"You see how she is," said Olive, when they came away.

"Yes, yes, yes," Halleck desolately assented.

"Sometimes she seems to me just like a querulous, vulgar, middle-aged woman in her talk; she repeats herself in the same scolding sort of way; and she's so eager to blame somebody besides Bartley for Bartley's wickedness, that, when she can't punish herself, she punishes her father. She's merciless to that wretched old man, and he's wearing his homesick life out here in the city for her sake. You heard her just now about his discouraging her plans?"

"Yes," said Halleck, as before.

"She's grown commoner and narrower, but it's hardly her fault, poor thing! and it seems terribly unjust that she should be made so by what she has suffered. But that's just the way it has happened. She's so undisciplined, that she couldn't get any good out of her misfortunes—she's only got harm; they've made her selfish, and there seems to be nothing left of what she was two years ago but her devotion to that miserable wretch. You mustn't let it turn you against her, Ben; you mustn't forget what she might have been. She had a rich nature; but how it's been wasted and turned back upon itself! Poor, untrained, impulsive, innocent creature—my heart aches for her! It's been hard to bear with her at times, terribly hard, and you'll find it so, Ben. But you *must* bear with her. The awfulest thing about people in trouble is that they are such *bores*; they tire you to death. But you'll only have to stand her praises of what Bartley was; and we had to stand them, and her hopes of what you would be if you were only at home, besides. I don't know what all she expects of you, but you must try not to disappoint her; she worships the ground you tread on, and I really think she believes you can do anything you will, just because you're good."

Halleck listened in silence. He was indeed helpless to be otherwise than constant. With shame and grief in his heart, he could only vow her there the greater fealty because of the change he found in her.

He was doomed at every meeting to hear her glorify a man whom he believed a heartless traitor, to plot with her for the rescue from imaginary captivity of the wretch who had cruelly forsaken her. He actually took some of the steps she urged: he addressed inquiries to the insane asylums, far and near; and in these futile endeavors, made only with the desire of failure, his own reason seemed sometimes to waver. She insisted that Atherton should know all the steps they were taking; and his sense of his old friend's exact and perfect knowledge of his motives was a keener torture than even her father's silent scorn of his efforts, or the worship in which his own family held him for them.

XXXVII

HALLECK had come home in broken health, and had promised his family, with the self-contempt that depraves, not to go away again, since the change had done him no good. There was no talk for the present of his trying to do anything but get well; and for a while, under the strong excitement, he seemed to be better. But suddenly he failed; he kept his room, and then he kept his bed; and the weeks stretched into months before he left it.

When the spring weather came, he was able to go out again, and he spent most of his time in the open air, feeling every day a fresh accession of strength. At the end of one long April afternoon, he walked home with a light heart, whose right to rejoice he would not let his conscience question. He had met Marcia in the public garden, where they sat down on a bench and talked, while her father and the little girl wandered away in the restlessness of age and the restlessness of childhood.

"We are going home to Equity this summer," she said, "and perhaps we shall not come back. No, we shall not come back. *I have given up.* I have waited, hoping—hoping. But now I know that it is no use waiting any longer: *he is dead.*"

She spoke in tearless resignation, and the peace of accepted widowhood seemed to diffuse itself around her.

Her words repeated themselves to Halleck as he walked homeward. He found the postman at the door with a newspaper, which he took from him with a smile at its veteran appearance and its probable adventures in reaching him. The wrapper seemed to have been several times slipped off, and then slit up; it was tied with a string now, and was scribbled with rejections in the hands of various Hallocks and Halletts, one of whom had finally indorsed upon it, "Try 97 Rumford street." It was originally addressed, as he made out, to "Mr. B. Halleck, Boston, Mass.," and he carried it to his room before he opened it, with a careless surmise as to its interest for him. It proved to be a flimsy, shabbily printed country newspaper, with an advertisement marked in one corner.

State of Indiana,   } ss.
    Tecumseh County,   }

In Tecumseh Circuit Court, April Term, 1879.

BARTLEY J. HUBBARD   }
      vs.   } Divorce.   No. 5793.
MARCIA G. HUBBARD.   }

It appearing, by affidavit this day filed in the office of the Clerk of the Tecumseh Circuit Court, that Marcia G. Hubbard, defendant in the above entitled action for divorce on account of abandonment and gross neglect of duty, is a non-resident of the State of Indiana, notice of the pendency of such action is therefore hereby given said defendant above named, and that the same will be called for answer on the 11th day of April, 1879, the same being the 3d judicial day of the April term of said court, for said year, which said term of said court will begin on the first Monday in April, 1879, and will be held at the Court House, in the town of Tecumseh, in said County and State, said 11th day of April, 1879, being the time fixed by said plaintiff, by indorsement on his complaint, at which said time said defendant is required to answer herein.

Witness my hand and the seal of the said court, this 4th day of March, 1879.

                                     AUGUSTUS H. HAWKINS,
{ SEAL }   *Clerk.*
Milikin & Ayres, Att'ys for Plff.

Halleck read this advertisement again and again, with a dull, mechanical action of the brain. He saw the familiar names, but they were hopelessly estranged by their present relation to each other; the legal jargon reached no intelligence in him that could grasp its purport.

When his gaze began to yield, he took evidence of his own reality by some such tests as one might in waking from a long faint. He looked at his hands, his feet; he rose and looked at his face in the glass. Turning about he saw the paper where he had left it on the table; it was no illusion. He picked up the cover from the floor, and scanned it anew, trying to remember the handwriting on it, to make out who had sent this paper to him, and why. Then the address seemed to grow into something different under his eye; it ceased to be his name; he saw now that the paper was directed to Mrs. B. Hubbard, and that by a series of accidents and errors it had failed to reach her in its wanderings, and by a final blunder had fallen into his hands.

Once solved, it was a very simple affair, and he had now but to carry it to her; that was very simple too. Or he might destroy it; this was equally simple. Her words repeated themselves once more: "I have given up. He is dead." Why should he break the peace she had found, and destroy her last sad illusion? Why should he not spare her the knowledge of this final wrong, and let the merciful injustice accomplish itself? The questions seemed scarcely to have any personal concern for Halleck; his temptation wore a heavenly aspect. It softly pleaded with him to forbear, like something outside of himself. It was when he began to resist it that he found it the breath in his nostrils, the blood in his veins. Then the mask dropped, and the enemy of souls put forth his power against this weak spirit, enfeebled by long strife and defeat already acknowledged.

At the end Halleck opened his door, and called, "Olive, Olive!" in a voice that thrilled the girl with strange alarm where she sat in her own room. She came running, and found him clinging to his door-post, pale and tremulous. "I want you—want you to help me," he gasped. "I want to show you something—Look here!"

He gave her the paper, which he had kept behind him, clutched fast in his hand as if he feared it might somehow escape him at last, and staggered away to a chair.

His sister read the notice. "Oh, Ben!" She dropped her hands with the paper in them before her, a gesture of helpless horror and pity, and looked at him. "Does *she* know it? Has she seen it?"

"No one knows it but you and I. The paper was left here for me by mistake. I opened it before I saw that it was addressed to her."

He panted forth these sentences in an exhaustion that would have terrified her, if she had not been too full of indignant compassion for Marcia to know anything else. She tried to speak.

"Don't you understand, Olive? This is the notice that the law requires she shall have to come and defend her cause, and it has been sent by the clerk of the court there, to the address that villain must have given in the knowledge that it could reach her only by one chance in ten thousand."

"And it has come to you! Oh, Ben! Who sent it to *you?*" The brother and sister looked at each other, but neither spoke the awe-stricken thought that was in both their hearts. "Ben," she cried, in a solemn ecstasy of love and pride, "I would rather be you this minute than any other man in the world!"

"Don't!" pleaded Halleck. His head dropped, and then he lifted it by a sudden impulse. "Olive!"—but the impulse failed, and he only said, "I want you to go to Atherton with me. We mustn't lose time. Have Cyrus get a carriage. Go down and tell them we're going out. I'll be ready as soon as you are."

But when she called to him from below that the carriage had come and she was waiting, he would have refused to go with her if he durst. He no longer wished to keep back the fact, but he felt an invalid's weariness of it, a sick man's inadequacy to the further demands it should make upon him. He crept slowly down the stairs, keeping a tremulous hold upon the rail; and he sank with a sigh against the carriage cushions, answering Olive's eager questions and fervid comments with languid monosyllables.

They found the Athertons at coffee, and Clara would have them come to the dining-room and join them. Halleck refused the coffee, and, while Olive told what had happened, he looked listlessly about the room, aware of a perverse sympathy with Bartley, from Bartley's point of view; Bartley might never have gone wrong if he had had all that luxury; and why should he not have had it, as well as Atherton? What right had the untempted prosperity of such a man to judge the guilt of such men as himself and Bartley Hubbard?

Olive produced the newspaper from her lap, where she kept both hands upon it, and opened it in dramatic corroboration of what she had been telling Atherton. He read it and passed it to Clara.

"When did this come to you?"

Olive answered for him. "This evening—just now. Didn't I say that?"

"No," said Atherton, and he added to Halleck, gently: "I beg your pardon. Did you notice the dates?"

"Yes," answered Halleck, with cold refusal of Atherton's tone of reparation.

"The cause is set for hearing on the 11th," said Atherton. "This is the 8th. The time is very short."

"It's long enough," said Halleck, wearily.

"Oh, telegraph!" cried Clara. "Telegraph them instantly that she never dreamt of leaving him! Abandonment! Oh, if they only knew how she had been slaving her fingers off for the last two years to keep a home for him to come back to, they'd give *her* the divorce!"

Atherton smiled and turned to Halleck: "Do you know what their law is now? It was changed two years ago."

"Yes," said Halleck, replying to the question Atherton had asked and the subtler question he had looked, "I have read up the whole subject since I came home. The divorce is granted only upon proof, even when the defendant fails to appear, and if this were to go against us,"—he instinctively identified himself with Marcia's cause,—"we can have the default set aside, and a new trial granted, for cause shown."

The women listened in awe of the legal phrases; but when Atherton rose, and asked, "Is your carriage here?" his wife sprang to her feet.

"Why, where are you going?" she demanded, anxiously.

"Not to Indiana, immediately," answered her husband. "We're first going to Clover street, to see Squire Gaylord and Mrs. Hubbard. Better let me take the paper, dear," he said, softly withdrawing it from her hands.

"Oh, it's a cruel, cruel law!" she moaned, deprived of this moral support. "To suppose that such a notice as this is sufficient! Women couldn't have made such a law."

"No, women only profit by such laws after they're made: they work both ways. But it's not such a bad law, as divorce laws go. We do worse, now, in some New England States."

They found the Squire alone in the parlor, and, with a few words of explanation, Atherton put the paper in his hands, and he read the notice in emotionless quiet. Then he took off his spectacles, and shut them in their case, which he put back into his waistcoat pocket. "This is all right," he said. He cleared his throat, and lifting the fierce glimmer of his eyes to Atherton's, he asked, drily, "What is the law, at present?"

Atherton briefly recapitulated the points as he had them from Halleck.

"That's good," said the old man. "We will fight this gentleman." He rose, and from his gaunt height looked down on both of them, with his sinuous lips set in a bitter smile. "Bartley must have been disappointed when he found a divorce so hard to get in Indiana. He must have thought that the old law was still in force there. He's not the fellow to swear to a lie if he can help it; but I guess he expects to get this divorce by perjury."

Marcia was putting little Flavia to bed. She heard the talking below; she thought she heard Bartley's name. She ran to the stairs, and came hesitantly down, the old wild hope and wild terror fluttering her pulse and taking her breath. At sight of the three men, apparently in counsel, she crept toward them, holding out her hands before her like one groping his way. "What—what is it?" She looked from Atherton's face to her father's; the old man stopped, and tried to smile reassuringly; he tried to speak; Atherton turned away.

It was Halleck who came forward, and took her wandering hands. He held them quivering in his own, and said gravely and steadily, using her name for the first time in the deep pity which cast out all fear and shame, "Marcia, we have found your husband."

"Dead?" she made with her lips.

"He is alive," said Halleck. "There is something in this paper for you to see,—something you *must* see"—

"I can bear anything, if he is not dead. Where—what is it? Show it to me." The paper shook in the hands which Halleck released; her eyes strayed blindly over its columns; he had to put his finger on the place before she could find it. Then her tremor ceased, and she seemed without breath or pulse while she read it through. She fetched a long, deep sigh, and passed her hand over her eyes, as if to clear them; staying herself unconsciously against Halleck's breast, and, laying her trembling arm along his arm till her fingers knit themselves among his fingers, she read it a second time and a third. Then she dropped the paper, and turned to look up at him. "Why!" she cried, as if she had made it out at last, while an awful, joyful light of hope flashed into her face, "*It is a mistake!* Don't you see? He thinks that I never came back! He thinks that I meant to abandon him. That I—that I— But you *know* that I came back, —you came back *with* me! Why, I wasn't gone an hour,—a *half*-hour, hardly. O Bartley! poor Bartley! He thought I could leave him, and take his child from him; that I could be so wicked, so heartless— Oh, no, no, no. Why, I only stayed away that little time because I was *afraid* to go back! Don't you remember how I told you I was afraid, and wanted you to come in with me?" Her exultation broke in a laugh. "But we can explain it now, and it will be all right. He will see—he will understand—I will tell him just how it was— Oh, Flavia, Flavia, we've found papa, we've found papa! Quick!"

She whirled away toward the stairs, but her father caught her by the arm. "Marcia!" he shouted, in his old raucous voice, "you've got to understand! This"—he hesitated, as if running over all terms of opprobrium in his mind, and he resumed as if he had found them each too feeble—"*Bartley* hasn't acted under any mistake."

He set the facts before her with merciless clearness, and she listened with an audible catching of the breath at times, while she softly smoothed her forehead with her left hand. "I don't believe it," she said, when he had ended. "Write to him, tell him what I say, and you will see."

The old man uttered something between a groan and a curse. "Oh, you poor, crazy child! Can nothing make you understand that Bartley wants to get rid of you, and that he's just as ready for one lie as another? He thinks he can make out a case of abandonment with the least trouble, and so he accuses you of that; but he'd just as soon accuse you of anything else. *Write* to him? You've got to *go* to him! You've got to go out there and fight him in open court, with facts and witnesses. Do you suppose Bartley Hubbard wants any explanation from you? Do you think he's been waiting these two years to hear that you didn't really abandon him, but came back to this house an hour after you left it, and that you've waited for him here ever since? When he knows that, will he withdraw this suit of his and come home? He'll want the proof, and the way to do it is to go out there and let him have it. If I had him on the stand for five minutes," said the old man, between his set teeth—"*just five minutes*—I'd undertake to convince him from his own lips that he was wrong about you! But I am afraid he wouldn't mind a letter. You think I say so because I hate him, and you don't believe me. Well, ask either of these gentlemen here whether I'm telling you the truth."

She did not speak, but, with a glance at their averted faces, she sank into a chair, and passed one hand over the other, while she drew her breath in long, shuddering respirations, and stared at the floor with knit brows and starting eyes, like one stifling a deadly pang. She made several attempts to speak before she could utter any sound; then she lifted her eyes to her father's: "Let us—let us—go—home! Oh, let us go home! I will give him up. I *had* given him up already; I told you," she said, turning to Halleck, and speaking in a slow, gentle tone, "only an hour ago, that he was dead. And this—this that's happened, it makes no difference. Why did you bring the paper to me when you knew that I thought he was dead?"

"God knows I wished to keep it from you."

"Well, no matter now. Let him go free if he wants to. I can't help it."

"You *can* help it," interrupted her father. "You've got the facts on your side, and you've got the witnesses."

"Would you go out with me, and tell him that I never meant to leave him?" she asked simply, turning to Halleck. "You—and Olive?"

"We would do anything for you, Marcia!"

She sat musing, and drawing her hands one over the other again, while her quivering breath came and went on the silence. She let her hands fall nervelessly on her lap. "I can't go; I'm too weak; I couldn't bear the journey. No!" She shook her head. "I can't go!"

"Marcia," began her father, "it's your *duty* to go!"

"Does it say in the law that I have to go if I don't choose?" she asked of Halleck.

"No, you certainly need not go if you don't choose!"

"Then I will stay. Do you think it's my duty to go?" she asked, referring her question first to Halleck, and then to Atherton. She turned from the silence by which they tried to leave her free. "I don't care for my duty any more. I don't want to keep him, if it's so that he—left me—and—and meant it—and he doesn't—care for me any—more."

"Care for you? He *never* cared for you, Marcia! And you may be sure he doesn't care for you now!"

"Then let him go, and let us go home."

"Very well," said the old man; "we will go home, then, and before the week's out Bartley Hubbard will be a perjured bigamist."

"Bigamist?" Marcia leaped to her feet.

"Yes, bigamist! Don't you suppose he had his eye on some other woman out there before he began this suit?"

The languor was gone from Marcia's limbs. As she confronted her father, the wonderful likeness in the outline of their faces appeared. His was dark and wrinkled with age, and hers was gray with the anger that drove the blood back to her heart; but one impulse animated those fierce profiles, and the hoarded hate in the old man's soul seemed to speak in Marcia's thick whisper, "I will go."

XXXVIII

The Athertons sat late over their breakfast in the luxurious dining-room, where the April sun came in at the windows overlooking the Back Bay, and commanding at that stage of the tide a long stretch of shallow with a flight of white gulls settled upon it.

They had let Clara's house on the hill, and she had bought another on the new land; she insisted upon the change, not only because everybody was leaving the hill, but also because, as she said, it would seem too much like taking Mr. Atherton to board, if they went to housekeeping where she had always lived; she wished to give him the effect before the world of having brought her to a house of his own. She had even furnished it anew for the most part, and had banished as far as possible the things that reminded her of the time when she was not his wife. He humored her in this fantastic self-indulgence, and philosophized her wish to give him the appearance of having the money, as something orderly in its origin, and not to be deprecated on other grounds, since probably it deceived nobody. They lived a very tranquil life, and Clara had no grief of her own, unless it was that there seemed to be no great things she could do for him. One day, when she whimsically complained of this, he said: "I'm very glad of that. Let's try to be equal to the little sacrifices we must make for each other; they will be quite enough. Many a woman, who would be ready to die for her husband, makes him wretched because she wont live for him. Don't despise the day of small things."

"Yes, but when every day seems the day of small things!" she pouted.

"Every day *is* the day of small things," said Atherton, "with people who are happy. We're never so prosperous as when we can't remember what happened last Monday."

"Oh, but I can't bear to be always living in the present."

"It's not so spacious, I know, as either the past or the future; but it's all we have."

"There!" cried Clara, "that's *fatalism!* It's *worse* than fatalism!"

"And is fatalism so very bad?" asked her husband.

"It's Mahometanism!"

"Well, it isn't necessarily a plurality of wives," returned Atherton, in subtle anticipation of her next point. "And it's really only another name for resignation, which is certainly a good thing."

"Resignation? Oh, I don't know about that!"

Atherton laughed, and put his arm round her waist—an argument that no woman can answer in a man she loves: it seems to deprive her of her reasoning faculties. In the atmosphere of affection which she breathed, she sometimes feared that her mental powers were really weakening. As a girl she had lived a life full of purposes, which, if somewhat vague, were unquestionably large. She had then had great interests,— art, music, literature,—the symphony concerts, Mr. Hunt's classes, the novels of George Eliot, and Mr. Fiske's lectures on the cosmic philosophy; and she had always felt that they expanded and elevated existence. In her moments of question as to the shape which her life had taken since, she tried to think whether the happiness which seemed so little dependent on these things was not beneath the demands of a spirit which was probably immortal and was certainly cultivated. They all continued to be part of her life, but only a very small part; and she would have liked to ask her husband whether his influence upon her had been wholly beneficial. She was not sure that it had; but neither was she sure that it had not. She had never fully consented to the distinctness with which he classified all her emotions and ideas as those of a woman; in her heart she doubted whether a great many of them might not be those of a man, though she had never found any of them exactly like his. She could not complain that he did not treat her as an equal; he deferred to her, and depended upon her good sense to an extent that sometimes alarmed her, for she secretly knew that she had a very large streak of silliness in her nature. He seemed to tell her everything, and to be greatly ruled by her own advice, especially in matters of business; but she could not help observing that he often kept matters involving certain moral questions from her till the moment for deciding them was past. When she accused him of this, he confessed that it was so, but defended himself by saying that he was afraid her conscience might sway him against his judgment.

Clara now recurred to these words of his as she sat looking at him through her tears across the breakfast table. "Was that the reason you never told me about poor Ben before?"

"Yes, and I expect you to justify me. What good would it have done to tell you?"

"I could have told you, at least, that if Ben had any such feeling as that, it wasn't *his* fault altogether!"

"But you wouldn't have believed that, Clara," said Atherton. "You know that, whatever that poor creature's faults are, coquetry isn't one of them."

Clara only admitted this fact passively.

"How did he excuse himself for coming back?" she asked.

"He didn't excuse himself; he defied himself. We had a stormy talk, and he ended by denying that he had any social duty in the matter."

"And I think he was quite right!" Clara flashed out. "It was his own affair."

"He said he had a concrete purpose, and wouldn't listen to abstractions. Yes, he talked like a woman. But you know he wasn't right, Clara, though *you* talk like a woman too. There are a great many things that are not wrong except as they wrong others. I've no doubt that, as compared with the highest love her husband ever felt for her, Ben's passion was as light to darkness. But, if he could only hope for its return through the perversion of her soul,—through teaching her to think of escape from her marriage by a divorce,—then it was a crime against her and against society."

"Ben couldn't do such a thing!"

"No, he could only dream of doing it. When it came to the attempt, everything that was good in him revolted against it and conspired to make him help her in the efforts that would defeat his hopes if they succeeded. It was a ghastly ordeal, but it was sublime; and when the climax came,—that paper, which he had only to conceal for a few days or weeks,—he was equal to the demand upon him. But suppose a man of his pure training and traditions had yielded to temptation,—suppose he had so far depraved himself that he could have set about persuading her that she owed no allegiance to her husband, and might rightfully get a divorce and marry him,—what a ruinous blow it would have been to all who knew of it! It would have disheartened those who abhorred it, and encouraged those who wanted to profit by such an example. It doesn't matter much, socially, what undisciplined people like Bartley and Marcia Hubbard do; but if a man like Ben Halleck goes astray, it's calamitous; it 'confounds the human conscience,' as Victor Hugo says. All that careful nurture in the right since he could speak, all that lifelong decency of thought and act, that noble ideal of unselfishness and responsibility to others, trampled under foot and spit upon,—it's horrible!"

"Yes," answered Clara, deeply moved, even as a woman may be in a pretty breakfast-room, "and such a good soul as Ben always was naturally. Will you have some more tea?"

"Yes, I will take another cup. But as for natural goodness"—

"Wait! I will ring for some hot water."

When the maid had appeared, disappeared, reappeared, and finally vanished, Atherton resumed. "The natural goodness doesn't count. The natural man is a wild beast, and his natural goodness is the amiability of a beast basking in the sun when his stomach is full. The Hubbards were full of natural goodness, I dare say, when they didn't happen to cross each other's wishes. No, it's the implanted goodness that saves,—the seed of righteousness treasured from generation to generation, and carefully watched and tended by disciplined fathers and mothers in the hearts where they had dropped it. The flower of this implanted goodness is what we call civilization, the condition of general uprightness that Halleck declared he owed no allegiance to. But he was better than his word."

Atherton lifted, with his slim, delicate hand, the cup of translucent china, and drained off the fragrant Souchong, sweetened, and tempered with Jersey cream to perfection. Something in the sight went like a pang to his wife's heart. "Ah!" she said, "it is easy enough for us to condemn. *We* have everything we want!"

"I don't forget that, Clara," said Atherton, gravely. "Sometimes when I think of it, I am ready to renounce all judgment of others. The consciousness of our comfort, our luxury, almost paralyzes me at those times, and I am ashamed and afraid even of our happiness."

"Yes, what right," pursued Clara, rebelliously, "have we to be happy and united, and these wretched creatures so"—

"No right—none in the world! But somehow the effects follow their causes. In some sort they chose misery for themselves,—we make our own hell in this life and the next,—or it was chosen for them by undisciplined wills that they inherited. In the long run their fate must be a just one."

"Ah, but I have to look at things in the *short* run, and I can't see any justice in Marcia's husband using her so!" cried Clara. "Why shouldn't you use me badly? I don't believe any woman ever meant better by her husband than she did."

"Oh, the meaning doesn't count! It's our deeds that judge us. He is a thoroughly bad fellow, but you may be sure she has been to blame. Though I don't blame the Hubbards, either of them, so much as I blame Halleck. He not only had everything he wished, but the training to know what he ought to wish."

"I don't know about his having everything. I think Ben must have been disappointed some time," said Clara evasively.

"Oh, that's nothing," replied Atherton, with the contented husband's indifference to sentimental grievances.

Clara did not speak for some moments, and then she summed up a turmoil of thoughts in a profound sigh. "Well, I don't like it! I thought it was bad enough having a man, even on the outskirts of my acquaintance, abandon his wife; but now, Ben Halleck, who has been like a brother to me—to have him mixed up in such an affair in the way he is—it's intolerable!"

"I agree with you," said Atherton, playing with his spoon. "You know how I hate anything that sins against order, and this whole thing is disorderly. It's intolerable, as you say. But we must bear our share of it. We're all bound together. No one sins or suffers to himself in a civilized state, or religious state—it's the same thing. Every link in the chain feels the effect of the violence more or less intimately. We rise or fall together in Christian society. It's strange that it should be so hard to realize a thing that every experience of life teaches. We keep on thinking of offenses against the common good as if they were abstractions!"

"Well, *one* thing," said Clara, "I shall always think unnecessarily shocking and disgraceful about it, and that is Ben's going out with her on this journey. I don't see how you could allow that, Eustace."

"Yes," said Atherton, after a thoughtful silence, "it *is* shocking. The only consolation is that it is *not* unnecessarily shocking. I'm afraid that it's necessarily so. When any disease of soul or body has gone far enough, it makes its own conditions, and other things must adjust themselves to it. Besides, no one knows the ugliness of the situation but Halleck himself. I don't see how I could have interfered; and upon the whole I don't know that I ought to have interfered, if I could. She would be helpless without him, and he can get no harm from it. In fact, it's part of his expiation, which must have begun as soon as he met her again after he came home."

Clara was convinced, but not reconciled. She only said, "I don't like it."

Her husband did not reply; he continued musingly: "When the old man made that final appeal to her jealousy,—all that there is really left, probably, of her love for her husband,—and she responded with a face as wicked as his, I couldn't help looking at Halleck."

"Oh, poor Ben! *How* did he take it? It must have scared, it must have disgusted him!"

"That's what I had expected. But there was nothing in his face but pity. He understood, and he pitied her. That was all."

Clara rose, and turned to the window, where she remained looking through her tears at the gulls on the shallow. It seemed much more than twenty-four hours since she had taken leave of Marcia and the rest at the station, and saw them set out on their long journey with its uncertain and unimaginable end. She had deeply sympathized with them all, but at the same time she had felt very keenly the potential scandalousness of the situation; she shuddered inwardly when she thought what if people knew; she had always revolted from contact with such social facts as their errand involved. She got Olive aside for a moment and asked her, "Don't you *hate* it, Olive? Did you ever dream of being mixed up in such a thing? I should die— simply *die!*"

"I shall not think of dying, unless we fail," answered Olive. "And, as for hating it, I haven't consulted my feelings a great deal; but I rather think I like it."

"Like going out to be a witness in an Indiana divorce case!"

"I don't look at it in that way, Clara. It's a crusade to me; it's a holy war; it's the cause of an innocent woman against a wicked oppression. I know how *you* would feel about it, Clara; but I never *was* as respectable as you are, and I'm quite satisfied to do what Ben, and father, and Mr. Atherton approve. They think it's my duty, and I am glad to go, and to be of all the use I can. But you shall have my heart-felt sympathy through all, Clara, for your involuntary acquaintance with our proceedings."

"Olive! You *know* that I'm proud of your courage and Ben's goodness, and that I fully appreciate the sacrifice you're making. And I'm not ashamed of your business: I think it's grand and sublime, and I would just as soon scream it out at the top of my voice, right here in the Albany Depot."

"Don't," said Olive. "It would frighten the child."

She had Flavia by the hand, and she made the little girl her special charge throughout the journey. The old Squire seemed anxious to be alone, and he restlessly escaped from Marcia's care. He sat all the first day apart, chewing upon some fragment of wood that he had picked up, and now and then putting up a lank hand to rasp his bristling jaw, glancing furtively at people who passed him, and lapsing into his ruminant abstraction. He had been vexed that they did not start the night before; and every halt the train made visibly afflicted him. He would not leave his place to get anything to eat when they stopped for refreshment, though he hungrily devoured the lunch that Marcia brought into the car for him. At New York he was in a tumult of fear lest they should lose the connecting train on the Pennsylvania road, and the sigh of relief with which he sank into his seat in the sleeping-car expressed the suffering he had undergone. He said he was not tired, but he went to bed early, as if to sleep away as much of the time as he could.

When Halleck came into their car, the next morning, he found Marcia and her father sitting together, and looking out of the window at the wooded slopes of the Alleghanies through which the train was running. The old man's impatience had relaxed; he let Marcia lay her hand on his, and he answered her with quiet submission, when she spoke now and then of the difference between these valleys, where the wild rhododendrons were growing, and the frozen hollows of the hills at home, which must be still choked with snow.

"But, oh! how much I would rather see them!" she said at last with a homesick throb.

"Well," he assented, "we can go right back—afterward."

"Yes," she whispered.

"Well, sir, good morning," said the old man to Halleck, "we are getting along, sir. At this rate, unless our calculations were mistaken, we shall be there by midnight. We are on time, the porter tells me."

"Yes, we shall soon be at Pittsburg," said Halleck, and he looked at Marcia, who turned away her face. She had not spoken of the object of the journey to him since they left Boston, and it had not been so nearly touched by either of them before. He could see that she recoiled from it; but the old man, once having approached it, could not leave it.

"If everything goes well, we shall have our grip on that fellow's throat in less than forty-eight hours." He looked down mechanically at his withered hands, lean and yellow like the talons of a bird, and lifted his accipital profile with a predatory alertness. "I didn't sleep very well the last part of the night, but I thought it all out. I shan't care whether I get there before or after judgment is rendered; all I want is to get there before he has a chance to clear out. I think I shall be able to convince Bartley Hubbard that there is a God in Israel yet! Don't you be anxious, Marcia; I've got this thing at my fingers' ends as clear as a bell. I intend to give Bartley a little surprise!"

Marcia kept her face averted, and Halleck relinquished his purpose of sitting down with them, and went forward to the state-room that Marcia and Olive had occupied with the little girl. He tapped on the door, and found his sister dressed, but the child still asleep.

"What is the matter, Ben?" she asked. "You don't look well. You oughtn't to have undertaken this journey."

"Oh, I'm all right. But I've been up a good while, with nothing to eat. That old man is terrible, Olive!"

"Her father? Yes, he's a terrible old man!"

"It sickened me to hear him talk, just now—throwing out

his threats of vengeance against Hubbard. It made me feel a sort of sympathy for that poor dog. Do you suppose she has the same motive? I couldn't forgive her!" he said, with a kind of passionate weakness. "I couldn't forgive myself!"

"We've got nothing to do with their motive, Ben. We are to be her witnesses for justice against a wicked wrong. I don't believe in special providences, of course; but it does seem as if we had been called to this work, as mother would say. Your happening to go home with her, that night and then that paper happening to come to you—doesn't it look like it?"

"It looks like it, yes."

"We couldn't have refused to come. That's what consoles me for being here this minute. I put on a bold face with Clara Atherton, yesterday morning at the depot; but I was in a cold chill all the time. Our coming off, in this way, on such an errand, is something so different from the rest of our whole life! And I *do* like quiet, and orderly ways, and all that we call respectability! I've been thinking that the trial will be reported by some such interviewing wretch as Bartley himself, and that we shall figure in the newspapers. But I've concluded that we mustn't care. It's right, and we must do it. I don't shut my eyes to the kind of people we're mixed up with. I pity Marcia, and I love her—poor, helpless, unguided thing!—but that old man *is* terrible! He's as cruel as the grave where he thinks he's been wronged, and crueller where he thinks *she's* been wronged. You've forgiven so much, Ben, that you can't understand a man who forgives nothing; but *I* can, for I'm a pretty good hater myself. And Marcia's just like her father, at times. I've seen her look at Clara Atherton as if she could kill her!"

The little girl stirred in her berth, and then lifted herself on her hands, and stared around at them through her tangled golden hair. "Is it morning, yet?" she asked sleepily. "Is it to-morrow?"

"Yes; it's to-morrow, Flavia," said Olive. "Do you want to get up?"

"And is next day the day after to-morrow?"

"Yes."

"Then it's only one day till I shall see papa. That's what mamma said. Where is mamma?" asked the child, rising to her knees, and sweeping back her hair from her face with either hand.

"I will go and send her to you," said Halleck.

At Pittsburg the Squire was eager for his breakfast, and made amends for his fast of the day before. He ate grossly of the heterogeneous abundance of the railroad restaurant, and drank two cups of coffee that in his thin, native air would have disordered his pulse for a week. But he resumed his journey with a tranquil strength that seemed the physical expression of a mind clear and content. He was willing and even anxious to tell Halleck what his theories and plans were; but the young man shrank from knowing them. He wished only to know whether Marcia were privy to them, and this, too, he shrank from knowing.

XXXIX

THEY left Pittsburg under the dun pall of smoke that hangs perpetually over the city, and ran out of a world where the earth seemed turned to slag and cinders, and the coal-grime blackened even the sheathing from which the young leaves were unfolding their vivid green. Their train twisted along the banks of the Ohio, and gave them now and then a reach of the stream, forgetful of all the noisy traffic that once fretted its waters, and losing itself in almost primitive wildness among its softly rounded hills. It is a beautiful land, and it had, even to their loath eyes, a charm that touched their hearts. They were on the borders of the illimitable West, whose lands stretch like a sea beyond its hilly Ohio shore; but as yet this vastness, which appalls and wearies all but the born Westerner, had not burst upon them; they were still among heights and hollows, and in a milder and softer New England.

"I have a strange feeling about this journey," said Marcia, turning from the window at last, and facing Halleck on the opposite seat. "I want it to be over, and yet I am glad at every little stop. I feel like some one that has been called to a death-bed, and is hurrying on and holding back with all her might, at the same time. I shall have no peace till I am there, and then shall I have peace?" She fixed her eyes imploringly on his. "Say something to me, if you can! What do you think?"

"Whether you will—succeed?" He was confounding what he knew of her father's feeling with what he had feared of hers.

"Do you mean about the lawsuit? I don't care for that! Do

you think he will hate me when he sees me? Do you think he will believe me when I tell him that I never meant to leave him, and that I'm sorry for what I did to drive him away?"

She seemed to expect him to answer, and he answered as well as he could: "He ought to believe that—yes, he must believe it."

"Then all the rest may go," she said. "I don't care who gains the case. But if he shouldn't believe me—if he should drive me away from him, as I drove him from me"— She held her breath in the terror of such a possibility, and an awe of her ignorance crept over Halleck. Apparently she had not understood the step that Bartley had taken, except as a stage in their quarrel from which they could both retreat, if they would, as easily as from any other dispute; she had not realized it as a final, an almost irrevocable act on his part, which could only be met by reprisal on hers. All those points of law which had been so sharply enforced upon her must have fallen blunted from her longing to be at one with him; she had, perhaps, not imagined her defense in open court, except as a sort of public reconciliation.

But at another time she recurred to her wrongs in all the bitterness of her father's vindictive purpose. A young couple entered the car at one of the country stations, and the bride made haste to take off her white bonnet, and lay her cheek on her husband's shoulder, while he passed his arm round her silken waist, and drew her close to him on the seat, in the loving rapture which is nowise inconvenienced by publicity on our railroad trains. Indeed, after the first general recognition of their condition, no one noticed them except Marcia, who seemed fascinated by the spectacle of their unsophisticated happiness; it must have recalled the blissful abandon of her own wedding journey to her.

"Oh, poor fool!" she said to Olive. "Let her wait, and it will not be long before she will know that she had better lean on the empty air than on him. Some day he will let her fall to the ground, and when she gathers herself up all bruised and bleeding— But he hasn't got the all-believing simpleton to deal with that he used to have; and he shall pay me back for all—drop by drop, and ache for ache!"

She was in that strange mental condition into which women fall who brood long upon opposing purposes and desires. She wished to be reconciled, and she wished to be revenged, and she recurred to either wish for the time as vehemently as if the other did not exist. She took Flavia on her knee, and began to prattle to her of seeing papa to-morrow, and presently she turned to Olive, and said:

"I know he will find us both a great deal changed. Flavia looks so much older—and so do I. But I shall soon show him that I can look young again. I presume he's changed too."

Marcia held the little girl up at the window. They had now left the river-hills and the rolling country beyond, and had entered the great plain which stretches from the Ohio to the Mississippi; and mile by mile, as they ran southward and westward, the spring unfolded in the mellow air under the dull, warm sun. The willows were in perfect leaf, and wore their delicate green like veils caught upon their boughs; the May-apples had already pitched their tents in the woods, beginning to thicken and darken with the young foliage of the oaks and hickories; suddenly, as the train dashed from a stretch of forest, the peach orchards flushed pink beside the brick farmsteads. The child gave a cry of delight, and pointed; and her mother seemed to forget all that had gone before, and abandoned herself to Flavia's joy in the blossoms, as if there were no trouble for her in the world.

Halleck rose and went into the other car; he felt giddy, as if her fluctuations of mood and motive had somehow turned his own brain. He did not come back till the train stopped at Columbus for dinner. The old Squire showed the same appetite as at breakfast: he had the effect of falling upon his food like a bird of prey; and as soon as the meal was dispatched he went back to his seat in the car, where he lapsed into his former silence and immobility, his lank jaws working with fresh activity upon the wooden toothpick he had brought away from the table. While they waited for a train from the north which was to connect with theirs, Halleck walked up and down the vast, noisy station with Olive and Marcia, and humored the little girl in her explorations of the place. She made friends with a red-bird that sang in its cage in the dining-hall, and with an old woman, yellow and wrinkled, and sunken-eyed, sitting on a bundle tied up in a quilt beside the door, and smoking her clay pipe as placidly as if on her own cabin threshold. " 'Pears like you ain't much afeard of strangers, honey," said the old woman, taking her pipe out of her mouth, to fill it. "Where do you live at when you're home?"

"Boston," said the child, promptly. "Where do *you* live?"

"I *used* to live in Old Virginia. But my son he's takin' me out to Illinoy, now. He's settled out there." She treated the child with the serious equality which simple old people use with children; and spat neatly aside in resuming her pipe. "Which o' them ladies yonder is your maw, honey?"

"My mamma?"

The old woman nodded.

Flavia ran away and laid her hand on Marcia's dress, and then ran back to the old woman.

"That your paw, with her?" Flavia looked blank, and the old woman interpreted, "Your father."

"No! We're going out to see papa—out West. We're going to see him to-morrow, and then he's coming back with us. My grandpa is in that car."

The old woman now laid her folded arms on her knees, and smoked obliviously. The little girl lingered a moment, and then ran off laughing to her mother, and pulled her skirt. "Wasn't it funny, mamma? She thought Mr. Halleck was my papa!" She hung forward by the hold she had taken, as children do, and tilted her head back to look into her mother's face. "What *is* Mr. Halleck, mamma?"

"What is he?" The group halted involuntarily.

"Yes, what is he? Is he my uncle, or my cousin, or what? Is *he* going out to see papa, too? What is *he* going for? Oh, look, look!" The child plucked away her hand, and ran off to join the circle of idle men and half-grown boys who were forming about two shining negroes with banjos. The negroes flung their hands upon the strings with an ecstatic joy in the music, and lifted their black voices in a wild plantation strain. The child began to leap and dance, and her mother ran after her.

"Naughty little girl!" she cried. "Come into the car with me, this minute."

Halleck did not see Marcia again till the train had run far out of the city, and was again sweeping through the thick woods, and flashing out upon the levels of the fields where the farmers were riding their sulky-plows up and down the long furrows in the pleasant afternoon sun. There is something in this transformation of man's old-time laborious dependence into a lordly domination over the earth, which strikes the westward journeyer as finally expressive of human destiny in the whole mighty region, and which penetrated even to Halleck's sore and jaded thoughts. A different type of men began to show itself in the car, as the Western people gradually took the places of his fellow-travelers from the East. The men were often slovenly and sometimes uncouth in their dress; but they made themselves at home in the exaggerated splendor and opulence of the car, as if born to the best in every way; their faces suggested the security of people who trusted the future from the past, and had no fears of the life that had always used them well; they had not that eager and intense look which the Eastern faces wore; there was energy enough to spare in them, but it was not an anxious energy. The sharp accent of the seaboard yielded to the rounded, soft, and slurring tones, and the prompt address was replaced by a careless and confident neighborliness of manner.

Flavia fretted at her return to captivity in the car, and demanded to be released with a teasing persistence from which nothing she was shown out of the window could divert her. A large man leaned forward at last from a seat near by, and held out an orange.

"Come here to me, little Trouble," he said, and Flavia made an eager start toward this unlooked-for friend.

Marcia wished to check her; but Halleck pleaded to have her go.

"It will be a relief to you," he said.

"Well, let her go," Marcia consented. "But she was no trouble, and she is no relief." She sat looking dully at the little girl after the Westerner had gathered her up into his lap. "Should I have liked to tell her," she said, as if thinking aloud, "how we were really going to meet her father, and that you were coming with me to be my witness against him in a court—to put him down and disgrace him—to fight him, as father says?"

"You mustn't think of it in that way," said Halleck gently, but, as he felt, feebly and inadequately.

"Oh, I shall not think of it in that way long," she answered. "My head is in a whirl, and I can't hold what we're doing before my mind in any one shape for a minute at a time. I don't know what will become of me—I don't know what will become of me!"

But in another breath she rose from this desolation, and was talking with impersonal cheerfulness of the sights that the car-window showed. As long as the light held, they passed through the same opulent and monotonous landscape; through little towns full of signs of material prosperity, and then farms and farms again; the brick houses set in the midst of evergreens, and compassed by vast acreages of corn-land, where herds of black pigs wandered, and the farmers were riding their plows, or heaping into vast winrows for burning the winter-worn stalks of the last year's crop. Where they came to a stream the landscape was roughened into low hills, from which it sank again luxuriously to a plain. If there was any difference between Ohio and Indiana, it was that in Indiana the spring night, whose breath softly buffeted their cheeks through the open window, had gathered over those eternal corn-fields, where the long, crooked winrows, burning on either hand, seemed a trail of fiery serpents writhing away from the train as it roared and clamored over the track.

They were to leave their car at Indianapolis, and take another road which would bring them to Tecumseh by daylight next morning. Olive went away with the little girl, and put her to bed on the sofa in the state-room, and Marcia suffered them to go alone; it was only by fits that she had cared for the child, or even noticed it.

"Now tell me again," she said to Halleck, "why we are going."

"Surely you know."

"Yes, yes, I know; but I can't think—I don't seem to remember. Didn't I give it up once? Didn't I say that I would rather go home, and let Bartley get the divorce, if he wanted?"

"Yes, you said that, Marcia."

"I used to make him very unhappy; I was very strict with him, when I knew he couldn't bear any kind of strictness. And he was always so patient with me; though he never really cared for me. Oh, yes, I knew that from the first! He used to try; but he must have been glad to get away. Poor Bartley! It was cruel, cruel, to put that in about my abandoning him when he knew I would come back; but perhaps the lawyers told him he must; he had to put in something! Why shouldn't I let him go? Father said he only wanted to get rid of me, so that he could marry some one else— Yes, yes; it was that that made me start! Father knew it would! Oh," she grieved, with a wild self-pity that tore Halleck's heart, "he knew it would!" She fell wearily back against the seat, and did not speak for some minutes. Then she said, in a slow, broken utterance: "But now I don't seem to mind even that any more. Why shouldn't he marry some one else that he really likes, if he doesn't care for me?"

Halleck laughed in bitterness of soul, as his thought recurred to Atherton's reasons.

"Because," he said, "you have a *public* duty in the matter. You must keep him bound to you, for fear some other woman, whose husband doesn't care for her, would let *him* go, too, and society be broken up and civilization destroyed. In a matter like this, which seems to concern yourself alone, you are only to regard others."

His reckless irony did not reach her through her manifold sorrow.

"Well," she said, simply, "It must be that. But, oh! how can I bear it? how can I bear it?"

The time passed; Olive did not return for an hour; then she merely said that the little girl had just fallen asleep, and that she should go back and lie down with her—that she was sleepy too.

Marcia did not answer, but Halleck said he would call her in good time before they reached Indianapolis.

The porter made up the berths of such as were going through to St. Louis, and Marcia was left sitting alone with Halleck.

"I will go and get your father to come here," he said.

"I don't want him to come! I want to talk to you—to say something— What was it? I can't think!"

She stopped, like one trying to recover a faded thought; he waited, but she did not speak again. She had laid a nervous clutch upon his arm, to detain him from going for her father, and she kept her hand there mechanically; but after a while he felt it relax; she drooped against him, and fell away into a sleep in which she started now and then like a frightened child. He could not release himself without waking her; but it did not matter; her sorrow had unsexed her; only the tenderness of his love for this hapless soul remained in his heart, which ached and evermore heavily sank within him.

He woke her at last when he must go to tell Olive that they were running into Indianapolis. Marcia struggled to her feet: "Oh, oh! Are we there? Are we there?"

"We are at Indianapolis," said Halleck.

"I thought it was Tecumseh!" She shuddered. "We can go back; oh, yes, we can still go back!"

They alighted from the train in the chilly midnight air, and found their way through the crowd to the eating-room of the station. The little girl cried with broken sleep and the strangeness, and Olive tried to quiet her. Marcia clung to Halleck's arm, and shivered convulsively. Squire Gaylord stalked beside them with a demoniac vigor. "A few more hours—a few more hours, sir!" he said. He made a hearty supper, while the rest scalded their mouths with hot tea, which they forced with loathing to their lips.

Some women who were washing the floor of the ladies' waiting-room told them they must go into the men's room, and wait there for their train, which was due at one o'clock. They obeyed, and found the room full of emigrants, and the air thick with their tobacco-smoke. There was no choice; Olive went in first and took the child on her lap, where it straightway fell asleep; the Squire found a seat beside them, and sat erect, looking round on the emigrants with the air of being amused at their outlandish speech, into which they burst clamorously from their silence at intervals. Marcia stopped Halleck at the threshold. "Stay out here with me," she whispered. "I want to tell you something," she added, as he turned mechanically and walked away with her up the vast lamp-shot darkness of the depot. "*I am not going on!* I am going back. We will take the train that goes to the East; father will never know till it is too late. We needn't speak to him about it."

Halleck set himself against this delirious folly: he consented to her return; she could do what she would; but he would not consent to cheat her father. "We must go and tell him," he said, for all answer to all her entreaties. He dragged her back to the waiting-room; but at the door she started at the figure of a man who was bending over a group of emigrant children asleep in the nearest corner—poor, uncouth, stubbed little creatures, in old-mannish clothes, looking like children roughly blocked out of wood, and stiffly stretched on the floor, or resting woodenly against their mother.

"There!" said the man, pressing a mug of coffee on the woman. "You drink that! It'll do you good,—every drop of it! I've seen the time," he said, turning round with the mug, when she had drained it, in his hand, and addressing Marcia and Halleck, as the most accessible portion of the English-speaking public, "when I used to be down on coffee—I thought it was bad for the nerves; but I tell you, when you're travelin', it's a brain-food if ever there was a brain"—

He dropped the mug, and stumbled back into the heap of sleeping children, fixing a ghastly stare on Marcia.

She ran toward him.

"Mr. Kinney!"

"No, you don't! No, you don't."

"Why, don't you know me—Mrs. Hubbard?"

"He—he—told me you—was dead!" roared Kinney.

"He told you I was dead?"

"More'n a year ago! The last time I seen him! Before I went out to Leadville!"

"He told you I was dead," repeated Marcia huskily. "He must have wished it!" she whispered. "Oh, mercy, mercy, mercy!" She stopped, and then she broke into a wild laugh: "Well, you see he was wrong. I'm on my way to him now to show him that I'm alive!"

XL

HALLECK woke at daybreak from the drowse into which he had fallen. The train was creeping slowly over the track, feeling its way, and he heard fragments of talk among the passengers about a broken rail that the conductor had been warned of. He turned to ask some question, when the pull of rising speed came from the locomotive, and at the same moment the car stopped with a jolting pitch. It settled upon the track again; but the two cars in front were overturned, and the passengers were still climbing from their windows, when Halleck got his bewildered party to the ground. Children were crying, and a woman was led by with her face cut and bleeding from the broken glass; but it was reported that no one else was hurt, and the trainmen gave their helplessness to the inspection of the rotten cross-tie that had caused the accident. One of the passengers kicked the decayed wood with his boot. "Well," he said, "I always like a little accident like this, early; it makes us safe the rest of the day." The sentiment apparently commended itself to popular acceptance. Halleck went forward with part of the crowd to see what was the matter with the locomotive; it had kept the track, but seemed to be injured somehow; the engineer was working at it, hammer in hand; he exchanged some dry pleasantries with a passenger who asked him if there was any chance of hiring a real fast ox-team in that neighborhood, in case a man was in a hurry to get on to Tecumseh.

They were in the midst of a level prairie that stretched all round to the horizon, where it was broken by patches of timber; the rising sun slanted across the green expanse, and turned its distance to gold; the grass at their feet was full of wild flowers, upon which Flavia flung herself as soon as they got out of the car. By the time Halleck returned to them, she was running with cries of joy and wonder toward a windmill that rose beautiful above the roofs of a group of commonplace houses, at a little distance from the track; it stirred its mighty vanes in the thin, sweet inland breeze, and took the sun gayly on the light gallery that encircled it.

A vision of Belgian plains swept before Halleck's eyes. "There ought to be storks on its roof," he said absently.

"How strange that it should be here, away out in the West!" said Olive.

"If it were less strange than we are here, I couldn't stand it," he answered.

A brakeman came up with a flag in his hand, and nodded toward Flavia. "She's on the right track for breakfast," he said. "There's an old Dutchman at that mill, and his wife knows how to make coffee like a fellow's mother. You'll have plenty of time. This train has come here to stay—till somebody can walk back five miles and telegraph for help."

"How far are we from Tecumseh?" asked Halleck.

"Fifty miles," the brakeman called back over his shoulder.

"Don't you worry any, Marcia," said her father, moving off in pursuit of Flavia. "This accident makes it all right for us, if we don't get there for a week."

Marcia answered nothing. Halleck began to talk to her of that Belgian landscape in which he had first seen a windmill, and he laughed at the blank unintelligence with which she received his reminiscence of travel. For the moment, the torturing stress was lifted from his soul; he wished that the breakfast in the miller's house might never come to an end; he explored the mill with Flavia; he bantered the Squire on his saturnine preference for steam power in the milling business; he made the others share his mood; he pushed far from him the series of tragic or squalid facts which had continually brought the end to him in reveries in which he found himself holding his breath, as if he might hold it till the end really came.

But this respite could not last. A puff of white steam showed on the horizon, and after an interval the sound of the locomotive's whistle reached them, as it came backing down a train of empty cars toward them. They were quickly on their journey again, and a scanty hour before noon they arrived at Tecumseh.

The pretty town, which in prospect had worn to Olive Halleck's imagination the blended hideousness of Sodom and Gomorrah, was certainly very much more like a New England village in fact. After the brick farmsteads and coal-smoked towns of Central Ohio, its wooden houses, set back from the street with an ample depth of door-yard, were appealingly familiar, and she exchanged some homesick whispers with Marcia about them, as they drove along under the full-leaved maples which shadowed the way. The grass was denser and darker than in New England, and, pretty as the town was, it wore a more careless and unscrupulous air than the true New England village; the South had touched it, and here and there it showed a wavering line of fence and a faltering conscientiousness in its paint. Presently all aspects of village quiet and seclusion ceased, and a section of conventional American city, with flat-roofed brick blocks, showy hotel, stores, paved street, and stone sidewalks, expressed the readiness of Tecumseh to fulfill the destiny of every Western town, and become a metropolis at a day's notice, if need be. The second-hand omnibus, which reflected the actuality of Tecumseh, set them down at the broad steps of the court-house, fronting on an avenue which for a city street was not very crowded or busy. Such passers as there were had leisure and inclination, as they loitered by, to turn and stare at the strangers; and the voice of the sheriff, as he called from an upper window of the court-house the names of absentee litigants or witnesses required to come into court, easily made itself heard above all the other noises.

It seemed to Halleck as if the sheriff were calling them; he lifted his head and looked at Olive, but she would not meet his eye; she led by the hand the little girl, who kept asking, "Is this the house where papa lives?" with the merciless itera- tion of a child. Halleck dragged lamely after the Squire, who had mounted the steps with unnatural vigor; he promptly found his way to the clerk's office, where he examined the docket, and then returned to the party triumphant. "We are in time," he said, and he led them on up into the court-room.

A few spectators, scattered about on the rows of benching, turned to look at them as they walked up the aisle, where the cocoa matting, soaked and dried, and soaked again with per- petual libations of tobacco-juice, mercifully silenced their foot- steps; most of the faces turned upon them showed a slow and thoughtful movement of the jaws, and, as they were dropped or averted, a general discharge of tobacco-juice seemed to ex- press the general adoption of the new-comers, whoever they were, as a necessary element of the scene, which it was useless to oppose and about which it was idle to speculate. Before the Squire had found his party seats on one of the benches next the bar, the spectators had again given their languid attention to the administration of justice, which is everywhere informal with us, and is only a little more informal in the West than in the East. An effect of serene disoccupation pervaded the place, such as comes at the termination of an interesting affair; and no one seemed to care for what the clerk was reading aloud in a set, mechanical tone. The judge was busy with his docket; the lawyers, at their several little tables within the bar, lounged in their chairs, or stalked about laughing and whispering to each other; the prosecuting attorney leaned upon the shoulder of a jolly-looking man, who lifted his face to joke up at him, as he tilted his chair back; a very stout, youngish person, who sat next him, kept his face dropped, while the clerk proceeded:

"And now, on motion of plaintiff, it is ordered by the Court that said defendant be now here three times called, which is done in open court, and she comes not; but wholly makes de- fault therein. And this cause is now submitted to the Court for trial, and the Court having heard the evidence, and being fully advised, find for the plaintiff—that the allegations of his complaint are true, and that he is entitled to a divorce. It is therefore considered by the Court that said plaintiff be and he is hereby divorced, and the bonds of matrimony heretofore existing between said parties are dissolved and held for naught."

As the clerk closed the large volume before him, the jolly lawyer, as if the record had been read at his request, nodded to the Court, and said, "The record of the decree seems correct, your honor." He leaned forward, and struck the fat man's expanse of back with the flat of his hand. "Congratulate you, my dear boy!" he said in a stage whisper that was heard through the room. "Many happy returns of the day!"

A laugh went round, and the judge said severely:

"Mr. Sheriff, see that order is kept in the court-room."

The fat man rose to shake hands with another friend, and at the same moment Squire Gaylord stretched himself to his full height before stooping over to touch the shoulder of one of the lawyers within the bar, and his eyes encountered those of Bartley Hubbard in mutual recognition.

It was not the fat on Bartley's ribs only that had increased: his broad cheeks stood out and hung down with it, and his chin descended by the three successive steps to his breast. His complexion was of a tender pink, on which his blonde moustache showed white; it almost vanished in the tallowy pallor to which the pink turned as he saw his father-in-law, and then the whole group which the intervening spectators had hitherto hidden from him. He dropped back into his chair, and intimated to his lawyer, with a wave of his hand and a twist of his head, that some hopeless turn in his fortunes had taken place. That jolly soul turned to him for explanation, and at the same time the lawyer whom Squire Gaylord had touched on the shoulder responded to a few whispered words from him by beckoning to the prosecuting attorney, who stepped briskly across to where they stood. A brief dumb-show ensued, and the prosecutor ended by taking the Squire's hand, and inviting him within the bar; the other attorney politely made room for him at his table, and the prosecutor returned to his place near the jury-box, where he remained standing for a moment.

"If it please the Court," he began, in a voice breaking heavily upon the silence that had somehow fallen upon the whole room, "I wish to state that the defendant in the case of Hubbard *vs.* Hubbard is now and here present, having been prevented, by an accident on the road between this place and Indianapolis, from arriving in time to make defense. She desires to move the Court to set aside the default."

The prosecutor retired a few paces, and nodded triumphantly at Bartley's lawyer, who could not wholly suppress his enjoyment of the joke, though it told so heavily against him and his client. But he was instantly on his feet with a technical objection.

The judge heard him through, and then opened his docket at the case of Hubbard *vs.* Hubbard. "What name shall I enter for the defense?" he inquired formally.

Squire Gaylord turned with an old-fashioned state and deliberation which had their effect, and cast a glance of professional satisfaction in the situation at the attorneys and the spectators. "I ask to be allowed to appear for the defense in this case, if the Court please. My friend, Mr. Hathaway, will move my admission to this bar."

The attorney to whom the Squire had first introduced himself promptly complied: "Your honor, I move the admission of Mr. F. J. Gaylord, of Equity, Equity County, Maine, to practice at this bar."

The judge bowed to the Squire, and directed the clerk to administer the usual oath. "I have entered your name for the defense, Mr. Gaylord. Do you desire to make any motion in the case?" he pursued, the natural courtesy of his manner further qualified by a feeling which something pathetic in the old Squire's bearing inspired.

"Yes, your honor, I move to set aside the default, and I shall offer in support of this motion my affidavit, setting forth the reasons for the non-appearance of the defendant at the calling of the cause."

"Shall I note your motion as filed?" asked the judge.

"Yes, your honor," replied the old man. He made a futile attempt to prepare the paper; the pen flew out of his trembling hand. "*I* can't write," he said in despair that made other hands quick to aid him. A young lawyer at the next desk rapidly drew up the paper, and the Squire duly offered it to the clerk of the Court. The clerk stamped it with the file-mark of the Court, and returned it to the Squire, who read aloud the motion and affidavit, setting forth the facts of the defendant's failure to receive the notice in time to prepare for her defense, and of the accident which had contributed to delay her appearance, declaring that she had a just defense to the plaintiff's bill, and asking to be heard upon the facts.

Bartley's attorney was prompt to interpose again. He protested that the printed advertisement was sufficient notice to the defendant, whenever it came to her knowledge, or even if it never came to her knowledge, and that her plea of failure to receive it in time was not a competent excuse. This might be alleged in any case, and any delay of travel might be brought forward to account for non-appearance as plausibly as this trumped-up accident in which nobody was hurt. He did his best, which was also his worst, and the judge once more addressed the Squire, who stood waiting for Bartley's counsel to close. "I was about to adjourn the Court," said the judge, in that accent which is the gift of the South to some parts of the West; it is curiously soft and gentle, and expressive, when the speaker will, of a caressing deference. "But we have still some minutes before noon in which we can hear you in support of your motion, if you are ready."

"I am mready, your honor!" The old man's nasals cut across the judge's rounded tones, almost before they had ceased. His lips compressed themselves to a waving line, and his high hawk-beak came down over them; the fierce light burned in his cavernous eyes, and his grizzled hair erected itself like a crest.

He swayed slightly back and forth at the table, behind which he stood, and paused as if waiting for his hate to gather head.

In this interval it struck several of the spectators, who had appreciative friends outside, that it was a pity they should miss the coming music, and they risked the loss of some strains themselves that they might step out and inform these *dilettanti*. One of them was stopped by a man at the door. "What's up, now?" The other impatiently explained; but the inquirer, instead of hurrying in to enjoy the fun, turned quickly about, and ran down the stairs. He crossed the street, and, by a system of alleys and by-ways, modestly made his way to the outlying fields of Tecumseh, which he traversed at heightened speed, plunging at last into the belt of timber beyond. This excursion, which had so much the appearance of a chase, was an exigency of the witness who had corroborated on oath the testimony of Bartley in regard to his wife's desertion. Such an establishment of facts, purely imaginary with the witness, was simple enough in the absence of rebutting testimony; but, confronted with this, it became another affair—it had its embarrassments, its risks.

"Mready," repeated Squire Gaylord, "mready with facts and *witnesses!*" The word, in which he exulted till it rang and echoed through the room, drew the eyes of all to the little group on the bench next the bar, where Marcia, heavily veiled in the black which she had worn ever since Bartley's disappearance, sat with Halleck and Olive. The little girl, spent with her long journey, rested her head on her mother's lap, and the mother's hand tremulously smoothed her hair, and tried to hush the grieving whisper in which she incessantly repeated, "Where is papa? I want to see papa!"

Olive looked straight before her, and Halleck's eyes were fixed upon the floor. After the first glance at them, Bartley did not lift his head, but held it bent forward where he sat, and showed only a fold of fat red neck above his coat-collar. Marcia might have seen his face in that moment before it blanched and he sank into his chair; she did not look toward him again.

"Mr. Sheriff, keep silence in the Court!" ordered the judge, in reprimand of the stir that ensued upon the general effort to catch sight of the witnesses.

"Silence in the Court! Keep your seats, gentlemen!" cried the sheriff.

"And I thank the Court," resumed the Squire, "for this immediate opportunity to redress an atrocious wrong, and to vindicate an innocent and injured woman. Sir, I think it will prejudice our cause with no one, when I say that we are here not only in the relation of attorney and client, but in that of father and daughter, and that I stand in this place singularly and sacredly privileged to demand justice for my own child!"

"Order, order!" shouted the sheriff. But he could not quell the sensation that followed; the point had been effectively made, and it was some moments before the noise of the people beginning to arrive from the outside permitted the Squire to continue. He waited, with one lean hand hanging at his side, and the other resting in a loosely folded fist on the table before him. He took this fist up as if it were some implement he had laid hold of, and swung it in the air.

"By a chance which *I* shall not be the last to describe as providential,"—he paused, and looked round the room as if defying any one there to challenge the sincerity of his assertion,—"the notice, which your law requires to be given by newspaper advertisement to the non-resident defendant in such a case as this, came, by one chance in millions, to her hand. By one chance more or less, it would not have reached her, and a monstrous crime against justice would have been irrevocably accomplished. For she had mourned this man as dead,—dead to the universal frame of things, when he was only dead to honor, dead to duty, and dead to her; and it was that newspaper, sent almost at random through the mail, and wandering from hand to hand, and everywhere rejected, for weeks, before it reached her at last, which convinced her that he was still in such life as a man may live who has survived his own soul. We are therefore *here*, standing upon our right, and prepared to prove it God's right and the everlasting truth. Two days ago, a thousand miles and a thousand uncertainties intervened between us and this right, but *now* we are here to show that the defendant, basely defamed by the plea of abandonment, returned to her home within an hour after she had parted there with the plaintiff, and has remained there day and night ever since." He stopped. "Did I say she had never absented herself during all this time? I was wrong. I spoke hastily. I forgot." He dropped his voice. "She did absent herself at one time,—for three days,—while she could come home to close her mother's dying eyes, and help me to lay her in the grave!" He tried to close his lips firmly again, but the sinuous line was broken by a convulsive twitching. "Perhaps," he resumed with the utmost gentleness, "the plaintiff returned in this interval, and, finding her gone, was confirmed in his belief that she had abandoned him."

He felt blindly about on the table with his trembling hands, and his whole figure had a pathos that gave the old dress-coat statuesque dignity. The spectators quietly changed their places, and occupied the benches near him, till Bartley was left sitting alone with his counsel. We are beginning to talk here at the East of the decline of oratory; but it is still a passion in the West, and his listeners now clustered about the Squire in keen appreciation of his power; it seemed to summon even the loiterers in the street, whose ascending tramp on the stairs continually made itself heard; the lawyers, the officers of the court, the judge, forgot their dinner, and posed themselves anew in their chairs to listen.

No doubt the electrical sphere of sympathy and admiration penetrated to the old man's consciousness. When he pulled off his black satin stock—the relic of ancient fashion which the piety of his daughter kept in repair—and laid it on the table, there was a deep, inarticulate murmur of satisfaction which he could not have mistaken. His voice rose again:

"If the plaintiff indeed came at that time, the walls of those empty rooms, into which he peered like a thief in the night, might have told him—if walls had tongues to speak as they have ears to hear—a tale that would have melted even *his* heart with remorse and shame. They might have told him of a woman waiting in hunger and cold for his return, and willing to starve and freeze, rather than own herself forsaken; waiting till she was hunted from her door by the creditors whom he had defrauded, and forced to confess her disgrace and her despair, in order to save herself from the unknown terrors of the law invoked upon her innocent head by his villainy. This is the history of the first two weeks of those two years, during which, as his perjured lips have sworn, he was using every effort to secure her return to him. I will not enlarge now upon this history, nor upon that of the days and weeks and months that followed, wringing the heart and all but crazing the brain of the wife who would not, in the darkest hours of her desolation, believe herself willfully abandoned. But we have the record, unbroken and irrefragable, which shall not only right his victim, but shall bring yonder perjurer to justice."

The words had an iron weight; they fell like blows. Bartley did not stir; but Marcia moved uneasily in her chair, and a low, pitiful murmur broke from behind her veil. Her father stopped again, panting, and his dry lips closed and parted several times before he could find his voice again. But at that sound of grief he partly recovered himself, and went on brokenly.

"I now ask this Court, for due cause, to set aside the default upon which judgment has been rendered against the defendant, and I shall then ask leave to file her cross-petition for divorce."

Marcia started half-way from her chair, and then fell back again; she looked round at Halleck as if for help, and hid her face in her hands. Her father cast a glance at her as if for her approval of this development of his plan.

"Then, may it please the Court, upon the rendition of judgment in our favor upon that petition—a result of which I have no more doubt than of my own existence—I shall demand under your law the indictment of yonder perjurer for his crime, and I shall await in security the sentence which shall consign him to a felon's cell in a felon's garb"—

Marcia flung herself upon her father's arm, outstretched toward Bartley.

"No! No! No!" she cried with deep, shuddering breaths, in a voice thick with horror. "Never! Let him go! I will not have it! I didn't understand! I never meant to harm him! Let him go! It is *my* cause, and I say"—

The old man's arm dropped; he fixed a ghastly, bewildered look upon his daughter, and fell across the table at which he stood. The judge started from his chair; the people leaped over the benches, and crushed about the Squire, who fetched his breath in convulsive gasps. "Keep back!" "Give him air!" "Open the window!" "Get a doctor!" cried those next him.

Even Bartley's counsel had joined the crowd about the Squire, from the midst of which broke the long, frightened wail of a child. This was Bartley's opportunity. When his counsel turned to look for him, and advise his withdrawal from a place where he could do no good, and where possibly he might come to harm, he found that his advice had been anticipated: Bartley's chair was vacant.

XLI

THAT NIGHT, when Halleck had left the old man to the care of
Marcia and Olive, for the time, a note was brought to him from
Bartley's lawyer, begging the favor of a few moments' interview on very important business. It might be some offer of
reparation or advance in Marcia's interest, and Halleck went
with the bearer of the note. The lawyer met him hospitably
at the door of his office. "How do you do, sir?" he said, shaking
hands. Then he indicated a bulk withdrawn into a corner of
the dimly lighted room; the blinds were drawn, and he locked
the door after Halleck's entrance. "Mr. Hubbard, whom I
think you know," he added. "I'll just step into the next room,
gentlemen, and will be subject to your call at any moment."

The bulk lifted itself and moved some paces toward Halleck; Bartley even raised his hand, with the vague expectation
of taking Halleck's, but seeing no responsive gesture on his
part, he waved a salutation and dropped it again to his side.

"How d'ye do, Halleck? Rather a secret, black, and midnight
interview," he said jocosely. "But I couldn't very well manage
it otherwise. I'm *not* just in the position to offer you the freedom of the city."

"What do you want, Hubbard?" asked Halleck, bluntly.

"How is the old Squire?"

"The doctor thinks he may rally from the shock."

"Paralysis?"

"Yes."

"I have spent the day in the 'tall timber,' as our friends out

446

here say, communing with nature; and I've only just come into town since dark, so I hadn't any particulars." He paused, as if expecting that Halleck might give them; but, upon his remaining silent, he resumed. "Of course, as the case now stands, <u>I know very well that the law can't touch me</u>. But I didn't know what the popular feeling might be. The Squire laid it on pretty hot, and he might have made it livelier for me than he intended: he isn't aware of the inflammable nature of the material out here." He gave a nervous chuckle. "I wanted to see you, Halleck, to tell you that I haven't forgotten that money I owe you, and that I mean to pay it all up some time yet. If it hadn't been for some expenses I've had lately,—doctor's bills, and so forth,—I haven't been very well, myself,"—he made a sort of involuntary appeal for Halleck's sympathy,— "and I've had to pay out a good deal of money,—I should be able to pay most of it now. As it is, I can only give you five hundred of it." He tugged his portemonnaie with difficulty up the slope of his pantaloons. "That will leave me just three hundred to begin the world with; for of course I've got to clear out of *here*. And I'd got very comfortably settled after two years of pretty hard work at the printing business, and hard reading at the law. Well, it's all right. And I want to pay you this money, now, and I'll pay you the rest whenever I can. And I want you to tell Marcia that I did it. I always meant to do it."

"Hubbard," interrupted Halleck, "you don't owe me any money. Your father-in-law paid that debt two years ago. But you owe some one else a debt that no one can pay for you. We needn't waste words. What are you going to do to repair the wrong you have done the woman and the child"— He stopped; the effort had perhaps been too much.

Bartley saw his emotion, and in his benighted way he honored it. "Halleck, you are a good fellow. You are *such* a good fellow that you can't understand this thing. But it's played out. I felt badly about it myself, at one time; and if I hadn't been robbed of that money you lent me on my way here, I'd have gone back inside of forty-eight hours. I was sorry for Marcia; it almost broke my heart to think of the little one; but I knew they were in the hands of friends; and the more time I had to think it over, the more I was reconciled to what I had done. That was the only way out for either of us. We had tried it for three years, and we couldn't make it go; we never could have made it go; we were incompatible. Don't you suppose I knew Marcia's good qualities? No one knows them better, or appreciates them more. You might think that I applied for this divorce because I had some one else in view. Not any more in mine at present! But I thought we ought to be free, both of us; and if our marriage had become a chain, that we ought to break it." Bartley paused, apparently to give these facts and reasons time to sink into Halleck's mind. "But there's one thing I should like to have you tell her, Halleck: she was wrong about that girl; I never had anything to do with her. Marcia will understand." Halleck made no reply, and Bartley resumed, in a burst of generosity, which marked his fall into the abyss as nothing else could have done. "Look here, Halleck, I can't marry again for two years. But, as I understand the law, Marcia isn't bound in any way. I know that she always had a very high opinion of you, and that she thinks you are the best man in the world: why don't *you* fix it up with Marcia?"

Bartley was in effect driven into exile by the accidents of his suit for divorce which have been described. He was not in bodily danger after the first excitement passed off, if he was ever in bodily danger at all; but he could not reasonably hope to establish himself in a community which had witnessed such disagreeable facts concerning him; before which, indeed, he stood attainted of perjury, and only saved from the penalty of his crime by the refusal of his wife to press her case.

As soon as her father was strong enough to be removed, Marcia returned to the East with him, in the care of the friends who continued with them. They did not go back to Boston, but went directly to Equity, where in the first flush of the young and jubilant summer, they opened the dim old house at the end of the village street, and resumed their broken lives. Her father, with one side palsy-stricken, wavered out every morning to his office, and sat there all day, the tremulous shadow of his former will. Sometimes his old friends came in to see him, but no one expected now to hear the Squire "get going." He no longer got going on any topic; he had become as a little child—as the little child that played about him there, in the still, warm summer days and built houses with his law-books on the floor. He laughed feebly at her pranks, and submitted to her rule with pathetic meekness in everything where Marcia had not charged them both to the contrary. He was very obedient to Marcia, who looked vigilantly after his welfare, and knew all his goings and comings, as she knew those of his little comrade. Two or three times a day she ran out to see that they were safe; but for the rest she kept herself closely housed, and saw no one whom she was not forced to see; only the meat-man and the fish-man could speak authoritatively concerning her appearance and behavior before folks. They reported the latter as dry, cold, and uncommunicative. Doubtless the bitter experiences of her life had wrought their due effect in that passionate heart; but probably it was as much a morbid sensitiveness as a hardened indifference that turned her from her kind. The village inquisitiveness that invades, also suffers much eccentricity; and after it had been well ascertained that Marcia was as queer as her mother, she was allowed to lead her mother's unmolested life in the old house, which had always turned so cold a shoulder to the world. Toward the end of the summer the lame young man and his sister, who had been several times in Equity before, paid her a visit; but stayed only a day or two, as was accurately known by persons who had noted the opening and closing of the spare-chamber blinds. In the winter he came again, but this time he came alone, and stayed at the hotel. He remained over a Sunday, and sat in the pulpit of the Orthodox church, where the minister extended to him the right hand of fellowship, and invited him to make the opening prayer. It was considered a good prayer, generally speaking, but it was criticised as not containing anything attractive to young people. He was understood to be on his way to take charge of a backwoods church down in Aroostook County, where probably his prayers would be more acceptable to the popular taste.

That winter Squire Gaylord had another stroke of paralysis, and late in the following spring he succumbed to a third. The old minister who had once been Mrs. Gaylord's pastor was now dead; and the Squire was buried by the lame man, who came up to Equity for that purpose, at the wish, often expressed, of the deceased. This at least was the common report, and it is certain that Halleck officiated.

In entering the ministry, he had returned to the faith which had been taught him almost before he could speak. He did not defend or justify this course on the part of a man who had once thrown off all allegiance to creeds; he said simply that for him there was no other course. He freely granted that he had not reasoned back to his old faith; he had fled to it as to a city of refuge. His unbelief had been helped, and he no longer suffered himself to doubt; he did not ask if the truth was here or there, any more; he only knew that he could not find it for himself, and he rested in his inherited belief. He accepted everything; if he took one jot or tittle away from the Book, the curse of doubt was on him. He had known the terrors of the law, and he preached them to his people; he had known the Divine mercy, and he also preached that.

The Squire's death occurred a few months before the news came of another event to which the press of the State referred with due recognition, but without great fullness of detail. This was the fatal case of shooting which occurred at Whited Sepulchre, Arizona, where Bartley Hubbard pitched his tent, and set up a printing-press after leaving Tecumseh. He began with the issue of a Sunday paper, and made it so spicy and so indispensable to all the residents of Whited Sepulchre, who enjoyed the study of their fellow-citizens' affairs, that he was looking hopefully forward to the establishment of a daily edition, when he unfortunately chanced to comment upon the domestic relations of "one of Whited Sepulchre's leading citizens." The leading citizen promptly took the war-path, as an esteemed contemporary expressed it, in reporting the difficulty with the cynical lightness and the profusion of felicitous head-lines with which our journalism often alleviates the history of tragic occurrences: the parenthetical truth in the closing statement, that "Mr. Hubbard leaves a (divorced) wife and child somewhere at the East," was quite in Bartley's own manner.

Marcia had been widowed so long before that this event,—consequence or penalty, as we choose to think it,—could make no outward change in her. What inner change, if any, it wrought, is one of those facts which fiction must seek in vain to disclose. But, if love such as hers had been did not deny his end the pang of a fresh grief, we may be sure that her sorrow was not unmixed with self-accusal as unavailing as it was passionate, and perhaps as unjust.

One evening, a year later, the Athertons sat talking over a letter from Halleck, which Atherton had brought from Boston with him. It was summer, and they were at their place on the Beverly shore. It was a long letter, and Atherton had read parts of it several times already, on his way down in the cars, and had since read it all to his wife. "It's a very morbid letter," he said, with a perplexed air, when he had finished.

"Yes," she assented. "But it's a very *good* letter. Poor Ben!"

Her husband took it up again, and read here and there a passage from it.

"But I am turning to you now for help in a matter on which my own conscience throws such a fitful and uncertain light that I cannot trust it. I know that you are a good man, Atherton, and I humbly beseech you to let me have your judgment without mercy: though it slay me, I will abide by it. . . . Since her father's death, she lives there quite alone with her child. I have seen her only once, but we write to each other, and there are times when it seems to me at last that I have the right to ask her to be my wife. The words give me a shock as I write them; and the things which I used to think reasons for my right rise up in witness against me. Above all, I remember with horror that *he* approved it, that he advised it!

". . . . It is true that I have never, by word or deed, suffered her to know what was in my heart; but has there ever been a moment when I could do so? It is true that I have waited for his death; but, if I have been willing he should die, am I not a potential murderer!"

"Oh, what ridiculous nonsense!" Clara indignantly protested.

Atherton read on: "These are the questions which I ask myself in my despair. She is free, now; but am I free? Am I not rather bound by the past to perpetual silence? There are times when I rebel against these tortures; when I feel a sanction for my love of her, an assurance from somewhere that it is right and good to love her; but then I sink again, for, if I ask whence this assurance comes—I beseech you to tell me what you think. Has my offence been so great that nothing can atone for it? Must I sacrifice to this fear all my hopes of what I could be to her, and for her?"

Atherton folded up the letter, and put it back into its envelope, with a frown of exasperation. "I can't see what should have infatuated Halleck with that woman. I don't believe now that he loves her; I believe he only pities her. She is altogether inferior to him: passionate, narrow-minded, jealous—she would make him miserable. He'd much better stay as he is. If it were not pathetic to have him deifying her in this way, it would be laughable."

"She had a jealous temperament," said Clara, looking down. "But all the Hallecks are fond of her. They think there is a great deal of good in her. I don't suppose Ben himself thinks she is perfect. But"—

"I dare say," interrupted her husband, "that he thinks he's entirely sincere in asking my advice. But you can see how he *wishes* to be advised."

"Of course. He wishes to marry her. It isn't so much a question of what a man ought to have, as what he wants to have, in marrying, is it? Even the best of men. If she *is* exacting and quick-tempered, he is good enough to get on with her. If she had a husband that she could thoroughly trust, she would be easy enough to get on with. There is no woman good enough to get on with a bad man. It's terrible to think of that poor creature living there by herself, with no one to look after her and her little girl; and if Ben"—

"What do you mean, Clara? Don't you see that his being in love with her when she was another man's wife is what he feels it to be—an indelible stain?"

"She never knew it; and no one ever knew it but you. You said it was our deeds that judged us. Didn't Ben go away when he realized his feeling for her?"

"He came back."

"But he did everything he could to find that poor wretch, and he tried to prevent the divorce. Ben is morbid about it; but there is no use in our being so."

"There was a time when he would have been glad to profit by a divorce."

"But he never did. You said the will didn't count. And now she is a widow, and any man may ask her to marry him."

"Any man but the one who loved her during her husband's life. That is, if he is such a man as Halleck. Of course, it isn't a question of mere right and wrong, of gross black and white— there are degrees, there are shades; there might be redemption for another sort of man in such a marriage; but for Halleck there could only be loss—deterioration—lapse from the ideal. I should think he might suffer something of this even in her eyes"—

"Oh, how hard you are! I wish Ben hadn't asked your advice. Why, you are worse than he is! You're *not* going to write that to him?"

Atherton flung the letter upon the table, and drew a troubled sigh. "Ah, I don't know! I don't know!"

Notes

Page 3, line 20 Fast Day: traditionally a "first of spring" day proclaimed as a day of contrition.

Page 107, line 24 Tylor: Edward Tylor, pioneer ethnologist, wrote *Primitive Culture*, 1871.

Page 205, line 26 Eastlake movement: Charles Eastlake, British Victorian interior decorator, established a "rustic" style.

Page 206, line 16 Papanti's: Count Lorenzo Papanti conducted for generations of children the dancing school in which, especially in private classes, what Cleveland Amory called "Proper Bostonian" little girls met the little boys who would grow up fitted to become fashionable husbands.

Page 313, line 36 *bolla:* right Latin is *bulla* (as in the ball-like Papal seals, dangling on ribbons, which give their name to "a Papal Bull." How Howells arrived at *bolla* is a matter for conjecture.

Page 328, line 1 presidential canvas: reference to the Hayes-Tilden campaign dates the action of the novel as centering on 1876.

Page 450, line 29 Whited Sepulchre: see "Introduction," p. xxii.

Appendix

Did Howells "Have a Nervous Breakdown" While Writing *A Modern Instance*?

As new facts have come to light, the old picture of Howells at work on *A Modern Instance* has sharpened in focus. He had cleared his decks for action on his biggest task to date and he worked under relentless pressure. Perhaps he brought too much stress on himself. He set deadlines for finishing sections, so he could fulfill a cherished dream of taking his family back to Europe. He let *Century* print the early installments before he had in fact finished the novel.

The bulletins he sent in letters to family and friends throughout the late spring, all summer, and well into autumn of 1881 tell of buoyant progress. He thought it a good novel, great with promise, and he was piling up pages. Of course he felt the strain, but he pushed on. Quite suddenly, however, family tensions mounted critically. His lovely, gifted elder daughter, Winifred, relapsed into the illness that, after long and bitter suffering, would kill her, still in youth, in 1889. As Howells wrote to T. B. Aldrich on 6 August 1881, "It is most kind of you to ask this hospital to visit you, but for the hospital it is impossible. Winny is doomed to an indefinite season in bed. . . . We have not yet organized a nurse, and Mrs. Howells has worn herself out waiting on W., so that *she* is in bed, too" (Lohmann, 2, p. 292). But Howells worked on as hard as he could; that was his custom, and, besides, he had to.

As matters turned out, however, illness stopped the author himself early in November. As late as 6 November 1881

Howells wrote a brisk, lucid letter to James R. Osgood, supplying him a scheme with which to open business negotiations about the new travel book he proposed to write from Europe (Lohmann, 2, p. 301). On 15 November he sent a letter to his father, apologizing because he could not make a promised trip home to Ohio: "I am down with some sort of fever. . . . It's the result of long worry and sleeplessness from overwork, nothing at all serious" (Mildred Howells, 1, p. 303).

In the event, his first conviction that he was not seriously ill turned out to be wrong, almost dead wrong. He was down "seven incredible weeks" (Lohmann, 3, p. 16), and of course he had to struggle against exhaustion for at least that much longer, fighting to finish the book. It would be spring before he felt normal, and he could not leave for Europe until July.

I now believe I was mistaken in arguing from the evidence available in 1954 that Howells suffered a nervous breakdown in November 1881, and that not so much mere work as the impact of Winifred's "nervous" collapse, multipled by psychic stress from the "strong" nature of his fictional materials—sexuality, passion, jealousy, demonism, and divorce —broke him. There was warrant for supposing, from Howells's recurrent neurotic crises in adolescence and young manhood, that psychic stress could have broken him. Because of the vagaries of medical diagnosis and the circumlocution customary in polite discussion of physical events typical of the day, it was impossible to establish a physical etiology and therefore tempting to hypothesize a psychosomatic cause for Howells's prostration.

Now, however, my hypothesis has split on a rock of fact, a firm bit of physical pathological evidence. Its context suggests that more such matter-of-fact information, now perhaps lost, once existed. At any rate, a letter Howells wrote to his father on 15 December 1881 casts new light on his illness and "breakdown." Written from Cambridge, it reports, "We have come down to this boardinghouse, so that I can be handy to the doctor at all hours. There has been a very persistent and tedious recurrence of the stricture, and Belmont was so far off that I suffered a great deal before I could get at the doctor; now I reach him in a few minutes" (Lohmann, 2, p. 302).

At least for laymen, it is only in the absence of evidence regarding physical pathology that one may reasonably guess at psychosomatic etiologies. Uremic toxicity resulting from a "very persistent" and recurrent urethral blockage could account for many of Howells's reported symptoms. The blockage also readily accounts for the reticence of his reports to Mrs. Annie Fields and Charles Eliot Norton. Only to his father could Howells write the truth. It would be idle to speculate about what the "fever" was that knocked Howells down. Standard medical practice in our time would place him, once down and suffering his "stricture," in a hospital bed, continuously catheterized until he was convalescent. There remains no reason in good logic to believe any longer in the hypothesis that Howells suffered a "nervous breakdown" while composing *A Modern Instance*.

—Edwin H. Cady

Pg 268
Theatre/paper/preaches

Swedenborg + Darwin
Pg 417 what's any possible connection